Freed from his harness, ~~~~ ~~~~
the door's spongy weatherstripping to the roof of
the car so we were seeing eye-to-eye.

"So do *you* have any idea what's going on here?"
I asked.

"His true body is coming through into this
plane," the ferret told me, staring wide-eyed at
Smoky's increasingly monstrous form. The ferret
sounded smart, his voice like that of an excitable
middle-aged librarian inside my head. Finally, some
good luck.

"It's what?" I asked.

"This animal body . . . it's just a flesh vessel for
my consciousness. I am not a ferret, and the entity
that has inhabited Smoky's body is most assuredly
not a cute little doggy. If I'm not mistaken, he's
changing into something close to his true form,"
the ferret said. He had a little bit of an accent, I
realized. A Canadian librarian.

"But why?"

"Clearly the magic from the portal has . . .
altered him."

"But how?" I did realize I was starting to sound
like a three-year-old.

"I'd hazard to say it's a side effect of whatever
disastrous magic caused that portal to open."

"Which is a fancy way of saying you don't
know?" The pain was making me crabbier than
usual.

The ferret reared back, looking offended.

Spellbent

LUCY A. SNYDER

BALLANTINE BOOKS • NEW YORK

A Del Rey Mass Market Original

Copyright © 2009 by Lucy Snyder
Excerpt from *The Devil in Miss Shimmer* by Lucy A. Snyder
copyright © 2009 by Lucy Snyder

Published in the United States by Del Rey, an imprint of The Random House Publishing Group, a division of Random House, Inc., New York.

DEL REY is a registered trademark and the Del Rey colophon is a trademark of Random House, Inc.

This book contains an excerpt from the forthcoming book *The Devil in Miss Shimmer* by Lucy A. Snyder. This excerpt has been set for this edition only and may not reflect the final content of the forthcoming edition.

ISBN 978-0-345-51209-3

Printed in the United States of America

www.delreybooks.com

9 8 7 6 5 4 3 2 1

For Carol,
who always believed

Acknowledgments

Although writing is inevitably a solitary occupation, making a book is anything but. First, big thanks go to my husband, Gary A. Braunbeck, for his encouragement and advice over the years. I'd also like to thank my first readers: Sara, David, Greg, Dan, Trista, Jerry, and the other members of Writeshop. And, of course, I must thank my agent, Robert L. Fleck, for getting my novel out into the world, and I must thank my editors at Del Rey (Liz Scheier and Shauna Summers) for taking my book and helping me make it even better. And finally, I'd like to express my appreciation for Laura Jorstad's sharp-eyed copyediting, Jessica Sebor's always-prompt assistance, Dreu Pennington-McNeil's fine cover design, and Dan Dos Santos's truly spectacular cover art.

prologue

My name is Jessie, and I'm the reason why your life is about to change forever. Maybe you're only just starting to realize that the world is spinning strange, and you're looking for answers. But maybe you already know what's happened, and you're looking for *me* so you can either buy me a drink or kick my ass.

God help me, I could have stopped them. I'm sure of that. My only defense is that I honestly thought I was doing the right thing, but my best intentions are black pavement now.

All I can do now is tell you my story and let you decide for yourself whether I'm a heroine or a villain or just another tool. I've had some time to gather my thoughts, and other people's thoughts for that matter; it's amazing what magic can coax from the dead. So if I start telling you about events I wasn't around to see, know that my memories are solid even if the original owners are dust. I'll be happy to give you the eyewitness tour if you bring good beer.

Begin at the beginning, right? I still can't find memories from the ancients who planted this disaster, so let's start with the night my own life went off the rails . . .

chapter one

A Simple Storm-Calling

Cooper woke me up before the nightmare did. He caught me square in the shin with a jerking kick and I bolted up, my heart hammering like a small demon trying to break through my rib cage. Already the dream had slipped from my mind, leaving nothing behind but my wrecked nerves. Cooper twitched and ground his teeth. Sweat plastered his curly black hair against his forehead, and his tattooed arms shook as he crushed the pillow against his chest.

I wanted to hold him close, wake him up. I hated seeing the man I loved in that kind of pain. It didn't matter that he was the teacher and I, his apprentice. But I knew he'd lash out at anyone near him when he came out of the dream. So I wiped the sweat out of my eyes and scooted away from him on the bed.

"Cooper," I called. My throat felt like it was lined with steel wool, and I could taste pennies where I'd bitten the inside of my lip. "Wake up."

No response.

My heart was slowing, finally, but my hands still shook as I wiped my eyes again. I'd never had nightmares before I started sleeping with Cooper. The first couple of times we'd both gotten bad dreams the same night, I dismissed it as coincidence. But after a dozen nights? It was pretty clear that the terror I saw in his fractured sleep mirrored the terror fading inside my own head.

We were having the same damn nightmare . . . and lately I was having it whether I was sleeping beside him or not.

He writhed and groaned.

Cooper's white fox terrier, Smoky, was cowering under my computer desk, whining. The dog was giving me a scared look: *Wake him up before something bad happens.* I'd seen the dog take on creatures ten times his seventeen pounds when he thought his master was in danger; he'd once torn the ear off an ogreish no-neck who was preparing to brain Cooper with a tire iron in a bar parking lot. But when the nightmare came on, fierce little Smoky was helpless.

I could hear the rustling of my six-month-old ferret racing around in his cage in the corner.

What's going on inside your head? I wondered, staring down at Cooper.

I slid off the bed, took a deep breath, and let loose a shout that shook the floor: *"Cooper!"*

He jerked awake, arms windmilling, punching the air, kicking the sheet off the bed. "No, I won't, I won't, get away from me—"

"Cooper, calm down! You're okay, you're okay."

"What? Where—where am I?" he gasped, staring around in the dimness.

"In our apartment. Remember?" I climbed back onto the bed and crawled to him across the twisted bedclothes.

"J-jessie?" he stammered, his eyes finally seeming to focus. "Oh man am I glad to see you."

He caught me in a strong hug and kissed me. His naked skin was slick with sweat, and beneath his

usual pleasantly garlicky smell was the faint, sharp
odor of brimstone. Smoky padded out from under the
desk and hopped up onto the bed.

"Are you okay?" I asked.

"Yeah. Think so. Dream can't really hurt me, right?
I can't even remember what it was all about." He
laughed nervously and patted Smoky's smooth head.
"Serves me right for falling asleep when I didn't
need to."

"You almost *never* get enough sleep. You go till
you finally pass out from sheer exhaustion. Then you
get REM rebound and a worse nightmare than you'd
have gotten otherwise."

I chose to ignore the little voice inside my head re-
minding me that I, too, had been going without sleep.
When things got bad, I'd been taking sleeping pills to
blunt the dreams. But not very often; the drugs left
me groggy and stupid the next day.

"Hmm, much sense you make, young Jedi," he
said. "But sensible man I am not."

He stretched, his spine popping. I couldn't help but
admire the play of muscles across his lean torso. He
was thirty-eight but easily passed for thirty; there
wasn't an ounce of fat on him. Some dumb relationship calculator I'd found online—the kind that di-
vides your age by two and adds seven years and tells
you that's the youngest you can date—said that I
wasn't old enough for him.

I know I'm immature in some ways, but inside me
there's a cranky old lady yelling at the damn kids to
get off her lawn. She's been there awhile. I've decided to call her Mabel.

When I was a teenager, most of the other girls got
on my very last nerve—all the stuff they obsessed over

just seemed stupid and trivial to me. I mean, seriously, who gives a shit about what shade of eye shadow to wear to a pep rally? I'd rather skip the whole thing and read a book. I thought Ohio State would be better than high school, but mostly it was just bigger.

Maybe I'd have felt different about things if my mom hadn't died when I was eleven. After she was gone, there was nobody around to make me feel particularly excited about makeup and shoe shopping. I started the existential angst early, started feeling like I was way older than the other kids, and that never got better. The day I turned twenty-three, I felt ancient, even with Cooper there to celebrate with me.

Cooper, on the other hand, is nothing if not bubbling with youthful energy. He could be fifty and would still be hotter than half the twentysomething guys I've met. Of course, most of the guys I've seen at OSU would only have six-packs if they bought them at the 7-Eleven. And the boys I've dated didn't have Cooper's brains, or his heart, or his guts. And his southerly anatomy isn't too shabby, either. Top that with him being the real thing when it comes to magic . . . well, whoever made the relationship calculator can kiss my rosy pink butt.

"What time is it?" he asked.

"A little past nine—the sun's just gone down."

Cooper rubbed his face and scratched his chin through his short dark goatee. "How's the sky?"

"Dry. The nearest cloud is in Indiana, I think."

"Well, then it's time for us to earn our rent money." He reached over the side of the bed to retrieve his jeans. "Three thousand from the farmers for a nice little rainstorm—not a bad payment for a night's work, huh?"

The doorbell rang downstairs.

"I'll get it," Cooper said, slipping on his Levi's.

He thumped downstairs. I peeled off my sweat-soaked T-shirt and panties, tossed them in the hamper, then started digging through the dresser for some fresh clothes. Everything in there was a hopeless jumble, but at least it was clean. A year back, Cooper pissed off a sylph and she nixed all his housecleaning charms; it took us forever to get our laundry mojo working again. As curses go that one was pretty minor—probably the faery equivalent of writing on your face in Sharpie marker while you're passed out—but there are few things more embarrassing to a modern witch or wizard than being forced to use a Laundromat.

I heard the front door creak open, and then our neighbor's cheerful greeting: "Hey, man, everything okay over here? I heard someone holler."

"Hey, Bo," replied Cooper. "Yeah, we're fine, sorry if we disturbed you."

"Oh, ain't nothing, just makin' sure you folks is okay," Bo replied. "Miz Sanchez brought me some of her tamales earlier 'cause I fixed her tire, and she told me to make sure you folks got a couple dozen."

I heard a paper grocery bag rattle open. "Hey, these smell great," said Cooper. "That was really nice of her."

"She's real grateful for what you two done for her little girl."

I clearly remembered the afternoon Mrs. Sanchez was running from door to door, panicked to near incoherence because her six-year-old daughter had disappeared from the apartment complex's pool. Cooper knew enough Spanish to ask for one of the girl's dolls. After that it was easy enough to go back to the privacy of our apartment and cast a spell to track the kid's spirit to the other side of the complex. We found the little girl in a run-down garden apartment. Thankfully, she was okay; the creepy old pedophile who rented the place hadn't done anything more than feed her ice cream.

Once the girl was safe with her mother—and no one the wiser that we'd used magic to find her—I called the cops on my cell phone while Cooper impressed upon the old man that he was never, ever to go near a child again. The old guy was so frightened by Cooper that he practically raced to the police cruiser like jail was going to be some kind of safe haven.

Cooper can be pretty fierce when he gets angry. To me, that's one of his sexiest traits. It's not just about being able to tear the house down; it's about being willing to do it in a heartbeat to protect the people who genuinely need your help.

"Anyone would've done the same," said Cooper. "Please be sure to thank her for us."

After a quick dinner of Mrs. Sanchez's tasty tamales and salsa, Cooper and I and the two animals piled into the Dinosaur—Cooper's big, black, much-tinkered-with 1965 Lincoln Continental. Smoky hopped onto the backseat while I sat shotgun with my ferret in his walking harness and leash.

Cooper talked to Smoky over his shoulder as he drove. The white terrier seldom made any noise as he replied telepathically. Familiars almost never seem to be "talking" to their masters, so the masters' sides of the conversations can seem a little schizophrenic if they don't remember to think instead of speaking out loud. I know of several witches and wizards who just can't keep their mouths shut; when Bluetooth headsets came on the market, a lot of chatty Talents ran out and bought them to reclaim some of their dignity.

"Yes, about midnight," Cooper said. "What? No. You have to pee? You should have said something earlier. No, you'll just have to wait."

With a heavy, long-suffering sigh, Smoky lay down on the black leather upholstery and covered his snout with his paws.

I felt my cell phone buzz in the right thigh pocket of my cargo pants. I pulled out my phone and flipped it open.

"Hello, vibrating pants," I said into the receiver.

The woman on the other end burst into laughter. "Jessica, you are such a weirdo sometimes!"

No one still called me Jessica but Mother Karen, an older white witch I had met through Cooper. "Pot, kettle, black, Karen. How are you?"

"I'm fine. What are you two doing tonight?"

"We're off to drown some farmers' sorrows."

"Calling a rainstorm? Good girl, my morning glories are starting to wilt. Well, I was doing some baking tonight and thought I'd invite you two over if you were free."

"Who's that?" Cooper asked.

"Mother Karen. She's baking."

"Ooh!" Cooper's eyes lit up. "I want me some haish brownies," he said in his best hillbilly accent. "An' summa thet cherry pah!"

Karen heard him and laughed. "Tell that man he is not to so much as sniff my cannabis brownies ever again. Last time he got stoned he turned my kids into spider monkeys and they broke half the dishes in the house. But I will save him a cherry tart or two."

"You get pie," I told him. "*Las drogas es verboten.*"

"I never get to have any fun." Cooper pouted.

"Speaking of breaking things, did you want to ride with me to hapkido practice this week?" Mother Karen asked.

"Yes, thanks. We're doing knife and sword defenses, right?"

"Right you are. And remember, belt tests are in three short weeks."

"Oh, cool, I totally forgot!" I was up for my purple belt; I figured it would be at least another year before I was ready for my black belt test, mostly because I kept missing class.

Mother Karen laughed. "Ah, to be young and still excited about belt tests. Meet me at my house around six on Tuesday?"

"Okay, sounds like a plan."

I said good-bye, turned off the phone, and slipped it back in my pocket. Then I realized Cooper had taken I-71 south toward downtown Columbus. "I thought we'd be doing this someplace out in the country, near the farms."

Cooper laughed, a touch nervously, it seemed to me. "I . . . just don't feel like being out in the boonies. I figured we could do this in the Grove. Any magic we work there will be amplified for miles."

To most people, the Grove is just the middle of Taft Park. The park's made up of two dozen acres smack in the middle of downtown, extending from the east side of the Statehouse to the Columbus Art Museum. The central dozen acres were old-growth forest, virtually unchanged since the first European explorers set foot in them.

But to the city's Talents, the Grove is the focal point of a strong upwelling of Earth magic and is one of only two places of power in the entire state. It's home to some of the only enchanted trees left in the Midwest, and, as the occasional normal kid on a ghost hunt finds out, the Grove is a lot bigger on the inside than it looks on the outside. The Talented families in the city have worked hard behind the scenes to make sure the Grove stays wild and unmolested by developers and Parks & Recreation officials bent on "improving" it.

The problem was, if any of the vast majority of the populace who didn't know wizards existed saw us performing magic, Cooper would get into quite a bit of trouble with the local governing circle. A few people, like the farmers paying us to call down some rain, know Talents exist. But those few are put under a geas to keep the secret and not speak to outsiders about magic. In the wake of the medieval witch hunts—which murdered a lot of harmless mundane women and almost nobody using actual black magic—Talent leaders had decided it was best that most mundanes knew as little as possible about the magical world.

"If we get a really good storm going, the skyscrapers will give better lightning protection," Cooper said.

He put his right hand on my leg and moved his fingertips in a light, teasing circle on the inside of my thigh. Tingly. "I have a feeling we're going to get things very, very wet tonight, don't you?"

You just want to fuck me downtown where someone might see us, I thought, then found myself sitting there with a dirty grin on my face as my inner exhibitionist pushed my worries under the covers. Erotomancy was just the thing for working forces of nature. I lifted his hand and put it over my left breast so he could feel my nipple hardening beneath my thin T-shirt.

"Why, ah have no idea what you are talkin' about, Mista Marron," I said. "Ah think you might be trying to take advantage of me. Ah think you are planning to put that great big ol' cock of yours inside me and make me just *scream*."

His fingers gently squeezed my nipple, sending a shiver of delight down my spine. "Stop with the southern belle dirty talk . . . you know it gets me hot."

"Why, Mista Marron, isn't that what you want?"

"What I want is to stop this car, throw you onto the hood, and take you right here by the side of the road."

He had that certain horny-loony gleam in his eye; he wasn't kidding one little bit about stopping the car. He was going to do it—do *me*—right out there in the light of the oncoming traffic so the truckers could get a quick rearview mirror peep show at seventy miles an hour. And he'd be able to get us both off before the highway patrol showed up—and if he couldn't, he'd be able to cast a mirage spell and make the cops and everyone else think the car was parked miles away from our actual location.

You should stop this, I thought. *Take his hand off your tit and put it back on the steering wheel.*

Instead I squeezed his hand tighter against my breast and said, "I want you."

It was the nightmares' fault this was happening. I

knew he woke up so crazy with relief at finding himself alive with all parts intact that he wanted to send us both into orgasmic oblivion right out in the open where gods and monsters and mundanes could see us.

I knew because I felt exactly the same way. Cooper had always been a bit of an exhibitionist, but I had warmed to it during the year of nightmares as my own way of giving the Darkness the finger. The Darkness could take us to dreamland and torture us, it could murder us in a thousand ways and leave us shivering on our sheets in confusion and terror, it could leave us psychically scarred, afraid to sleep, but it could not break us. We wouldn't let it.

As Cooper's foot touched the brake, my ferret wiggled out of the crook of my right arm, hopped onto my chest, and nipped Cooper's thumb.

"Ow! Dammit!" Cooper jerked his hand away.

The ferret chittered at both of us, his little beady eyes glittering.

I laughed. "Guess he doesn't want us getting our freak on until it's rainstorm time."

"Just what I need, a weasel chaperone," Cooper grumped. "But at least it's a sign of intelligent response. Is he talking to you yet?"

"No, not yet. Should I be worried? I mean, I could've picked wrong."

"You got a good strong empathy buzz off him at the animal shelter, right?"

I pursed my lips. We'd gone to dozens of shelters and pet stores looking for an animal to be my familiar. Birds, snakes, rats, cats, frogs, dogs, rabbits, iguanas . . . my mind was reeling by the time we'd gotten to the Ferret Rescue League. When the attendant put the second slinky ball of fluff in my hands, I felt a strange warm humming buzz along my spine. And before I had a chance to think, I'd already said *This is the one. Let's take him and go home.*

And honestly? I'd sort of been hoping for a cat or dog. The ferret was sheer adorableness, sure, but we couldn't let him out of his cage without him immediately finding the most damn inaccessible place in the apartment to dive into and hide. Like the bedsprings, or the coils behind the refrigerator. Cooper finally had to cook up a ferret retrieval charm.

However, the ferret was still a bit stinky. The musky oils in his fur took half a dozen hand washings to get off my skin. Cooper refused to do a deodorant charm on the grounds that a ferret ought to smell like a ferret, and I was Just Being Picky. So I became resigned to the ferret funk, and waited for the magic to happen.

"Yeah, I *think* I did," I said. "But how do I know what something's supposed to feel like if I've never felt it before?"

Cooper shrugged. "You just know. I've seen a dozen apprentices pick their first familiars, and so far things seem normal to me. I wouldn't worry about him yet. He isn't fully grown. Sometimes it takes a while for a familiar to awaken. Probably he just needs a little more exposure to magic."

Cooper snapped his fingers and the radio tuner's face lit up, the dial spinning over to his favorite oldies station. "Stairway to Heaven" was just fading out.

The DJ's voice broke in. "Hope all you night birds have found your own little bit of heaven tonight, even if it *is* too darn hot out. Don't you wish it was Christmas? A little Christmas in July? Here's some Doug and Bob McKenzie to make you think cool thoughts . . ."

"The Twelve Days of Christmas" lurched through the speakers.

Cooper jerked and swatted the air. The speakers squealed as the radio sparked in the dashboard. The stench of scorched wiring filled the car.

"Jesus, Cooper, you didn't have to break it!"

"I hate that goddamn song." The color had left his face, and a muscle in his left eyelid was twitching.

"I know. But *jeez*." He'd never been able to explain to me why he so disliked any version of the song, no matter how silly, but usually he could suffer through a few stanzas until he could change the station or leave the room. I'd never seen him react so violently to it before.

"What are you going to do if we get carolers next December, kill them?" I asked.

He didn't reply. The bad post-nightmare madness was back in his eyes. I rolled down my window to air out the car.

"Hey, are you okay?" I asked him gently. "If you're not feeling well, we should put this off until tomorrow night."

"No." He shook his head as if to clear it. He gave me a quick, unconvincing smile, then fixed his eyes back on the road. "I'm fine. Let's do this thing. I told the Warlock we'd hit the Panda Inn for karaoke and a late dinner tonight."

You mean late drinks, I thought, irritated, but didn't say anything. I couldn't really fault Cooper for wanting to hang out with his half brother; it was good to see Cooper happy, and he and the Warlock always had fun. The Warlock's boozy come-ons were tolerable. I just wished their nights out didn't always end with Cooper puking up Suffering Bastards and Mai

Tais at five in the morning. As with stinky ferrets, Cooper refused to use any anti-poisoning charms on the grounds that a night of drinking ought to feel like a night of drinking.

We left the freeway and drove up Broad Street. On one side loomed the St. Joseph Cathedral, which had been home to more than its share of miracles because it was so close to the Grove; on the other was the high stone garden wall that surrounded most of the park. The fence had gone up in the 1960s when traffic got bad enough that wandering Grove creatures started running a real risk of getting squashed by cars.

The only open side faced the Statehouse, and it was also the only part that attempted to masquerade as a standard city park. There was half an acre of mowed lawn, some decorative cherry trees, a goldfish pond surrounded by concrete benches, and a few picnic tables. A line of ward-charmed rocks marked the border between the lawn and the western edge of the Grove. The wards were subtle, but effectively kept most mundanes out of the Grove and reminded most Grove denizens to stay put.

Cooper turned the Dinosaur left onto Third Street and then took another left into Taft Park's tiny parking lot. He gunned the motor to get the huge car over the curb and drove it across the grass, dodging picnic tables and startling a small flock of sleeping Canada geese. The tires left no marks on the turf; Cooper had long ago enchanted the wheels.

"Yuck. Grass is probably covered in goose shit," he said as the geese flew off, honking alarm. "Annoying birds."

"Could we use it for anything?"

"Use what?" he asked. He hit the brake and put the car in park. We were about a dozen yards away from the fishpond.

"Goose poop."

That's the core of ubiquemancy: Magic is in everything. The spellcaster just has to figure out what kind of magic, how it can be used, and then invoke it in a spur-of-the-moment chant that sounds like a Pentecostal speaking in tongues to those who can't understand the primal languages. Unlike other magical disciplines, ubiquemancy seldom involves calling on spirits directly. Instead it relies on instinct, improvisation, and imagination to focus ambient magical energies.

Some people think that we can do any kind of magic with ubiquemancy, and while that's theoretically true, in practice it's a whole lot trickier, especially if things have Gone Terribly Wrong. It's not just about coming up with the right words. It's a lot like singing—some spells are about as hard as "Mary Had a Little Lamb," but some of them are as challenging as *La Bohème*. Few singers can do a difficult aria the first time out of the gate, and if they don't have the right natural range they might never be able to do it. And even if a singer has range and skill, being able to improvise and perform a brand-new aria right there on the spot while the audience is ripping the chairs out of the aisles and throwing them at your head . . . well, like I said, it's tricky. But then again, you can get lucky sometimes.

Ubiquemancy worked very well with Cooper's manic, live-for-the-moment mind-set. People who dismiss the style call Cooper and our kind Babblers;

the name's stuck enough that even those who respect the art use it.

Magical talent is the biggest thing that makes a good Babbler. And Cooper had talent in spades. On his good days, he was one of the best wizards I had ever seen; I couldn't have asked for a better master. Unfortunately, on his bad days he had a tendency to give in to his self-destructive streak and drink himself senseless. At least after we became lovers he'd cut way back on his alcohol intake.

I sometimes got frustrated with ubiquemancy's magical anarchy and Cooper's pat "Oh, you just *know*" replies to my questions. Sometimes I thought I would have been better off learning a more formalized magic like Mother Karen's white witchcraft.

But darned if Cooper's crazy magic didn't *work*.

"Goose shit," Cooper mused. He turned off the ignition. "It'd be great for curing barren earth . . . fire tricks . . . controlling geese . . . summoning predatory animals . . . spoiling food and water . . . plant growth . . . and maybe flight. Lots of stuff we don't need to do tonight."

"Should we go to the pond?"

"No, we don't want to be right by water. Over there by those oaks looks good. Let's get undressed."

I tied the ferret's leash to the stick shift and pulled off my T-shirt, sports bra, and sneakers. I shimmied out of my cargo pants and panties, folded my clothes, and stacked them on the dashboard.

Cooper was already standing naked on the grass, stretching and scratching his back. "No, it's better if you stay in here," he told Smoky.

The dog whined.

"What? Oh, right." Cooper opened the rear door. Smoky jumped out, ran over to a picnic table, and peed on the tubular steel leg. He gave himself a good shake, kicked grass onto his mark, and happily trotted back to the car.

Cooper shut the car's doors after Smoky was back inside, then met me on the other side.

"Think wet thoughts," he told me, lightly touching the small of my back and running his hand down to my ass. My skin prickled into goose bumps at his touch. "Think low pressure. The clouds are our audience; make them come."

We walked across the grass to the edge of the trees. Cooper backed me up against the trunk of a red oak.

"This tree's roots touch those in the heart of the Grove," he whispered, planting small kisses on my face. "We're all set to broadcast; let's make it good."

He closed his eyes and started planting soft kisses down my neck, over my breasts. My hormones lit up like Madison Square Garden on New Year's Eve. *This is the best job ever,* I thought.

He started moving against me, breathing rhythmically in preparation for the chant. I closed my eyes and followed his body's rhythm. There was a brief, stretching sting as he pushed up into me, but after that it was beautiful. I wrapped my legs around his waist and ignored the scratching of the bark against my back. Once we really got going the pain might actually start working for me. I don't think of myself as a masochist, but my wires sometimes get a little crossed.

Anyway. I was glad to have the chant to focus on, or else it would all be over too quickly. Cooper could last for hours, provided I came quietly. But the nightmares had left me with too much pent-up anxiety to have a nice polite little orgasm. I'd be biting, screaming, demanding the obscene application of Popsicles . . . yeah, I figured the distraction of the spell was going to be a good thing. Silly me.

The old, old words started tumbling out of him, first as sounds that might have been little more than grunts of the ancient pre-humans who lived at the sea and rivers, worshipping the spirits they saw in the cool waters. Then his round grunts grew angles, grew more refined; my mind was filled with an image of a sunburned warlock standing in the reeds of the Nile, begging the gods for rain.

The words were coming out of me, too; my language was different, a tongue that spoke of mists and crashing waves, of broad, gray thunderstorms rolling over windswept North Atlantic islands.

I felt the air around us stir, felt the tiny hairs on my arms and the back of my neck rise. The tops of the trees began to rattle as the wind rose.

Cooper's chant rose to match, changed to something more musical, Western and Eastern in the same breath. I caught a flash of storm clouds boiling above a vast American plain as a medicine man dressed in deerskin and buffalo hide raised his ropy arms to the sky. I could smell the damp plains earth and sweating leather on Cooper's skin.

My chant shifted to match; I spoke the shadow of an old priest in a bear-pelt cloak, standing in the dry forest of a new, green land, pouring the last of his mead on the thirsty earth and asking the Father God to grant him and his men a touch of rain.

Then Cooper's body jerked, and his chant was chopped short by his sudden, pained gasp. I heard the scream in my mind, smelled entrails being pulled from a still-living body and thrown on a charcoal fire.

"Oh God!" Cooper turned and gave me a hard shove away from him. I tumbled backward over the grass.

I rolled to my feet, feeling confused and exposed, wishing my clothes weren't all in the car. "Cooper, what the—"

His body had gone rigid; the cords of his neck stood out, and his tattooed sigils glowed faintly purple in the dim light. The air was growing ominously electric, the clouds above them darkening into a slate-gray spiral.

"Get away!" He sounded as if something was choking him. "Far. Fast. *Now!*"

I knew better than to argue or waste time asking questions. I sprinted back for the car, fear churning in my stomach. Nothing like this had happened before. Cooper had said that the ritual couldn't be interrupted, no matter what.

I got to the Lincoln, ran around to the driver's side, and dove into the seat. Smoky was whining on the front seat, his paws pressed against the window. Before I could get the door closed, he'd jumped over me and was running toward his master.

Cooper started to scream. His voice sounded like a band-saw blade grinding against a rusty iron post.

Should you run away like this? I wondered as I cranked the key in the ignition and slammed the car into drive. *Don't think. Just do it. Cooper knows this stuff way better than you do.*

The storm was gathering with alarming speed. Thunder rumbled. In the rearview mirror I saw the wind whipping a dust devil around Cooper's rigid form. The sound of the gale was drowning out his scream.

I hit the accelerator just as a massive bolt of lightning shot down from the sky.

The earth around Cooper exploded. A shock wave whipped across the park, and I was thrown forward into the steering wheel as the back of the Lincoln jerked off the ground.

Ohshitohshitohshit!

The car tilted, and the gale blasted into the Lincoln's passenger side, lifting it and knocking it over onto the driver's side. I fell hard against the window, helpless, as the car spun like a carnival ride across the grass. My clothes and the ferret flew off the dashboard. The weasel scrabbled for purchase on my sweaty skin to keep from being hung by his leash.

The car slammed into a steel-framed picnic bench bolted to a concrete slab beside the goldfish pond and stopped.

I untangled myself from the steering wheel and set the frightened ferret on top of the passenger-side headrest. I grabbed my scattered clothes and got dressed as quickly as I could. The ferret had left a dozen pinprick scratches on my side and hip. Once I was no longer in danger of being arrested for public indecency, I unrolled the passenger-side window and stuck my head out to see how Cooper was doing, hoping against hope this would turn out to be just another one of those funny little Babbling-gone-wacky incidents where he'd be standing there amid smoke and debris with singed hair and a sheepish *Oops did it again* look on his face.

No such luck. There was a steaming crater the size of a child's wading pool where he'd been. I couldn't tell how deep it was, but the charred sides reflected a bright red glow, as if from live coals or lava.

"Cooper! Cooper, where are you?" I shouted, feeling sick bile rise in my throat.

No answer.

Smoky lay near the crater, his flanks heaving as he gasped for breath. His body looked strangely bloated.

I bent down to make sure the ferret's lead was still secured to the stick shift. "You stay in here," I told him, my voice shaky, not certain if he understood. "I'll come get you when I'm sure it's safe."

I pulled myself up through the window and slid down the curved door, landing lightly on the grass. Where was Cooper? Had he been knocked unconscious and thrown into the trees? Or was the crater all that was left?

No, no, no. He couldn't be dead. He just *couldn't*.

"Smoky?" I called. "Smoky, where's Cooper?"

The terrier was trying to get to his feet, dragging his hindquarters as if he'd broken his back. Bloody foam flecked his muzzle. He saw me and started to howl.

Oh, Jesus, poor thing, I thought.

The crater smelled like a gangrenous wound, like bad magic, and I was getting the same stink off Smoky.

I stepped closer to the crater. And then it hit me: I was looking at an intradimensional portal. I couldn't have been more stunned if I'd put a cake in the oven, left it to cook, smelled smoke, and opened the oven to discover the cake had transformed into an angry firedrake. Actually, the cake-to-firedrake I could have explained away as a prank from the Warlock, but this? This was off-the-chart bad and unexpected.

How in the name of cold sweat and stomach cramps had we created *an intradimensional portal* from a simple storm-calling chant?

After a couple of beats, my brain shifted out of shock and into more practical questions: Where did the portal lead? I had no clue, but by the look of it, it sure wasn't a beachside resort. Had Cooper been pulled inside? It seemed likely. I couldn't see any trace of him nearby. If he'd been blown apart in the explosion, there'd still be blood or—I swallowed sickly against the thought—scattered bits of his flesh.

My first instinct was to call Mother Karen and get her to send help, but I realized I couldn't just stand there and do nothing while I waited for the cavalry. God only knew what might come through. Might come through at any moment. I realized I had to do my best to get that sucker *closed*, and fast.

I'd heard Cooper and the Warlock talking about travel between dimensions; portals were hugely dangerous. The longer they stayed open, the worse things got. And creating one was supposed to be a complicated ordeal involving extended rituals and the blood of red-haired virgins and stuff like that. I never imagined that anyone could open one by *accident*.

Smoky started having some kind of seizure. The howls and growls coming from him were sounding less and less dog-like. I couldn't think of any Earthly creature that made a shriek like metal sheets being rent in half, a rumble like wet bones being crushed beneath a dire war machine. I ran toward the crater, giving the little dog a wide berth.

I came within a few yards of the crater's edge and stopped. I'd expected to see the bottom crawling with lava or hellfire, but there was only a void of utter blackness. My head swam with vertigo, bile rose in my throat, and every cell in my body thrummed with pain: I was staring into the heart of Nightmare.

I closed my eyes, certain the horrible Dark would surely melt my brain into epileptic gelatin. I could still feel it with every nerve and every pore, an evil heat that would cook me and everybody else down to ash.

Stumbling away from the portal, I bent and grabbed a handful of sod and dirt and hurled it at the crater, shouting what I hoped would work as a sealing chant. I circled, staring at the ragged edge of the crater, pushing the nightmare shadows out of my mind with images of closing doors, healing wounds, windows blocked shut with nails and boards.

The longer I stayed near the portal, the more afraid I was that I would trip and fall inside, that it would grow and swallow me up. And I was desperately afraid I was too weak to get it closed. An ice pick of pain lanced behind my eyes; I was burning through so much magic energy that my blood sugar was getting low. If the spell didn't start working soon, I was going to pass out.

I chanted the words for "close" in every language my mind could bring forth, all the while casting handfuls of good, fresh dirt into the vile portal like antibiotics into an infection.

Finally, *finally*, it was working. I felt the ground start to move under my feet, and the sides of the crater started to pull together. Yard-wide jagged cracks opened in the park's lawn as the crater's edges sealed, a puckered scar in the earth.

I took a step back, breathing hard, pressing against my temples to try to ease my throbbing skull. *You did it. You actually did it.*

A metallic scream dispelled my sense of relief. I turned, dreading what I might see. Smoky was still thrashing. His body was stretching and growing; I could hear his bones crackling. Blade-like reptilian spines erupted from his back. He was fairly steaming with the bad magic I'd felt from the portal.

I backed away. I'd never even *heard* of anything like this happening to a familiar. Definitely time to call for help.

I pulled my cell phone out of my pant pocket and called up Mother Karen's number. I pressed the phone to my ear.

"Jessica, is that you?" Mother Karen didn't sound like herself. "Jessica? It's so dark, it's hard to hear you."

It wasn't Karen. I felt my knees buckle as I recognized the voice. "Aunt Vicky?" I stammered.

"Jessica, I've been waiting so long for you. When will you come visit me? It's so cold in here, and the snakes won't leave me alone—"

I shut off the phone and stared at it, shivering. My aunt Victoria had been dead for over five years; she'd murdered her philandering husband, Bill, with rat poison, then killed herself with a bottle of sleeping pills and a fifth of gin as she cried over his body.

I'd found the corpses four days later after I got worried because nobody was answering the phone; flies had found them much sooner. It was a memory I'd tried hard to purge from my mind.

I turned the phone on again. The menu was no longer in English. The characters resembled Cooper's tattoos: sigils that came from no known human language; symbols he'd described seeing in his dreams.

"Oh *fuck*," I whispered.

Smoky was still growing, changing. His body was hugely elongated now, and a third set of stocky, clawed legs was sprouting from the bottom of his rib cage. His skin was splitting, his white hide hanging in bloody tatters over swelling gray scales.

I was shaking with panic. The pain in my head was making it hard to think; I had *no* idea what I could do. Thunder rumbled, and the first raindrops started pattering down from the sky.

I can help, I heard in my mind. *Let me out of this car and I can help*.

The ferret? I didn't expect him to be able to communicate so soon.

I dropped my phone back in my pocket and hurried toward the Lincoln. "Hang on tight," I called, hoping the ferret would hear and understand. "I'm gonna turn the car over."

I spoke the word of a long-dead tribe that described the act of putting a turtle or beetle back on its feet. I made a sweeping movement with both hands. The headache throbbed anew, but I ignored it. I wasn't going to keel over just yet.

The Lincoln creaked over and whammed back down on its wheels. A moment later the ferret poked his head up in the open window.

I ran to the car and started to unbuckle the ferret's harness, wishing I could remember more about what I was supposed to do with a newly awakened familiar. According to Cooper, familiars could be tremendously knowledgeable, veritable furry little walking magic encyclopedias, provided you were lucky enough to get an experienced one. If the ferret was as green as I was, though, it would be *Magic for Dummies* time and we were probably screwed.

Freed from his harness, the ferret clambered up the door's spongy weatherstripping to the roof of the car so we were seeing eye-to-eye.

"So do *you* have any idea what's going on here?" I asked.

"His true body is coming through into this plane," the ferret told me, staring wide-eyed at Smoky's increasingly monstrous form. The ferret sounded smart, his voice like that of an excitable middle-aged librarian inside my head. Finally, some good luck.

"It's what?" I asked.

"This animal body . . . it's just a flesh vessel for my consciousness. I am not a ferret, and the entity that has inhabited Smoky's body is most assuredly not a cute little doggy. If I'm not mistaken, he's changing into something close to his true form," the ferret said. He had a little bit of an accent, I realized. A Canadian librarian.

"But why?"

"Clearly the magic from the portal has . . . altered him."

"But how?" I did realize I was starting to sound like a three-year-old.

"I'd hazard to say it's a side effect of whatever disastrous magic caused that portal to open."

"Which is a fancy way of saying you don't know?" The pain was making me crabbier than usual.

The ferret reared back, looking offended. "I admit I've never seen anything like this before, but I am certainly capable of educated conjecture."

The rain was coming down harder; it looked like Cooper and I had called up a real gully washer of a storm.

"Why wasn't I affected?"

"Well, you're not a transdimensional being like us familiars, are you?" the ferret replied. "Badly controlled portal magic will inevitably affect us; I was lucky to be farther away."

"So what are you?" I asked. "What's your true form?"

The ferret blinked. "You might find my true form . . . upsetting. I would seem somewhat alien in my natural state."

"Alien how?"

The ferret shuffled his feet uncomfortably. "Can't I just tell you later, once we've gotten to know each other a bit better? I've been a familiar for more than three hundred years, and during my service I've unfortunately encountered many humans who are prejudiced against—"

"Okay, fine, whatever." I held up my hands; we really didn't have time to argue. Whatever he was, I was stuck with him, at least for a while. "Do you have a name?"

"My name in your language is 'Palimpsest.' You can call me Pal, if you like."

Smoky roared. He'd grown positively huge; his scaled body was over twenty feet long, and I guessed he'd stand as tall as me once he got his six sets of taloned legs working under him. His tail was long and covered in the blade-like scales. His red-eyed head looked more crocodilian than canine, and his maw was filled with serpentine teeth the length of my hand.

Smoky roared again, and bright green flame erupted from his mouth. His transformation seemed nearly complete.

"A dragon? All this time, he was really a dragon?" I asked.

"For lack of a better name, yes, a dragon. But he shouldn't be here." Pal's whiskers quivered as he sniffed the air. "I . . . something's not right here. I can feel a shift. I think he's warping reality."

"Warping? How?" I asked, thinking of my brief chat with my dead, damned aunt.

"I don't have a good sense of exactly what's happening yet. But I worry that once torn, the fabric of your world could keep tearing. You were right to close the portal as you did; now you've got to deal with Smoky."

My stomach sank. "Deal with him how?"

"Subdue him, however you have to. He's too dangerous to let run around loose."

Was he talking about killing Smoky? Jesus. I sure wasn't looking forward to that. "Would Cooper's shotgun work, or do I need to summon up the Caladbolg or some damn thing like that?"

"The shotgun should work as well as anything else," Pal replied.

I popped the Lincoln's trunk and got into our duffel bag of supplies; I found a packet of Advil and a warm bottle of Gatorade. Hoping the combination would kill my headache, I popped the two pills and chugged the drink. I found a PowerBar gel packet and stuck it in my thigh pocket for later, just in case.

Next, I opened up the long black gun case. Inside was a twelve-gauge, pump-action nine-shot Mossberg 590 "Intimidator" with a black plastic stock. It was fully loaded with cartridges that contained eighteen pellets of mixed silver and iron buckshot: a little something for any sort of hostile creature Cooper and I might encounter out in the woods or in the bad parts of the city. We'd started toting firearms after a close call with a pack of drunk werewolves in Logan County. I hoped the shot would be enough to penetrate Smoky's thick scales, if it came to that.

A sheathed silver dagger and a bandolier of twenty extra cartridges lay in foam cutouts above the shotgun. Below the shotgun was a holstered Colt .380 "Pocketlite" automatic pistol and a seven-shot clip loaded with silver bullets half-jacketed in iron. Cooper had enlisted the Warlock's help to put various minor enchantments on the weapons to improve their accuracy and stopping power; Cooper's skills definitely lay in making love and not war.

Some mundanes—specifically the farmers— wondered why we relied on firearms for defense instead of magic. Sure, there are binding spells and such . . . but think of the opera singer trying to perform in a riot. If you're in a panic, squeezing a trigger is a whole lot more reliable than trying to cast a spell.

Make no mistake: There *are* killing words. But using a killing word on a familiar or a human being is as serious as deciding to ram your car full-speed into a crowd of pedestrians; it should never be done unless you're left with no other choice, and even in a clean-cut self-defense situation the consequences are severe. There's an allowance for word-killing demons and other bad characters, but most Babblers won't go near that kind of magic, no matter what. Once you've crossed the border into necromancy, it's hard to get your spirit clean again. You start losing your ability to do white magic, and pretty soon all you're good for is death magic on the fast lane to hell.

And there's the little detail that grand necromancy is illegal and will get you imprisoned or worse. So, killing words? I was sure I'd never use them. Guns and knives seemed far less dangerous.

I slung the bandolier across my body, loaded the Colt, and clipped the holster and the dagger to the waistband of my cargo pants, then hefted the shotgun. Palimpsest ran across the roof onto the trunk lid and hopped onto my shoulder, perching on one of the shotgun cartridges.

Cooper had taken me out to the range every few weeks so we could practice target shooting; the first time I'd fired the shotgun the recoil had damn near knocked me flat. The bruise under my collarbone would have lasted a week if Cooper hadn't healed it. But since then, I'd learned to properly brace myself and could handle the gun pretty well. I'd been good with the Colt from the start; the small gun fit my hand perfectly.

I slammed the trunk shut. Smoky had wobbled to a full twelve feet and was snorting the air, apparently searching for the scent of something. His scaly skin steamed in the rain, smelling of hate and pain and rage.

I raised the shotgun to my shoulder, my heart pounding. His eyes looked most vulnerable. I hated everything about this situation.

"Smoky," I said, struggling to keep my voice and hands steady. "Smoky, look at me, boy."

Smoky ignored me and launched himself across the park toward the Statehouse. He moved like a giant centipede across the street and down the ramp to the Capitol Square's underground parking garage.

"Don't let him get away!" Pal exclaimed. "The farther he goes, the worse the damage might be!"

Cursing, I pelted after Smoky, even though I knew there was no way I could keep up with him. The rain was cold against my skin, and my hair and clothes were getting soaked. At least the downtown area was nearly deserted. Except on the evenings when there was a Blue Jackets hockey game at Nationwide Arena or a concert at the Ohio or Palace theaters, the city's downtown pretty much rolled up its sidewalks and shut down after seven o'clock on Sunday night.

My foot hit something soft and slippery, and I nearly twisted my ankle. I looked down and realized I was standing in a pool of blood.

"Jesus! What the . . ."

There were three corpses, best as I could tell. It looked like they'd been turned inside out, exploded. Bits of flesh and bone were everywhere. I saw shreds of gray maintenance uniforms amid the gore. I felt intensely sick and fought down the urge to vomit.

"God. Poor guys. How—how could Smoky *do* this?" I asked the ferret. "We were barely thirty seconds behind, and these guys look like they swallowed dynamite sandwiches . . . how did this happen?"

"I don't know," Pal replied, his sinuous body weaving to and fro as he sniffed the air.

The rest of the garage was empty except for a maintenance van and a motorcycle. A wide smear of blood trailed to the far end of the garage, where Smoky was nosing around the underground entrance to the Riffe Center. I didn't see any blood on his muzzle. The glass doors to the center were smashed; huge pieces of thick plate glass lay shattered on the concrete.

"I didn't hear him do that," I said. "Is there something else out here? Is he tracking something? Did something come through the portal?"

The ferret sniffed the air. "I can't say."

How could he not know? I tried to force down my panic. "Are you saying you don't know, or you know but won't tell me?" My words came out angrier than I intended, but I didn't feel like apologizing for my tone. I began to walk toward Smoky, hoping he wouldn't slither into the Riffe Center before I got close enough to either shoot or try some kind of a binding spell.

"I don't know if anything else is here," the ferret replied. "Why would you think I'd withhold information from you?"

"Let's see," I replied. "Cooper's been sucked away to God-knows-where by some evil force and his little dog's turned into a monster. Tom, Dick, and Harry on the night cleaning crew just got turned into stew meat. And my familiar suddenly wakes up and starts telling me what to do . . . yet won't tell me what it really is. And it can't tell me the most *important* thing I need to know, which is whether or not I've got some other freak show to deal with besides Hopalong Smaug here."

"Are you saying you don't *trust* me?" The ferret sounded supremely offended.

"Yes, that's exactly what I'm saying," I said, stopping. "Fear? Check. Worry? Check. About to pee my pants? Check. Trust in my new mystery familiar? Nope, sorry, just ran out. How do I know you're not some . . . some evil spirit who came through the portal to possess the body of my ferret?"

"You're paranoid," he said.

"Convince me," I replied.

"I'm not sure how I can do that," the ferret said, agitated. "There are spells to prove I'm telling the truth, but I imagine you don't know them. And we can't spare the time to perform them."

"Okay. Go back to the car and wait for me. I'll come back for you when I'm done."

"You can't do this by yourself, you're not experienced—"

"I know how to shoot. And I know Smoky. Go."

The ferret reluctantly climbed down my back and humped back up the garage ramp into the rainy night.

Did I just do a phenomenally stupid thing? I wondered. *He's right, I can't do this alone . . . but I guess I'm going to have to try.*

I paused. Maybe I didn't have to do this Palimpsest's way. Maybe Smoky was still sane enough to listen to me and stay put. Maybe I could find a landline in the building that actually connected to the real world. I could phone Mother Karen to find someone who knew about this kind of stuff and could put things back the way they were supposed to be.

And then we could figure out how to get Cooper back.

Maybe.

chapter two

Slaying the Dragon

I lifted the shotgun to my shoulder and trotted toward Smoky, who was still sniffing the pieces of shattered door glass. Smoke rose from his nostrils with each exhalation.

I am so *about to get myself barbecued,* I thought. *I wish Cooper were here; he'd know exactly what to do.*

Tears welled up in my eyes. Where was he? Was he okay? If he'd been sucked into that black pit of nightmares I'd seen . . . dammit, I should have insisted we wait another day to summon the rain. We never should have gone out that night.

I could have been curled up on the couch with Cooper, watching an old movie with little terrier-sized Smoky on his lap and my ferret on my lap, eating popcorn and laughing and smiling and kissing instead of being wet and scared and alone and not knowing what the *hell* I was doing in this stinking parking garage.

I was about a dozen yards from Smoky. Close enough for a clean, strong hit with the shotgun, although I didn't want to do that. In the yellow lights of the garage, he was truly frightening: part dog, part Asian dragon, part centipede, all wrong. Green slime caked the edges of his lips—blood, poison, or both?

His eyes, I realized, were faceted like an insect's. Would he recognize me through his new eyes, or would I look as monstrous to him as he did to me?

I set the shotgun muzzle down and leaned the stock against my damp leg so it would be close at hand. While Smoky had never been able to speak to anyone but Cooper, I hoped to get some kind of friendly response, and I figured pointing a firearm at him wasn't the best tactic.

I whistled at him. "Smoky! Smoky, whatcha looking at there, buddy?"

His head jerked up from the smashed glass, and he stared at me. His lips drew back from his dagger-like teeth in a snarl. Green poison dripped from the tips. A growl like an anvil dragging across concrete rolled out of his throat.

Not the response I'd been hoping for.

"Smoky, don't be like that. It's me, Jessie. You know me, I'm your *friend*. I fed you just this morning. Cooper's missing, and I need your help if we're gonna get him back."

I slowly reached into my pocket, hoping I had a rubber band or hair tie in there, but could only find a loose thread from the stitching. It would have to do. I broke it off and began to chant old words for "bind."

At the first weak touch of my magic, Smoky lunged at me, fast as a striking cobra.

No time to finish. I snatched up the shotgun, swung the muzzle up toward Smoky, and squeezed the trigger. It blasted into his open mouth.

Smoky roared and jerked back, shaking his head like a dog with a wasp-stung nose. I pumped the gun, aimed for his eye, and fired again.

Smoky bucked, and I didn't see his tail flailing toward me until it was too late. The tail slammed into my left shoulder, knocking me off my feet and the shotgun out of my hands.

I tumbled across the concrete and landed back-first against the cinder-block wall, knocking my head painfully. I lay there, dazed, expecting to feel Smoky's hot breath on my skin as his jaws clamped down on my prone body—

—but instead I heard glass breaking. I turned my head in time to see Smoky's tail disappearing through what was left of the doors to the Riffe Center. The shotgun lay ten yards away from me.

"Oh great," I moaned, awkwardly sitting up. I'd banged up my knees and elbows and hands pretty well during my tumble. "*This* is going well."

At least you're not barbecue, I reminded myself. *Or giblet surprise.*

I scratched an itch on my left forearm, and my hand came away sticky with blood. Smoky's tail had torn my T-shirt and opened a three-inch gash in my shoulder. I couldn't see anything but blood in the wound.

I tried to raise my left arm and was answered with a bright blue spike of pain from the muscles and joint. It even hurt to make a fist. I had to take care of the arm before I could think about tracking down Smoky.

Bracing myself against the wall with my good arm, I climbed to my feet. There was wriggling movement on the floor near the broken glass. I retrieved the shotgun and slowly approached it.

Smoky's green blood had spattered on the floor, and a strange moss was growing from it. As I watched, the moss sprouted thorny tendrils that wiggled out across the concrete like earthworms seeking dirt. Or tentacles seeking meat.

I stepped back out of tendril reach. *You don't know* what *that is; don't even* think *about touching it,* I thought. *This ain't biology class; don't experiment.*

But if a few drops of blood produced *this* . . . he was bound to bleed a lot more if I had to kill him. Would the reality warp end with him, or would the moss survive him and sustain it?

I jogged through the broken doors and entered the basement floor of the Riffe Tower. Moss was spreading across the pinkish marble stairs leading to the foyer. I hoped he wouldn't go too far before I could catch up.

To my right was the locked gate to a little cafeteria; I'd eaten there after I'd been to an art exhibit on the main floor. It wasn't exactly gourmet dining, but I knew the place would have what I needed.

It took me a couple of minutes of searching for words for "rust" to rot the steel Master Lock enough that I could bash it open with the butt of the shotgun. I heaved the gate out of the way. The kitchen was locked, too, but I was getting better at finding good words for "corrosion." The doorknob's comparatively flimsy lock gave after a minute of chanting.

The kitchen was lit in the red glow from the EXIT signs. I set my shotgun down by the door. A white steel medical kit was bolted to the back wall between the grill and one of the prep tables; I opened it and found a roll of gauze and an Ace bandage.

"Mustard, mustard, where are you, mustard . . . ?" There it was, right below the prep tables. I pulled the huge plastic jar off its shelf and set it on the steel tabletop.

I heard a roar and frightened shouts upstairs.

Three firecracker pops of a pistol. Then a loud thumping and shattering glass. The scream of a man in pain.

Girl, you better hurry, I thought.

My arm ached, and my palm had gone numb. Maybe Smoky *had* put a little something special into my wound. Or maybe his cut had damaged a nerve.

Cooper had shown me how to make a healing poultice out of mustard and onions from our weenie roast fixings when we'd gone swimming at Buckeye Lake and I cut my foot open on a broken bottle. But mustard and onions weren't much use for poison. Would ginger work? Garlic? My memory pinged: basil. People once used basil in poultices to draw out venom. Hindus? Medieval Europeans? My memory failed. No matter.

I found all the herbs I needed in a cabinet; the powdered garlic was relatively fresh, but the dried basil was sad and stale. I dumped what was left of the tin onto a cutting board, mixed in an equal portion of chopped onions from the refrigerator, a few pinches of dried garlic, and enough mustard to make a paste. I kneaded the mixture as I spoke the ancient words for "health" and "healing," then pulled up the remains of my T-shirt sleeve and pressed a handful of the paste against the angry wound.

Pain jagged from the wound down my arm and into my chest. I managed to keep from screaming, kept up my chant as I tried to think cool thoughts, healing thoughts. I visualized the pain and poison leaving my body and my flesh closing beneath my fingers.

It was done. I pulled my hand away. The wound had knitted into a red seam. It looked like it might not even scar. As a precaution against the wound being pulled open, I wrapped my shoulder in gauze and then the Ace bandage, then flexed my arm. I felt a twinge when I rotated the arm backward, but all things considered the joint felt pretty solid.

There was a phone bolted to the wall near the door; would I be able to get through to anybody on a landline? I lifted the receiver and put it to my ear. Instead of a dial tone, I heard a hollow, faint roar.

I jiggled the cradle. "Hello?"

"I need to get warm." My aunt's voice was thin, barely more than a whisper. "It's so cold in here. Let me warm up inside you. I can slip in through your ear and you'll hardly know I'm there at all—"

Shit.

I slammed the receiver back in its cradle, grabbed the shotgun, and headed back to the stairway.

Then stopped.

The marble steps were completely covered in waving, curling vines and meat-purple fern-like fronds. The vines shuddered and stretched out toward me, yearning for my heat or blood or both.

I backed off and ran down the corridor to the other set of stairs that led up to the first floor. I jogged up the steps and peeked out around the corner.

The entire floor between the basement stairway and the entrance to the art gallery was covered in a jungle of undulating fronds. A viney lump twitched in the middle of the floor. The vines shifted, and I saw a section of white uniform shirt. A walkie-talkie crackled.

I forced my gaze from the dying security guard

and realized that half a dozen round pods were
growing near his body. They looked like football-
sized red grapes. As I stared at the translucent pods,
I realized I was seeing tiny embryos like curled eels
growing inside. Thick, thorny umbilical vines pulsed
between the guard's body and the pods.

Oh hell. How fast were Smoky's pups growing? I
raised my shotgun and took aim . . . then lowered
it. Jesus. I didn't have enough ammo if every drop of
his blood was going to turn into a hungry, baby-
spawning briar patch.

On the bright side, I wouldn't have to worry about
trying to contact anyone if this got much worse. The
entire downtown would look like an inferno of bad
magic to anyone even remotely sensitive.

Surely the governing circle knew what was going
on by now, and would do something to help. They
are a group of seven powerful witches and wizards
who act as the local government for the Talents in
Columbus and a few counties beyond. They arbitrate
disputes, set policies, and enforce the laws set forth
by the Virtii, ancient air spirits who had been tasked by
the powers that be with overseeing Talented humankind.

Past that, I was stupidly hazy on the details, like
who was part of the circle, how many people worked
for them, how much power they had, and how
quickly they could turn my life to utter shit if I pissed
them off. The circle doesn't shine a very strong light
on its activities, but my ignorance was mostly my
own fault. I'd never been much for paying attention
to local politics, and my understanding of our laws
was pretty much at a kindergarten "white magic
good, necromancy bad" level. But I wasn't living in

abject ignorance—at least I did know that Benedict Jordan was their leader.

Mr. Jordan pretty much owned Columbus. He was a direct descendant of the two most powerful Talented families who'd founded the city, and he had been head of the governing circle for at least twenty years. He was also the controlling partner of the Jordan, Jankowitz & Jones law firm downtown and sat on the city council. Rumor had it that he was worth billions; he owned the high-end clothing store chain The Exclusive, and it seemed like he owned half the buildings in the trendy Short North.

So, I figured with so much trouble downtown, and him having so much money tied up in it, he would be bound to send the cavalry out to help us *tout de suite*. Yeah. I seriously needed to work on my clairvoyance.

Smoky had smashed through the plate-glass doors; vines were devouring the glass where his blood had smeared.

I stared down at the shotgun in my hands. It was like trying to stop a forest fire with a can of gasoline. And unless I found a piece of rope or a good intact spiderweb, another try at a binding spell would probably be useless. What on Earth could I use to stop Smoky that wouldn't involve him shedding more blood?

Gee, maybe if I swore real hard he'd faint, I thought darkly. *Or maybe I could jump into his mouth and hope he chokes on me?*

Then my mind flashed on Cooper's brief lecture on the uses of goose droppings. Offal could always be used to control the creature that produced it . . . if you could just figure out how. And Smoky had left plenty of fur on the car seats and some hide on the grass.

"I'm an idiot." I ran back down the stairs.

The lights went off just as I entered the tunnel leading to the garage. I hunted vainly in my thigh pockets for my penlight, found nothing but a wad of dryer lint. Fortunately, Cooper had showed me lots of dryer lint tricks during our hours of shame at the Laundromat. I used the wad and a dead word for "cold flame" to light a green faery fire in the palm of my left hand. It didn't cast much illumination, but it was enough to let me hurry through the dark and tremendously forbidding garage.

Cooper wouldn't need to use these crappy little props for rinky-dink spells, Old Lady Mabel complained as I skirted the starving thatch of Smoky's vines. *He'd be calling down the ghost of Thomas Edison to juice the whole building and light it up like Christmas. He'd have shrunk Smoky right back down before he left the park. We'd be at the Panda Inn by now.*

As I emerged from the garage, I realized something was terribly wrong with the sky. The slate-gray clouds had become a pearly white flatness streaked with ruby highlights. The air hung still and dead. The white of the sky cascaded down like an ethereal waterfall at the edge of the Grove; I could barely see the trees beyond.

"Mother*fucker,*" I whispered, shivering with a mixture of frustration and fear.

Someone—presumably a wizard employed by the governing circle—had cast an isolation sphere on the entire downtown area. I'd done a paper on isolation spheres in my freshman enchantments class at

OSU, so I knew in painful detail what kind of trouble I was in. The sphere would be invisible to any mundanes outside it, but anyone attempting to approach the barrier would find himself with a sudden compulsion to turn around and go back the way he'd come. Inside, the sphere was much like trapping a spider under a jar, and I the unlucky cricket trapped with it.

The white color of the sky meant we were totally locked down. Nothing could get in or out, not man nor spirit nor spell nor electrical signal. But that wasn't the bad part.

The ruby highlights meant the governing circle mages had hugely sped up time within the globe. And *that* meant that the governing circle had sensed the reality tear and had decided the easiest way of dealing with it was to isolate it, time-accelerate it, and wait an hour to see if whatever was causing trouble starved or died in the years that had passed within the globe. They'd be able to call a tornado in to mask any magical destruction to the city. Apparently Mr. Jordan had decided to go for an insurance write-off.

The cavalry wasn't coming to save me or anyone else.

"Goddammit, this isn't *fair*! I need *help* down here!" I screamed at the blank sky.

"Be quiet," the ferret fussed. "They'll hear you."

Palimpsest was sitting on the hood of the Dinosaur. I hurried across the street.

" 'They'? It's a 'they' now, for certain?" I asked.

"I thought you didn't *want* my help," Pal replied crossly.

"Mostly I need your nose. Help me find where

Smoky left his skin. *This*"—I shook the shotgun at him—"was a very, very bad idea. I need to work an old-fashioned control spell."

"I might not know everything—"

"No! *Really?*"

"—but I don't think you're ready for an incantation of that complexity, which is why I suggested the shotgun in the first place."

"And your suggestion got us *this* lovely bit of helpful intervention from the local pointy-hats." I jabbed my middle finger toward the sky. "So if I *can't* take care of this my ownself, *you're* going to be here for a very, very long time. So try to be a little supportive, *please*?" I asked.

The ferret seemed to shrink into himself. "I'm sure now that Smoky is tracking something, but I don't yet know what it is. I caught smells of rage and pain and hunger . . . I think it did kill those men in the garage."

"How?"

"Malevolent spirits will often attempt to possess the bodies of weaker creatures. But if the spirits are especially powerful and uncontrolled, the hosts often experience violent, fatal physical reactions."

I paused, wincing as I thought of the men. "You mean they explode."

"Yes, that would be one such reaction."

I took a deep breath. "Okay. We've gotten off on the wrong foot. I'm sorry if I've been a horrendous ungrateful bitch, but this whole thing has me royally freaked. So can we start over, and try to get ourselves out of this mess?"

"I accept your apology. And yes, I'd quite like to get out of here as well. I'll find that hide you wanted." He hopped off the car and scurried over to the grass where Smoky had made his transformation.

I followed, and soon we'd gathered a good handful of fur and limp, bloody, stinky hide. I wished I'd thought to bring along some hand sanitizer.

I'd never tried a control spell, and had only seen Cooper do them a few times. In *theory* it was all pretty straightforward: I just had to get inside the target creature's head and take command.

Yep. Straightforward like busting through a brick wall with your bare hands. Hell's bells.

I gingerly squeezed the handful of bloody hide and glanced at Pal, who was sitting on the picnic bench. "If I start barking, don't you dare laugh at me."

"Perish the thought," he said.

"Okay then." I took a deep breath and closed my eyes.

I started a simple divination chant, asking the spirit residue on the hide and blood to lead me to Smoky. Palimpsest had told me the truth about the dog body being a mere puppet; though the flesh and blood was real, it felt as spiritually dead as a discarded Halloween mask. I focused on the faint, darker, alien essence that curled around the cells like aether.

Ancient words for "hunt" spilled from my lips in a dozen languages I could never name. I felt rather than saw Smoky standing on a deserted street, belching fire.

I knew his true name, his true nature. *Kyothalahüi, Servant of Flame.*

"Become!" I barked in Smoky's ancient, secret language.

I felt myself slip into his scaly skin, into his fragmented mind. My senses were crippled by his anger and pain, drowned by the ocean of information from a dozen too many legs and a hundred too many eyes. I couldn't control it, couldn't understand it. The fire stopped, and the body stumbled.

I saw a dark, twisted form. Smoky's faceted eyes wouldn't focus for me. What was it?

The twisted thing darted forward. I felt a slashing pain at my throat, my belly. The thing was digging inside me, and I couldn't stop it—

—I broke the connection, collapsing back onto the grass.

"Oh hell," I gasped, rising onto my knees. "I messed up. Oh God, I messed up . . ."

"What happened?" asked Pal.

"There was this *thing*. A demon. Smoky was attacking it when I entered his mind, and the demon . . . I think it killed Smoky."

A brief blast of cold, sulfurous wind rippled across the landscape. In its wake, the trees and grass lost their color. In the white light from the blank sky, the world suddenly looked as though it had been carved from bleached bone.

"*Now* it killed Smoky," Pal replied. "And the demon is changing the reality in our isolation sphere."

My brain was just beginning to process what I'd sensed inside the dragon. "He never meant to hurt us—he was always focused on killing the monster that came into our dimension, but we all looked so alien to him, he couldn't really see that we were his friends. Oh *hell*."

Smoky might have calmed down once the demon was dead, and I had no doubt that the demon *would* be dead if I hadn't interfered.

I swallowed down the sick bile rising in my throat. I wanted to cry.

"Did he wound it?" Pal asked.

"I—I think so. He was burning it. But it was still strong enough to tear him up."

"Let's hope he weakened it. Because . . . well, you know what we have to do now," Pal said.

We had to do what strong, terrifying Smoky hadn't quite managed: kill the demon. And hope it didn't kill us first.

chapter three

Wutganger

Something bit my finger; I did a double take when I saw that it was the *grass*.

"What the—" I scrambled to my feet.

The bone-gray grass had become unnaturally animated; the blades were widening, splitting open to reveal tiny, toothed maws that snapped at my sneakers.

"Oh dear!" exclaimed Pal, who abruptly leaped off the picnic table onto my shoulder.

The wooden top of the picnic table was shaking, tearing itself loose from the galvanized bolts holding it to the steel frame.

I hurried over to the relative safety of the road. The toothy sod was trying to heave itself free of the soil.

"What in the hell is *this*?" I asked Pal.

"I'm afraid I misjudged the nature of the reality shift," he said, his voice quavering. "I don't think Smoky was the cause of this; I think he was holding the decay in check."

My heart sank. "Great. How bad will this get?"

"Very bad, I expect. The demon's affecting organic matter. It's only a matter of time before the very asphalt holding this road together is corrupted," he replied. "Do you know where Smoky fell?"

"Yeah. It's not far; I'm pretty sure he was just a few blocks south of the mall on High."

I crept down the street with the Mossberg on one shoulder and Pal on the other. The air hung damp and still and stank of ozone and sulfur.

"I had a bad thought," I said, scanning the nearby buildings nervously.

"What?" Pal asked.

"The grass—it *died*. Whatever it's turning into, it's not *alive* in the strictest sense of the word, is it?"

"No, it's not."

"So okay. If we don't stop the demon, it'll keep doing what it's doing, right? Killing things and reanimating them?"

"Almost certainly."

"So could the demon, you know, trick whoever's monitoring the sphere into thinking everything in here's good and dead and it's A-okay to lift the barrier? And then all this shit could spill out into the rest of the world?" I asked.

Pal paused. "I would think that whichever magical hazards specialist your governing circle has monitoring the situation would be canny enough to recognize that threat."

"And I'd have thought they'd have, you know, *helped* us, instead of leaving us in here to get slurped by the glop. But hey, I live on Naïve Lane in Happy Candycane Acres, what do I know?"

Something screeched; I turned my head toward the noise. One of the trees by the Statehouse sidewalk had torn itself free of the ground. It was scrabbling toward us on a snaky mass of muddy roots. The trunk had split open lengthwise into a seeping mouth lined with thorny teeth. Its branches flailed at us.

"Oh look, isn't that nice? The tree is *screaming* at us. Eat a bag of hell, Mr. Tree!"

I took aim with the shotgun and blasted it once, twice. The tree blew apart. Pinkish gray bits of fleshy wood twitched on the pavement.

"Oh look, Mr. Tree's still moving!" I fired into the largest nearby chunk, the butt of the gun slamming hard into my shoulder. The pain was deeply satisfying.

"Stop, you're wasting your ammunition," Pal hissed. "What's the matter with you?"

"What's the matter with *me*, Mr. Ferret?" I asked, plucking cartridges off my bandolier and shoving them into the gun's loading tube. Both my shoulders hurt now, and my fingers were tingling. "Why, I guess I'm feeling a little *hostile* about this whole situation."

The murderous rage coursing through my veins was nothing short of exhilarating. I wanted to tear the world open and dance in its guts.

"Stupid girl, it's affecting you! Keep your head!" Pal snapped.

"Keep your own damn head, *weasel*."

He was digging his little pinprick claws into my skin, and I'd have liked nothing better than to pick him up and slam him down on the dinosaur-blood asphalt and see his stinking little brains splatter everywhere—

"Are your fingers going numb? That's the *nerves* dying. You let the rage take you, your flesh will turn to cold meat, and he'll shape you as he pleases."

I stared down at my fingertips. They had gone pale; the blood had been squeezed right out of them. Fear squelched my anger. I slung the shotgun over my shoulder and rubbed my hands together to try to get the circulation going again.

"How did you know?" I asked.

"Because I can't feel my paws." Pal took a deep breath. "The demon's broadcasting rage and hate. If we let ourselves indulge in either of those emotions, we're gone."

We started down the street again.

Be serene, I told myself. *Be cool. Be calm and collected as a cow in a field. A cow waiting to be led off, get bashed in the head and carved into steaks.*

Images of abattoir carnage filled my mind, and in an instant I pictured myself blasting the heads off chain-saw-wielding slaughterhouse workers.

"This is *not* very damn easy," I said, desperately forcing my mass-murder daydream away. "I've got to go kill a demon that's much, much stronger than I am, and I can't get angry? How am I supposed to get my adrenaline going if I can't get angry? I've got a *lot* to be angry about right now."

"Determination doesn't have to be anger," Pal replied. "Think about how much you love Cooper and want him back. Keep that love front and center, and *know* that you will get him back, and nothing will stand in your way."

Okay, feel the love, I thought, shifting the ever-heavier shotgun to my left hand. Feel the love, feel the love. Bunnies in shining armor. Love love love.

We walked down High Street past the mall. The store windows were eerie in the flat light. A dead sparrow flopped toward us, chirping hatred. When we turned right on West Town, I beheld a sight I was completely unprepared for.

Smoky lay dead on the sidewalk, and a scorched

thing was tearing off his scales, gnawing his flesh. My eyes just wouldn't focus on it.

What is it? I thought to Pal.

The thing sensed me, shrieking as it pulled its jagged head from the corpse and turned on us.

Suddenly I was sitting in a filthy stone-lined pit, staring down at a bloody hacksaw in my left hand and my own sawed-off leg in my right.

"Don't make me do the second one," I heard myself plead to someone standing above.

And then the pain hit me.

I screamed and fell to my knees, shutting my eyes as if that could shut out the agony sawing on every nerve. The shotgun clattered to the pavement.

"It's a Wutganger," Pal squeaked, his voice thin and shaky. "It's an illusion! See past it! Fight it!"

How could I stand and fight when my guts were falling out? I tried to gather them up, but something clamped down on my left forearm.

The lance of pain as the Wutganger bit through my ulnar nerve jerked me out of the illusion to a far worse reality. The Wutganger was the very incarnation of Cooper's blotted-out nightmares. The face was a leathery patchwork of dead cooked flesh stitched together with twisted wire, the teeth broken shards of glass pounded into pustulant gray gums. Its eyes were live coals, steaming hate and sulfur from the dead sockets.

I screamed as it worried my arm, my bones crunching. I scrabbled at my waist, found the sheathed silver dagger, and pulled it free. The monstrosity tore my forearm apart and howled in my face, its blast-furnace breath blistering my skin.

Mouthing an ancient word for "oblivion," I

rammed the dagger deep into its charred chest, right where its heart ought to be.

The Wutganger exploded. Its molten-lava blood spurted across the left side of my face, down my shirt and pants.

I fell backward, clutching my eye with my right hand.

One moment the sky was the flat condemning white and the next it was open and vast and black. Lightning flashed and sheets of rain pounded down on me, washing away the hideous blood.

I did it, I thought.

Then I heard the freight-train roar. Oh God. The governing circle had called down a tornado.

"We've got to get out of here!" Pal barked, tugging at my shirt.

I couldn't see out of my left eye at all, and there was nothing below my left elbow but a few inches of ragged, bleeding stump around jutting fragments of bone. Shards of broken plate glass gleamed in the wound.

I'm going to bleed to death, I thought numbly.

"You've got to move!" Pal bit my side.

I lurched to my feet and staggered away from the corpses of Smoky and the Wutganger. Pal clung to my waist.

The tornado roared behind me, loud as an apocalypse. I turned and saw the huge, ropy black funnel descend on High Street. The cloud-bound top was big as a city block, and seemed to fill the entire sky.

The funnel plowed into the Riffe Tower. The skyscraper's windows exploded into wet glitter and the pink marble façade blew away like a dusting of talcum power. Steel beams screamed as the tornado twisted them, tearing the huge building up by its roots to get at Smoky's pups.

I turned and ran from the monster storm, blood and God-knew-what-else running down my face, my arm a torch of pain, my heart straining in my chest.

I kept running after my vision went entirely black, kept running until I hit a curb and went sprawling on the sidewalk. The tornado roared nearby, the ground shaking.

I tried to get up, but I'd lost too much blood. Consciousness failed me, and I knew no more.

chapter four

Palimpsest: The Cavalry

I only just barely managed to avoid being crushed when Jessie tumbled onto the pavement; I cannot tell you how much I loathe and despise being put into small animals. You can't carry anything of any consequence, and people are always accidentally stepping on you. Bad for your dignity, worse for your bones!

But that's a tangent. I was scrambling for a hold on her wet shirt as she rolled over onto her back. She made a valiant effort to get up, then collapsed. The Wutganger's blood had burned away half her face; what remained was white as library paste. I could feel her heart slowing like a watch winding down.

The tornado roared through the intersection where the Wutganger and the slain flameservant lay, then sucked back up into the black sky.

I wondered what kind of dubious magic Cooper had been meddling in to bring on the demon. It couldn't have just been a garden-variety imp, oh no— it had to be a Wutganger. They are one of the worst kinds of demons, created from a strong, Talented soul that has been tormented so terribly and for so long that it breaks. The sane, rational part of the soul projects all its capacity for evil and destruction into the lesser fragment to keep itself from being entirely destroyed.

Wutgangers are spirits of mindless rage, pain, and hate. Usually they possess the bodies of the living—and clearly this Wutganger had tried that in the garage. But for one to pull itself together out of dead flesh and inanimate objects like that . . . sweet Goddess.

I knew I had to try to get help, so I wiggled into Jessie's pocket, grabbed the antenna of her cell phone with my teeth, and backed out. Have I mentioned how very, very much I hate small-animal bodies? I was starting to wonder which ancient, vengeful god I'd offended to end up in this predicament. It was unusually bad luck to have been spirited into a little vermin-eater, worse luck to be mastered by such a young, inexperienced Talent in such a whacking mess of danger. My previous master was an old, sedate wizard, and I had lived a very comfortable existence in the body of a bear.

If Jessie died . . . oh Goddess, if she died I'd be trapped in the ferret, mute and practically powerless, for who knew how long. Even worse, the time wouldn't count toward ending my servitude. I still had sixty years left on my sentence; if Jessie lived, she might be the last master I'd ever need to have before I earned my freedom.

All that sounded a bit selfish, didn't it? Of *course* I cared whether she lived or died—I'm not a monster! But I had only known her for a few hours; she was still virtually a stranger. Jessie hadn't yet had the chance to grow on me, not unlike a winsome fungus.

So: I was determined to summon the cavalry, as Jessie would put it. I braced my back paws on the bottom of the phone and heaved it open. The buttons and screen lit up, and for a moment I could do nothing more than gape dumbly at them, trying to make sense of the device. I'd only seen cellular telephones on television. My previous master lived in the wilderness outside Whitehorse, Canada, and saw no need for modern technology. The old wizard had only grudgingly subscribed to satellite TV to keep his grandchildren entertained; I found myself watching quite a lot of American programming during my master's afternoon naps.

I had seen Jessie answer the call from the woman she called Mother Karen; perhaps I could get through to her. But how could I possibly communicate? The ferret's throat could only produce clucks, chuckles, and hisses. What else would she understand? The old telegraph code, maybe? Would she understand the code for "SOS"? It was the best I could think to do.

I found the button I hoped would redial the phone and pushed it with my forepaws. Soon I heard the other phone ringing.

An older woman answered the phone: "Hello, Jessica?"

I started clucking the short-short-short, long-long-long, short-short-short of an SOS.

"Hello, who is this?"

I kept clucking the SOS. A few seconds later the line went dead.

I hissed in frustration, then crawled up under Jessie's burned, sodden shirt and curled up over her heart. What little magical power I possessed in this wretched wisp of fur and meat I could use to keep her heart beating, but for how long? Her heart couldn't pump air, and air was all she'd have left in her veins if her arm didn't stop bleeding. If I'd still been in a bear—or better, an ape or monkey—I could have fashioned a tourniquet. Given my overseer's dislike of me, though, I suppose I should be glad I hadn't been put into a snake or toad.

An eternity later, I heard a truck or van pull up close by. Booted feet thudded onto the pavement.

"There she is," a man said. "Get her legs and we'll put her in back."

I peeked out through Jessie's collar. The vehicle was an ambulance, and the men were dressed as EMTs . . . but they didn't have a gurney. And they smelled of machine oil and gunpowder instead of Betadine and bandages. I was, to say the least, suspicious of their true intentions, so I tried to sense them more deeply. The man who'd spoken had a mind that felt cold and hard; the second man vibrated with fear and indecision.

"She's hurt bad," said Fear. "Shouldn't we heal her up or something first?"

"Mr. Jordan said stasis only; he wants to see the damage. He'll handle the rest," said Cold. "So get her feet and we'll get out of here."

Fear man knelt, reaching for Jessie's legs. I puffed my fur up as much as possible, hissed, and lunged for his fingers.

"Hey!" Fear snatched his hand away. I was most pleased.

"Ignore it," Cold said. "Just her familiar, and it can't do shit."

I wished more than ever that I had the power of speech so I could give that lout a piece of my mind. But just then a minivan veered onto the street and skidded to a stop near the ambulance. A gray-haired woman in a denim dress and a teenage boy in a Blue Jackets hockey jersey jumped out of the van. The woman smelled like chocolate and cherries, and the boy smelled of goaty sweat and peanut butter. He lagged behind, looking scared, but the woman hurried up to the men.

"What are you doing to her?" the woman demanded.

"We're taking her to Riverside Hospital," Cold replied smoothly.

"No you're not. That ambulance is empty. You don't even have a stretcher. Who are you?"

The first man frowned and made a small motion with his fingers; I recognized it as a common memory-wipe spell.

The woman countered it effortlessly with a wave of her hand. "Tell me who you are, or I'm calling the governing circle!"

"We *are* the governing circle, ma'am. Benedict Jordan wants this girl brought in for questioning—"

"Questioning? Look at her, she's nearly dead!"

"This is none of your concern—"

"It is very much my concern! I'm her master's proxy, and I'm a licensed healer. I hereby invoke my rights and I'm taking her with me! You two can just . . . just shove on back to whatever hole you crawled out of!" Her voice was shrill with fear, but she wasn't backing down.

Cold stepped toward her, then stopped, looking irritated and baffled. "Mr. Jordan won't be happy about this."

"He can be unhappy as he wants to be, but he's not so much as talking to this girl on the phone until she's out of danger."

"You're the witch with the foster kids, right?" Cold said, eyeing the teenager. "You should really think about what might happen to your kids if you weren't around to take care of them."

"Get out of here!"

"Suit yourself." Cold shrugged, and then smiled as if he'd suddenly realized that this annoying interruption in his assignment meant he'd get off work early that night. He gestured for his assistant to follow him back to the ambulance.

Once the men were gone, the woman quickly cast a stasis spell on Jessie. The bleeding instantly stopped, thank Goddess, but I decided it was prudent to stay right where I was on her chest, just in case her heart started to fail.

"Jimmy, please help me put her in the car," the woman said, picking up Jessie's cell phone. She closed it and slipped it into a pocket of her dress.

"Yes, Mother Karen," the boy replied.

Karen looked at me curiously as she and the boy pulled off Jessie's bandolier and then carefully lifted her body. "I didn't know Jessica had a familiar. Are you new?"

I nodded.

"Good thing you were around tonight, little fellow. I didn't realize what you were trying to do until after I hung up, but . . . well, I got here. Just in time, it looks like."

Karen and Jimmy laid my mistress across the backseat of the minivan. Karen looked down at Jessie's burned face and bitten-off arm and shook her head.

"What on Earth did you get yourself into tonight, Jessica?"

chapter five

Palimpsest: Virtus

I stayed curled on Jessie's chest as Karen drove north on High Street. Under the stasis spell, the girl's heartbeat had slowed to maybe ten beats a minute, and her blood oozed through her veins like syrup.

"Jimmy, please cast that stealth charm of yours on the car."

"But you said I wasn't supposed to—" the boy began.

"I said you were not to use it for racing your friends on the freeway," Karen said sharply. "This is different. We need to hurry."

"Okay." The boy closed his eyes and began to recite a Japanese racing charm.

The car shimmered around us, then went translucently blue.

Mother Karen stomped down on the accelerator. We sped up the street at ninety miles per hour, zipping right through slower vehicles. I caught quick glimpses of the interiors of tall vans and SUVs as we passed through them, the occupants oblivious but for one little girl in a car seat who goggled at us as we zoomed beneath her feet.

Karen slowed slightly as she turned off onto a side street, and after a few twists and turns the boy stopped his recitation. The minivan turned visible again, and she braked as the tires crunched on a gravel driveway in front of a big, barn-red house.

The front door opened, and a couple of teen girls in shorts and halter tops stepped onto the front porch.

Karen rolled down her window and called, "Girls, please clear off the kitchen table and put down one of the medical drops."

The girls disappeared back into the house as Karen and Jimmy got Jessie out of the backseat. They carried her into the house, through a short hallway into a bright country-style kitchen, and laid Jessie down on a rectangular table covered in a green plastic tablecloth. I hopped off her chest onto the top rung of one of the ladder-back wooden chairs.

"Oh my God, what happened to her?" asked one of the girls, reeking of fear as she stared at Jessie's burned face and bitten-off arm.

"There was some trouble downtown," Karen said. "It's nothing for you to worry about. I need you girls to keep the other kids out of here—they're too young to see this, and I need quiet to work on her. There should be juice boxes and snacks in the little fridge in the playroom if anyone wakes up hungry or thirsty."

Karen opened a nearby cabinet, pulled out a briefcase-sized white medical kit, and opened it on the kitchen counter. "I know this is kind of gruesome, but I need you to help me with this, Jimmy."

He swallowed, turning a bit green. "Okay . . ."

From my vantage on the back of the chair, I peered at Karen as she pulled on a pair of disposable latex gloves. She lifted up Jessie's stump to inspect it. "Can you smell that, Jimmy?"

"Yes." The boy looked as though he might vomit.

"That burned-hair smell is demon ichor. The rotten-chicken smell is demon venom—it's full of putrescine and draculins among other things. It causes hemorrhagic fever when it gets in the human bloodstream, only it's not contagious, fortunately." Karen turned Jessie's arm this way and that, the bloody bits of glass gleaming in the soft yellow light. "This is really nasty. I need you to get six extra boxes of gauze, then get the Tupperware box labeled BONE STARTER out of the basement chest freezer."

"Yes ma'am." He ran down the hall, clearly relieved that he had been given a reason to leave the kitchen.

Karen got a pair of kidney-shaped plastic pans out of the cabinet along with a squirt bottle of saline. She set one bowl under Jessie's wounded arm and the other near the girl's face.

"I'll have to do this in two stages," she told me. "The bone won't grow if there's still poison in her, so first thing is to get all the demon goo out of her system and make sure she doesn't have an infection."

Karen rinsed Jessie's stump with the saline, then got tweezers and a pair of small, sharp scissors out of the kit. She pulled bits of gravel, glass, and corroded wire from the wound and trimmed away the ragged dead flesh and bone.

"I'm guessing from the smell of the venom that this was some kind of Plagueshadow or maybe a Wutganger?" Karen asked me.

I chirped and nodded from my chair-top perch.

Karen shook her head as she rinsed off the stump again. "I hope you realize that you're both tremendously lucky to be alive right now."

I most certainly did, but had no way of easily conveying that, so I mutely watched her work.

A half-grown ginger cat crept into the kitchen, peering up at me curiously. "Are you prey?" the kitten asked.

"No, I am *not* prey," I replied sharply. "And I don't want to play with you, either."

"Oh." The kitten looked crestfallen, then looked at Karen. "Will she make me tasty wet food?"

"Not now, kitten."

"Will *you* make me wet food?"

"Can't work the can opener, sorry." It had often occurred to me that being able to communicate with other animals is usually far less useful than people seem to think it is.

"Her paw's all gone," the kitten said, gazing up at Jessie's unconscious form.

"Yes, you're quite observant." I sighed.

"A dog got me and ate up my leg. Karen fixed me. She makes good paws," the kitten chirped.

I spotted a moth fluttering down the hall in the entryway.

"Kitten, look behind you! Prey!"

"Prey?" The kitten mewed and bounded away in pursuit.

Saved by the bug, I thought.

Karen had finished debriding Jessie's arm. The older witch gathered jars of herbs and unguents from the cupboard and refrigerator and started pounding together a poultice with a mortar and pestle. Jimmy came back in with the frozen bone kit and extra gauze, and he and Karen spread the green paste thickly on Jessie's wounds and bandaged her up.

Karen and Jimmy gathered up Jessie and carried

her down the hall into a small guest bedroom. I leaped onto Jimmy's shoulder as he passed by; he seemed surprised but didn't try to shoo me off. The pair laid Jessie down on the plush double bed, and I scurried down Jimmy's arm and took my place beside Jessie's head. Karen cast the charm to cancel the stasis. The girl gasped and shuddered as her heart started to beat normally again.

Karen stretched and glanced at the clock on the wall. "It's nearly midnight now, so I should let the poultice work for a few hours then check her temperature and give her a potion," she told Jimmy. "It looks like I'm going to be up all night. But you've got school tomorrow, so you should go to bed soon and try to get a little rest."

Karen stopped, cocking her head to the side to listen to something I couldn't hear. "Were you expecting some of your friends tonight?" she asked Jimmy.

The boy shook his head.

"Well, then there surely shouldn't be any other Talents on our street tonight," Karen said, hurrying out of the room. I hopped off the bed and ran along behind her.

Karen slid open the door to the hallway closet and searched through it. She found what looked like a long canvas rifle case, then unzipped it and pulled out an ivory-colored staff. It bore sigils for fire and light carved into its gleaming surface. I thought it might be polished dragon bone or mammoth tusk, and it gave off the emanations of very old, very strong enchantments.

Carrying the staff as if it were a loaded shotgun with a hair trigger, Karen flung open the front door and stepped out onto the porch. I followed close behind. Three black sport utility vehicles were speeding up the street and slid to a stop at the curb in front of Karen's house. A dozen men in dark suits piled out of the cars and strode up the gravel driveway. I recognized Cold and Fear among them.

"Don't come any closer," Karen warned, pointing the staff at them. "What do you want?"

"You know what we want," said Cold, stepping forward. "Mr. Jordan is adamant that the girl be turned over to him tonight. Give her to us, and we won't bother you again."

"You can't have her," Karen replied grimly. "You're trespassing; get out of here."

Cold sighed and squeezed the bridge of his nose as if he was trying to ward off a headache. "Look. We all have better things to do right now. Don't make us do this the hard way."

"So go away. That's not hard at all," Karen replied.

Cold sighed again then nodded at the men behind him. They marched toward the house.

Karen began chanting an invocation in one of the ancient star languages humans aren't supposed to know. I was impressed; clearly she was not your average suburban housewitch. She jumped off the porch onto the lawn and stabbed the end of the staff into the earth.

The staff burst in a blue bolt of lightning that shot straight up into the clouds and held there, a giant roaring Jacob's Ladder spark between Earth and sky. The men and Karen were all knocked to their knees by the shock of the explosion, and for a moment I was certain I'd been deafened.

A round, bright portal opened where the bolt pierced the clouds, and a creature that looked like an enormous crystalline orrery began to drift down to Earth. My mouth went dry as I realized it was a Virtus. How had Karen managed to call a Virtus? The guardian spirit's ten diamond eyes orbited around a pulsing magma heart, and as it slowly spiraled toward the house it left behind a trail of glowing mist that curled into mathematical symbols before it evaporated.

Fortunately, any mundane neighbors who might have been awakened by the noise in the street wouldn't be able to see or hear what was happening on the lawn. I could feel that the house and its yards had a camouflage enchantment, presumably to keep the children's practice sessions out of sight of the neighbors. The magic seemed strong enough to shield even the huge Virtus from view.

Mother Karen had gotten to her feet, her palms blistered from the exploding staff, her knees caked with mud and grass.

"Hear my plea!" she shouted up to the Virtus in its own ancient language. "These men have come to unlawfully abduct a girl under my protection."

The Virtus's inhuman jewel eyes all focused on Karen. "You claim a mark of duty to this girl?"

"Yes. I am her master's rightful proxy," she replied.

Trembling, Karen held her scorched palms up to the guardian. A glowing tentacle of plasma emerged from the Virtus's heart and probed Karen's left palm. A sigil glowed bright in her hand, and she gasped in pain.

"She has the proper mark," the Virtus said in English, turning on the men, who had all gone pale. "Present your counter. Now."

"Our . . . our master is Benedict Jordan—" Cold began.

"Irrelevant. Present your counter."

"We, uh, we don't have one, but Mr. Jordan—"

"Irrelevant." The Virtus flared bright as the sun, and the proud men cowered in its harsh light. It was a truly beautiful scene. "If you do not have a counter, you have no right to the girl."

The Virtus's plasma tentacle shot down and drew a burning circle around the house. "You shall not cross this line without permission from my kind, or you will be expunged. Leave this place now, or I will remove you."

Jordan's men couldn't get back to their vehicles fast enough.

"Thank you," Karen said to the Virtus as she knelt before it.

"Why have you spent your token on such trivia?" the spirit demanded. "Kings have warred for the artifact you possessed to save their entire tribes, and you use it for a single girl?"

"It seemed like the thing to do at the time," Karen replied, her voice shaking.

"Foolishness," the Virtus replied, and disappeared back into the night sky, leaving behind only the smell of ozone and the smoking ward circle.

Karen got back to her feet, more slowly this time. "Well, that's that."

She dusted herself off as best she could with the backs of her hands, then looked past me into the house. I turned to follow her gaze; her teenagers were clustered on the stairs, smelling frightened.

"Nothing more to see, kids," Karen said, sounding profoundly tired. "Everybody go back to bed. But since you're still awake, Jimmy, please help me get my hands cleaned up . . ."

chapter six

The Luckiest Girl in Ohio

I gradually woke up in a bright, sunlit room; I didn't really *want* to be awake. My face was wrapped in gauze, and the slightest movement hurt like hell. It took me a moment to realize I was in Mother Karen's guest suite.

The ache from my bandaged left eye spread back through my skull; both temples throbbed. My left arm was bandaged up under my breasts. I tried to shift my legs but couldn't. A fat calico cat dozed between my feet.

"You're awake?" Pal popped up beside my pillow.

"Sorta . . . ," I mumbled.

"She's awake!" Pal chirped to the cat, who stood up, gave a leisurely stretch, and hopped off the bed. I guessed she had gone off to fetch Mother Karen.

I licked my cracked lips; my tongue felt as though it had been coated in glue. "How long was I out?"

"Thirty-six hours," Pal replied. "You nearly died."

Pal quickly told me about everything that had happened while I was unconscious.

"Jesus," I said. Calling down the Virtus was no mean feat, and was a tremendous drain on anyone's magical reserves. The summoning was supposed to be limited to fairly senior wizards when they had a life-or-death issue that needed mediation.

"I mean, I know things got screwed up something fierce, but I tried to fix it," I said. "Couldn't they have waited till later to try to question me?"

"I don't believe they really meant to question you," Pal replied quietly. "I suspect they meant to take you someplace where your body wouldn't be found and leave you to die."

"Fuck me," I said.

"Language, Jessica, language!" Mother Karen stood smiling in the doorway with a steaming mug in her hands. Her cheer seemed forced.

"What's going on, Karen? Why did those guys want me dead?" I asked.

"Oh, nonsense, of course they didn't want you *dead*," Karen said lightly, casting a quick, irritated glance at Pal. "It was all a huge misunderstanding, and . . . well, you haven't done a thing wrong, and so you shouldn't worry about anything."

Karen came to the side of the bed and helped me sit up a little. "Drink this," she said, bringing the mug to my lips, "and when you wake up, you'll be feeling much better."

The healing potion tasted like frosted mint brownies. I just had time to think that Karen made the best-tasting potions in probably the entire country before I fell fast asleep.

I woke with a mighty need to pee. I sat up, and a nauseating wave of dizziness made me immediately wish I hadn't.

"Right on time," Karen said. She was knitting a long blue scarf in a wooden rocking chair by the bed.

"I'm gonna bust," I said as Karen set aside her needles and helped me get out of bed.

"No you're not. The toilet is just over here."

Karen led me out into the guest bath.

"Sorry can't be polite gotta go." I fumbled down my pajama pants with my free right hand—when did I get into pajamas?—and plunked down on the toilet.

"No problem, covering my eyes, won't look," Karen replied.

Sweet relief. "Thank God. Hey, nice ducks," I said, noticing the cute blue-and-white duck-patterned wallpaper for the first time.

"Oh, thanks," said Karen. "We put that up last month."

An awkward silence as my cascade continued unabated.

"By the way," Karen said, "did you know that the human bladder can hold nearly a liter of urine?"

"Oh, well that would explain a lot right now," I replied. "Not to be a nitpicker, but why didn't you magic some of this out of me while I was asleep?"

"I did. Twice."

"Oh." I finally finished, wiped, and pulled on the flannel pants.

"You had a lot of poison in you. You're lucky to be alive." Karen helped me wobble to the sink.

"So Pal says. Speaking of, where is he?"

"Curled up with one of the cats, I think."

"No, I'm here." Pal humped into the doorway. "I felt you wake up, but Snoogums was sleeping on my tail."

I gave Karen a look. "You have a familiar named 'Snoogums'?"

"Oh goodness no, it's just a pet. The five-year-old named him. I had nothing to do with it."

I paused. "Is there any news about Cooper?"

Mother Karen shook her head.

"So who's gone looking for him?"

"Nobody, as far as I know."

A swell of fear and frustration rose in a hot tide inside me. "Someone's got to go after him, he could be—"

"Wait." Karen held up a hand, took a deep breath. "Listen. Worry about Cooper later; we need to take care of you first. I need to take off your bandages to make sure you're healing up properly. I . . . couldn't fix as much as I wanted to. There were some complications with the governing circle."

"The men came back again," Pal said. "With a scroll from a different Virtus."

I felt sick all over again.

"I don't want you to worry, no matter what you see, okay?" Karen said quickly. "It can all be fixed. Later, when things are sorted out."

Karen got a pair of scissors out of the drawer under the sink. She cut the sling-like bandage binding my left arm to my body, then unwound the wrapping on my arm.

Five inches below my elbow, my forearm ended in a stub of puckered, purple scar tissue. My knees went rubbery.

"My hand. But I . . . I can still feel it," I stammered.

"That's normal. Your nerves are still inflamed, and so your brain doesn't know it's gone yet," Karen said gently.

"*What the fuck am I supposed to do without my hand?*"

"Listen!" Karen's tone was worried, but stern. "I

wanted to give you your hand back, but right now I *can't*. The representatives from the governing circle came here last night; they summoned the Virtus to put me under a geas. I am forbidden under pain of death from doing more than necessary to get you healthy again until the head of the governing circle says I can."

"Mr. Jordan did this? Why? What the fuck did I ever do to *him*?" Tears streamed hot and bitter down my right cheek to my lips.

"I don't know. I honestly don't. I think this has to do with Cooper. Where is he? What happened to you two down there?"

"We were calling the storm, and—and something went wrong. Cooper accidentally opened a portal; I think it sucked him in. A demon came out. A Wutganger. Someone put an isolation sphere on us, and—"

I broke down sobbing. "Oh God, it got so fucked up. Cooper's gone, and I don't know how to get him back. These poor guys got killed by the demon, and I got poor Smoky killed and he was just trying to help us oh God I didn't know what I was doing and j-just made it worse—"

Karen hugged me. "Shh, shh, it's okay, it's all over—"

"No it's not, if it was all over, I'd have my hand back. I'd have Cooper back." I took a shuddering breath and squeezed my eyes shut, trying to stop myself from crying.

"This is maybe not the best time, but unfortunately it can't wait. I need to take the bandages off your face," Karen said.

I stood still and miserable. Karen carefully cut the

gauze away and peeled it off. Her own face went pale.

"I think maybe we should put you back to bed for a little while no honey please don't look in the mirror—"

I stepped past Karen. And looked. And wished the demon had killed me after all.

My left eye was not still covered by a patch, as I'd hoped. My eyeball had been eaten out of my head by the Wutganger's blood; a white plastic ball held my lidless socket open. The flesh of my left cheek had been melted practically down to the bone; the skin and muscle Karen's potion had regrown was thin, red-streaked, and pitted.

"It's fixable!" Karen said. "Please don't freak out, it's fixable. Really. This didn't turn out like I hoped; that tissue will sunburn like crazy, maybe they'll let me do a bit more under the terms of the geas . . ."

"I—I'm a monster," I whispered. The Wutganger had made me into a version of itself after all.

"No you're not, you've just got a bit of a scar—"

"A bit of a scar?" I began to laugh hysterically. "Oh yes, and I am just the Princess of Luck, too, aren't I? I am just soaking in luck! Sweet Jesus on a pogo stick, I can't go out in public like *this*." I shook my stump at my reflection. "I can't go to work like this."

Oh God. *Work.*

I turned to Karen, my heart pounding. "What day is it? What time is it?"

"It's Wednesday, a little shy of seven AM."

"Crap in a hat, I was supposed to work yesterday. You didn't call me off, did you?"

Karen shook her head. "No, I'm sorry, I didn't know—"

"Oh hell, rent was due yesterday, I am *so* boned—"

"Please, Jessica, calm down. You'll make yourself sick."

"Okay." I took a deep breath. "Okay."

"Look, your supervisor and landlord should understand; you've obviously had a bad accident."

I suddenly realized that I didn't have enough money for rent in my checking account, and I didn't know how to access Cooper's account. "You wouldn't happen to have two hundred I could borrow until I can get the rainstorm money from the farmer's co-op, do you?"

Karen shook her head. "That would violate the terms of the geas as well."

"Motherf—" I stopped myself and took another deep breath. There was no sense in taking my frustration out on Karen. "Could you write me a note for my boss?"

"That I think I can do."

"So what else do you have to do—or not do—because of this geas they put you under?"

"Well, at eight AM sharp I have to call Benedict Jordan's office to tell him that you're well enough to meet with him. And then presumably he'll be out to see you."

"About what? About Cooper?"

"I wish I knew," Karen replied.

chapter seven

Meeting Mr. Jordan

I didn't feel like going back to bed. I didn't much feel like doing *anything*, really, but curling into a ball of uselessness wasn't an option. I had an hour to get ahold of myself, cowgirl up, and see what it was that Mr. Jordan wanted.

Karen brought me an old gray T-shirt and a pair of one of her older teens' jeans to replace the clothes ruined by the demon's blood. She taught me a simple shoelace-tying charm, then left to start breakfast. I took a shower and got dressed, and then Pal and I went into the conservatory to wait for The Man.

"What does Jordan want with *me?*" I asked Pal. "He can wave his pinkie finger and have a hundred guys snap to it. There's nothing I can possibly do for him that he can't get already."

Mother Karen had put us in the conservatory sunroom off the formal dining room so we'd be out of the way of the kids as they got ready for school. I had a hard time keeping track of exactly how many kids Karen was fostering; it was at least twelve and maybe as many as twenty. The house was tucked away on a dead-end lane that backed up into the woods lining the Olentangy River. Anyone who saw it from the street would just think it was a standard three- or four-bedroom Old Worthington colonial. Inside, it had been enchanted, expanded and re-expanded to give every child a bedroom, plus an enormous indoor playroom and a big fenced backyard equipped with a sound-dampening enchantment so that Karen's elderly neighbors wouldn't be disturbed.

"I expect he wants an explanation for what happened the other night," Pal replied. He was perched on a chessboard on the rattan coffee table. "The man on the TV news said that the tornado destroyed the Riffe Tower and critically damaged the Ohioana Bank Building and part of the Statehouse. The heart of downtown is closed and they don't yet know when it can be reopened. This disaster has cost a lot of people a great deal of money."

I rubbed my good eye. "So he's going to, what, make me pay it all off somehow? I couldn't do that even if I lived two hundred years."

"I don't know what he's going to do," Pal replied. "Would you like to play chess while you wait for him?"

I shook my head. "You'd beat me. My concentration's shot. I think I'll just watch the pterodactyls and the sunrise."

The exterior of Karen's house couldn't accommodate the conservatory addition, so she had it enchanted so that the windows looked eastward over the ancient, majestic Appalachians. As the sun rose above the verdant evergreen forests in the valleys, quetzals wheeled on updrafts between the peaks, large and in charge of the blue Cretaceous skies. Pteranodons dove and cried near their huge cousins, their membranous wings striped with bright blues and greens. A few drab, primitive crow-like birds flapped awkwardly in the magnolias near the windows.

"Magnificent creatures," Pal said, watching a quetzal maneuver delicately with its twenty-foot wings, light and diaphanous as a living sail. "A pity they died out on this world."

"Well, they lasted way longer than we've been around," I said. "If humans survive another fifty million years on this planet, *then* we can start feeling sorry for them."

"Your people will survive," Pal said. "You'll change and evolve like any species, and you might find your descendants physically unrecognizable. But the spiritual elements that make your people unique will survive."

"You're sure about that? We do seem to have an endless capacity for boning things up."

And by "we" I mean "I," I thought miserably.

"The higher entities have invested too much time in humanity to let it destroy itself. If the Virtii felt your people were doomed, familiars would be nothing more than animals, nothing more than handy vessels for wizards to extend their senses. We indentured spirits would be assigned elsewhere."

"How did you get here?" I asked. "I mean, I sort of understand the process of a spirit entering a familiar, but how did you come to be mine?"

"Why was I assigned to you? It was purely random, as far as I know," Pal said. "How did I become an indentured spirit? Erm. Well. Let's just say that humanity has no particular monopoly on messing up."

I smiled despite myself. The ruined muscles in my left cheek cramped sharply. "Ow."

"Try not to hurt yourself," said Pal.

I heard a small child skipping through the

dining room, chanting, "Birdy lizard birdy lizard birdy lizard."

A little girl in pink Powerpuff Girls pajamas ran into the conservatory, holding her arms out to the flying dinosaurs beyond the glass. Then she realized she wasn't alone and stopped in her tracks. She stared openmouthed at me for two beats, then let out an ear-bleeding shriek.

"*Monster lady!*" the little girl yelled. She ran away wailing in terror.

"Oh good," I said, holding my ear. "I'm scaring off little kids. I'm just all set for Halloween, aren't I?"

Karen came in through the dining room.

"I called Mr. Jordan's office," Karen said. "He'll be here very shortly."

"Swell. Hey, could I get you to help me bandage this back up?" I gestured toward my face. "My 'little bit of a scar' is making me feel pretty gruesome right now."

Karen looked pained. "He said he wanted you without bandages."

I felt intensely uncomfortable, as if he'd demanded to see me naked. "Why?"

"He does damage assessment. He wants to see the damage."

"That's nice. Does he want my shirt off, too? 'Cause I think my boobie got burned." I angrily pulled out my collar and peeked down my shirt. "Yep, I see a new Band-Aid! More scars he's gonna wanna see! I could totally do the Big Damage Lapdance for him. I could see if I can pop my fake eye into his waistband or something."

"Jessica!"

"No, really, I can totally do this. It'll be a *hoot*." I pressed on my spongy left temple, and the white plastic ball popped painfully into my palm. I stared at it.

"Is this a Ping-Pong ball?" I asked.

"I washed it first!" Karen said, exasperatedly snatching it out of my hand. "Let's get this back in, because Mr. Jordan will be here any minute. You need to straighten up and take this seriously. Believe it or not, your life could be much, much worse than it is now if Mr. Jordan decides he doesn't like you. That means no cussing, no talking back. Hold still."

I leaned my head back as Karen inserted the ball back in my eye socket.

"I *am* taking this seriously. And I can't believe you stuck a Ping-Pong ball in my head."

"It was what I had, and it filled the space. The eight-ball was a little too big."

"You could've shrunk it. Just sayin'."

"No, I *could've* given you the potion downtown and left you lying there on the pavement with an empty socket," Karen replied crossly. "And I didn't, did I?"

I sensed real anger and regret behind her words. "Whoa, what did I do?"

"It's not what you've done, it's what I'm afraid you're *about* to do. Which is to make a very, very powerful wizard your enemy. I love you to death, Jessica, but I've got eighteen kids to worry about, and I love each and every one of them with all my life."

"I know that, Karen . . . you know I'd never do anything to put your family in danger."

"Make this man happy, Jessica. Give him whatever he wants, and we can all get on with our lives." Karen paused, seemed to listen to something in the distance. "He's on the front porch. I better go let him in." She disappeared down the hall.

A few minutes later a tall man in a dark blue Armani suit with a red silk tie strode into the sunroom. His face was smooth, his short, wavy hair dark with just the right amount of gray at the temples. He had the kind of broad white smile you see on presidential candidates, and he carried a glossy burgundy leather portfolio that probably cost a hundred bucks in some tony executive store downtown.

"You must be Jessica!" he boomed, sticking his hand out to me. I uncertainly shook his hand. His grip was dry and painful, the back of his hand furry with dark hair.

"Let's sit down and get started, shall we?"

When Mr. Jordan spoke, Pal laid his ears back. I hoped the lawyer wouldn't hold our entire conversation twenty decibels louder than necessary. I sat down in the wicker chair on the other side of the chessboard.

He's trying to make you feel small, Pal said inside my head.

Mr. Jordan gave Pal a laser-like glance with his icy blue eyes. "Why don't you run along and play with the cats?"

Had Mr. Jordan heard Pal? No, that would be fifteen shades of illegal. Not even a bigwig like Jordan was allowed to listen in on telepathy between a familiar and master.

"I'd like him to stay here," I said, my voice shakier than I'd have liked.

"Fine." Jordan sat down in the chair facing me. "So, tell me, what brought you to our fine midwestern city?"

"What? Um, well, I came here to live with my aunt Vicky when I was in high school."

"Things not going so well back home in Texas?" Mr. Jordan flipped open the portfolio.

"Things were okay, really . . . it's just my dad remarried, and his new wife had a young daughter, and she got pregnant right away with the twins . . . it was just sort of . . . crowded, I guess. It seemed best for me to come out here."

I tried not to think about how sour my home life had turned. Mom died suddenly, just a month after my eleventh birthday. My relationship with my father had always been a little uneasy, tainted with impatience and resentment. We never seemed to have much in common, and I would have suspected I was adopted, except that I looked so much like both my parents. I mostly resembled Mom, but nobody denied my physical resemblance to my father.

After my father met Deborah at his company, he had less and less time for me. I was thirteen when they got married; my father moved us away from our cozy Craftsman home (and the few friends I had) in Lakewood out to a cookie-cutter neighborhood in Plano so that he and my stepmother could be closer to work. By the time the twins were born, I felt like a ghost in their four-bedroom house.

"I suppose that fire you started in your bedroom had *nothing* to do with Mr. Feathers sending you here, then?" Jordan asked.

I gave a start. How did he know about that? "It—it was an accident," I stammered. "Nobody knew

I had a Talent, and I had a bad dream about fire, and—"

Jordan waved my explanation away. "Of course, of course. An accident. Pyrokinesis is quite common among certain teenagers who are denied regular outlets for their abilities. Mr. Feathers sent you here to live with your mother's sister quite soon after, correct?"

"He called her that day and they made arrangements, yeah."

"Sent you by Greyhound bus, didn't he? Just a week after the fire?"

"Yeah . . ."

"You'd think a man with his income could have afforded an airplane ticket, wouldn't you?"

"It was Aunt Vicky's idea—they didn't know how bad my nightmares might get, and what might happen while I was asleep, so they thought the bus might be less dangerous."

"Ah. Do you speak with Mr. Feathers often?"

Why was he calling my father "Mr. Feathers"?

"Sometimes," I said. I belatedly realized it had been well over a year since I'd even tried to contact him. The last two times I'd called the house, he hadn't picked up or replied to my voice mails. My e-mails had also gone unanswered. "He's pretty busy with his job and my brothers and sisters—"

"They're not your siblings."

"What?"

"Joseph Feathers is not your biological father. Your father was Ian Shimmer."

"*What?*" I felt profoundly shocked, but the shock was mixed with a weird sense of relief and vindication. My real father hadn't rejected me after all. Or had he? Did my biological father even know I existed? Did my mother have an affair? I couldn't believe she would cheat; she and my father—I mean, Joe—always seemed perfectly happy together.

"I suppose you want proof." Mr. Jordan pulled a sheet of paper out of the folder and handed it to me. I took it with a quivering hand and scanned it. The only thing I could really see was Shimmer's picture; I had his eyes and nose. Which, possibly not coincidentally, looked an awful lot like Joe's eyes and nose. The brief text was hard to read, hard to take in.

Shimmer had been my mother's first husband. I'd never known she had a previous marriage. Maybe Joe hadn't, either; it seemed like the kind of thing he'd have thrown in my face sooner or later.

"Shimmer died . . . in prison? Why was he in prison?" I asked.

"The case has been sealed and I cannot divulge any details," Jordan replied, "except to tell you that your mother was convicted in the same case. Due to her pregnancy, she was not incarcerated, but she was forbidden from performing any magic under pain of death. She married Joseph Feathers very soon after. Apparently she met him at a coffee shop."

Jordan's expression was scornful; clearly he thought my mother had hooked up with the first likely guy who came her way after the trial, a man of means who would keep her comfortable and who could be duped into thinking the baby she carried was his own.

"She was a witch?" I had always thought my Talent was from some long-recessed family trait.

"A sorceress, actually. A necromancer, the same as Ian Shimmer."

Black magic? Death magic? I remembered my mom as a warm, loving person. No. It wasn't possible.

Is he lying? I desperately thought to Pal.

No, I don't think he is. Pal was sitting on the edge of a fern's pot, his eyes wide.

"She . . . she never did any of that kind of magic that I ever knew," I faltered.

"Of course not," Mr. Jordan replied, his voice hard as a judge's gavel. "She was completely forbidden from performing even the simplest charm, although we couldn't prevent her from using mundane emotional and psychological manipulation on your stepfather. She was forbidden to possess magical materials or spell books or to teach others magical arts. And as a consequence of her finally disobeying her orders, she was dead less than an hour after she cast her last spell."

I had never been able to forget coming downstairs in the morning to find my mom cold and still on the kitchen floor; the coroner told the family she'd had an undiagnosed brain aneurysm that burst.

"What spell?" I asked.

"Do you remember feeling sick and having headaches in the month before your mother died?"

Was there *anything* this guy didn't know about? "Yes; she told me the doctor said it was a sinus infection."

"It was, in fact, brain cancer. An aggressive ependymoma. Even with surgery, radiation, and the best hospital care, you had a vanishingly small chance of survival."

"She . . . she gave her life to cure me?"

"Oh, not just *her* life; she was a necromancer, remember? She slipped into Children's Medical Center of Dallas that night and smothered a young boy named Peter Gonzales who was awaiting a heart transplant. Your mother stole his life energy to cure you. She managed to ward off the automatic death-spell invoked after she completed her incantation; the Hunter spirit didn't catch her until she was back home."

"That's a lie! She wouldn't kill a little boy!" I knew I wasn't supposed to raise my voice to the man, but I couldn't help it.

"Oh, but she'd done worse. I can show you the documentation if you'd like." Mr. Jordan shuffled through his papers.

"Keep it." I was biting down hard on the inside of my cheek to keep myself from tearing up. I would *not* cry in front of this man.

"As you wish." Jordan closed the folder. "So. With you the proverbial red-haired stepchild back in Texas, you came out here to live with your mother's sister Victoria. Who, while she never had much magical ability herself, took a keen interest in fostering yours.

"You may not know this, but the day after the fire, Mr. Feathers was determined to put you in a mental institution. But Victoria recognized that the fire in your bedroom was the result of your Talent manifesting itself rather than teenage sociopathy; she convinced him to turn over your guardianship to her. You were most fortunate he called her first rather than the county hospital; your life would be very different and much worse right now if you had been committed. In many ways, you owe Victoria your life."

Just a couple of days after I arrived in Columbus,

Aunt Vicky had arranged for me to start getting magic lessons at the Folklore Department at Ohio State. As at most large universities, the OSU Folklore Department was mainly a front for secretly educating Talented students in magic. The faculty offered a few mundane lower-level classes for ordinary students, but most of the rest of their offerings took place in the tall, windowless folklore tower in the center of campus. The department was well funded by local benefactors such as Mr. Jordan, and so the administration never really questioned why hundreds of students majored in a subject with seemingly no commercial value in the working world.

"Vicky was really cool about everything," I agreed. "She did all right by me, for sure."

"Then why did she die?"

I paused uncertainly. Surely he knew all about Vicky's death? It had happened in his backyard, after all. "Well, her husband, Bill, started sleeping around on her, and I guess when she found out, it was just too much for her. She poisoned him and then herself."

"Do you think she was depressed?"

"Well, yeah, I'm sure she must have been. She was never, you know, the most chipper person in the world, but I think she would've had to be seriously depressed to do what she did."

"Then why didn't you do something to help her?"

I couldn't say anything for a moment. "I would have helped her, if I'd known what was going on—"

"And why didn't you know about all the bad things that were happening in your aunt's life?"

"It was my first year in college," I protested, feeling sick. "I was in the dorm, and I had a full load of classes—"

"Her house was less than a ten-minute drive from campus. You couldn't spare regular visits to the one person in your life who had genuinely helped and supported you? Who did *she* have for support besides her unfaithful husband? She should have had you."

"I didn't know—"

"A big part of knowing what's going on is being *interested* enough to try to find out. It doesn't seem to me that you were very interested in your aunt's life. How long did she lie there rotting in her house before you thought to see if she was all right?"

"Four days." The words died as they left my throat.

"I don't think I heard you. Please speak up."

"Four days." I tried to push the nasty images out of my mind. The horror of finding the decomposing bodies had been quickly followed by the bleak realization that I was alone in the world. Anguished, not knowing who else to turn to, I'd called my instructor Cooper that night; he was the only person I'd met at the huge university with whom I'd felt any real connection.

He was a tremendous comfort as I grieved for my aunt; I don't know how I would have managed without him. And, yes, we'd gone to bed pretty quickly after the class quarter finally ended, but I'd been aching for his touch for weeks. Afterward, he stuck by me, introduced me to a world I could not have imagined. It wasn't just the magic. Through him, I finally met people like Mother Karen, people who became genuine friends instead of just more acquaintances I couldn't really be myself around. I wasn't going to let *anyone* make me feel ashamed of our relationship.

But oh God, poor Vicky . . .

"She was lying there dead for four days before I found her," I finished quietly.

"So. I will ask you again: Why do you think your aunt died?"

"She died because I was self-centered and too caught up in my own crap to care about anyone else. She died because I was eighteen and stupid."

"Do you think you're any smarter now?"

"Yes."

"You haven't finished college. That doesn't seem very smart, does it?"

"I'm just a couple of quarters away from my degree. We've had too much work for me to take classes the past year."

" 'We' being you and Cooper Marron, I suppose? I did note, however, that much of your work is completely nonmagical in nature and involves mundane duties at a construction company."

"You say that like I'm lugging spackle or something. I put together their ads and newsletter. I work there because I *like* it there."

"It's not work befitting an apprentice sorceress. It's not even work befitting a Talented teenager. And it's not the kind of work that Cooper Marron feels he needs to pursue, is it?"

"Cooper gets loads of contracts, and I'm not advanced enough to help with all of it. We need steady money, so I work a part-time job I enjoy; it's not a big deal."

"And why aren't your skills advanced enough to participate in Cooper's contract work?"

"Because . . . because I'm just not there, yet. Cooper says ubiquemancy's kind of a tricky art; it just takes a while to get the hang of it."

"Or maybe that's just a convenient excuse for Cooper."

"What do you mean by that?"

"It seems that he's turned you from his apprentice into his common woman without you noticing. He's got you warming his bed, cleaning his home, paying his bills while your studies languish."

"That's not true!"

"Are you denying that you've had a sexual relationship with Cooper Marron that began either during or soon after he taught your freshman introduction to ubiquemancy class at OSU?"

"No," I said, "but we didn't start seeing each other until after the class finished."

"Nonetheless, his relationship with you was—and is—unethical. It's a clear violation of the codes of student–teacher conduct. Surely I don't need to explain these basic rules to you. Did you never wonder why the department didn't invite him back to teach?"

"He didn't want to go back . . . he doesn't like teaching huge classes. He prefers one-on-one sessions."

"I'll just bet he does."

I fought down the urge to smack the supercilious half smirk off his face. "Look, you're making our relationship out to be this sleazy thing, and it's not! We're partners, and we love each other."

"You say you're partners, but you've already admitted to me that he has you doing mundane work to support his interests. Any ethical master would have enabled you to leave the mundane world behind by now."

"That's not fair . . . I mean, look at you, wearing

that lawyer suit and tie. You spend most of *your* life in the mundane world. How is your life as a lawyer so much more magically worthy than my little office job? Is it just because you make loads more money than I do? You governing circle wizards keep telling the rest of us how money is this lousy, no-good distraction from all the crap we're supposed to focus on—"

I realized I'd gone too far, and quickly shut up.

Mr. Jordan frowned at me. "The difference is that I do not rely on mundanes for my survival. They rely on me for *theirs*. And the work I do is crucial to our community's continued harmonious existence with the mundane world.

"For instance, that disastrous little stunt you and Cooper pulled the other night caused nearly half a billion dollars in damage and crippled the city's downtown. And *I* am the one responsible for cleaning up your mess. My company will have the city back in working order before the week is over. We will restore commerce and harmony, and soon everyone but the families of the dead night workers will forget about the whole ugly incident.

"You, on the other hand, waste your time and Talent in front of a computer. The worst part is that you still rely on the outside world for survival. That kind of reliance is the very definition of a mundane."

He paused, staring at me. "You need to decide which world you belong to."

"I belong in this world," I replied. "I'm completely dedicated to my magical studies."

"Completely dedicated. Mm-hm. A dedicated student is a respectful student, wouldn't you say?"

Where was he going with this? "Yes, I suppose so . . ."

"No. There's no 'suppose' here. Any serious student wants to be a respected member of the magical community, and one has to *give* respect to get it. Ignoring and disobeying the laws and rules of a community disrespects that community."

"But—"

"Cooper Marron has a long history of scorning the laws of our world. And you, young lady, disrespected our rules when you let yourself become involved with him as his lover. Both of you have disrespected our world with your casual use of magic, and the incident downtown is a direct consequence of your sloppy behavior.

"Your family has a history of violence and destructiveness, and at this point I'm not at all convinced that you won't follow in your mother's and father's footsteps and become an outlaw even worse than Cooper Marron. How can I trust that you'll be a responsible, productive member of our society? How can I let you remain part of our world?"

Is he talking about banishing me? I asked Pal.

Yes, he is, the ferret replied.

"I never meant any disrespect to you or anyone else by seeing Cooper," I said. "I never wanted to do anything but be with the man I love. I am really sorry for what happened the other night; I tried as hard as I could to make things right and I just couldn't."

"You did do surprisingly well, all things considered." Jordan's tone was grudging. "Nobody who was aware of the situation expected you to survive. Clearly you're a strong Talent. It would be a pity if you had to be banned from continuing your studies."

"What do you want me to do?"

A parchment and black quill pen made from a raven's feather appeared on the chessboard in front of me.

"I want you to sign this agreement that states that you will not, upon pain of banishment and two years' incarceration, attempt to find Cooper Marron or bring him back to this plane of existence."

I stared at the parchment. "I . . . I can't sign this."

"You must. These are the terms of your remaining in the community, as decided by the governing circle. We think this is in the community's best interests as well as your own."

"But earlier . . ."

Don't make him angry, Pal warned. *You're in a heaping lot of trouble as it stands.*

". . . earlier you blamed me for not living up to my responsibilities to Aunt Vicky. For turning my back on her when she needed help most. And now you want me to turn my back on the man I love, right when he needs help most? How is this supposed to make me a more responsible member of the community?"

"Wherever he is, Cooper is lying in a bed he made a long time ago." His voice held the snap of a coffin closing.

"Cooper's helped plenty of other people in this city when they've been in trouble. Why won't you help him?"

"Cooper is a bad influence. I can't risk any more death and destruction because of him. I particularly can't risk him returning to this city insane and out of control. No. He stays where he is. And you sign this agreement that you'll leave well enough alone. After you do that, I'll make sure you get assigned to a new, more suitable master."

"And if I don't sign?" I asked.

"I can't prevent you from working what magic you know how to use, but you will be anathema. No member of this community may assist you in any fashion until you sign. Most major cities in North America have courtesy agreements with us, so you'd be excluded most anyplace you might wish to move to."

"I . . . I have to think about this."

Mr. Jordan nodded. "You have an hour. After that, the anathema decree will take effect, and Mother Karen will have to remove you from her home."

Mr. Jordan nodded toward the front of the house. "Cooper's car is outside. Aside from some body damage it appears to still be in working order. We've taken the liberty of removing the weapons from the trunk. We can fix the car, and your hand and your eye, after you sign. It's up to you."

Mr. Jordan got up and left the room, left me staring down at the parchment. A few moments later I distantly heard him speak a few curt words to Mother Karen, and then the slam of the front door echoed down the hallway. Pal crawled out of the fern pot and onto my shoulder. My blind eye socket ached, and my missing hand felt like it was on fire.

"You should sign that so we can get Mother Karen to take care of your arm," Pal said.

"No. I can't. It's not right." I shook my head, trying to clear the cloud of regret and anxiety Jordan had stirred up. "I can't believe the nerve of that guy, making me feel all guilty about letting Vicky down and then telling me I should abandon Cooper. And he comes in here acting like this bullshit is for my own good—does he *really* think I've forgotten he left me out there to die? Damn him to hell if he thinks I'm going to sign this."

I grabbed the parchment and tried to tear it in half with my teeth. It wouldn't rip. Swearing, I balled it up in my hand and threw it behind the fern.

"You *do* realize that signing that agreement is in your best interests right now?" Pal said, shifting his paws nervously.

"You don't actually think that jerk's *right,* do you?"

"No. I think he's railroading you," Pal replied. "It's clear he's going to do anything he can to keep you from even starting to look for Cooper. Which, considering you lack the experience to successfully find your master on your own in the first place, much less do battle with the horrors that surely lie wherever he's gone, strikes me as a very suspicious kind of overkill.

"But I think things will go badly for you if you don't bow to Mr. Jordan's wishes. And we have at best a slim chance of getting Cooper back in one piece. So I'd be derelict in my duties if I didn't tell you that for your own sake you should sign the paper, find a new master with whom you are *not* likely to become romantically involved, and get on with your life."

"You said 'we.' Does that mean *you'll* help me find Cooper, at least?" I asked.

"It's my mission to help you in any way that I can," Pal said. "But I need to know that you understand that from here on out, life will be hard for you, and there might be no good outcome to this. Your eye, your hand—that's just the beginning of what you might lose."

I squeezed my fist. "I *have* to find him. It's as simple as that. But first I gotta get myself bandaged back up; I wonder if Mother Karen has a sling?"

chapter eight

A New Record

"I really think you should reconsider," Mother Karen said, worried, as I worked at getting the Dinosaur's dented door open. "You realize that, five minutes from now, I won't be able to so much as take you to hapkido practice, right?"

"I'm not going back to the dojo, not until this is over, anyway. Please give my apologies to the sensei, if you're allowed to do that kind of thing," I replied, alternately yanking and kicking the door.

"Why not use a spell for that?" Karen asked.

"Not as satisfying as brute force right now," I replied, the door finally coming open with a metal-scraping squeak. "Hop on up," I said to Pal, who jumped off the car's roof to my good shoulder.

Karen handed me my cell phone and a couple of extra boxes of gauze. "Don't forget these—and try to keep that arm in the sling as much as possible the next few days."

"Thanks. And I will." I tossed the boxes on the passenger seat and turned on my cell phone, expecting to see a message or two from the Warlock wondering what had happened to me and Cooper. But there was nothing: no messages, nor any missed-call alerts.

"Did the Warlock call you while I was unconscious?" I asked.

Mother Karen frowned. "No, he didn't . . . were you expecting him to?"

"Well, yeah, kinda. Cooper and I were supposed to get together with him for dinner, but then all the shit downtown happened . . . ah, hell, he probably met someone new at his bar to fall madly in bed with and he forgot about everyone else."

Feeling abandoned and frustrated, I clipped the cell phone to the waistband of the cast-off jeans.

Mother Karen reached up and adjusted one of the bandages on my head. "The tissue's still really thin over the bone, and if it tears you could get a pretty nasty infection. You won't be able to get proper healer care, so if anything goes wrong you should see a physician." Karen made a face. "They'll want money—a lot of it—and half the time they don't know what they're doing. If all this goes on for more than a week, though, you'll need to see someone about getting a proper glass eye and some corrective surgery."

"If any of this goes bad on me, I'll have to try to take care of it myself . . . I don't know *anyone* who has the money for regular surgery, much less plastic surgery," I replied. "Our next-door neighbor got a bill for ten grand when he busted up his leg in a motorcycle accident. They only kept him overnight. We did what we could for him afterward, but if he'd had to rely on the hospital for care, he still wouldn't be walking right."

"I've heard that hospital work is quite lucrative for healers," Karen admitted. "I've never done it myself. I feel bad for all the people dying and crippled out there, but there's not enough of us to take care of all of them. How do you choose who gets helped and who doesn't? It seems to all hinge on money and class status; I'm just not comfortable with that."

"Cooper told me that most religious hospitals don't let witches help, so I figure that limits things."

"Not as much as you'd think," Karen replied. "The modern popes have gone from promoting witch hunts to publicly pretending we just don't exist. Some doctors at Christian hospitals make quiet referrals for their sickest patients. Other hospitals have an attached wing that isn't *technically* part of the hospital where they can do procedures that the church frowns upon. Important people can't just be left to *die*, can they?"

Karen looked sad and disgusted.

"Speaking of fixing things," I asked, eyeing the bandages over my stump, "got any advice for what to do if I *do* get an infection? I think this is starting to seep a little."

"I'd try a little spell with moldy cheddar and wood ash. But I'm afraid my time is up, and you've got to go." Karen smiled sadly. "Your anathema light just came on."

"My what?"

"Your anathema light," Pal said. "It's a sort of red, pulsing glow."

I looked down at myself; I didn't see anything. "It's all over me?"

"All over, I'm afraid," Mother Karen said. "Any Talent will see it, and know that they're supposed to stay away from you. Nonmagical folks won't be able to consciously sense it, but you might make them nervous. Strangers, anyway."

"Lovely. Well, we better get on home." I got into

the Dinosaur and awkwardly heaved the door shut. Pal hopped into the backseat.

"Good luck to you, Jessica. For what it's worth, I hope you can bring Cooper back."

"Me, too." I started the car. "But if I don't make it through this . . . name a kitten after me or something, okay?"

Driving the Dinosaur with only one arm was rough, but I quickly learned to steady the steering wheel with my knees when I had to shift. I was halfway to the apartment when I realized the parchment and black-feathered pen were lying on the passenger seat beside the boxes of gauze. The contract still bore faint wrinkles from my attack on it in the conservatory.

Had it followed me into the car?

Was that thing in here when we left Mother Karen's place? I thought to Pal, who was curled up in the backseat.

"No," Pal replied. "The seat was empty three minutes ago."

How did it find me? Are we being tracked? I thought of the phone at my waist—someone like Mr. Jordan could pretty easily tap its GPS chip to keep tabs on me.

At least nobody else could listen in on what Pal and I were talking about, as long as I kept my own mouth shut. Although my brain interpreted his remarks as regular speech, everything he said came to me telepathically, and the confidentiality of his discourse was protected by some of the most fundamental rules of our magical society. I remembered Cooper telling me that nobody on Earth—not even the governing circle—was allowed to tap telepathy between a familiar and his or her master. In extreme circumstances, the familiar's otherworldly handlers could record the discourse, but there was a lot of wizardly red tape involved, and the handlers didn't share information with Earthly magical authorities unless serious formal charges had been made.

"There could be tracking spells on the car, or your clothes, or the parchment could be attuned to your unique physical or spiritual profile," Pal replied. "Most likely, though, the tracking charm is simply part of the anathema spell."

Swell, I thought back. *Well, for now, let's pretend we don't notice it. I bet they have the car bugged, too. I'd rather Mr. Jordan didn't know what I have planned.*

"What *do* you have planned?" Pal asked.

I'm still working on that one.

"Ghetto, sweet ghetto," I said aloud as I pulled into the Northglade Apartments' parking lot.

The complex had been the pinnacle of trendy yuppiedom around the time I was born; now it was near the bottom of its slow decline. The air stank from the Budweiser plant down the street. Gutters glittered with bits of broken bottles. Tired-looking mothers watched broods of shrieking kids pounding across the weed-riddled blacktop in their supermarket sneakers.

A couple of South American men in undershirts sat smoking Lucky Strikes on the front porch of one of the three-bedroom units. I knew they had probably ten guys sharing the place; they all held down two and three jobs apiece at nearby fast-food joints. What they didn't spend on smokes or beer or food, they sent back home to their families. Half would come home to sleep while the others worked, hot-bunking like sailors on a submarine at war.

The apartments had survived a decade of neglect because they were well built. They were quite spacious for the money, and in a complex full of screaming spouses and booming stereos and barking dogs, nobody ever complained about Cooper and me chanting (and sometimes blowing things up) at odd hours of the night.

My neighbor Bo was out on his front porch in a frayed lawn chair, petting his pit bull Gee. She started wagging her tail furiously when she saw the Dinosaur pull up in the spot between Bo's old truck and my little Toyota Celica.

Gee was the sweetest-tempered dog I had ever known. Bo found Gee out in the country two years before; she'd been shot through the lung, and two of her legs and most of her ribs had been broken. Some Neolithic asshole had been beating and starving her to try to turn her vicious, and when she still wouldn't fight, he shot her and left her for dead on the side of the road. Bo came knocking on our apartment door that night to see if we knew of a good veterinarian. Cooper numbed the dog's pain, set her bones, and healed her.

Later, when Gee was resting comfortably on a pile of old blankets in Bo's apartment, Cooper told me he had an errand to run and left in the Dinosaur. He came back three hours later with swollen knuckles and something that might have been blood on the toes of his Doc Martens.

He slept more peacefully that night than I had ever seen.

"Yo, Jessie, 'sup?" Bo waved at me as I killed the engine.

"Oh, this and that," I said as I forced the door open and slowly got out. The arm was starting to hurt something fierce again. Pal hopped up on my shoulder, mostly to avoid being slurped on by Gee as she came bounding over to greet me.

"Sweet Jesus in heaven, girl, what happened to you?"

"Had a little accident." I paused, considering whether to tell Bo the truth or not. He'd known ever since we fixed up Gee that we used magic, but he'd agreed to keep quiet about it and hadn't asked too many questions since then. I always got the feeling he was trying not to seem nosy.

"Like a car accident? Where Cooper at? He okay?"

I decided I was too tired and sore to lie. "You know the other night when there was that tornado downtown?"

"Holy Jesus, you get caught up in that?"

"Well, sort of." I glanced around to make sure nobody else was in earshot. "Cooper and I were trying to call a rain shower, but we got a demon instead. The tornado was to cover up the damage the demon did. I got munched by the demon and Cooper got sucked off to another dimension. I don't know if he's okay or not."

Bo looked aghast. "You got your hand bit off?"

"Lost my eye, too. Not a good night, all things considered."

"Can your folks fix that, like y'all fixed Gee and her leg?"

"Yeah, they *can,* but for right now they're not

gonna. I'm kind of on everybody's shitlist right now."

" 'Cause of all the damage downtown?"

"Mostly because I want to find Cooper and bring him back, and Mr. Jordan doesn't want him found."

"But Cooper's your man, you *got* to try and find him. You gotta do right by family. It ain't right that they wanna keep you from helping him."

"Yeah, it ain't right, but that's what they're doing."

"Can I do anything? You two been real good to me and Gee. I got maybe fifty dollars to help with that," he said, pointing at the paper taped to my door, "and I'll get more at the end of the week. Miz Sanchez might be able to help, too. I know she'll want to."

I walked to my door and pulled the paper off. It was an eviction notice. "Oh, this is just getting better and better."

"Don't go gettin' all stressed about that, now," Bo said. "They always give an eviction notice first moment you're late 'round here. Takes 'em six weeks to evict anyone, so they want to get a good early start on laying the hammer down on folks."

"They want a seventy-five-dollar late fee on top of the rent and the water bill," I said, reading the notice. "That comes to seven hundred and thirty dollars. And they want it as a cashier's check. Joy. I might be taking you up on that offer, Bo."

"No problem, just let me know," he replied.

I unlocked the door and stepped into the apartment. It had been built as the mirror image of Bo's rental: a fairly basic two-bedroom town house with a drafty cinder-block basement. The bedrooms were spacious enough for most people, but got pretty cramped in a hurry if you had to find a place to put a library of arcana and a few hundred canisters of spell ingredients.

Cooper and I had decided not to magically expand the interior of the apartment as Mother Karen had done with her house. We didn't know if we'd be staying there more than another year or two, and undoing that kind of enchantment was complicated and noisy and tended to leave magical residue that would be disconcerting for future tenants.

So Cooper bought a two-bedroom shack way out in the woods in Athens County for a few thousand dollars, banished the termites and roaches and mold, and set up warding spells that would dissuade any rural burglar. He set up a trans-spatial door in the upstairs hallway of the apartment, and we were able to use the shack as our library, storeroom, and practice room.

We could have expanded the shack and just kept a one-bedroom or efficiency apartment as a portal into the city, but we were concerned about people seeing us carry in boxes and furnishings that the apartment couldn't possibly hold. Curious neighbors usually became nosy neighbors. Northglade was in a handy location and allowed dogs. At the time, the extra expense seemed trivial.

"I better call Mr. Handley and see when I can get my paycheck," I said to Pal as I locked the front door behind us. Pal clambered down and humped over to Smoky's water bowl.

I sat down on our love seat by the living room phone and punched in the number for my day job.

Maria, the secretary, answered the phone. "Handley Construction, how may we help you?"

"Hi, Maria, it's Jessie . . . look, I had an accident earlier this week, and that's why I missed work and didn't call in. Is Mr. Handley there? Can I talk to him?"

"Oh. Jessie." Maria sounded uncomfortable. "I'll . . . see if he's available."

The line abruptly switched to easy listening.

Pal humped into the living room. "I think something went bad in the kitchen . . . what's going on?"

"Not sure . . . she put me on hold."

The phone clicked silent for a moment, and then Mr. Handley was on the line: "I'm surprised you'd be calling here, Miss Feathers."

What was with the "Miss Feathers" stuff? "Hello, Mr. Handley, I just wanted to—"

"Apologize for stealing three hundred dollars from petty cash? It's a little late for that."

"What?"

"Don't play innocent with me. Not after you lied on your job application about your criminal record," he said.

"I'm not a criminal. I didn't steal from you," I said, feeling lost at sea.

"I've got a copy of your arrest details right here in front of me," he replied sharply. "Don't you know this kind of thing is a public record? You were convicted of misdemeanor theft twice in the past three years."

"No, I never—"

"Stop. *Please*. The police tell me there's not enough evidence to have you charged. And you're not worth suing. I don't want to see you or hear from you again, clear?"

The line went dead. My heart was pounding in my ears.

"What was that all about?" asked Pal.

"I suddenly have a police record," I replied, acid rising in my throat. "Everybody at Handley thinks I'm a liar and a thief. I'm a hundred shades of fired. Oh God. Where am I going to get rent money?"

The farmers. Cooper and I *did* manage to call down rain, after all, and the tornado didn't touch the farms. The three-thousand-dollar fee would solve my most immediate problems. I flipped through the telephone book until I found the co-op's number.

After a couple of minutes on hold, I was connected with Cooper's farm contact, Mr. Maedgen.

"Yep, that was a right fine rainstorm," he said. "Tell Cooper his money's waiting for him here at the office."

"Oh good," I said. "Can I pick it up this afternoon?"

"Sure, as long as Cooper comes with you . . . we can't give the payment to anyone but him."

"But he *can't* come with me," I said, trying to keep my frustration out of my voice. "He had to go out of town on an emergency, and I don't know when he'll be back. We live together; I can show you the lease with both our names on it. Our rent's due, and we're going to be out on the street without that payment."

"Well, I'm sorry, miss, but the terms of the contract are that the money is to be paid to Cooper Marron and nobody else."

"But I helped him with the spell," I protested. "You owe me as much as you owe him."

"I'm sorry, but your name isn't on the contract. Rules are rules. I can't help you."

I thanked him, hung up, and sat there with my head in my hand.

"Bad news?" Pal asked.

"If I ever get Cooper back, there are going to be a few changes in how he writes up his work contracts," I said bitterly.

"Is there anyone who could lend you money for the time being?" Pal asked.

Well, there's the Warlock, I thought back. *But since he didn't bother trying to get in touch with me after we didn't show up at the Panda Inn Sunday night, maybe he's trying to stay out of all this.*

I punched in his number. A second later, I got a three-tone beep and a recorded female voice announcing, "I'm sorry, the number you have dialed has been disconnected . . ."

I hung up, feeling even sicker than before. "That's not a good sign."

"Could you try to open a mirror at the Warlock's home?" Pal suggested.

I shook my head. *He and Cooper refuse to keep enchanted mirrors around. They say they're too easy for other Talents to spy through.*

"And telephones aren't?"

I shrugged. *We all pick and choose. Cell phones are easy, and you can't play MP3s on a pocket mirror. Or at least the boys have never been able to work that kind of magic.*

I glanced down at my feet. Mr. Jordan's contract and the quill pen lay a few inches from my left sneaker. Swearing long and hard, I grabbed the contract, balled it up in my hand again, and threw it with as much force as I could muster across the living room.

"This completely sucks," I muttered, trying hard to not start weeping.

"Look, it's not all bad," Pal replied. "As Bo said, you have six weeks to avoid eviction."

"I suppose so," I said, taking a deep breath to get hold of myself. "But since Mr. Jordan's been so kind as to rewrite me as a convicted petty criminal, I don't think I have much of a chance of finding a job anytime soon. And there's no way in hell my dad— I mean, my stepfather—would lend me the money. So I figure eviction's unavoidable at this point."

"Well, Cooper owns the house in the woods outright, doesn't he?" Pal asked.

Yes, I thought back. *He got a load of money from that exorcism he performed up in Cleveland.*

"So if worse comes to worst, you can just move everything into the house, right?" Pal asked.

Sure, if all our stuff will fit, I replied. *My architectural skills are crap; I couldn't expand it any further.*

"Well, then let's go to the house and do some old-fashioned measuring, shall we? With the proper charms, I am quite sure you can get most anything into the house."

Pal crawled up on my shoulder, and we went upstairs. The steel door to the house was right there on the wall between the master bedroom and the bathroom, huge and red and completely out of place. I stopped. Cooper always made sure to hide the door when we left the apartment, just in case maintenance decided to pay an unexpected visit.

I know he hid that before we left, I thought to Pal.

"I'm sure he did, too." Pal sniffed the air. "Something's burning."

I went up to the door and put my palm against it. I, too, could smell burned wood and metal. *The steel's warm.*

Bracing myself, I spoke the key to release the lock. The door swung open to a burned wreck of smoldering boards and scorched fieldstones. Nothing of Cooper's house still stood but the fireplace and chimney. Only an intense fire could have caused this kind of damage, but the flames had not spread to the pines that were only a few yards away.

Clearly, this was no accident, and no act of a mere vandal. Cooper had been very careful to protect the house against fire. Nobody but a powerful wizard could have countered his spells.

I stared at the ashes where our library used to be. Dizzy, I fell to my knees in the doorway. "Oh God. Some of those books were older than Moses . . . they didn't *exist* anywhere else."

"I don't think they burned," Pal said. "There would be magical residue from their destruction, and I don't sense anything. Whoever did this absconded with anything of real value before they burned the house."

"Whoever"? I don't think there's any question about who did this, I thought grimly. *Why'd he bother leaving the apartment intact? Why not just burn it, too?*

"He wouldn't want that much collateral damage to the community," Pal replied. "Better to show you he can find your secrets and defeat your master's magic. Better to force you into eviction and break your will to oppose him."

The fitful wind was blowing smoke into the apartment; our bedroom fire detector started beeping shrilly. I shut the door and spoke the word to hide it, then hurried over to the detector to hit the reset button.

Jordan sure didn't waste his time putting the screws to us, did he? I thought as I opened the bedroom window to air the apartment out.

"No, he didn't. I am surprised at how far he's gone to pressure you, and how quickly he's put things in motion," Pal replied. "A man in his position needs the approval of a Virtus for such extreme actions. He must have convinced at least one of them that Cooper poses a serious threat."

But why? I asked. *What threat could he possibly pose to anyone?*

"I'm as much at a loss as you are," Pal said. "There's more to this than I can fathom right now. Even if Mr. Jordan was driven out of sheer sadism to torment you . . . well, he didn't rise to his current position through self-indulgence. He's committed nontrivial magical resources to breaking your will."

Well, Jordan can go screw himself, I thought. *If he thinks he can bully me, he's got another think coming.*

"If the Virtii approved of arson, they may approve of murder," Pal warned. "That's a rare and serious step, but it could happen."

Well, they didn't burn down this lousy wreck of an apartment complex, I replied. *So I guess they're not ready to kill anybody over this yet. At least nobody but Cooper.*

I looked around the bedroom. A few of the jewelry cases on my dresser looked as though they'd been moved slightly, but I couldn't be sure.

Jordan's goon squad went through this entire apartment, didn't they? I asked Pal.

"I can't be certain, but given the circumstances I'd say you'll probably find anything of any magical power to be mysteriously gone," he replied.

Well, if Jordan's got the keys to this place, and if I'm going to get evicted, I'm sure not going to stay here, I thought. *Let me take a nap, and then let's get this place packed up.*

"Where will we go?"

Someplace where Jordan can't find us, that's for sure.

chapter Nine

Supersonic Butterfly

I woke up groggy, socket and stump throbbing, as Pal poked my neck with his sharp little nose.

"What now?" I mumbled.

"Think to me, don't talk," he warned. "We need to find someplace else to stay as soon as possible."

I sat up, looking around the bedroom. Everything seemed pretty quiet. *What's happened?*

"My overseer summoned me to his lair," Pal replied. "They want me to abandon you and take an assignment with a new master."

So you're getting pressured, too? Swell.

I flopped back on the bed, then immediately regretted jostling my stump. As I rolled over onto my good side, I felt something crinkle beneath me. It was Mr. Jordan's parchment and the quill. Again. I shoved them off the bed.

"No, you don't understand," Pal insisted. "This is unheard of. We familiars are supposed to be above any local political trouble a Talent might get into. We can be recalled if a master is formally convicted of a crime and banned from using magic, but this . . . this under-the-table coercion isn't supposed to happen. *Ever.*"

I frowned. *So how much are they pressuring you?*

"Quite a lot, actually."

That definitely wasn't good news. *Are you going to leave me?*

Pal looked at me as if I was slightly crazy. "Of course not! First, it wouldn't be the right thing to do, and second, if that scaly bastard thinks he can treat me like a slave . . . well, I suppose I *am* a slave . . . but still."

Scaly bastard?

"My overseer is a white wyrm. I've had to suffer through his supercilious, egotistical twattery for nearly three centuries. I'll be damned if I let him get the upper hand in this."

But don't you have to do what he tells you to do?

"I have to make him *think* I'm doing as I'm told, yes," he said. "But unless you complain to him, or unless Mr. Jordan's agents catch you doing something illegal, he's none the wiser. During the first century of my sentence, I was directly monitored, and most everything I said or did with my master was recorded. My master joined a group of other witches and wizards who objected to the invasion of their privacy, and they lobbied the Virtii until the rules were changed to eliminate the eavesdropping."

Pal drew himself up proudly. "I have kept my nose impeccably clean until now. I have earned my right to privacy, and I will continue to use it to do what I believe is the morally correct course of action. Which is to help you out of this mess."

But what about the governing circle?

"Ah, see, that's the blind spot. The Virtii have never given local governing circles the right to track or interfere with familiars, and we trust-boon familiars are only subject to renewed monitoring if local officials can provide conclusive evidence of misdeeds. So if they don't catch you doing anything illegal, they won't catch me, either."

Pal cocked his head, seeming to consider his own words, and his whiskers twitched nervously. He jumped off the bed and hopped up on the windowsill, peering out anxiously as if scanning for strangers watching the apartment. "But therein lies the rub—unless we're very careful, you *are* likely to be caught doing something they can declare is illegal. I don't like what's happened here at all. Mr. Jordan couldn't have managed all this in the space of just a few days . . . he's had to gain influence in some very high, very specific places. I think he planned for all this a long time ago."

Are you saying that Jordan caused the accident at the park? I asked, dumbfounded.

"No," Pal replied. "I don't think that at all. It was far too messy and destructive. But I do think that Mr. Jordan suspected something like this might happen, and he put in place a contingency plan to deal with you very aggressively in case it did."

If he thought Cooper was going to do something, why did he let it happen at all? I wondered. *Why not simply warn us?*

"I don't know," Pal said. "But for both our sakes, we've got to figure it out. Did Cooper ever speak of Mr. Jordan?"

No, never. He only met him once at a big to-do downtown, as far as I know. They never had anything to do with each other.

"Well, we should get this apartment sorted," Pal replied. "Do you know any packing charms?"

No, not really . . . we mostly did things the mundane way when we moved in here.

"Strictly speaking I'm not supposed to show you that kind of thing, though it's really not that hard . . . but first, you need to box up all your smaller breakables."

We didn't keep any of our moving boxes, but Bo might have something at his place, I replied. *I need to see if he wants our food anyhow.*

We went downstairs and into the kitchen. A sour, funky smell assaulted my nose; had Cooper left the milk sitting out again? No, the counters just had a couple of dirty plates, and we'd emptied the trash the previous day.

I pulled open the fridge, and the stench made me gag. My jar of gherkins were covered in fuzzy mold. The milk we'd bought three days ago was solid gray-green sludge in its translucent plastic jug. The plastic bag of baby carrots had turned to rotting brown goop. And the bag of Mrs. Sanchez's tamales—oh God.

I quickly shut the door, swallowing bile.

"There goes my damage deposit," I coughed.

"We can clean that with a spell," Pal said.

"Not if it means having to open the fridge again." My eye was watering.

Clearly, whoever had torched the shack had decided to add that extra little bit of spite and spoil our food. Probably they accelerated time within the refrigerator. I opened up the cabinets to check our dry goods. The soup and tuna cans bulged with botulism gas, and the oatmeal teemed with weevils.

"Rat bastard sons of bitches."

The only food the goon squad had left untouched in the kitchen was the forty-pound bag of Smoky's

Science Diet. My mood sank even lower when I saw the dog kibble. Poor Smoky . . .

No. I blinked down the tears welling in my eye. I couldn't afford to get depressed. I swept the ruined spices, cans, and boxes into the kitchen garbage can.

I probably can't trust my toothpaste or lotions or anything like that, can I? I thought to Pal.

"I wouldn't recommend it," he replied.

Fine. Makes packing simpler, anyway.

I pulled a handful of garbage bags out of the box and stomped through the apartment bagging tubes of cream, tins of powder, and bottles of soap, shampoo, and lotion. Even the brand-new bag of ferret chow we'd bought for Pal was moldy. It took me most of an hour, and at the end I had three bags to haul out to the Dumpster.

Bastards probably blanked all our DVDs, I thought bitterly as I heaved the bags into the top of the steel bin. My stump hurt worse than ever, and my good arm and lower back ached. *They probably zapped our electronics and crapped spyware all over my hard drive.*

"Well, once the wards are deactivated, burning a building and spoiling food are fairly easy," Pal replied. "They might have left the rest alone. Pack everything you want to keep unless something seems obviously compromised."

I pondered the bag of dog food when I went back into the kitchen. *Do you think that's really okay? I wouldn't want to give it to Bo and have Gee get sick, but I wouldn't want to waste it, either.*

Pal crawled down off my shoulder and hopped

onto the bag. He sniffed at the kibble, licked a piece, then bit into it.

"It's not very tasty, but I don't think it's been tampered with," he said.

Why'd they leave the dog food alone? I wondered.

"So they could say that technically they didn't leave us to starve."

"Creeps."

I hefted the bag against my hip and went next door, Pal following behind. Bo answered my knock.

"Hey, you okay? You lookin' kinda pale," Bo said.

"I think so." I couldn't hold the bag up any longer, so I let it slide down my leg to the concrete porch. "Hey, can Gee eat this brand? Smoky, um, he . . . he didn't make it the other night."

"Your little dog got killed? Man. I sure am sorry to hear that." Bo shook his head.

"Yeah, me, too." I couldn't fight back the tears this time, couldn't fight back the soul-deep fatigue of everything I'd been through. My vision swam, and my knees buckled.

"Whoa, got you!" Bo exclaimed, catching me before I could pitch backward.

I clung to his broad shoulders, tried to pull myself up, got a whiff of his aftershave and sweat that suddenly reminded me so much of Cooper, reminded me so much of what I'd lost and might never have again, and before I knew it I was weeping like a child into Bo's T-shirted chest.

He held me and patted my back awkwardly. "That's okay. You been through a lot. Let it all out."

I was finally able to take a deep, ragged breath and stand up. I'd left the wet outline of my nose and eye on his green shirt. "I got snot on you."

He shrugged and smiled. "If that's the worst I get on me today, then it's a pretty good day."

My socket and arm were hurting worse than ever. "I hate to ask, but do you have any ibuprofen?"

"Like Advil? Yeah, I got that. You look like you could use somethin' to eat, too."

"I sure would appreciate it," I replied. "The creeps trashed all our food while I was gone, except for this." I nudged the dog food bag with the toe of my sneaker. "Everything else is rotten."

Bo frowned. "Why they do that?"

"Showing me who's boss. Trying to scare me away from looking for Cooper, I guess."

"That ain't cool," replied Bo. "You'd think they got better things to do."

"Yeah, you'd think," I agreed.

"Well, come on in," Bo said, lifting the dog food easily. "I ain't got no more tamales, but I can make you a ham sandwich."

"Does he have any eggs?" Pal asked. "I'm feeling a bit peckish myself."

"Do you have a raw or hard-boiled egg I could give to my ferret in a little bowl?" I asked as I followed Bo into his apartment.

"I think I got some left . . . you go on, have a sit on the couch."

I went into his living room, stepping over toy trucks and wrestling action figures. "Are your kids with you this week?"

"No, they with their mama," Bo replied, sticking his head out the kitchen pass-through. "I guess I should gather up all those toys, but I kinda like havin' 'em out. It's like my boys is still here even though they ain't, ya know?"

"Yes, I think I do," I replied.

The coffee table was strewn with empty Zima bottles and Subway sandwich wrappers. *Playboy* magazines were scattered across the threadbare tan couch; I stacked a few of them to the side and sat down.

I heard Bo crack open a can of soda, and then he came into the living room carrying a Coke and a bottle of Advil.

"I found you some pills in the kitch—oh." He froze openmouthed for a moment as his eyes fell on the stack of magazines. "I forgot I had them things out. I, uh, I just—"

"—read them for the articles, right? No big thing, Bo."

Lips pursed in embarrassment, he cleared away some wrappers and set the pill bottle and Coke can down on the coffee table in front of me. I popped the lid off the bottle with my thumb and dumped four pills onto my lap. I set the bottle aside, popped the pills into my mouth, and washed them down with a slug of soda.

"You want cheese on this?" Bo called from the kitchen.

"Sure."

"Mustard?"

"No, thank you. I only use it for medicinal purposes."

"Huh?"

"Never mind."

Looking puzzled, Bo brought in the Velveeta and ham on white bread on a paper plate and a bowl of egg, then sat across from me in an old leather recliner. We chatted about the weather and the sorry state of the apartment complex while I ate and Pal lapped up his egg.

"They got a devil's nerve to evict *anyone* after all they ain't fixed 'round here," Bo said. "There's leaves and bugs in the pool all the time now—and my boys want to go swimming, you know? If they ain't bothering to get the bugs out, how do we know they're bothering to keep up with the chlorine and what-all to keep the germs down?"

"Don't worry," I replied. "Cooper took care of that when they filled the pool for the summer. The water might have trash floating in it, but nobody's gonna get hepatitis if a junkie takes a crap in it some night."

Bo wrinkled his nose at me. "That's a *nasty* thought, girl."

"Well, it could happen," I protested around a mouthful of sandwich. "My point is, the pool won't make your kids sick. Cooper made sure the water is and will remain fundamentally clean no matter what happens to it."

"Can I have some of that ham?" Pal asked as I was about to finish off my lunch.

Sure. I pulled the quarter-sized remnants of the lunch meat off the bread and laid it on the edge of his bowl. *But it's really not very good for you.*

"It's not that good for *you*, either." He chewed the rubbery ham daintily.

"I wondered if I could ask you another favor," I said to Bo as I set the paper plate on the coffee table.

"Sure, what?"

"I'm not going to fight this eviction thing, at least not right now, so I need to pack up my stuff. Do you have any moving boxes? And could I borrow you to help me get a few things packed today?"

"Sure," Bo said. "I got a bunch of boxes in the basement. I'll dig 'em out an' bring 'em up. You can hang up here if you want."

"Thanks, Bo. You're a sweetie."

After Bo went downstairs, I laid my head back against the couch, my eye half closed. The Advil was starting to kick in with a faint ringing in my ears along with sweet ebbing of the pain in my eye and arm.

I eased my arm out of the sling to stretch my elbow and shoulder and laid my crippled arm on the stack of magazines.

"Packing your things won't take very long," Pal told me. "Particularly if you don't mind him seeing you perform charms."

Well, he's seen them before, I thought back. *I don't see how it would hurt anything. I want to get this done, find a new place, and start looking for Cooper.*

"You can't search for Cooper if Mr. Jordan is monitoring your movements," Pal replied. He twitched his tail anxiously, as if he was trying to decide to do something risky but didn't want to say what.

I wasn't in the mood to have to pry out whatever was on his mind. *Well, I guess I don't have a choice, do I? I'll figure something out. One thing at a time.*

The ibuprofen was making me feel a bit sleepy and light-headed. I sank down deeper on the couch. The magazine was cool under my palm, and I could feel the smooth ridge of the spine. I absently started to pick at the staple with my thumbnail.

"Jessie!" Pal exclaimed, hopping up in my lap.

"What?" I sat up in alarm.

"Did you do that?" He was staring at my stump.

What? I looked around, trying to figure out what he was going on about.

"The magazine moved. You moved it."

I looked at the stack of magazines under my hand . . . no, it was under *nothing*. The hand was gone, yet when I closed my eye again I could still feel the slick paper, the cool ridge of the staple. I grasped the spine with my thumb and forefinger, lifted the magazine an inch and dropped it with a soft thud.

I opened my eye and stared at my stump, tried again. Nothing.

"That's a most unusual thing you just did," Pal said.

Well, apparently I can only do it with my eye closed, I replied, baffled. *This doesn't exactly help me drive stick any better.*

"I'm serious—reflexive parakinesis is quite a rare natural ability, even among Talents." Pal beat a little tattoo with his feet and then hopped sideways across the couch, back arched in ferretish excitement. "This is wonderful! Only some Talents can learn to do it at all. And most everyone who does has to concentrate and practice for dozens of hours before they manage as much as you just did."

Pal stopped his weasel war dance, shook himself sternly, and returned to my lap, apparently trying to look as dignified as possible. "Were your parents—?"

Transvestites? Elvis impersonators? FBI agents? You know as much as I do right now, I thought bitterly. *Seriously, though, what's the big deal? Cooper moves things telekinetically all the time.*

"Yes, but he does it through charm shorthand, which he had to spend months learning and internalizing like most anyone else," Pal replied. "What you just did wasn't a charm. It wasn't learned. It was natural to you."

I don't mean to be dense, but . . . so what? I ever-so-slightly moved a magazine with my mind. We're having a whole conversation with our minds. When I was sixteen I set fire to my freakin' bedroom with my mind. We're a mind-y bunch. This seems a little underwhelming by comparison.

"It's fairly impressive that a tiny monarch butterfly can migrate thousands of miles, is it not?" Pal asked. "It's fairly impressive that a circus dolphin can leap twenty feet out of the water through a flaming hoop, is it not?"

Well, yeah, we sure can't do those things without magic or technology, so it's plenty impressive.

"But most any monarch can fly thousands of miles, and most every healthy dolphin can leap high from the water, correct? No monarch would be particularly impressed by one of its brethren flapping from Brazil to Canada, would it?"

I guess not . . .

"So what would you think about an otherwise mundane monarch that could naturally fly fast enough to break the sound barrier?" he asked. "Would you sit there and say, 'Oh well, we have airplanes that can fly much faster than that little butterfly, and they can transport cargo and bomb cities and lots of other things. That little monarch couldn't carry a single grenade!'"

Hell no, if I saw a supersonic butterfly I'd be completely impressed. I'd be plenty impressed even if it was just wearing a little jet pack. Are you saying that my moving the magazine is up there with a Mach One monarch?

"It's nearly that rare, yes," Pal replied.

You asked about my parents. Why?

"I've been here on Earth for quite some time now. I've met thousands of Talents. I've met one other natural parakinetic, a Hawaiian boy whose family was supposed to be descended from the goddess Pele."

Are you saying my great-great-whatever was some kind of deity?

"Or possibly an incubus or some other type of spirit entity," he replied. "Studying the hereditary implications of spirit–human offspring is a bit of a hobby of mine, and I do get excited when I find new potential subjects."

I shifted in my seat, suddenly feeling a bit like a guinea pig. *I never really understood how that god–human thing was supposed to work anyway. Genetically, I mean. As I understand it, lesser deities are mostly natural forces that people worshipped and believed in for so long that they became aware and intelligent, right?*

"In most cases, yes. Imagination can be a powerful thing, even in mundanes."

And spirits like demons are the projection of souls or soul particles that can't exist in their natural state in this world, right? So gods and spirits don't have genes to pass along, unless they possess the body of some poor schmuck, and then they'd just be passing on the schmuck's genes, right?

"Well, it's not quite that simple. Spirit entities can certainly impregnate women—or any female animal, really—without having to possess the body of a man. What they do through their natural magic is to duplicate the genes in the woman's egg so it can start dividing into a blastula . . . but they have the power to make extreme changes to her genetic structure.

"Take Jesus the Christ, for instance," Pal continued. "My sources agree he must have begun as Mary's clone, but it's an utterly simple matter for a deity of Jehovah's power to turn an X chromosome into a Y. The human genome is just so much modeling clay to the creator entities."

Huh. Cool. So what generally happens to the descendants of a god's child?

"Well, it's highly unpredictable, which is why studying them is so interesting to me. You can have a hundred generations of perfectly mundane humans descended from a godchild, and then suddenly a baby will be born with wings, or the ability to pass through walls.

"The Virtii are nothing if not mathematically precise," Pal went on, "but even the Talent genes they wove into your species millennia ago have proven to be surprisingly variable in their expression. If we can learn the rules behind the seemingly random expression of godchild genes, we will understand life and magic that much better."

Are we just an experiment to the Virtii? My teachers and the pointy-hats always made a big to-do about us having some highfalutin role in the fate of the Universe and whatnot, but I can't see the Virtii needing our help, you know? Or really caring about what happens to us. I've never seen a Virtus for real, but from all I've heard they're heartless as rocks.

And why give just part of the human race Talent, and then turn around and micromanage us like they do to keep us from taking over the world from the mundanes? I continued. *They gave all the faery*

*races some kind of Talent, and from what I hear
they pretty much leave them alone. I know we humans are flawed and petty and power-hungry, but
goblins are even worse.*

"I can't disagree with you. It has seemed to me
that the Virtii are studying Talents—human or
otherwise—for their own ends, but what those
might be I couldn't say."

I was still thinking about godchildren. *I read an article that said there are about sixteen million descendants of Genghis Khan alive in the world today. I get
that he was big into the raping and pillaging. But
could he really outdo Zeus? Or even just a really
determined incubus?*

"Probably not," Pal replied. "At this point most
humans, mundane or Talented, have got some kind
of spirit or deity tampering in their genes."

*So my talent is rare . . . but almost any baby con-
ceived might have the potential for it? You're saying
we're living in a world where almost any butterfly
could be supersonic?*

"Well, yes," he said. "We live in a world of infinite
possibilities."

chapter ten

Disappearing Act

I was trying to wrap my mind around everything Pal had just told me when I noticed that Mr. Jordan's parchment and pen had materialized beside me. With a sigh, I shoved the contract behind the couch and threw the feathered pen into the litter on the coffee table.

Is that jerk ever going to give up? I wondered.

"Lawyers don't come with an off button," Pal replied, "so I'd have to say it's not very likely."

Bo puffed up the stairs with an armload of a dozen flattened boxes and a roll of clear packing tape around his sweaty left wrist.

"Found these under the stairs," he said. "Will these be enough?"

"Well, it should be a decent start. Thanks a bunch." There was a Budget/U-Haul rental place across the road; if worse came to worst I could always buy some extra boxes. I set Pal on my shoulder and got to my feet. "Got time to help me pack for a while?"

"Sure."

I led Bo next door and put him to work reassembling the boxes and packing up our CDs, DVDs, and remaining books. Pal told me to get the box of trash bags, and then we went upstairs to practice my packing charms.

"See those boots in the corner?" Pal asked as I shut the door to the bedroom.

I followed Pal's nod to Cooper's battered old black engineer's boots in the corner of the bedroom by the closet. "Yes?"

"Can you make them float? Not to make them rise like helium balloons, but to make them neutrally buoyant."

Yes, I've done that before. I closed my eye and re-membered a long-dead word for "weightless." As I chanted it softly, the boots rose slightly off the floor and drifted to the wall.

"Very good," thought Pal. "Now, let's work on your sweep. Do you have some suitcases?"

Sure. I slid open the closet and pulled our two rolling Samsonite cases down from the top shelf. One was a big gray hardcase, and the other was a smaller soft-sided model made from red ballistic nylon. *Now what?*

"Now you need to float everything in your closet and sweep it into those trash bags, then sweep the bags into that smaller case," he replied. "We'll save that big case with the combination locks for later."

Uh, no way that'll all fit. In case you hadn't no-ticed.

"So you'll just have to shrink the bags once they're full," Pal replied.

Oh.

"After that, you'll need a good, sturdy, shatter-proof container. Preferably nothing with holes, preferably something with a lid that can close very tightly."

How big does it have to be?

"No bigger than a shoe box," he replied.

Well, we've been buying liter-sized tall plastic jars to keep spell ingredients in. Most of them burned with the shack, but I have an empty one under the sink that I was using to store our Epsom salts. Will that work?

"It should work perfectly," Pal replied.

I went into the bathroom and dug the jar out from under the sink.

And now what? I came back into the bedroom.

"Well, you float your clothes and other belongings, sweep them into the trash bags and boxes, shrink the bags and boxes, sweep them into the suitcases, shrink the suitcases so they fit snugly in the jar, seal the jar, and you're done." Pal acted as if it were the simplest thing in the world.

Ah. Gotcha. I tried to think of a chant sequence to accomplish all that. My mind was a perfect blank. *Um.*

"Think of fall leaves, floating and swirling into a neat pile," Pal told me helpfully.

Right. Leaves. Floaty. Swirly. Shrinky. Yeah. My brain had seemingly transformed itself into an empty bait bucket.

"We *are* in a bit of a hurry, yes?" Pal prompted.

Look, I'm sorry, I haven't done this before, okay?

"Got a bit of Babbler's Block, have you?"

Shut up! Jeez! Give me a moment, would you?

Pal sighed. "Why don't I just teach you a standard packing charm instead? The English version involves double hand movements, which you can't do, so how about the Danse d'Emballage?"

"Danse"? This involves dancing?

"It's fun," Pal replied. "And it'll do something about the dreadful heat in here. Trust me. Just step left, step right, hop back, and spin while you repeat after me: '*Volez, mes effets, mouche, pesanteur de défi et rétrécissez les espaces vides . . .* '"

After a few awkward missteps, rhythmic trips, and tongue slips, my clothes and knickknacks were flying off the hangers and out of my dresser drawers, shrinking to the size of fluttering moths, and diving into neat rows in the trash bag I'd laid on my bed.

"That's pretty slick," I panted, taking a rest. My breath fogged in the suddenly cold air; apparently the packing charm drew power from ambient heat.

"You should put the furniture into boxes instead of bags," Pal said, shivering despite his fur.

"Okay. Let's go see how Bo's doing."

Pal crawled up on my shoulder. We went back downstairs and found that Bo had reassembled all the boxes. He was sitting by the stereo, sorting through my and Cooper's DVDs.

"You guys have some cool stuff," Bo said. He held up our copies of *Fight Club* and *Taxi Driver*. "Mind if I borrow these?"

"Sure, you can borrow anything you want," I replied. "I don't know how long my stuff will have to stay in storage, so somebody might as well enjoy the movies."

"Where you gonna go? You know you're welcome to stay at my place," Bo said, sounding hopeful.

"I really appreciate the offer, but honestly that could bring some bad attention down on you, and neither of us wants that," I said.

"You could shrink all those movies and books down and still have room in the box for your electronics," Pal said.

All right, I replied.

"Hey, Bo, could you stand and hold one of those empty boxes up, and sort of tilt it away from you a little?"

Bo got up off the floor and did as I asked, looking a bit puzzled.

"This is going to look a little weird," I said to Bo, "and I'd appreciate it if you didn't tell anyone else about this."

"Okay," he replied uncertainly.

I began the packing dance; I was learning to abbreviate the movements and recitation down to magical shorthand to get the same effect. It was less embarrassing, anyhow. Shrinking books and DVDs flew neatly into Bo's cardboard box, filling the right side, and I quickly filled the left side with the TV, stereo, and sundry players.

"Holy Jesus," said Bo, his eyes huge as he taped the box closed. He seemed unaffected by the arctic air. "Next time I gotta move, I'm calling you for sure, girl."

"Seriously, please don't tell anyone about this," I replied, rubbing my hand against my jeans to warm it up a bit. Cooper and I had never felt comfortable putting the silencing spell on Bo; it just didn't seem neighborly. Maybe that had been a mistake, but I'd asked so much of him I wasn't going to gag him now.

"I won't, I won't," he said. "But for real, you could make a killing doing that moving-and-storage thing."

"I could, except for the part where I can't let people see me doing this," I replied. "Or at least not very many. I can do magic for money as long as it's on the down low. I can't take an ad out in *The Columbus Dispatch* or anything."

"People not supposed to know there's real magic in the world, huh?"

"Exactly."

"That's too bad. Might give some folks hope who don't got it otherwise."

"Or it could scare people, or make them resentful that we can do things that they never can." I shook my head. "The 'why' doesn't matter—we've got pretty strict rules, and I could get in trouble."

"More trouble than you in now?"

"I could get thrown out of the city, or I could get sent to prison."

"You folks got your own prisons?"

"Yeah. People die in them." A lump rose in my throat as I thought of the father I never had a chance to know.

"I can see not wantin' to risk that," Bo said. "Jail ain't no fun even when it's safe."

I was eager to change the subject. "Well, if I could get you to hold a couple more boxes for me, I think I can get the rest of this place packed up . . ."

By 3 PM the apartment was empty and I held the plastic jar with the two miniaturized suitcases nestled against each other inside. At a casual glance, they merely looked like shaving kit bags.

"That is the coolest damn thing I seen all week," Bo marveled. "And it don't weigh a thousand pounds or nothin'. Perfect size to take with you."

"Well, actually, I can't take this with me," I replied, then thought to Pal, *Tracking charms probably all over my stuff, right*?

"Right," Pal replied.

"Well, you can leave it with me," Bo said. "That won't take up no space at all."

"Bad idea," Pal warned. "Don't involve the poor man more than he is."

"Once again, I really appreciate the offer, but having this could be real bad luck for you," I said. "I'll just . . . I don't know, I'll probably put this in a locker at the bus station or something."

"Them lockers ain't real safe," Bo said, "and they don't let you keep them more'n a couple days at most."

"Why not get a safe-deposit box at a bank?" Pal asked.

Oh yeah, I thought back. *Good idea.*

"I'll think of something," I told Bo.

We all left the barren apartment, and my eye fell on my Celica and the Dinosaur.

"Darn it, I should have left room in the jar for the cars," I said.

"Just take 'em 'round to the back lot," Bo said. "There's cars back there ain't been moved in a year. The management don't pay no attention at all."

It didn't take me long to drive the cars to the other side of the complex.

Are you going to get in trouble for showing me that packing charm? I asked as I locked up the Dinosaur and started walking slowly across the hot blacktop back to Bo's place. I carried the plastic jar in the crook of my arm.

"Possibly," he replied, "but that will surely pale in comparison with the trouble I'm about to get into."

What do you mean?

"Clearly, Mr. Jordan is up to something, and I believe he has somehow managed to trick the Virtii. Someone needs to get to the bottom of this."

By "someone" you mean me, right?

"Indeed. But Mr. Jordan will track you wherever you go because of the anathema spell," Pal replied.

Well, maybe if I just, you know, keep moving, he'll lose track of me?

Pal shook his head. "Men like him don't lose track." He paused. "But I know how to defeat the anathema spell they've put on you."

I stopped in my tracks. *You're kidding.*

"Indeed I am not."

Where'd you learn a thing like that?

Pal took a deep breath. "I've never liked . . . restrictions. I've gone out of my way to learn how to get past them, and my predilection for such things is what led to my being sentenced to several hundred years of indentured servitude as a familiar.

"I will likely go to prison if I am discovered assisting you," he continued, "but I'll be ashamed of myself if I don't lend you my full knowledge and abilities."

Wow. I sure do appreciate that. So how do we get this spell off me?

"There's something you need to know first," Pal said. "The removal—really, it's a spiritual transference—is only good for a day or so. You'll have to keep performing the spell, particularly if you're otherwise spotted and they get wise to what you've done."

What about you? Isn't someone keeping tabs on you?

"Not directly, and under normal circumstances they shouldn't be allowed to relay that information to people like Jordan," Pal replied. "But that wall of privacy will fall in a hurry if Jordan convinces my overseer that I'm helping you break the law."

I'll work fast, and stay out of sight. So what do we need to do?

"Well, there's no point in doing any of it until you find a place for your jar," Pal said. "You'd likely be tracked and the spell discovered almost instantly."

Right, I replied. *But what* will *we need to do?*

"We'll need to find tissue from a mundane human female, preferably blood instead of hair or nail clippings," he replied. "And then I'll show you how to perform a ritual to foist your anathema off onto the other woman temporarily. In essence, you'll be hiding your spiritual profile beneath that of the other woman, and vice versa."

So what happens to this other woman?

"Well, the anathema spell will be in full effect on her for a time," Pal said, "so she must be someone who doesn't come into regular contact with Talents. And it should be someone relatively close by at the time you perform the spell."

Will the contract follow her around like it's been doing to me?

"Presumably, yes. It might be alarming, but since Jordan didn't leave any of his mundane contact information on the parchment, I doubt she could ring him up to complain."

But what if someone else signs the thing?

"It wouldn't be your signature, would it? So it wouldn't matter," Pal replied.

But this other woman will have my spiritual profile, won't she? Won't that make her signature binding for me?

"No, not unless she forges your signature exactly," explained Pal. "Mr. Jordan will have created the charm to reject a signature that isn't legally yours. He'd have to consider your signing somebody else's name to the thing to get it to go away."

How would the spell know what my signature looks like?

Pal sighed. "Jessie, your signature is on every form you ever signed for college, for banks, for your apartment. It's on every receipt for everything you ever bought with your credit card. It's not that hard for even a mundane to dig up."

Oh. I suddenly felt naked under the hot sun. *So, aside from being haunted by a legal form, will anything bad happen to the woman I dump my anathema on? Will other people treat her badly?*

"Well, it's certainly possible," he said.

So I foist my anathema off on some other woman, and then she might go interview for a job she desperately needs and not get it? Or maybe she gets stopped for a traffic ticket and the cop decides to search her car? Or some jerk in a bar decides to harass her?

"Yes, all those things are possible."

Well, that just sucks! I don't want to mess up a stranger like that, and I sure as hell don't want to do that to a friend.

"Do you want to find Cooper or don't you?"

Of course I do!

"Then you have to get rid of your anathema," Pal said. "I don't like this any more than you do."

Could the person I switch with be dead? I asked hopefully, thinking that surely somebody in the apartment complex had an urn of their mother's or grandmother's ashes. *Or maybe someone* almost *dead, someone stuck in a nursing home?*

"Dead people don't make good spiritual trades,"

Pal replied. "And you need your trade to be up and moving around to draw your trackers away from you. It'd look suspicious if you suddenly appeared to be bedridden."

Oh. Well, crap.

We'd reached Bo's apartment. Bo had let Gee out onto his front patio and was sitting in his lawn chair brushing her brindled coat. Gee spotted me and came bounding over. I set down my jar and scratched the dog between the ears.

"Can I ask one last favor of you?" I asked Bo.

"Sure, what?"

"Can you take me down 161 to the Ohioana Bank on the intersection at High Street?"

"No problem. Mind if Gee comes along? She sure does like riding in the car."

We went to Bo's rusty old Chevy truck. Gee leaped in the moment Bo opened the driver's door and wedged herself behind the passenger seat. I climbed in cradling the jar, the sun-hot vinyl seat uncomfortable even through my jeans.

"I still think it'd be better if y'all folks could, you know, do your thing in public," Bo said as he started his truck and pulled out of his parking space. "Folks need magic and miracles to keep 'em going."

"I don't know. We have the rules for a reason. If witches were allowed to come out of the broom closet, sorcerers would take over pretty quickly," I said. "I mean, guys like Mr. Jordan have *already* taken over, but without the restrictions it'd be even worse."

"I can't see how having wizards in charge would be worse than the buncha fatcat crooks we got in charge now," Bo said. "Maybe it'd be better having a guy in charge who really could get stuff done."

"You'd just be trading mundane but mostly functional corruption for a magical dictatorship," I said, leaning back against the seat's headrest and closing my eye.

"Yeah, but your folks got actual skills 'n' wisdoms," Bo said. "They're better than regular politicians."

I cracked my eye open and gave him a hard look. "Do you think rich white people are better than poor black people, Bo?"

He gave a start, and stared at me as if I had sprouted devil's horns. "*Hell* no! I ain't never gonna believe that!"

"But rich white people pretty much control everything, right?"

"Yeah, 'cause they got to the American Pie first, and they cheat to keep it for themselves. They got The Man working for them. We just as good as they are. We just can't get in on the game most of the time 'cause it's rigged from the day we born."

"So you're saying that rich white people are born having most of the power, and they spend their money looking out for their own interests so they keep their power. And they mostly don't give a damn about anyone who isn't just like them, right?"

"Yeah, exactly."

"Bo, any wizard who'd want to be in charge is gonna be even less like you—and less interested in your problems—than the guys in power now," I said. "You think The Man's keeping you down now? Wait until The Man can turn you into a toad, or make you into his very own zombie slave. Trust me, you *don't* want wizards running your world. You just don't."

"It don't sound like you have much pride in your own people," Bo said.

I shrugged. "Before I knew I had Talent, I grew up like almost everybody else in my town. In my school, we had a few kids from richer families who rubbed it in our faces all the time that they were better than anyone else because they had cool toys and designer clothes their parents bought for them. I thought at the time that it was a load of crap to feel proud and superior about something you got handed to you as a matter of blind, dumb luck. And I still feel that way. My having magical Talent was just a roll of the dice. I can't take credit for it, and I'm an asshole if I start acting like I can."

"But you can take credit for what you *do* with what God gave you."

"Sure. I try to do the best I can with what I've been given. But almost everybody feels that way, don't they?" I asked. "I read this article in *Forbes* about women who are supposed to be the ten most accomplished heiresses in the world. One of the women won a bunch of awards for riding horses in steeplechases. Another woman is an actress who's won a couple of Emmys for a show she was on. And the rest are magazine models, or manufactured pop stars, or they're presidents of some company or other their families founded.

"And so I'm reading the article, thinking that these women come from families that are worth billions of dollars, families that have huge financial and political power. *Huge*. They could afford the best education, the best of everything. For the amount of knowledge and sheer opportunity they had at their disposal growing up, you'd think some of them could have become important inventors, or doctors, or renowned poets, or *something* really cool. But the most radical thing any of them has done is become a moderately successful TV actress. As a group, they're mostly good at being decorative and spending money to maintain their family's power, and *Forbes* is hailing them as heroines for this? That's some real gold-plated bullshit they're selling. Other people might buy it, but I sure don't."

"You real opinionated today," Bo observed as he turned right onto High Street.

"I get ranty when I'm in pain," I replied, rubbing my stump lightly through the sling.

Bo pulled into a tree-shaded parking spot by the tall brick bank building.

"Speaking of rich movie stars, think I got time to go see what kinda DVDs they got on the shelves?" Bo asked, nodding toward the Old Worthington Library across the parking lot.

"You don't need to wait for me, so you've got as much time as you want. I'm not going back to the apartment," I replied, "and I'll catch a bus or take a cab to wherever I go after this."

"I couldn't just leave you here . . . ," he said.

"No, really, I'll be fine. You and Gee and your boys are better off this way. And if everything goes okay, I'll see you guys again really soon."

I gave Bo a light hug and opened the truck's door. "I really appreciate everything you've done for me. Take care, okay?"

I got out, shut the truck's door, and went around to the side of the bank to their ATM with Pal riding on my shoulder like a pirate's parrot. Nobody else was in sight.

"I bet they've already nuked my credit union bank card," I said to Pal as I set my jar down on the sidewalk, then pulled my small leather change purse out of my front jeans pocket. I awkwardly worked the bank card out of its pocket with my thumb, stuck it in the ATM, and punched in my PIN. Rejected.

"Figures." I sighed, shoving the card back into the pocket on the side of the purse. I got out my MasterCard. "Maybe I'll luck out with this one?"

The credit card was still good; I took out a four-hundred-dollar cash advance and stashed everything in my change purse. "That's not much, and if I survive all this my credit's probably wrecked forever, but if I'm careful it'll do for now," I told Pal.

I picked up my jar, and Pal and I went back around to the front of the bank and went inside. A security guard stared at me and stepped forward.

"Miss, you can't bring pets in here," he said sternly.

"He's a service animal, like a guide dog," I replied smoothly. "If I was blind instead of a cripple, you wouldn't make me leave my guide dog outside, would you?"

The guard blanched when I said "cripple." "I, uh, but . . . but it's a *rat*."

"It's a ferret, not a rodent." I set my jar down on the carpeted floor. "He *eats* rats."

"I do?" asked Pal. "That's right, I do. How revolting. I must speak to my overseer about this business of being assigned to the bodies of small verminovores."

I reached into my pocket, pulled out my ATM receipt, squished it into a ball, and tossed it on the floor.

"Fetch," I told Pal.

He climbed down from my shoulder, humped over to the receipt, took it in his jaws, and returned to my shoulder. When I held my hand out, he obligingly dropped the paper in my palm.

"See? He's very helpful." I stuck the wad in my pocket and picked up my jar.

"Well, I suppose it's okay," the guard mumbled, uncertainly hitching up his gun belt, "but if it starts running around in here bothering people, you'll have to take it and leave."

"No problem; he'll stay put on my shoulder unless I tell him otherwise," I replied.

I went over to the couches beside the glass cubicles holding the empty banker's stations and sat down. A woman in a dark suit, who'd watched the entire exchange between me and the guard, hurried over, her hard heels tut-tutting across the polished floor.

"Can we help you?" the woman asked, eyeing my bandaged face, faded clothes, mystery jar, and ferret with a mixture of bafflement and distaste.

"Why yes. I need to rent a safe-deposit box," I replied.

"We require a cash deposit—"

"I have cash. Look, the sooner you help me get the box, the sooner you'll have my unattractive, proletarian self out of here and never see me again," I said, suddenly feeling too tired for tact.

The woman's tone turned wooden. "One of our banking specialists will help you soon." She turned on her Ann Taylor stilettos and strode toward the offices in the back.

A short time later a young man about my age in a brown suit came out of the back offices, smoothing his tie. He put on a nervous smile and held out his hand to me, although he didn't manage eye contact. "Hello, I'm Philip. My manager said you want to rent a safe-deposit box?"

I shook his sweaty hand. "Yes, I do."

My anathema must be tweaking these people out something fierce, I thought to Pal.

"I'd say so," my familiar agreed.

"Please follow me over to my desk," Philip said, gesturing toward the first banker's cube.

I got up and carried my jar and Pal to the chair on the other side of his desk. Philip was staring squarely at the blotter in the middle of his desk, as if he was afraid he might accidentally start staring at my face or arm.

"So, is . . . is that some kind of raccoon?" Philip asked.

"No, he's a ferret. Weasel family."

"Oh. He's got that little bandit mask, and, uh . . . well." He cleared his throat helplessly. "What size box do you want to rent?"

"Big enough to hold this." I set the jar on his desk. "Plus some smaller stuff like a change purse and a set of keys."

"Oh." He eyed the jar as if it might be a bomb. "What's that?"

"Personal effects." I shrugged. "Nothing explosive, poisonous, illegal, or contagious."

"Oh. Well, we have a five-by-five-by-twenty-four box that should hold that. It's forty dollars per year, payable in full in advance. We only take cash if you don't have an account with us. And I'll need to see your ID."

"That's fine." I dug out my change purse, and he got out the paperwork for me to fill out and sign. I paused at the home address and telephone number blanks, then proceeded to write in Mother Karen's information.

After I paid the rental fee, the young man went into the vault and returned shortly with a long, narrow box. It had keys in two locks in the top.

"Here you go," he said. "It takes both keys to unlock this. We keep one key here, and I'll give the other to you. If you lose your key, we have to drill out the lock, and that's pretty expensive. I think it's like a hundred dollars."

"Gotcha." I finished the form, signed it, and pushed it across the table to him. He undid both locks on top of the box, opened the lid, and passed the second key to me. I put the jar, my car keys, and my cell phone in the box, then pulled all the credit, ID, and bank cards out of my change purse and laid everything but my driver's license alongside the jar. I shut the lid; it locked automatically with a hollow click.

"Is there anything else I can do for you before I take this to the vault?" Philip asked.

"Do you have a blank envelope and a regular stamp I could buy from you? And maybe a blank piece of notepaper?"

"Uh, sure." Philip opened his desk drawer and found an envelope and stamp, then pulled a piece of paper out of the feed tray of his printer. He glanced at my bandaged arm and bit his lip. "Don't worry about paying me; it's just a stump—I mean *stamp*! Stamp."

He looked utterly mortified as he carefully set the items down on the desk in front of me.

"Thanks." I licked the stamp and stuck it on the

envelope, shook his trembling hand, and took the envelope and paper over to the stand that held the deposit slips. After I addressed the envelope to Mother Karen, I began to write a note:

> *Karen,*
> *I realize you can't do anything on my behalf until this is over with, but hopefully you can hang on to the key and ID until I can see you again. If I die or get put in prison or disappear for more than half a year, please go to the Ohioana on High to get the contents of my safe-deposit box. What's in there will need some expanding, but there are some movies and books your kids might enjoy. One of the teens might like the TV and stereo. If not, have a garage sale!*
> *Otherwise, I will see you soon to get this back from you.*
>
> *Thanks and all my best,*
> *Jessie*
>
> *P.S. If you go get my stuff, make sure you look like me!*

I folded the key and my driver's license inside the letter and sealed it all inside the envelope.

"Do you think that's safe?" Pal asked.

Not a hundred percent, no. But if something happens she has to have some way of getting to this stuff, right?

"But your driver's license—"

—is kinda useless at this point. It's a pain for me to drive one-armed right now, and it's not like I can write a check or use my credit card again until this is

over. All the license is gonna do is tell the local cops who I am. I'd rather just be able to smile sweetly, tell them I'm Jane Smith and I lost my cards in whatever horrible accident mangled me.

I stuck the envelope in my back pocket and went outside. I stood on the sidewalk, feeling—and probably looking—a bit lost.

"What's the matter?" Pal asked.

I guess it's time for me to disappear, I replied. *And I'm wondering where I can find a blood sample from a nasty woman.*

"Well, your other option besides finding an unpleasant person who deserves a bit of bad luck is to find someone so well off that a bit of bad luck won't matter to them," Pal said. "And this looks like a well-to-do neighborhood."

It is, I agreed. *Old Worthington residents mostly aren't hurting for money.*

"Well, surely the library over there has public restrooms, doesn't it? You might as well take a look inside. And really, you should do this as soon as you can. No doubt Jordan's agents know your current location because you used your cards at the ATM."

All right . . . I suppose I'm bound to find something with blood on it one way or the other in the women's room. I guess if the Fates don't hand me a bitch, I'll just have to look for the fanciest napkin in the bin and hope I've chosen correctly.

I looked skyward and said a brief prayer to whichever friendly spirits might be nearby: *Okay, I don't want to have to poop all over a decent person's day. And after the shitty few days I've had, is it too much to ask for a break here? I hope not. Amen.*

I paused. *P.S. It'd be swell if I didn't have to handle a stranger's tampon. Thanks much.*

I crossed the bank's parking lot to the library's lot, which was full of Volvos and SUVs of one sort or another. I fell in behind a group of middle school students and went into the building. The restrooms were past some short stairs to my left by the classrooms.

I was up the stairs and nearly to the door when I heard a little girl start throwing a tantrum inside.

"No! I want SpongeBob!" the little girl shrieked. I heard the hollow rap of small shoes kicking the counter.

I pushed open the restroom door and cautiously stepped inside. A well-dressed woman was trying to tend to a three-year-old girl in denim shortalls with a nasty scrape on her knee who was sitting by one of the sinks. A damp paper towel, pink with the little girl's blood, lay on the counter nearby. The woman held a tan fabric first-aid strip; the girl was pushing the woman's arm away indignantly.

"I want SpongeBob!" the child demanded.

"Honey, I don't have any SpongeBob Band-Aids—come on, I need to put this on your knee to keep the germs out. Stop being silly!"

What are the odds we could conjure up a SpongeBob SquarePants Band-Aid for the kid? I wondered to Pal.

"SpongeBob isn't in my repertoire," Pal replied darkly. "And Fates willing, he never will be."

The woman finally wrestled the bandage onto the little girl's knee and carried her out of the restroom past me, the child shrieking at the indignity of it all.

The bloody paper towel lay forgotten and forlorn on the counter. I approached it, holding my ear.

"Can I use kid blood instead of adult blood?" I asked.

"I don't see why not," Pal replied.

"Well, then looks like somebody out there still likes me," I replied. "At least enough to save me from the creeping horror of used feminine hygiene products. What now?"

"Pick up that paper towel and take it with you into a stall," he said.

I did as he asked, awkwardly latching the door behind me with the towel still in my hand. "Should I sit or stand?"

"Whichever best helps you concentrate. And you will need to concentrate very hard to get this to work," he replied.

I sat down on the toilet. Pal hopped off my shoulder onto the top of the paper dispenser.

"All right," said Pal. "I need you to focus on the child's blood. Concentrate. Tease out the spiritual essence lingering in the dying cells. Can you feel it?"

"Yes." I could feel the child in her mother's arms, still wailing and kicking as her mother carried her back to the family SUV, SpongeBob utterly forgotten, but the girl's fury still in full foam because she couldn't have ice cream.

"Keep focusing on the child's essence. Think of it as a cloak you could wear to hide yourself, and focus on your own essence cloaking the child. Keep that image in your mind, keep focusing, and repeat after me: *Vestri animus ut mei, meus animus ut vestri, os meus phasmatis, os meus vomica . . .*"

I stared unblinking at the bloody paper towel as I quietly repeated the chant, over and over. The towel began to darken, harden, the edges beginning to glow and smoke.

" . . . *Os meus vomica—*"

The paper towel exploded in a shower of purple sparks. Startled, I ducked and slipped sideways off the toilet, shaking my hand to put out the flames I was sure had engulfed my flesh. Then I realized my hand didn't hurt, and I stared at my pink, unburned palm. The paper towel hadn't even left ashes behind.

"Did—did it work?" I asked.

Pal had only narrowly avoided getting knocked off his perch. He looked me up and down. "Yes. I believe that worked nicely. You'll have to do that again this time tomorrow, maybe sooner if you perform a lot of other spells in the meantime. That sort of thing can make this counter-charm wear off. And to make best use of this, we should hie ourselves to wherever you plan to go."

I got up and Pal jumped back onto my shoulder. When I pushed out of the stall, I saw that a teenage girl in a Worthington Cardinals T-shirt had come into the restroom. The girl was standing with her back to the door, staring at me like I'd just beamed down from Mars.

Bet she heard me chanting, right? Or the explosion? Or me talking to you just now? I thought to Pal.

"Any or all of those are likely," Pal replied. "To be safe you should do a memory-wipe charm."

Cooper, for all his delighting to push the limits when it came to public displays of magic, had long ago made sure I learned a reliable, simple charm for erasing the last two minutes of a mundane's memory. It was, literally, a snap.

Trouble was, I had lost my desire to play by the governing circle's rules.

I noticed a pink plastic watchband on the girl's right wrist. "Hello there! Do you have the time?"

"Uh. Yeah." The girl nervously looked down at her watch. "It's four thirty."

"Jiminy crickets! We have time to catch the bus!" I replied, putting on a maniacal smile. "And we just looove the bus, don't we, Mister Weezypants?"

The girl backed out of the restroom and ran like hell.

" 'Mister Weezypants'?" Pal said as the door swung shut. "You shouldn't provoke people like that. And you should have erased her memory."

"Foo, she didn't see that much," I replied. "And if I can't mess with people in my condition, what good is it being armless and half blind and homeless and nearly broke, anyway?"

chapter eleven

Bus, Bar, and Box Store

Despite my cavalier words, I left the library as quickly and quietly as I could. Pal and I crossed Granville Road and walked down High Street to the post office, where I dropped my letter to Karen into one of the big mailboxes out front, abandoning it to the whims of fate and the postal carriers.

We walked a bit farther down High to the bus stop. The bench under the Plexiglas shelter was already crowded with summer-quarter Ohio State students heading back to campus, so I leaned against the signpost to wait for the southbound #2 to arrive.

"Out of curiosity, where are we going?" asked Pal.

Well, I replied, *I think the first thing I need to do is talk to the Warlock, if he hasn't blown town entirely. And if he's split, I need to see if I can track him down. If anyone has any ideas about what's happened to Cooper—and why—it's his own brother.*

I heard the bus rumbling down the street and dug in my pocket for six quarters. *Unless they've changed the schedule, this should eventually drop me just a couple of blocks from his bar in Victorian Village.*

"I don't think this is a very good idea," replied Pal. "Jordan's men have surely pressured and monitored the Warlock as much or even more than they've done to you. The anathema counter-charm won't hold if they've set up specific detection spells near the bar."

Well, it won't hurt to take a look around, will it? I asked. *I really do need to talk to him about everything that's happened. And you'd be able to sense the spells and warn me away, wouldn't you?*

"I could sense most spells, yes," he said, "but I can make no guarantees I'd be able to sense everything."

I was starting to feel seriously annoyed. *Well, do you have a better idea?*

Pal was silent for a moment. "No, I'm afraid not. I suppose we might as well take a careful look around."

The bus ground to a hissing halt in front of the stop. Pal and I got on after the college students; the driver either didn't notice Pal, or didn't care one way or the other.

The bus made its leisurely way down High Street and finally dropped us off at Fifth at five thirty. High Street was bumper-to-bumper with rush-hour traffic. I crossed the street after the light turned red and headed west down Fifth toward the Warlock's bar, Lingham Liquors Lounge.

I was a whole block away when the anathema sphere surrounding the bar became visible. The entire building was engulfed in a throbbing red glow that made my eye ache and my ears ring. Looking at it for more than a second made me want to throw up.

"Man," I said, leaning against a nearby brick wall and closing my eye, hoping the nausea would pass. "That's as subtle as a bullet in the head."

Pal couldn't look at it, either. "It's unsubtle, but

strong. I don't sense anything else at work here, but what else could they possibly need? No Talent can go near the place, and the Warlock can't get out."

You think he's still in there? I asked.

"They wouldn't bother warding an empty building."

What about his mundane regulars and staff?

"Well, that spell's nearly as powerful as the isolation sphere they cast to contain the Wutganger. It's bound to make approaching the bar a fairly anxious prospect for anyone even remotely sensitive to such things."

I'm glad to see I'm not the only one they felt like destroying financially, I thought bitterly. *Is there any way to get past it?*

"With magic, there's almost *always* a way," Pal replied. "But this one's going to be sticky. I have to give this a good hard think."

And I have to get some tea, and something to eat, I replied, still feeling shaky and headachy. *And then I really need to find a place to crash for the night.*

I backtracked down Fifth Avenue to Victorian's Midnight Café. I ordered an iced tea, an oatmeal cookie, a grilled egg sandwich, and a small cup of water for Pal at the counter, juggled the drinks and dessert, and sat down in one of the comfy purple chairs by the window to wait for the waitress to bring out the rest of my order.

An eighteen- or nineteen-year-old white kid with dreadlocks and a scruffy soul patch was up on the stage in the corner, reciting a rambling poem about Che Guevara, John Lennon, and, near as I could tell, marijuana. He finished his verse to a smattering of applause, then gathered up his canvas messenger bag and went to the community bulletin board. He pulled a flyer with tear-off tags out of his bag and tacked it up among the ads for yoga lessons and used sofas and bicycles. I could just make out the words ROOMMATE WANTED at the top of his paper.

Wait here and keep anyone from taking my seat, would you? I thought to Pal.

"All right," replied Pal, hopping off my shoulder onto the back of the chair.

I got up and approached the dreadlocked kid. I got a good whiff of him when I was three feet away. Yep, that poem had most definitely been about marijuana.

"Hi, I'm Jessie," I said. "You're looking for a roommate?"

He looked startled. "Whoa, did you have an accident or something?"

"Yes, it was extremely accidental. So, you need a roommate? What's your name?"

"Uh, yeah, I'm Kai. Me and my buds, we have this house on East Avenue, and this guy Boomer just totally bailed on us, I think he was in trouble with the cops or something—"

"Is it a room to share with somebody else, or is it a private room? 'Cause I need my own room, and my own bathroom would be sweet."

"Well, see, Boomer *was* in the attic room, and that's got its own bathroom, it's just a sink and a toilet and a shower but sometimes the shower don't work right, but Mikey wanted it so we were gonna rent out Mikey's old room on the third floor—"

"Can I talk you into letting me rent the attic room and have Mikey stay put?"

"Uh. Well, see Mikey and I go way back and he

was really cool and stuff when I was having trouble
with my folks and so I really owe him—"

"I can make it worth Mikey's while. And yours.
Everybody in the house would find me to be a *very*
worthwhile attic roommate."

"Like how?" he asked.

"Like I can get you as much liquor as you want,
whenever you want. For free," I replied. "And if you,
perhaps, were into cultivating certain species of indoor plants that have been a bit reluctant to grow, I
can help with that, too."

"Are you a farmer?" he whispered.

"Better." I leaned in close to his ear and spoke
low. "I'm a witch. The *real* kind. I can grow anything."

"You're shitting me," he said doubtfully.

"Nope, not one bit. I'll give you and your room-
mates a free demonstration at your place, say in two
hours?"

He agreed, and gave me a copy of his flyer with his
phone number and address. I folded it against my
thigh and stuck it in my back pocket.

The waitress arrived with my grilled egg sandwich
soon after I reclaimed my seat by the window.

"You want us to stay with *him*?" Pal said as the
dreadlocked kid left the café.

I sipped my iced tea. *What, you want me to drag
nice people into this swirling storm of shit that con-
stitutes my life right now?*

"Good point," replied Pal. "But wouldn't a hotel
room be more . . . sanitary?"

*Hotels cost money, which I don't have so much of
right now.* I set my tea aside and took a bite of the
sandwich. *Even if our Pot Poet's place turns out to*

be much worse than your standard student flop-house, well, you probably know a delousing spell and a decent cleaning spell, right? We'll be good.

"Never mind the spells . . . you've never met these people before," Pal said. "You have no idea if they're safe or not. And can I have some of that sandwich?"

I scooped out some of the cheesy scrambled egg filling and put it on a napkin so Pal could eat it on the floor.

I'm figuring Kai doesn't live with a junior Ed Gein. And even if he does, you know what? I'm not afraid of that right now, I replied. *I killed a demon last week. Yeah, maybe it was pure luck, but you know, maybe it wasn't. So I'm not afraid of some punk-ass stoner. I'm not afraid of some third-string football-player rapist. I've been afraid of so many things since Cooper disappeared . . . maybe people ought to start being afraid of* me *for a change.*

I savagely bit off another mouthful of bread and egg. *Handling a houseful of sophomore guys is the least of my worries right now.*

I finished my sandwich in silence, watching people come and go through the front door of the café. I'd been there with Cooper once when we were first dating, still so hot for each other that after a couple of espressos we'd ended up sneaking into the ladies' room to make out. Cooper had just bent me over the sink and was about to do me from behind when an overcaffeinated lady with a sudden attack of diarrhea started pounding on the latched door. Cooper had to quickly turn himself invisible, and I had to scramble to get my jeans back on, but I was able to let the lady inside with apologies before the situation became dire.

A college-aged couple was giggling and necking on the sidewalk outside. I suddenly felt acutely depressed. The café's bohemian charm had worn right off.

My cookie was in a zippered plastic bag; I pulled the treat out and stuck the bag in my pocket. Pal and I finished our snacks and left to catch the #84 bus. We arrived at the Lennox Town Center just after 7 PM.

"So, do you have any ideas about how to get past that anathema sphere?" I asked Pal as I started walking across the vast, sparsely parked asphalt lot toward the big brick Target store.

"Well," he said, "I did think of something. It's a type of dematerialization potion. After you drink it, it shifts you out of phase and turns you and whatever you happen to be carrying invisible and immaterial. But it wouldn't extend to, say, a horse or car you were riding. The potion lets you pass undetectably through any barrier, mundane or magical, short of a high-grade isolation sphere. And most of the ingredients are relatively common."

"Common enough to pick up here at Target?" I asked.

"Yes, I believe most of them should be available, and the rest we can locate later."

"So what's the downside?"

"It takes a minimum of twelve hours to brew, two hours of incantation to activate, and the resulting concoction must be consumed within twenty-four hours or it expires. And the effect doesn't last long once it's consumed."

"How long?"

"Well, a twelve-hour brew with two hours of

incantation will give you two minutes of demateri-alization," he replied. "An eighteen-hour brew with three hours of incantation might give you three minutes."

"So for an hour of dematerialization you'd need to brew the stuff for two weeks straight? And chant for three solid days? Jeez. No wonder I haven't seen this type of potion before. Are there any side effects?"

"Aside from the usual chance the potion simply won't work, typical side effects include nausea, vom-iting, diarrhea, disorientation, death or dismember-ment due to rematerializing inside a solid object, and sickness or death due to hantavirus or bubonic plague infections."

"Hantavirus? Bubonic plague?" I asked.

"The recipe calls for fresh rat's blood. Some peo-ple fail to cook the raw potion hot enough to kill the bacteria or viruses contained therein."

"Nice," I replied. "So try to not get us a sick rat, m'kay?"

"What makes you think *I'm* going to get the rat?" he asked indignantly.

"You're a ferret. Catching rodents is what you do."

"Oh. Yes. I keep trying to put that part of this new existence out of my mind, I suppose," he replied. "I mostly ate fish and fruit when I was a bear. Much nicer than raw rat."

What did you eat before? When you were in your real body, I mean? I'd reached the sidewalk, and a pair of women pushing a baby in a stroller were coming from the other direction.

"I was a vegetarian of sorts," he replied, "but the difference between animal and vegetable isn't as clearly defined on my home world as it is here."

How do you mean? I asked.

"Our plants can get out of the soil and move to a new location if they don't like where they're growing. Some of them are sentient. I tried not to eat those sorts of plants," he replied.

Oh. Well, I'm sure they found that very thoughtful of you, I replied.

We reached the front of the Target. The automatic doors swung in to admit me. A large, black-uniformed security guard with a greasy-looking buzz cut and cop mustache scowled at me from his station by the red plastic carts. He stank of garlic and hostility, and he seemed familiar to me.

"Hey, you can't bring that critter—" the guard began.

"He's a helper animal. Federal regulations say I can bring him in here."

"Yeah? Prove it." The guard crossed his arms over his chest belligerently.

"You ever hear of the Americans with Disabilities Act?" I asked, then paused, finally recognizing him. We'd gone to Upper Arlington High School together after I moved to Columbus. I didn't know his real name, but his nickname was Goat. He'd been a linebacker on the school football team, and had delighted in bullying other students. The rumor was he'd molested a girl at a party, but she'd been too frightened to press charges.

"I'm sure my lawyer would be happy to read the text of the act to you," I continued. "So let us through, please, unless you want to spend some quality time in court for a discrimination lawsuit."

"That seems the emptiest of empty threats," Pal

commented, "considering the only local lawyer either of us knows is Mr. Jordan."

This guy's a complete asshole. He hassles me, I'll shrink his balls to the size of field peas, I thought back savagely.

"My, you *are* getting crabby," Pal said. "But the Danse d'Emballage spell won't work on living flesh."

Then I'll shrink his underwear.

Goat stared at me. I stared back, unblinking. Jerks like him could smell fear.

Finally, he muttered "uppity crip bitch" under his breath and turned his back on me. I briefly considered shrinking his shorts on general principle, but decided against it. I yanked a cart out of a carrel and pushed it toward the snack bar.

"If you're truly interested in conserving your money, you should just get something from the snack aisles," Pal pointed out.

And you're turning into a real mother hen. I need a place to stash everything I'm about to shoplift; a cup with a lid will do nicely.

"You do realize that you'll be in a tremendous amount of trouble if you're caught using your Talent to steal," Pal said. "You'll be sent to prison for sure."

I don't have the cash to cover everything I need to get here, so I don't see a way around this. I got in line at the snack bar behind a guy ordering nachos.

"In theory, you'd get in less trouble making faery money from dead leaves," Pal replied.

"Hi, what can I get you today?" asked the girl at the counter, staring at Pal.

"Just a regular fountain drink, thanks," I replied, digging in my pocket for a dollar. The girl handed me an empty waxed paper cup in exchange for the money, and I went over to the soda dispenser to get some Sprite.

You're serious about the faery money? I filled my cup halfway with ice. *Seems like that sort of thing would be considered a worse crime.*

"Well, it all goes back to the ancient laws brought over from the Old World and what was socially accepted then. Not everything on the books makes sense from a modern perspective."

No kidding. I filled my cup partway with soda and stuck a lid and straw on it. *Faery money would seriously screw the poor cashier I'd give it to—at midnight the whole thing would turn back to old leaves.*

I shook my head. *They'd take whatever was missing from the till out of the cashier's paycheck. Even fifty dollars is a lot to somebody working a job like this. No. I couldn't do that.*

"The goods you steal will have to be paid for by someone."

But my shoplifting wouldn't be blamed on any one employee. Stores get robbed, and this isn't some mom-and-pop grocery that's hurting for cash. They'll have insurance. And I don't have a better idea. Do you?

"Not really," Pal admitted. "While we're in here, can you get me an actual bowl to eat out of so I have a little less wet napkin in my diet?"

Anything for my nice, helpful, never-sends-me-on-guilt-trips familiar.

I went to the snack aisle first and got some juice, soups, and snacks for myself and some lean canned chicken for Pal.

"Make sure to get some salt, ginger, vinegar, and

black and red pepper for the potion," Pal said. "And get a six-pack of little grape juice bottles; those are the right size to hold the potion, and frankly you'll need a strong-tasting sweet juice to make it a bit more palatable."

What about wine splits instead? I asked, thinking the alcohol in the wine might help kill off any nasties lingering in the rat's blood.

Pal shook his head. "Wine won't work as well; the fermentation products tend to increase undesirable toxins and lengthen the brewing time."

Heaven knows I don't want this taking any longer than it has to.

"We'll also need several types of herbs," he continued. "And this will need to brew over a flame rather than an electric coil, so you should get a camp stove as well."

Speaking of, what will I be brewing this in? Cooper had never been big on potion-making, and I hadn't studied it in school. *I don't think Target sells iron cauldrons.*

"My understanding is that stores like this generally sell their potions-grade iron and copper cauldrons as decorative plant containers in the garden center or home décor section," Pal replied. "But for our purposes, Pyrex would be best."

I picked up some soap, deodorant, shampoo, ibuprofen, antibiotic salve, bandages, Epsom salts, a ten-pack of latex gloves, a travel-sized bottle of hand sanitizer, a brush, and pack of dental toiletries on my way down the back aisle to the row where they stocked the herbal preparations.

This was the first time I'd sought out packaged herbal supplements in a megamart. Cooper was a

big believer in using common kitchen herbs and local weeds rather than relying on exotic items that
might not be readily available. I'd never really paid
any attention to what Target stocked before.

Okay, so I have a question. I picked up a white
plastic bottle of Saint-John's-wort capsules and gave
it a shake. *I know they'd probably still stock herbs
like this if the world were totally mundane.*

I set down the bottle and picked up a three-pack
of wolfsbane. *But what about* this *stuff? Do regular
people even use half the herbs they have out here?*

"I should hope not, but there are a lot of Talents in
this city. Surely many of them prefer to get their soda,
socks, and spell ingredients in one-stop shopping the
same as anybody else."

*Which reminds me, I should get some fresh
clothes while I'm here. My socks would probably
stand on their own if I took them off right now.*

"Please don't. But please do collect some aloe vera
juice, heliotrope, Atlantean quartz powder, Einhorn
powder, and vitreous humor draco niger."

Ew, squished dragon eyeballs. I looked over the
purple bottle of VHDN I found on a nearby shelf.
Does this stuff taste as bad as I think it'll taste?

"It's likely going to be far worse than you imagine," Pal admitted. "But it's key to the function of the
potion."

*This stuff will need to be refrigerated after I open
it,* I added, squinting at the small-print warnings on
the bottle. *Or, um, it explodes.*

"Then pick up a small refrigerator while you're
here. No point in stealing at all if you don't get everything you need."

I found a small dorm fridge in an aisle-end promotional display, then got a pillow, alarm clock, and some towels from an adjoining back-to-school section. The kitchen section yielded a quart-sized Pyrex saucepan and a wooden spoon made from black oak.

Wow, I thought to Pal as I looked over the array of tree species represented in the wooden spoon section. The store even stocked a carved mistletoe spoon bearing prominent warning labels that it was for decorative use only. *They really do cater to spellcasters here, don't they?*

"The regional buyers probably aren't aware of the nature of the materials that they order for the stores," Pal replied. "I'm sure the governing circles exercise some influence, but likely the stores are simply responding to customer demand, and anti-witchcraft forces at local churches don't know enough to protest against specific items."

I snagged a knapsack, Leatherman tool, sleeping bag, and folding cot along with a compact propane stove while I was in the sporting goods section. After that, I got packs of socks and undies and some basic T-shirts and jeans in the women's section, then went to the pet section and got Pal a bag of dry kibble and a couple of small crockery bowls to eat and drink from.

The cart creaked under the burden of my mountain of stuff, and it was getting hard to maneuver one-handed. I pushed it to a relatively isolated corner of the store and glanced up at the security cameras.

Does it seem to you those cameras in the ceiling move around? I asked Pal as I casually pulled the straw out of my mostly empty soda cup and popped the lid off.

"I think I do see them rotating, yes."

I pulled the zippered plastic bag left over from my café cookie out of my pocket and tucked it down in the top of the cup, the mouth of the bag forced open by the cup's sides. *Well, then we need a diversion, don't we?*

I closed my eye and felt for Goat the Security Guard. He was still standing by the carts near the entrance. I felt past the black polyester uniform slacks to the ratty, stained cotton jersey shorts beneath.

I whispered an ancient word for "shrink."

His surprised yelps could be heard across the entire store. People nearby craned their necks toward the ruckus, and the cameras swiveled away from my corner toward the front of the store. I quickly danced and softly chanted the shorthand version of the French packing spell; the contents of my cart shrank midair and fluttered into the cup-bound plastic bag like tiny insects. I sealed the bag, put the lid back on the cup, and tucked the straw back in, being careful to not pierce the plastic.

I abandoned the empty cart and headed toward the exit, pretending to sip my drink. *Smooth enough for you?*

"I admit I am impressed by your talent for larceny," Pal replied.

Be impressed if I can get the two of us out of this mess without prison sentences, I thought back.

Goat was nowhere near the entrance; I sensed he'd made a mad sprint to the men's room to pry out the magical wedgie I'd given him. I took a deep breath and plunged through the automatic doors. To my relief, the spellbound booty didn't make the security alarms go off.

"Where to now?" Pal asked.

To Kai's, of course, I replied. *So I can add marijuana trafficking to my criminal résumé.*

chapter twelve

Ganja Goddess

Pal and I managed to catch the very last bus back to the north campus area; it dropped us off on High Street across the street from the Blue Danube restaurant. Cooper loved the food at the Dube, particularly their savory patty melts and their hummus. And he thought their beer selection was one of the best in town outside the Warlock's place. However, I had deemed their restrooms far too cramped, dingy, and frequently visited for any type of making out, despite Cooper's insistence that all we'd need was to turn ourselves invisible and be very, very quiet.

Poor Cooper. I hoped he was okay. I couldn't let myself think too hard about what he might be going through, or else I'd start crying again. We'd figure out a way to get him back soon. If I said that to myself often enough, maybe I would start to believe it.

I walked to the corner of High and Blake and set my soda cup down on the curb. I pulled Kai's flyer out of my back pocket to double-check his address. "Yep, his place is on East Avenue, just a couple of blocks from here."

"Oh, good," replied Pal as he peered down Blake Avenue at the rows of dilapidated clapboard duplexes and crumbling brick town houses. "And all this time I was afraid we'd be staying in a *dump*."

"Hey, you're the one who said we needed a rat for this potion. Don't complain about easy hunting."

I picked up my cup and walked toward Kai's address. I found the place easily enough; it was a huge old Victorian single in dire need of a paint job. The broad front porch had surely been stately a hundred years before. Now the floorboards were warped and the railing supports were as broken and gray as a meth addict's teeth. Ragged lawn chairs surrounded a short plastic table covered in crumpled beer cans, with cigarette butts spilling from an old glass ashtray.

I went up the creaky wooden stairs and rang the bell. A burly young man in knee-length denim cutoffs and a BUCKEYES FOOTBALL T-shirt pulled open the door.

"Yeah?" he asked suspiciously.

"I'm Jessie," I said. "Kai told me to come by. I'm here to rent the room."

"Oh." He looked me up and down. "Come in, I guess."

"Charming young man," Pal whispered.

I stepped into the living room. There was the usual array of College Guy Furnishings: a sagging old brown couch, stained maroon velvet recliner, thrift-store end tables, and CD/DVD racks made of bricks and boards beside a shiny new wide-screen television and Sony gaming system. Rock posters adorned the walls. A half-empty bottle of tequila sat in the middle of the cluttered coffee table. The wooden floor was so old and worn that I got a pretty good view of the basement through the gaps in the boards; I saw the glow of fluorescent plant lights gleaming off the white enamel surface of a washer and dryer.

"Yo, Kai!" bellowed Buckeye Shirt. "That chick's here to see the room."

"Be up in a minute!" Kai yelled back from somewhere in the basement.

Two other young men stuck their heads into the living room from the kitchen. One was a slightly built guy with black hair and glasses, and the other was a tall, handsome boy with a mop of curly red hair. They gave each other a glance that said *This should be entertaining* and came into the living room, grinning like schoolkids about to play the best practical joke *ever*.

Nice, I thought. *I know that look. It's the look that says, "Ha ha! We're going to take this stupid deluded witchy girl apart at the seams and laugh her right out of the house."*

"You did express a disinterest in involving *nice* people in our current difficulties," Pal reminded me.

True enough, I thought back. *Hallelujah, it's raining jerks.*

"So how exactly *are* you going to handle these young gentlemen?" Pal asked.

I know a few party tricks, I replied. *Any Talent who ever went to OSU knows how to make faery liquor. It'll seem just like the real thing going down, but it'll turn to water a few minutes after they've drunk it. It'll be better for their livers, anyhow. And plant growth is pretty basic stuff.*

The dark-haired fellow in the glasses stepped forward and waved at me. "Hi, I'm Scott, and this is Patrick, and you already met Mikey." He pointed at Buckeye Shirt.

"Hi guys. I'm Jessie." I nodded at them and set my soda cup down on a clear spot on the end table beside the recliner. *Keep an eye on that, would you?* I thought to Pal.

"Certainly." He hopped off my shoulder onto the back of the recliner and took up a watchful position on the chair's arm near the cup.

"Nice ferret," said Scott.

"Thanks," I replied. "You're practically the first person I've met today who didn't think he was some kind of rodent."

"So is he supposed to be your familiar or something?" Patrick asked, looking like he was desperately trying to keep a straight face.

"Why, yes. Yes he is," I replied.

"So, um, where's your broomstick?" he countered, his face turning pink from his effort at not laughing.

"Broomsticks are *sooo* 1695," I replied, rolling my eye. "Modern witches use vibrators and drop acid just like everyone else."

"What?" He frowned, looking confused.

"Yeah, *flying on broomsticks* equals a big-ass euphemism for pagan women getting their freak on with broom handles greased up with morning glory butter," I said. "Sometimes strychnine. Not a good idea, but hey, back in the day they used to think a wolf's testicle wrapped in a greasy rag was a good barrier contraceptive. So, yeah, no broomsticks for me. But thanks *ever* so much for asking about my sex life when we've only just met."

Just then, Kai came thumping up the basement stairs with a couple of small, spindly marijuana plants growing in a rectangular clay pot. He set the pot reverently on the floor.

"Okay, so . . . make this grow," Kai said.

"Wait, don't I get to see the attic first?" I asked.

"Show us your stuff first, or show us some cash," Mikey said. "Ain't no way I'm giving up dibs on the attic unless you got proof of some real serious voodoo."

"Okay, fine. I'll do my thing on your lovely little pot plant here, but you don't get anything else until after I see the attic," I said, then thought to Pal, *You don't have diarrhea, do you?*

"What? No," he replied. "Why the sudden interest in the condition of my gastrointestinal tract?"

Because I just realized I need a fertilizer starter for this charm, and I won't gain the best credibility with these guys if I have to ask Kai for some Miracle-Gro. So I need you to poop in my hand, but not if it's going to be all runny and disgusting, I thought back.

"Ah. Indeed." He hopped off the couch and climbed up to my shoulder. I moved my hand under him so he could discreetly deposit a small, warm black pellet into my palm.

"I feel so close to you right now," Pal said.

Shut up and go back to the comfy chair, smart-ass, I replied, holding my cupped hand out toward the pot plants. *I haven't tried this trick in a while . . . I need to concentrate to do this right.*

Pal hopped back onto the chair.

"Okay," I said, "first I need you all to swear that what happens in this house stays in this house. You're not to discuss anything you're about to see with anyone else."

They looked at one another and shrugged doubtfully.

"Yeah, whatever," said Mikey.

"I need a promise that's just a teensy bit more formal," I replied. "I need you all to raise your right hands and say 'I will not speak of the magic I see.' Can you do that? Okay, on a count of three . . ."

After I counted down, they grudgingly raised their hands and repeated the words. As the boys said the final part of the promise, I spoke an ancient word for "bind," and the room briefly went cold as the spell took hold. They wouldn't be able to talk about my magic with outsiders no matter how hard they tried.

"Thanks, guys."

I closed my eye and focused on the stronger of the two plants. It had suffered greatly from lack of nutrients and proper water; a lesser plant would have died weeks before. Kai, despite his abiding love of the resinous bud, had a thumb browner than a politician's nose.

I began the chant, calling on the power of the trees and bushes nearby to help their herbaceous cousin grow tall and strong. Old, alien words for "growth" and "bounty" flowed off my tongue.

I felt Pal's pellet grow hot in my hand, and it burst with a small firecracker pop. A heartbeat later, I heard the college guys shout in surprise as the clay pot shattered. Pain stabbed through my skull. I stopped the chant and opened my eye.

The puny little plant had exploded into a seven-foot-tall bush. Shards of the broken clay pot lay around its tangled root-ball.

"Ho-ly shit," Patrick said, his skepticism drained clean away along with the blood from his face. "You're not a witch; you're some kind of ganja goddess."

"Ganja goddess, will you marry me?" asked Kai, tears of joy welling in his bloodshot eyes.

"I'm touched, Kai . . . but no. I'm already spoken for. May I see the room now?" I asked.

I collected Pal and my cup, and Kai took me upstairs to the sweltering attic room. It smelled of mildew and dirty feet. The room was about twenty feet long and maybe nine feet wide. The carpet was 1970s green shag and bore stains of unknown origin, and the floor was still littered with trash and milk crates left behind by the previous occupant. The walls had originally been white, I supposed, but it was hard to tell from the scuffs and stains. A noticeable nicotine line from cigarette smoke circled the room a few inches from the water-stained ceiling. Six-foot-square dormers were built into both faces of the roof; the left-hand one had been converted into a cramped bathroom with narrow closets on either side. There were windows in the dormers and in the wall at the far end; if I opened them all and set the stove in the dormer I wouldn't have to worry about choking on carbon monoxide.

A bare fluorescent light fixture—the sort of thing people usually installed in their garages—hung crookedly from the ceiling. There was a light switch to the right of the door. I flipped it experimentally; the fluorescent lights flickered on harshly. I flipped the switch down again.

"This'll do," I said. "Okay, here are the ground rules: You let me know before you come in, and you don't come in here when I'm not around unless it's a life-or-death emergency. I grew you enough pot to stone a small army, so we should be good there for a while. I'll make you liquor, but don't expect me to create it out of thin air. I'll need a finger of whatever you want me to make still in the bottle. I don't care when you have parties, but don't wake me up at four AM when you want more tequila. Sound fair?"

"Sounds fair," agreed Kai.

"Great," I said. "Now I really need a nap, so I'll see you in a while."

"Wait . . . aren't you gonna bring in any of your stuff?" Kai asked.

"I've already got it right here." I held up the soda cup, then set it down so I could close the door. "Bye now. Buh-bye, Kai."

I latched the door after Kai left; the slide-bolt seemed pretty flimsy, but anyone forcing it was bound to make more than enough noise to wake me from a sound sleep.

"You realize of course that the flowers from the plant you just magicked for them aren't going to be particularly rich in THC," Pal said.

Yes, I know, I thought back, just in case Kai was still in earshot. *They'll have to hang the plant up in the basement to cure for a while if they want a good smoke, anyway, and I hope to be gone from here well before then.*

"God, I'm so tired," I continued aloud, suddenly feeling the weight of the day pressing down on my very bones. I knelt, popped the lid off the soda cup, and pulled the plastic bag out. It looked like all the miniaturized goods floating inside had stayed dry. I desperately needed a nap on the cot.

"How do I unshrink and unfloat everything?" I asked Pal.

"Well, the counter-charm is essentially the reverse of the packing charm—"

"Jeez, more dancing? My feet are getting sore."

"—but it's usually much quicker, especially if you're not particular about where things go."

"All right; let's give this a try."

Pal coached me through the unpacking charm; soon everything was re-expanded and arrayed around me. My head hurt worse than ever. I unpacked the cot and set it up in the dormer, then unpacked the little fridge and plugged it in.

"I really do have to take a nap," I said as I un-rolled the sleeping bag atop the inflated mattress and tossed the pillow onto the cot. "Everything aches."

I took two ibuprofen tablets with a swig of warm Gatorade, then stuck the bottle in the fridge. I plugged in the little electric alarm clock.

"You have any idea what time it is?" I asked.

"I'm afraid not," he replied.

"Oh well. I'll take a wild guess and set the time to eight PM, and set the alarm to go off around mid-night. And then, potions, with a quick break to go dump my anathema again! And then, we're off to see the Warlock, and hopefully Lion will get his courage and Tin Man will get his heart and I will get my Cooper."

I went into the bathroom to avail myself of the toi-let. The shower stall was caked with soap scum and mildew, and the sink was furry with shaving leavings and something that was possibly chewing tobacco. The floor was covered in dust and curly black hairs, and the toilet looked like it hadn't been cleaned since the Truman administration. Fortunately, Boomer had left behind a roll of clean toilet paper in the cabinet under the sink, and having had to contend with

Greyhound station restrooms at a tender age, I was well practiced in squat-and-hover.

"I realize it's probably karmic payback for not bothering to clean the apartment before I left it today, but *damn* that's a nasty bathroom," I said to Pal as I emerged. "You said you know a good cleaning spell . . . ?"

"I never said that, actually, but in fact I do know a very good cleaning spell."

"Does it take long?"

"Probably half an hour to learn, a quarter hour to perform."

"Naptime first, then cleaning. Then potion." I shucked off my sneakers, crawled into the sleeping bag, and was soon fast asleep.

chapter thirteen

In the Wake of the Dream

I walked barefoot across cool green moss growing along a forested streambank. I had both my eyes and both my arms, and the spring sun felt wonderful on my skin. A few yards away, Cooper knelt bare-chested on a flat shale rock, washing a white T-shirt in the clear water of the stream. The morning sunlight shone on the wiry muscles of his back and shoulders.

Smiling, I walked up beside him. "Whatcha doing?"

"I can't remember where this came from, but it won't come out," he said, lifting the shirt from the water. Dark red blood stained the white cotton. "I've been scrubbing this for hours, but it won't come out."

The breeze shifted, strengthened. I thought I heard the tinkling of bells or a music box in the distance . . . it took me a moment to recognize the tune as "The Twelve Days of Christmas."

Somewhere in the distance, a baby began to scream.

The sun fled the sky, and the wind blew cold. Sleet stung my face. I looked down at Cooper; he was shivering on the rock, the stream completely frozen over, his hands covered in fresh blood steaming in the icy air.

"I didn't want to do it," Cooper whispered. "God help me, I didn't want to do it."

He cried out, convulsing in pain. His body stiffened and turned gray, a statue of ash that began to flake apart in the wind.

"Cooper!" I tried to grab him to shield him from the wind, but his body came apart in my embrace, blowing away on the freezing wind. A fist-sized lump of molten iron glowed where his heart had been, and the burning metal dripped out of his crumbling chest cavity, searing my left hand horribly, and suddenly I, too, was turning to ash and I couldn't stop it—

I came awake in the darkness, my clothes and the sleeping bag drenched in sweat. My eye socket and arm hurt worse than ever. I sat up, doubled over on the cot, cradled the stump of my arm, and vainly willed the pain away.

It was absolutely no comfort to realize that finally I was starting to remember the nightmares after I'd awakened.

Pal hopped up on the cot. "Are you all right?"

"No," I said, and began to sob from the pain in my body and in my soul and from the sheer injustice of everything that had happened oh God Cooper was gone and how would I ever get him back with the entire Universe wanting him gone and dead and what had he done and what was I going to do . . .

"Jessie, shh, Jessie, please, it'll be okay," said Pal.

"I can't do this," I wept. "I can't. It h-hurts too much."

"I know you've been through a lot, too much for any one person to be expected to handle, but you've got to pull yourself together," Pal said.

"I can't. I just want to sleep, and how can I sleep if I keep having nightmares . . . ?"

Somebody knocked on the door.

"G.G., you okay in there?" Kai asked.

"Yeah," I replied weakly. "Do you have any Vicodin or Percocets or anything like that?"

"I got some Robaxacets we got up in Toronto . . ."

"My arm is killing me . . . can I bum one?" I asked.

"Uh, okay . . . I gotta find the foils, though." I heard him head back down the stairs. I leaned against the door frame, wishing the Brick Fairy would descend and smite me across the head and make the pain go away.

Finally, Kai returned and I unlatched the door. "I'll pay you back for this," I said, taking the thick white pill from his hand.

"Hey, no worries . . . I hope you feel better," he replied.

I thanked him again, latched the door, downed the pill with a swig of Gatorade from the fridge, and collapsed back on the cot.

I slept fitfully at best, and did not feel the least bit better when Pal poked me awake with his sharp snout. Sunlight streamed through the window.

"Ugh, what time is it?" I asked, feeling queasy and feverish.

"Nearly noon," Pal replied. "It's only four hours until your anathema counter-spell starts to wear off."

"Four hours? Can't I sleep a little bit longer? I'm so tired . . ."

"No, you've *got* to get up. If you go back to sleep you might never wake up again," Pal replied. "You're burning up; unless my nose deceives me, you've got a nasty staph infection, and we need to take care of that before you get any worse."

"Infection?" I wriggled my throbbing arm out of the sling; my elbow was so swollen I could barely flex it. The bandages covering my stump were soaked with greenish yellow pus. "Aw, hell."

I threw off the sleeping bag and lurched up from the cot, my vision swimming, and stumbled to the bathroom to relieve my aching bladder. I switched the light on, and the sight of the forgotten filth suddenly made me absolutely furious.

"Can't any of the fraternity rejects around here learn to use a goddamn *sponge*?" I yelled into the tiny bathroom. "Damn this place to the nine hells, what kind of inbred dirt pig can *live* in this crap? Is it too much to ask for a clean fucking bathroom—"

I gasped, the muscles in my feverish body seizing up, my spine going rigid, and instead of my profane rant, old, old words spilled from my lips and a whirlwind rose in the cramped, moldy bathroom and then a bang and sunburst of light that blinded me and sent me to my knees.

"My goodness." Pal hopped over to me and nudged my thigh. "Are you all right?"

"Buh." I blinked several times to clear the spots in my vision. The bathroom floor in front of me shone bright and white and clean. The tub and sink and toilet looked like they were brand new. "Holy cats, did I do that?"

"Well, I certainly couldn't," Pal replied. "I suppose you don't know how you managed that, do you?"

"Uh-uh." Shaking, I got to my feet and went into the bathroom to use the toilet.

"You Babblers and your unreliable bursts of magical inspiration," Pal sighed.

I stared down at the white tiles as I peed. The

grout lines seemed to be undulating back and forth. "I think I'm starting to hallucinate."

"I can't say I'm surprised. We need to get that infection taken care of. Our best option is wood ash and moldy cheese, as Mother Karen suggested."

"Well, if these guys have cheese, it's almost guaranteed to be moldy," I replied as I finished up. "So we should be safe there. If not, I'll go door-to-door and pretend I'm a member of the Cheese Scouts or something."

Pal and I left my room and made our way downstairs. I was starting to notice flittering *things* lurking in dark corners that scuttled out of sight when I tried to look at them directly.

Oh, good, now I'm seeing little flitty things in the dark places—I'm hallucinating those, right? I wondered to Pal.

"Actually, probably not," he replied from his perch on my shoulder. "The world is full of fey creatures that normally even strong Talents don't see. Best to pretend you don't notice them, because to observe them is to affect them, and they don't like that."

Oh. I prudently stared down at my feet on the stairs, which was just as well because my balance as well as my depth perception were totally shot and I felt like I might trip at any moment.

Nonetheless, I got downstairs safely and wobbled through the living room into the kitchen. Mikey was on the couch drinking beer and watching two sweaty guys in tight shorts pummel each other in a cage fighting match; he didn't so much as grunt at me as I passed. Something that looked like a fleshy daisy with octopus tentacles instead of roots clung to the bottom of his beer. Its twin dozed on one of his hairy feet.

Shoals of indistinct fey creatures fled my feet as I entered the kitchen. I made a beeline for the old Maytag refrigerator, opened it, and ignored the weird mantis-like creatures lurking behind the pickle jar and a Taco Bell bag. A spiky little fey that looked like a cross between a mushroom and a puffer fish flopped away from the light as I pulled open the vegetable crisper. Bingo. Beside some flaccid carrots was a Ziploc bag of shredded cheddar; a full two-thirds of the cheese was mottled with green-gray *Penicillium* mold.

I grabbed the cheese and found a discarded Popsicle stick and disposable lighter in the huge pile of dirty dishes and debris on the kitchen counter.

"Better get a bowl, too. Some garlic wouldn't hurt, either," Pal said.

I found a relatively clean glass mixing bowl in one of the cabinets and some garlic powder.

All right, let's get this done, I thought to Pal. *I'd very much like to not be seeing the fey anymore. It's kind of hard not to stare at them. What would they do if I bothered them?*

"I'm surely not an expert, since I've never been able to see them myself," Pal admitted. "They share our plane but are not fully part of it. We're furniture to them, but nobody really knows how they perceive the world we interact with. Still, I've heard that in their perception, sentient attention is the equivalent of a strong spotlight shining down on them. They tolerate that sort of thing for a little while, but then they'll look for ways to make the light go away."

Lovely. I left the kitchen and went back into the living room.

Mikey glanced over at me, then belched and set

his empty beer down on the coffee table. The tentacle daisy leaped off the bottle at the last second and scuttled away to hide somewhere on the underside of the table.

"Y'know, if your face wasn't all fucked up, and if you wore some makeup and did something with your hair, you might be kinda hot," Mikey said, sounding bored.

I felt a sudden surge of anger rise through the haze of my fever. "And I might be vaguely attracted to you, if you weren't such a *dick*."

I said that last part with a lot more force and venom than I'd intended . . . and it didn't come out in English.

"Oh, *Jessie*," Pal sighed.

I'd turned Mikey into a giant, saggy, sweaty-smelling uncircumcised penis lolling on the couch. His hairy feet, looking ridiculous and tiny, stuck out where the testicles should have been. The tentacle daisy still clung to his toes, unperturbed.

Huh. This magical kick I'm getting from the fever is kind of handy, I thought to Pal.

"Your increased power is simply a temporary survival mechanism," he replied. "You're probably just a few hours from incapacitating delirium and coma."

Oh, goody.

Kai came down the stairs; he stopped dead on the landing when he got a clear view of the couch.

"Dude . . . that's just *wrong*," he croaked. "Is—is that Mikey?"

I nodded calmly. "He seems to be . . . in his element."

"Why did you do that?" Kai sounded close to panic.

I decided I felt too sick and tired to apologize for anything I had done or was going to do that day. "That's what he gets for being a prick to me."

"But . . . but he ain't got no mouth! Or nose! How can he breathe like that?"

I hadn't considered the respiratory consequences of turning somebody into giant genitalia.

How is he able to breathe like that? I asked Pal.

"He's able to breathe just fine," Pal assured me. "You didn't really turn him into a penis."

I didn't? He sure looks like a gargantuan wang to me.

"I believe you just put a perceptual charm on him. Anybody who looks at him thinks he's been transformed. He thinks it, too, or at least he thinks he can't speak or get off the couch. No harm done unless he needs to urinate or defecate while he's lying there, and honestly given the state of the couch I doubt anybody else living here will much notice if he does."

If it's just a perceptual thing, shouldn't I be able to see through it myself? Especially since I'm seeing the fey all over everything?

"Well, no, it doesn't work that way," Pal replied. "If a chair was painted red, it'd look red to you whether you were the painter or not, right? You could certainly cast a charm you could see past, but that *would* generally require an incantation with some conscious thought and planning put into it."

Huh. How easily do you think I can remove the charm?

"Obviously you didn't exert a lot of magical energy on this, so I'd say it should be fairly easy to reverse," Pal replied. "It might even wear off on its own after a while."

Cool.

I turned toward Kai. He had purple starfish riding in his dreadlocks. "I'll make a deal with you. I'm having a craptabulous day, and I could use some help. So if you help me for a couple of hours, I'll put Mikey back to normal."

Kai paled. "Okay . . ."

I led him upstairs to my room. The two flights winded me terribly, and bright spots bloomed in my vision.

"You okay?" Kai asked as I leaned against the door to catch my breath.

"Not so much, no," I replied. "But I'm gonna fix that."

I handed him the bowl with the spell ingredients and opened my door. "Please wash your hands, and then get the Leatherman tool out of that pile of stuff over there."

"Whoa!" Kai exclaimed, looking around the room. "When did you bring all this in here?"

"I had it with me when I arrived last night. It was in that cup of soda."

"No way!"

"Yes, way. After you've washed your hands and gotten the Leatherman out of the package, I need you to carve that Popsicle stick into little slivers in the bowl. And then I need you to burn the slivers down to ash, then knead the ashes, the moldy cheese, and a bunch of the garlic powder until you've got a paste."

"Uh, okay. How much is 'a bunch'?"

I eyed the jar lying atop the bag of cheese. "About a third of what's left in there. I'll get you guys more when I have the chance."

I walked over to my stuff pile and got the carton of Epsom salts. "I've got to take my bandages off and soak my arm for a little while before I do the spell. I look pretty gross under all this, so don't freak out, m'kay?"

Kai looked lost. "Okay . . ."

He went into the bathroom. "Whoa, you really cleaned in here!"

"Well, somebody had to," I replied.

"Did you, like, use *magic*?" he asked as he started washing his hands.

"Yeah, I did."

"Could you do this to the whole house?" he asked, excited.

"Possibly. Maybe. Let's talk about that in a couple of days, all right?"

He shook the water off his hands, and we traded places. I eased the sling off and carefully unwound the bandages on my arm. A sour stench slid up my nose as I peeled off the last of the gauze. The stump was well and thoroughly infected. The puckered scar had split open and was leaking brown pus, and angry red streaks ran up my arm clear to my shoulder. The lymph nodes in my armpit felt like grapes sliding around under my skin.

Kai stared in horror at my arm, but apparently curiosity kept him rooted to the spot.

"So, like, what happened to you?" he asked as I closed the stopper on the sink and turned on the hot water.

"I got my arm chomped off by a demon," I replied as I opened the carton and shook several ounces of Epsom salts into the steamy water. "Its blood burned my eye out of my head when I killed it."

"Whoa, you killed a *demon*? Like from *hell*?"

"Well, it sure didn't come from Cleveland." I stirred the salts in the water with my fingers to dissolve them, then eased my stump into the basin. My nerves were so damaged by the infection I barely felt the heat. I closed my eyes and rested my forehead against the cool mirror.

"How do you kill a demon?" he asked.

"Depends on the demon," I replied. "The one I dealt with took magic, a silver dagger, and a bunch of dumb luck."

"Was it going to kill you?"

"It killed three guys in a parking garage, and it wanted to exterminate the entire planet. It probably wasn't going to actually have the chance to kill anyone else besides me and Pal here, but we sure didn't want to die."

"Could you have, like, reasoned with it?" Kai asked.

"Not in this universe. It was about as reasonable as the black plague," I replied.

"So, I have a question about this magic stuff . . ."

"Shoot."

"In my physics class, my professor said that any kind of action takes energy. So where does the energy for magic come from?"

"Well, a chunk of the power for a spell always comes from the spellcaster. But that's usually just another thing to use calories on," I replied, shifting my arm. The warm salty water seemed to be drawing a lot of the crud out of my stump. "Strong spells take outside power, but there are all kinds of sources for magic. The kind you use depends of the type of magic you're doing."

"Like how?" Kai asked.

"I did some charms this morning that use heat from the air," I continued. "That's great on a hot day like today, but sucks when it's cold out. That's why haunted houses seem so chilly; poltergeists and wraiths tend to use heat to sustain themselves. Some spells use solar power . . . lots of full-moon rituals really source from reflected sunlight. Necromancers kill people or animals and use their life force. That's really powerful magic, but it trashes your soul. On the other hand, a lot of the magic people like me perform uses ambient spiritual energy, and that usually doesn't cost anybody anything."

"What's ambient spiritual energy?" Kai asked.

"In a way, it's a lot like solar power, only it's made by people. You know how the sun gives off a lot of energy just shining in space? We can use sunshine, or not use it, but it doesn't matter to the sun. People are the same way. Concentrating, dreaming, hoping, loving, getting mad, getting excited, it all gives off a kind of energy that hangs like an invisible cloud in areas where there are a lot of people."

"But what if you were out in the middle of nowhere? What would you use then?"

I shrugged. "There's always *something* a Talent can use. Sun. Wind. Heat. There are creatures all over this house that you can't see or touch, and they give off energy, too."

Kai glanced around the room, looking a little uneasy. The purple starfish in his dreadlocks breathed silently. "So how do you use spiritual energy and stuff like that?" he asked.

"It's not really a conscious thing if you've got magical Talent," I replied. "You don't have to think about metabolizing the Pepsi you drank to help you run down the block, right? You just do it, because that's how you're built."

"Did you have to learn this stuff, or did it just sort of come to you?"

"Oh yeah, I had to learn a lot. I was a teenager before I had any clue I could do any of this," I replied.

"Could you . . . could you teach me how to do some magic?" He bounced on his toes nervously.

Sophomores, I thought to Pal. *They look so cute when they get all hopeful like that.*

"Maybe," I told Kai. "I've got kind of a lot on my plate right now, but when things settle down I can give it a shot. First things first, though: Why don't you make the wood ashes and mix up the paste? I'm kinda gonna pass out soon if you don't."

"Oh. Yeah, sure."

Kai shaved and burned the Popsicle stick and made the paste while I kept soaking my arm. Soon he brought in an unappetizing orange-gray mush in the glass bowl.

"Fantastic," I said. I lifted my stump from the sink, popped the drain, and gathered up a handful of the gritty, pungent paste. I closed my eyes and held the paste against the infected wound, beginning a chant much like the one I'd used to heal the wound from Smoky's tail in the Riffe Tower.

As I chanted, the swelling in my arm gradually went down and the fever left my head. When I looked up again, the starfish in Kai's dreadlocks had disappeared. I pulled the gooey handful away, shook it off into the toilet, and rinsed myself in the sink. My arm looked healthy and pink.

"See? Lots nicer than a trip to the emergency

room, and quicker than a shot of penicillin," I said. "Could you bring me a towel, the boxes of fresh bandages, and the antibiotic salve?"

"Sure." Kai left the doorway and came back with the items I'd requested. I put salve on my scars, and Kai helped me put on fresh bandages and get my sling back on.

"I need to change the bandages on my head, too," I said, "And make sure I haven't got an infection started there, either."

"Have you considered brushing your hair while you're at it?" Pal asked drily.

Shush, I thought back. *This whole bed-head thing I've got going is part of my new look.*

"Oh, so this sweaty unkemptness is a 'look' now, is it?" Pal replied.

Well, I'm too poor and damaged to manage "pretty" or "fashionable," so I might as well just go with "scary" or "eek, a witch!"

"Right now, it's more like 'plague victim.' Seriously, brush your hair."

Fine. "Hey, Kai, could you bring me my brush as well?" I began to unwind the bandages on my head.

"Okay," Kai replied.

I'd gotten the bandages off when Kai returned. He flinched when I turned toward him to take the brush from his hand.

"Sorry," I said. "I did warn you it was a bit gross."

I brushed out my hair and smoothed my unruly auburn locks in place behind my ears. My ruined face was indeed fairly horrifying, but didn't look infected. I popped the ball out to check my eye socket. As far as I could tell, it was fine.

"Is that a Ping-Pong ball?" Kai asked.

"What can I say? My health plan sucks." I slipped the ball back into my socket and put some of the salve on the worst parts of my face. Kai helped me with the bandages again, and soon I felt and looked quite a bit better.

"Give me a minute to change clothes, and then if you don't mind, I need you to give me a ride up to Worthington. There's a little errand I need to run. Won't take long, I promise."

"Uh, okay. I'll meet you downstairs . . ."

Kai left, and I shut the door and dug out some fresh clothes while Pal got a snack at his bowl.

"The anathema counter-charm will work best if you can get close to the little girl's location and hand your aura off to somebody nearby," Pal said as he crunched on his kitten kibble. "Can you sense where she is?"

I closed my eyes and let my mind wander away from my body. "Yes. I'm pretty sure I can find her."

"Good. After that, we'll need to get back here as quickly as possible to get the potion started."

I shucked off my sling and sweaty clothes and put on fresh jeans and an olive-green T-shirt. It took me a couple of tries to recite Mother Karen's shoelace-tying charm correctly, but in the end I got my sneakers back on. I stuck my much-used plastic bag, a pair of latex gloves, and the little bottle of hand sanitizer in my pocket, just in case.

"Let's do this thing," I said to Pal. He hopped up on my shoulder and we went downstairs to meet Kai.

chapter fourteen

Potion Motion

I splurged on some burgers and sodas for Kai and myself at a nearby McDonald's drive-through, and then I directed him up High Street to Worthington.

Once we got onto the side streets, I gave directions with my eye half closed as I concentrated on the little girl's location. "Take a left when you can, then go straight for a while . . . okay, take another left, and then . . . stop."

The girl was close by. I looked around, and across the street was the Mon Petit Chou Child Care. Bingo.

"I need to go into that day-care center, but don't park right in front. Please go around over there to the side where it's sort of out of sight."

Kai parked in the shade of a tall elm and killed the engine.

"I won't be gone very long. Pal, you stay here with him, please."

Pal climbed down off my shoulder, and I got out of the car and walked across the street and through the day care's parking lot toward the front doors. Cooper and I had talked about having a baby in a few years once our living and work situations were a bit more stable. I dearly hoped we'd still have the chance to make a family someday. Mon Petit looked like a nice place, at least from the outside; I couldn't see any kids from the parking lot but I could hear happy shrieks and laughter coming from the fenced play yard in the back.

I put on my friendliest smile and pushed through the door.

The young woman at the counter looked up. "May I help you?"

"Yes, hi, my name's Karen, and I was staying at home with my little girl—she's just turned two—but I was in this bad accident recently and I just can't keep up with her anymore. She's staying with my sister, but that's really not working out, so I'm looking for a good day care for her. Just for a couple of days a week."

The woman at the counter smiled at me pityingly. "Well, that's certainly understandable. I can give you a tour, if you'll just give me your driver's license—"

"I lost it in the wreck; I haven't got a replacement yet, sorry," I said.

"Do you have any other form of picture ID, like an old student ID?"

"No, I'm sorry, it all burned up with my purse."

"Well, I'm afraid I can't let you look around without it."

I sighed. "I was afraid of that . . . oh well, I can come back after I've been to the DMV. Just hate dealing with the lines down there, you know? And the people are so grouchy. Do you have any brochures or anything like that I could take home to show my husband?"

"Sure." The woman brightened. "I can do that." She pulled a glossy *Welcome to Mon Petit Chou!* brochure out of a cubbyhole behind the counter and folded up a *Little Cabbages Newsletter* to go along with it.

"Thank you so much." I took the papers and slipped them into my sling. I paused, hoping I looked queasy.

"Is everything all right?" asked the young woman.

"I'm a little . . . the medicine they gave me, it doesn't, you know, sit right sometimes." I made the universal motion for "projectile vomiting" with my hand. "I think I need to get to a toilet . . . is there a ladies' room I could use?"

"Sure, yes, go down the hall to your right, the staff toilet's the first door on your left," the woman said quickly, leaning back in her chair away from me.

"Thanks *so* much." I hurried down the hall to the single-toilet restroom and locked myself in. There was a small stainless-steel trash can with a step-open lid between the toilet and the sink. I fished out my plastic bag and one of the latex gloves, pulled the glove on with my teeth, pressed the pedal to open the lid, and started sifting through the trash.

I quickly found a freshly used maxi pad, thoughtfully folded and wrapped in a layer of toilet paper. Setting the pad aside on the floor, I poked the baggie inside out. I picked up the pad through the bag and pulled it through, turning the bag right-side out again with the pad nestled neatly inside. I sealed the plastic zipper against the floor, then rolled my glove off against my jeans and tossed it in the trash. I stuck the bagged pad in my back pocket, flushed the toilet for effect, and left the restroom.

"Thanks again!" I waved cheerfully to the relieved-looking woman at the desk on my way out the door.

"Mission accomplished," I told Kai and Pal as I got back to the car.

Can I wait until I get back to our room to perform the counter-charm? I wondered to Pal. *It'll freak poor Kai out something fierce if I whip out a bloody maxi pad here in the car and start chanting.*

"You have a little less than an hour before yesterday's counter-charm runs out," Pal replied. "You should be safe, unless Kai makes an unexpected stop."

"Home, James!" I said. "I've got potions to make and spells to break."

Kai got us back to the house with thirty minutes to spare. Mikey was back to his old self on the couch, seemingly unaware that he'd been the biggest dick I or Kai had ever seen. I thanked Kai for his help, locked myself in the attic room, and foisted my anathema off on an OSU student who was supervising the children running amok in the play yard behind the day-care center.

"Your aura looks fine," Pal said after I finished the incantation and disposed of the ashes in the toilet. "Though having to do this every day will become tedious if this situation drags on much longer."

"No kidding," I said. "So let's get started on that dematerialization potion."

I started to gather the herbs and other ingredients together when Pal said, "Oh. We've forgotten the rat."

"That's totally your department," I replied.

Pal sighed. "I suppose it is. I'll see what I can find under the house."

I took Pal downstairs and sat in one of the battered

lawn chairs beside the front door sipping a Gatorade while he humped down the creaky wooden steps to slip under the porch.

A few minutes later there came a quick rustling, followed by a terrified squeak and a furious thrashing. Pal popped up shortly thereafter, his teeth buried in the neck of a small dead rat. He dragged the corpse up the stairs between his front legs. I collected the little rat in my plastic bag.

"That should give you enough blood," Pal said, seeming sheepish.

"What's the matter?" I asked.

"It . . . it's *delicious*," Pal admitted. "I've never tasted anything as wonderful as that little rat."

"Well, see, there you go! Natural prey. Of course it tastes good to you. Nothing to be ashamed of," I replied. "Let's go back upstairs."

I set up the camp stove upstairs under an open window. Pal showed me how to mix the ingredients for the potion in the Pyrex saucepan and led me through the two hours of incantation to prime the raw slurry for brewing. Then I set the saucepan over the stove's low propane flame and flopped down on my cot to have a rest.

"So what do we do for the next twelve hours while that's cooking?" I asked Pal. It was just past seven, and the low-hanging sun's rays were long and golden through the trees outside.

"We keep an eye on the pot and stove to make sure it doesn't overcook, or overturn and start a fire," he replied.

"I should have stolen something to read," I said, rubbing my good eye.

"They probably have books downstairs," Pal said. "They *are* students, after all."

"Hm. There's probably nothing but current-semester textbooks and *Sports Illustrated* downstairs."

"Kai seems literate. Surely he has some Marx or a copy of *The Motorcycle Diaries*. Or you could practice your parakinesis. Regaining even part of the use of that arm would be quite handy, no pun intended."

I sat up. "Now, that's a good idea."

I spent most of the evening and night alternately napping and trying to pick up and hold one of the empty plastic grape juice bottles with my phantom limb. By the time the potion finished brewing shortly after sunrise, I was able to pick up a bottle and carry it around for two minutes before I lost my concentration and dropped it.

"That's really quite impressive," Pal said as I turned off the flame to let the potion cool. "If you keep that up, you'll be able to eat with that hand again in less than a week."

"Is it supposed to be this color?" I asked, staring down into the pot of pinkish translucent potion. It smelled like rotting curry.

"Well, the color varies depending on the liquid base, but for grape juice, pink is a good color," Pal assured me. "Colorless is best, but you don't get that with anything less than twenty-four hours of brewing."

"No time for that," I replied. "This should give us two minutes of dematerialization per dose, right?"

"Indeed."

"Is there a way to test it?" I asked. "I don't want

to go down there and find out this stuff doesn't work."

"Yes. Once it's cool enough, dip one of your fingers into the potion, quickly. Make sure your hand's clean first."

"And then what?"

"Then wait a couple of seconds and see if you can move your finger through nearby objects."

"Okay." I washed and dried my hand at the sink, then went back to the potion pot and stuck my index finger in up to the second knuckle. The liquid was still quite hot; I yanked my hand away, then boggled as I saw that the skin on my finger had disappeared.

"Burn yourself?" Pal asked.

"I don't think so," I replied, fascinated by the sliding yellow tendons and pulsing blue blood vessels in my seemingly skinned digit. "But is it supposed to tingle?"

"A little, yes."

I made a fist; my index finger went straight through my palm. "Oh, weird!"

I pressed my finger into my thigh; it passed through my flesh as if it was air until my knuckle hit my skin. I wiggled my finger through the floor, the walls; after a minute or so, it became more difficult, and I started to feel the texture of the plaster and wood I was moving through.

"You'd better stop now, or you'll get stuck," Pal warned.

"Right," I replied. I pulled my hand away from the wall, my skin visible again, and spread my fingers wide until I was sure the potion had worn off. "Well, it seems to work fine. Do I just bottle it up now,

and . . . what? We can go back to the Warlock's bar
and check the place out?"

"Certainly."

I let the potion cool a bit more, then poured it into
the six plastic grape juice bottles and capped them
tightly. I loaded the bottles, my extra bandages,
medicines, the Leatherman, some clean clothes, and
some snacks for me and Pal into my knapsack. The
ferret climbed up to my shoulder and we headed
downstairs.

We walked to the stop on High Street and caught
the next bus; we got off near the Warlock's place
just a little before 9 AM. Traffic nearby was still
fairly heavy, but relatively few people were on the
sidewalks at that hour, since almost everyone who
had to be up in the morning was already ensconced
at work.

"He's even more of a night owl than we are," I
said, taking a quick peek around the corner of a
nearby building at the pulsing, horrible anathema
sphere surrounding the bar. We were maybe fifty
yards away. "He won't even be awake at this hour."

"I don't know about that," Pal replied. "It would
be pretty hard to sleep inside that sphere. It can't be
pleasant, though if he has any skill, he's likely been
able to buffer the effect somewhat."

"Right." I fished one of the bottles out of my
knapsack. "So we take this and run for it?"

Pal nodded. "You'll need to be closer, though, and
start running right after you drink the potion so you
have some momentum; it's hard to get any speed
going if you try to run after the potion takes effect.
You'll have maybe three or four seconds. While
you're enchanted, it will feel more like swimming,

and you might sink through the ground. When you feel yourself coming out of it, try to jump into the air so you don't get stuck in something when you re-materialize.

"Give me the potion first," he continued. "I've used it several times before, so don't worry about me; I can hang on. The last of your enchantment should be enough to carry me through as baggage. Just focus on getting us into the empty space of a room and not the floor or a wall."

I set the bottle down on the pavement, secured the zips on my knapsack, then eased my arm out of its sling and through the other shoulder strap of the sack. I tightened the straps as best I could, then retrieved the bottle and gripped the cap in my teeth to unscrew it.

I spat the cap aside and angled the bottle so Pal could drink from the wide mouth. My hand trembled. "Cheers."

"It will be fine," Pal reassured me, shuddering as he lapped up the nasty pink liquid. "Start walking toward the sphere. Drink the potion as fast as you can, then start running."

"Okay, here goes nothing." I strode down the sidewalk toward the sphere, trying not to look at it directly. I tipped the bottle back into my mouth and swallowed the bitterly foul solution in three big glugs. Almost immediately, my stomach cramped and began to tingle.

I'm gonna throw up, I thought.

"Don't," replied Pal, his voice strangely distant. "Surely you can keep it down for two minutes. Grit your teeth and run!"

I ran. My stomach felt like it was full of angry

buzzing bees, and the bees spread from my stomach to my intestines and liver and up my throat and the bees were in my brain and in my legs oh God I couldn't feel my legs and the world around me looked strange and dark like the negative of a photograph—

"Keep going! It's not far now!" Pal said.

—every cell in my body was vibrating, shimmying out of phase with the world as my legs lost touch with the ground. I was swimming in a vacuum, my bee-filled stomach twisting, and then there was a blue flash and faint static shock as I passed through the anathema sphere, what was that, a wall? A wall, black lights, everything looked wrong, I was spinning, spinning into shining white earth—

"Go up! Go up!" Pal yelled in my ear.

I swam toward where I thought "up" was.

"No, you're still going down! Go the other way!"

I turned myself over, starting to feel the faint texture of the soil and rock, and desperately swam up through the strata, through the damp basement, and popped up into the dimly lit barroom just as my body shifted back into proper phase—

—and suddenly I was falling.

chapter fifteen

The Warlock

I hit the polished wooden floor hard, cutting the inside of my lip on my front teeth. My vision didn't clear right away, but my innards rebelled against both potion and sudden gravity and started heaving.

"Here, use this." Somebody set a plastic bucket down on the floor beside my head.

I tried to say thanks but suddenly everything in my stomach was coming up and I just had time to get up on my hand and knees before I started vomiting, copiously and painfully. First came the potion, now dark and bitter as nightshade wine, then orange bile, then nothing. My body was racked with dry heaves a full three minutes after my stomach was empty.

Finally, my innards relaxed, and I rolled away from the bucket onto my back, drenched in clammy sweat. The bottles in my knapsack dug uncomfortably into my ribs, but I didn't have the energy to care.

The Warlock stood over me wearing old black jeans and a black velvet bathrobe that was loosely belted beneath his thickly pelted chest. He carried an unopened dark glass bottle of ginger ale. His fingers were armored with silver rings, and on a silver chain he wore an oblong bronze pendant of a bas-relief sword against a shield. Where Cooper was wiry and smooth, the Warlock was burly and furry, but they both had the same curly black hair, sharp gray eyes, and quick smile.

As I looked at him more closely, though, I realized he seemed sick: He was much paler than usual, his lips slightly blue, and his eyes looked sunken. His full beard and mustache were sprung with loose curls and wild hairs. It looked like he hadn't trimmed or waxed them in days, and usually he was quite vain about his facial hair.

"Looks like somebody's been home-brewing demat potions," the Warlock said, glancing into the bucket. "The question is, did you bring enough for the whole class?"

"I've—I've got five doses left," I coughed.

"Good girl," the Warlock said, flicking the metal cap off the bottle with his thumb and offering it to me. "This should make you feel a little better."

"Thanks." I managed to sit up and took the bottle from him. The ginger ale was sharply sweet and cool, and felt wonderful going down.

The Warlock frowned at the bandages on my face. "Did . . . have you lost your eye?"

"Unfortunately, yeah. Why?"

A terrible realization seemed to eclipse his face for a moment, but his expression quickly cleared. "It's . . . nothing. I'll tell you later."

He cleared his throat uncomfortably. "Well, I'm glad to see Cooper's been teaching you the good stuff, unless the potion was Spiderboy's idea." He jerked his head toward Pal, who was sitting on one of the bar stools, looking a bit woozy.

"Spiderboy?" I asked, completely baffled.

"Your familiar's a quamo. If he were in his real form, he'd be a big arachnid, tall as me."

"This fellow is quite perceptive," Pal admitted.

"How did you know?" I asked the Warlock.

"When people come into my bar, I like to know exactly who they are," he replied, then raised his hands to the rafters. "We seek, and magic almost always provides the solution. And speaking of knowing who everybody is—you're not wearing your own aura, young lady. What's up with that?"

"Mr. Jordan put an anathema on me after the accident downtown. He doesn't want me looking for Cooper. Pal showed me how to dodge the curse by trading spiritual profiles with other people."

The Warlock shook his finger at Pal in mock admonishment. "You're a naughty one, aren't you? Clever, but *very* naughty. Wouldn't want to be you when your jailers get wise to what you've been doing."

The Warlock walked behind the bar and poured himself a tall glass of dark ale from the tap. He toasted me with the glass before he took a drink: "Here's to our health."

He drained half the ale, set the glass aside, and said, "Tell me what happened downtown. Everything."

I got to my feet and sat down at the bar beside Pal. "I figured you'd heard all about it by now."

The Warlock shook his head grimly. "No, nothing, though of course I got some ideas. Coop and me, we've always had this connection, since before I can remember. Something big happens to either of us, the other feels it. So last weekend, I was in here working the room, making the new customers feel at home, when *boom*, I feel like I been hit by lightning, and I know Coop's in trouble. But before I can do anything else, I'm down for the count. Opal gets me awake maybe half an hour later, but goons from the Circle Jerk are here herding my customers out the door. They've got a scroll from a Virt saying they're putting the place under indefinite isolation. Won't say why. Won't say shit to me. They just clear out everybody but me and Opal, and then slap the sphere on the whole building."

The Warlock shook his head and took another long drink of his ale. "Phones don't work, cable doesn't work, can't get anything but static on the radio. At least we got electricity and running water. They had a mundane kid drop some groceries in the front foyer yesterday, so I guess they don't mean to starve us. Don't know what the hell I'm gonna do if I run out of decent beer, though."

I shuddered to think how much he'd been consuming if he was in any danger of drinking his own bar dry. "They didn't tell you *anything*?" I asked. "I thought they, you know, *had* to tell you something before they put you under house arrest or whatever this is supposed to be."

The Warlock shrugged. "I'm no poster boy for upstanding citizenship. Only the good kids get niceties like legal rights when serious shit goes down, because the Circle Jerks know they can scare the good kids into being useful to them. Us malcontents just keep being a pain in their butts no matter what. Jordan made it clear years ago he only tolerates me because everyone likes my bar. So tell me, what the hell happened to make him change his mind?"

We both had two more drinks apiece as I told him my story. When I finished, the Warlock looked grim.

"Not surprised Jordan's been leaning on you like that. Good for you for not caving. I wasn't sure you'd have it in you to fight back if something like this happened," he said, rubbing his temples as if he had a headache.

I wasn't sure if I should be offended or not. "You know what's happened to Cooper, don't you," I said.

"I have . . . suspicions, yeah," the Warlock replied.

"Tell me," I insisted.

The Warlock wouldn't meet my eyes. "I gotta go to the little boys' room first." He left his seat behind the bar and retrieved the bucket from the middle of the floor. "I'll be back in a few minutes . . . if you guys are hungry, there's plenty of stuff for sandwiches in the fridge." He gestured toward the kitchen behind a set of swinging doors, then turned and went down the hall to the men's restroom.

"That man's rather frightened," Pal said.

"That'd be a first," I replied. "Nothing scares the Warlock."

"Well, this most certainly has," Pal said. "I can smell it all over him."

I finished the last of my third bottle of ginger ale and set it by my other empties. "So, you're a giant spider."

"Well, that's an oversimplification. We're not spiders; we bear only a superficial resemblance to arachnids—"

"Eight legs? Lots of eyes? Breathe through your abdomen? Little pinchy mouthparts?"

"Well, yes, but—"

"Dude. You're a *spider*."

"This isn't fair. I haven't once given you a hard time about being a hairless water ape," Pal said.

"Okay, okay, I'm sorry, but . . . spiders are *completely* inhuman."

"I never claimed to be human, did I?" Pal replied testily.

"Yeah, but . . . but we get along really well. Well, *now,* anyway. You're sympathetic, you understand me . . . how's that possible if you're really a big spider alien?"

Pal sighed. "Jessie, I've had *practice.* You've been alive for a little over two decades—I've been a familiar for more than three *centuries.* Don't you think I could learn a little something about human psychology and culture in all that time? And, well . . . it's really not that hard to think and feel like a mammal once you've occupied their bodies for a while. Sometimes it's rather hard to remember what it was like to live in my true form."

"Won't it be weird when you finally get to go back to your own body and your own people?" I asked.

Pal shifted uncomfortably. "Yes. I imagine I'll have an adjustment period. Sometimes I'm . . . I'm not sure I *can* go back. I didn't exactly fit in even before I was arrested."

He shook himself and bounced on the bar stool as if he was trying to cheer himself up. "Ah well! I can certainly find a position in academia eventually. I'm sure one of my nestmates will give me a place to stay until I can find a suitable situation."

The Warlock came back to the bar and stowed the rinsed-out plastic bucket on a lower shelf.

"You were saying you had suspicions about what's happened to Cooper?" I said.

"Yeah, I was." The Warlock poured himself another

ale, looking troubled. "Did Coop ever tell you about our childhood?"

I shook my head. "Not much. He said you two were raised in foster homes, and I got the feeling that he didn't like talking about it, so I never pressed him."

"Okay, then." The Warlock took a long drink before he said anything else. "Coop was maybe six or seven, and I was about nine months old. A sheriff's deputy found Coop carrying me down a back road in Licking County, about eight miles outside Cedar Hill. We were filthy, thirsty, and Coop had near-total amnesia—he didn't know anything but his own name. He didn't have anything but the clothes on his back, and I didn't have anything but a diaper and this on my neck." He touched his sword-and-shield pendant.

"The last time we talked about this, Coop still said that he couldn't remember a thing from his life before he was walking down that road. The story goes that he freaked out when the child psychologist was talking to him at the sheriff's station and Coop set the room on fire. The local Talents got involved after that, and got us out of there. They figured out that we were brothers, but didn't think Coop and I had the same father, so I was John Doe for a long time.

"That's why I just go by Warlock—I figure if I can't use my given name, might as well call myself what I am and nothing more."

"Couldn't they use a spell to find out who your parents were?" I asked.

"That's where the Circle Jerks and our foster folks got suspiciously hazy," the Warlock replied. "Anytime

I asked, they just hemmed and hawed about it. Coop—he just flat didn't want to know. That pissed me off for a long time, till I got a bit older and figured out that some things really are best to let lie. But when I was sixteen, I was mad that the people around me were lying to me, so I started trying to find out on my own where we'd come from.

"I got hold of some old spell books and tried doing divination spells on my blood to trace my lineage. But no matter what I tried, I just couldn't get the magic to work. So then I tried to find a diviner to do the spells for me, but everybody wanted way more money than any teenager could come up with, or they told me they didn't have time, or whatever. One way or another, I got the brush-off when they figured out who I was.

"So I started doing mundane detective legwork as best I could. I didn't get any answers—I kept running into dead ends and locked doors. The only thing I found was a newspaper story in the *Cedar Hill Ally* from the same day the deputy found us on the road. The story talked about a fire in the woods, and a farmhouse the firefighters found out in the middle of nowhere that had burned straight to the ground. I figured out that the fire was less than three miles from where we'd been picked up, so I decided I'd go out there myself and have a look around."

The Warlock took another long drink from his glass.

"So what did you find out there?" I asked.

"It took me a while to find the place," the Warlock replied. "It's far out in the hills in a tangle of woods and dirt roads that nobody's ever going to pave. But I knew it the moment I saw it: a half-acre clearing, still charred and lifeless after fifteen years, with the burned wreck of a house and stone-lined basement out in the middle. I took one step onto the bare dirt and the evil of the place hit me like a punch in the gut, and before I knew it I was back in my Mustang burning rubber to get back to Columbus.

"I didn't sleep right for months after I went to that place. I don't know what happened there, but it was very, very bad, and Coop and I were part of it."

The Warlock was silent for a moment. "I quit looking for answers after that. Scared, I guess. But I came to realize I have certain . . . *shortcomings* when it comes to magic. Dirty gray and red magic I've always been good at, but the high-end white stuff has always been hard for me. Never been able to heal for shit; if it weren't for Opal, I'd be dead from a pickled liver by now."

"Is she any good at regrowing arms or eyes?" I asked, hopeful.

The Warlock shook his head. "She's good with your typical bar fight injuries because, surprise, that's what we get around here. If your arm was busted she could fix it, but complex regeneration's a little more than she's had to deal with. Sorry."

"No problem. Thought I'd ask the obvious," I replied, pushing down a sudden swell of frustration. "So what's the deal with 'The Twelve Days of Christmas'? Cooper's always hated that song like crazy."

The Warlock shook his head. "Can't say I like that tune much myself . . . makes me want to puke every time I hear it. I don't know why. But I'm sure it's because of what happened to us. About ten years ago I decided to get myself an in-depth spiritual exam, and I didn't get half the answers I was looking for . . . but I did find out I'm missing a chunk of my soul."

I was boggled. "How can you be missing a part of your soul?"

"Trauma. Black magic. Probably a mix of both," the Warlock replied. "I'm not missing a *big* piece, mind you, or I wouldn't much seem like a human being. But it was enough to screw up my ability to use white magic from the get-go, because it makes me look like a demon to the spirits that be."

"Do you have any idea where the rest of your soul is?" I asked.

"Based on the dreams I've been having lately, I'm pretty sure the rest of my soul is in a hell. I think Cooper's in there, too. All of him. I got the feeling that his getting dragged in there was inevitable . . . if it didn't happen during his life, it'd happen when he died. You get touched by something that turns into a hell, it's not gonna let you go easy. It's probably got my number, too, and it's just waiting for me to screw up a big spell or die. I know damn well that if I try to go rescue him, I'll be just as stuck as he is."

I thought of the Wutganger and wondered whose soul it had been a piece of. "That demon I fought downtown—"

"Not mine," the Warlock replied. "That I'm very sure of."

He paused. "I love my brother, Jessie, I do. But . . . I can't go after him. I just can't. I'd lay down my life for him if I thought I stood a chance of helping him, but I'm Mr. Snowball here. And . . . there are things worse than dying. Even if it's inevitable . . . I'm sorry, I can't do it."

"You don't have to go after him," I replied. "I'll do it. I'll bring him home, one way or another."

"Jessie, this is *hell* we're talking about. There are lots of hells in this universe—anybody who dies with a big load of guilt or hate's just as likely to create their own as they are to pass on to the Great Beyond—but the one thing they've all got in common is that they're worse than most people can possibly imagine. You go looking for Cooper—even supposing you don't get killed right away by whatever's in there, supposing you get out alive—you'll be changed by it. Cooper will have been changed by it. Your lives will *not* be the same.

"You don't want to do this, trust me," he finished, not really sounding like he thought he'd be able to talk me out of anything.

"I can't leave him down there," I said. "I can't live with myself knowing I could have done something, but wasn't brave enough to try. I should have helped my aunt Vicky, but I totally failed her; I can't do that to Cooper. I *have* to do this. Can you at least help me find a way into where he's trapped?"

"Yeah. I . . . I can find that field again. Opening a portal there shouldn't be too hard."

"You've done portals before?" I asked.

"No . . . but the barrier between that hell and our world is precious thin out there."

The Warlock shivered and pulled his robe closed, looking even sicker than he had before, and I finally put two and two together.

"You're spiritually bound to Cooper, aren't you?" I asked. "If he dies, you die."

The Warlock had gone a shade paler, but he forced a smile. "Which is good news, right? I'm still up and around, so that means hell hasn't killed him yet. And . . . his death is no guarantee of my death. There are . . . measures I can take."

He fingered the sword-and-shield pendant at his neck.

My mouth went dry, thinking of Mr. Jordan's story of how my mother saved me from cancer. The Warlock, for all his fighting and dodgy deals and insatiable appetite for sex, had always claimed he never committed nonconsensual violence. He never even took a familiar because he said he didn't believe in taking advantage of those who'd been forced into magical servitude.

"What kind of measures?" I asked. "Necromancy? After all your talk of not hurting other people?"

"Get off that high horse right now, Jessie," the Warlock said, softly but with real menace. "You eat meat the same as me; you're willing to accept the death of other creatures to support your own life."

"But not the death of *people*," I insisted. "And I know good and well it would take nothing less than human sacrifice to stop what's going to happen to you if Cooper dies."

He paused. "Come upstairs with me to our apartment. There's something you should see. Both of you, I suppose," he added, flicking his eyes toward Pal.

Pal climbed up on my shoulder, and I followed the Warlock through the kitchen to a flight of polished wooden stairs that led to the second floor. The Warlock's breathing became labored near the top. I could feel the wards on the stairs; uninvited visitors would be overcome with nausea and vertigo before they got even halfway up. His apartment entrance was certain to have a subtler and more deadly set of protections.

He unlocked the door and led me in. The air in the room was heavy with the smell of tobacco, incense, and dirty litter boxes. He flipped on the living room light. The walls were decorated with paintings and framed sketches, mainly nudes of men and women I figured were some of the Warlock's many lovers. He wasn't a bad artist, either; though some of the drawings were a little flat, he had a real talent for capturing faces and expressions. The hardwood floors were littered with piles of books and drifts of dust and cat hair. A gray Persian stared at me irritably from the black leather couch beside the huge television set.

"It's in the back," the Warlock said, beckoning me to follow him down a broad, arched hallway that was far too long to exist solely within the confines of the building. "You want anything to eat? I think Opal made some tuna salad."

"No, I'm good, thanks. Where *is* Opal, by the way?"

"She's down in the garage. The anathema sphere cranked her claustrophobia up to eleven, so she's been messing with our Land Rover. She's trying to get it magicked up so it can get through the sphere without frying out the electrical system or blowing up the fuel tank. I was glad she found something to keep her occupied, but I figured it wasn't gonna help us much since we didn't have the stuff on hand to keep the sphere from frying *us*. But now that you're here, and you brought goodies, maybe all that work wasn't for nothing."

"If she doesn't finish, we can just shrink the Rover down and stick it in your pocket and walk out with it," I said.

"When you've got a new hammer, everything looks like a nail, doesn't it?" Pal commented.

Shush. It's a most excellent hammer, I thought back.

The Warlock looked at me, his eyebrows raised. "Surely you don't think the sphere is the only barrier Jordan's put up between here and there, do you?"

"Well . . . no, I suppose not," I replied, feeling sheepish.

"Then I'd really feel much better about our chances if she got the Rover magicked up before we buzz on out of here to take you to certain death."

"Gosh, thanks, Warlock, that just warms the very cockles of my heart—have you ever considered selling the bar and starting a new career as a life coach?"

"Y'know, I keep suggesting that to Opal, but for some weird reason she thinks it wouldn't go over too well."

"Seriously, though," I said, "the potions I made expire tomorrow around sunrise—do you think she'll actually have the truck properly enchanted by then?"

The Warlock nodded, looking distracted. "I have a feeling she'll get it worked out in time. She's been at it for thirty hours straight. She yelled at me to quit looking over her shoulder last time I went in there. Lady's gotta have her space when she's like that."

"You're going to have to deal with your anathema before then," Pal reminded me.

"Oh, crap, yeah, my anathema," I said. "I'll need to leave to get some tissue in Worthington and do another counter-spell before four PM."

"Do you have enough potion to get in and out of here and still cover us?" the Warlock asked.

"Yeah. I've got enough left—we should be good, as long as we're out by tomorrow morning. Do you have forty dollars I can borrow for the cab?"

"How 'bout I give you sixty, and you can bring us back some pizzas for dinner. There's a place called Antolino's just around the corner. I want mine with anchovies and black olives. And here's the room I wanted to show you."

He stopped and opened a door to a room lit only by the blue glow of fluorescent aquarium lights. Four rectangular hundred-gallon aquaria were lined up against the back wall, their aerators bubbling softly. At first glance, I thought the pink things crawling on the smooth rocks and swimming through the red and green algae fronds were some kind of salamanders or frogs.

Then I took a closer look and saw that the big-headed, short-tailed creatures had a distinctly human form. The largest was maybe six inches long, the smallest perhaps four. Their lids were sealed shut over huge dark eyes, and their toothless mouths gulped air at the water's surface or gummed juice from the algae's fronds. Fragile webbing stretched between their tiny fingers.

"We call 'em the Jizz Kids," the Warlock said. "We started out with, oh, I guess fifty or sixty. Now there's two dozen. They were small as brine shrimp when we discovered them. Good thing they were that big, or Opal wouldn't have even seen 'em and would have flushed the whole batch. We lost over half in the first few weeks when we were trying to figure out what kind of environment suits them best. The water's a little salty, about what you'd get in a river delta near the ocean, but pure ocean water dehydrates them. Had to special-order the river weed from Japan."

I was staring into the nearest aquarium, my face nearly against the glass. "Holy shit. These are homunculi."

The Warlock smiled. "Glad to see Cooper hasn't been ignoring your classical education."

"How did you get these?"

"Well, when you come right down to it, it's because me and my lady are hopeless slobs." He laughed. "It's not a story for the dinner table, that's for sure.

"Opal and I were down in this little place we have in the mountains about four months ago. Strong Earth magic site, though nothing like the Grove. Anyhow, she was on her period and really wasn't in the mood for anything, so I ended up going into the bathroom to jack off—"

"Wait, whoa. This has already gone way past the 'too much information' line," I said.

"No, really, this is important," the Warlock insisted.

"No, really, my lunch is going to make friends with your floor if you give me any more details," I replied. "Just hit the highlights, if you feel *that* compelled to share this lovely story of yours."

"Well, there was some . . ." He made swirling motions with his index fingers. ". . . mixing of male and female personal substances after we both forgot to flush, got the idea?"

"God help me, I do."

"Okay. Not five minutes later, she got an emergency call from her sister in Gahanna. Her basement flooded, you know the drill. So we had to come back to the city.

"We drove back down to the cabin the following weekend. Opal went into the bathroom. People five counties over probably heard her holler when she lifted the toilet lid and found the kids swimming around in there. I bailed them all out and put them in a couple of mason jars, then took them back up here and started buying aquarium supplies."

"That's completely disgusting," I said.

"Yet kind of cool, you have to admit," the Warlock said. "They're coming along pretty well. Don't know if it was something in the water up there, or the 'shrooms we were taking, or what. We've tried to repeat the experiment—"

"Details: do not want!"

"—but no luck so far. So what we have is possibly all there will ever be, and there's still a lot we don't know about them. They seem to be developing sort of like regular human fetuses—they're absorbing their tails, for one thing—but I don't think anyone will confuse them with regular human kids once their eyes have opened and they're ready to live on dry land. If they're *ever* ready for land life."

The homunculi seemed to sense the Warlock's presence, and they were crowding at the glass near him.

"Looks like the kids are hungry," he said, and pushed aside his robe so he could get into the pocket of his black jeans. He pulled out a steel penknife and a purple healing crystal, then lifted the covers of the aquaria, drew the blade across his palm, and squeezed thick drops of blood into the water. The homunculi jostled one another to drink the Warlock's blood.

"They like yogurt, too," he said as he sealed the wound on his hand with the crystal. "But they like my blood best."

"So you're planning to use some of them in a sacrifice ritual?"

"*If* I have to. I don't *want* to, understand that." He turned to face me. "They won't take Opal's blood anymore; they're *my* kids. I don't know how long they'd last on yogurt and river weed. If *I* die, a lot of them are gonna die, too."

chapter sixteen

Manic Mechanic

The Warlock led me and Pal down to the basement garage. Opal, a tall, attractive, whip-thin woman with a shock of short bleached white hair, was hunched over the silver Land Rover's huge engine. She wore a grubby blue mechanic's jumpsuit and was smoking a clove cigarette and muttering a steady stream of automotive obscenities. I had often thought that if the Warlock and Opal were alcoholic beverages, the Warlock would be a smooth but strong stout-and-cider Snakebite and Opal would be a shot of Strawberry Surprise—the surprise being that the high-proof drink contained pure mouth-torturing capsaicin and not the slightest bit of strawberry, despite its pretty pink appearance.

I didn't doubt that they loved each other, in their way. But their open relationship got so volatile at times that I'd asked the Warlock on one of our Panda Inn evenings how he and Opal had managed to share space for so long. He'd given me and the rest of the bar a long, drunken, pornographic oratory. Apparently Opal fucked like a mink in heat and as far as the Warlock was concerned, any amount of her crazy, caustic behavior paled in comparison.

Opal held a replicator wand, and she'd created a marble-sized version of the anathema sphere at the tip. The concrete floor was littered with tools, greasy shop rags, plastic vials of spell ingredients, and crushed cans of Diet Mountain Dew.

"Hey, uh, baby—" the Warlock began.

"What what WHAT ALREADY?" Opal screeched. The mini sphere at the wand's tip went out. "Can't work with you breathing up my coo—oh, hey, Jessie, 'sup?"

I pointed to my knapsack. "I got demat potion. Enough for everybody. But it expires tomorrow morning around seven o'clock."

"Booyah!" Opal yelled. "You got any Einhorn powder? Gotta have that. Gas tank's gonna blow the moment we hit the sphere if I don't have that."

"I have some back at the house—"

"Rock. Go get it. Get me some cigs, too. Down to my last pack. Jakarta Blacks." Opal spoke hard and fast as a machine gun. She looked at the Warlock, irritated anew. "*Told* you we should stock those in the machines."

"I can't go get it right now—I've got to go up to Worthington first," I replied. "I can bring the powder with me when I come back."

"Hm. Guess I can wait. Rather have it sooner. Gas tank's easy if I got the Einhorn; the electrical's making me nuts."

"Why don't you take a break, try to get some sleep, baby?" the Warlock asked gently.

Opal sucked her clove down to the filter, crushed it against the sole of her left combat boot, and flicked it aside. "Sleep's for the weak and sickly."

"Yeah, and if you don't get some sleep, you're gonna be weak and sickly," the Warlock replied. "Go on upstairs and lie down for a bit, will you?"

Opal sighed. "Fine." She walked over to a nearby workbench and sorted through the debris of parts and tools and manuals until she found a small notebook and a pencil.

"Catch," Opal said, throwing them to the Warlock. "Make a list. Cigs. Coffee beans, French roast. Couple of other things I'll be needing, too . . ."

I gave two bottles of the potion to the Warlock for his and Opal's use in case something bad happened to me, and then Pal and I left the bar. My dematerialized trip through the sphere went slightly better this time, and after I quit heaving into a nearby trash can, I caught a cab back to Kai's house. He was sitting on the living room floor in gray gym shorts and a faded Scooby-Doo T-shirt eating Corn Pops and watching cartoons when I came through the front door.

"Hey, G.G., 'sup?" Kai asked sleepily.

I pulled one of the Warlock's twenty-dollar bills out of my pocket and held it toward him. "Mind driving me around to a couple of places?" I asked. "It can wait until you've finished breakfast and stuff."

"Uh, sure," he replied, taking the twenty from my outstretched hand. "Where we going?"

"I just need to go back to the place you took me yesterday, and to a grocery store, and then you can drop me off in Victorian Village if you don't mind." I paused. "Listen. I gotta go do this thing tonight, and . . . well, I might not be coming back. After tomorrow, if it's been more than, say, a week and you haven't seen me, just figure I'm gone for good. You can have what's left of my stuff upstairs; it's not much, but there's a little refrigerator up there you could sell or use or whatever. Oh, yeah, there's a bottle labeled VHDN in the fridge—don't just throw it in the trash, or it might explode and catch the house on fire. Safest thing to do is to flush it down the toilet a spoonful at a time. Don't dump the whole thing down at once, or it could explode in the plumbing."

"Oh. Explode." Kai looked dazed. "Uh, when you say you'll be gone for good . . . what do you mean?"

"My . . . best friend is in some trouble. I'm going to go try to bail him out, but I stand to get into just as much trouble as him if I get caught," I replied.

"Are, like, the cops after you?"

"Not exactly . . . it's more that I might have to keep an appointment in Samarra," I replied darkly.

"Oh. Is that, like, in Thailand?"

I winced inwardly and bit my lip. "No. Strictly speaking I think it's in Iraq."

"No way! That's, like, totally dangerous. Be careful out there, G. G."

"As careful as possible, trust me."

I retrieved the Einhorn powder and a few other herbs from my attic room, then went downstairs to meet Kai. He drove me back up to the day care center and waited in the car with Pal while I left to find a new tissue sample.

As I walked across the parking lot to the front doors, I saw the same young receptionist sitting behind the front desk. I belatedly realized that my previous bluff wasn't going to work twice, and I still didn't have any identification.

"Hello again!" the woman said. "Did you get your driver's license replaced?"

"Yep, sure did." I smiled at her as I approached the counter, wracking my brains to figure out what the heck I was going to do.

Then I spied a dead leaf that had blown inside. It was lying on the floor against the bottom of the counter.

"Let me get my ID out for you—oh, darn it, my shoe's come untied," I said, bending down to grab the leaf. "My husband ties my shoes for me when I leave, but this pair's always coming undone. I need to get some loafers, or something with Velcro."

I closed my eyes and imagined the veins pulsing quietly inside the receptionist's pert nose. Whispered an old word for "hemorrhage" as I snapped the leaf's stem.

"Oh!" I heard the receptionist exclaim.

I straightened up. Blood was spilling from the young woman's nose, down her chin and neck, and onto her pretty white blouse. I felt a pang of guilt; her clothes were probably ruined, and they didn't look cheap. The receptionist seemed to shake off her shock, then grabbed handfuls of Kleenex from a nearby dispenser and pressed them to her face.

"Oh my goodnez," she said. "Dis has nebber happened to be before. Maria! I godda bad nosebleed an' godda go do de res'room—cub help dis lady!"

"Okay, be out in a sec," Maria called from what I presumed was an interior office.

The receptionist didn't wait for Maria; she pushed up from her seat and hurried down the hall. I peeked over the ledge. Drops of the woman's blood had spattered on a couple of brochures; I snatched one up and headed back to the car.

Kai drove me to a small grocery store on North

High in Clintonville to get the odds and ends on Opal's list. Kai agreed to go to the pizza shop with me and help carry the pies back to the Warlock's bar.

I left Antolino's pizzeria with Kai following close behind, the three medium pizza boxes stacked in his arms. I rounded the corner toward the bar, and the red glow of the anathema sphere spiked into my retina like an ice pick.

"Ugh." I flinched and looked away.

Kai nearly ran into me. "What's the matter?"

"Do you see that bar up ahead? Lingham Liquors?"

"Yeah?"

"Do you see anything weird around the building?" Kai looked puzzled. "No, why?"

"Long story. Can you . . . can you go through the glass doors, put the pizzas on the cigarette machine in the foyer, and ring the bell on the second set of doors that goes into the bar?"

"Uh, sure, I guess . . ."

Kai walked past me toward the bar. I couldn't watch to see what happened when he crossed the sphere's barrier. He came back a couple of minutes later, empty-handed.

"All done," he said. "Is there something I'm missing here?"

"Did you feel anything when you went up to the front door?" I asked him, then thought to Pal, *He should have felt something if he had any sensitivity, right?*

"Right," Pal replied from my shoulder.

Kai shook his head, looking puzzled. "Like what?"

"A headache, or chills, or maybe just a case of the heebie-jeebies," I replied.

He shook his head again. "No, nothing."

"Then there's nothing for you to worry about," I said. I extended my hand to him. "Listen, if I don't see you again, it's been nice meeting you. Have a good life. If I do see you again, I probably won't be able to help you learn any magic, but I'll clean the house for you, how 'bout that?"

Still looking supremely confused, Kai shook my hand. "Okay, G.G., take care of yourself. See ya later, I hope!"

Kai went back to his car, and I ducked into a nearby alley so Pal and I could take another dose of the demat potion.

After I got over my rematerialization sickness in the women's room of the bar, I checked the front entrance and discovered that the pizzas were still sitting on the cigarette machine. I brought them inside a pie at a time, set them on the bar, and went upstairs to the apartment. The door was open, and the Warlock and Opal were standing in the living room, arguing.

"I'm not letting you go out there by yourself!" Opal declared. "I'm coming with you. *End* of story."

"Baby, come on, I really think it would be better if you stayed here and watched the critters," the Warlock protested.

"This goes right, we're only gone overnight," she replied. "The kids and the cats can deal."

"But if this goes wrong, we could be gone forever," he warned.

"If that happens, I wanna be with you!"

I cleared my throat from the doorway. Between the Warlock and Opal, they'd surely had sex with a quarter of the Talents in Columbus. "There must be *somebody* you could call to come critter-sit once you get outside the sphere."

The Warlock looked at Opal. "Well, there's Oakbrown . . ."

Opal shook her head. "Couldn't cook a demat to save his own life. And the Jizz Kids freak him out. Wouldn't even go in the room. Mariette?"

"She's not talking to me right now," the Warlock replied, looking embarrassed.

"How come?" Opal asked, frowning.

"I kinda put the moves on her boyfriend, and he didn't turn me down. He said she'd be cool with it, and . . . well, she wasn't."

"Then Rosko?" Opal asked.

"The last time he was up here, a ring of mine went missing. I don't trust him not to shop through our stuff."

"Hey, I got your Einhorn powder, and the pizzas are getting cold downstairs," I said. "Mother Karen would probably come house sit, but Jordan put a geas on her and house-sitting might violate that. There's a mundane kid named Kai I could call . . . he'd probably be able to look after the place for a while."

The Warlock frowned. "The sphere's strong enough to hurt a lot of mundanes."

"Not this kid," I replied. "He brought the pizzas up to the front door and didn't even get a twinge."

"He reliable?" Opal asked.

"So far he seems pretty darn reliable for a pothead," I replied.

"There's no way that would work out." The Warlock shook his head. "Even if he follows directions, even if he shows up right when he's supposed to, no mundane's gonna be able to take care of the kids properly. Not even if he's a science whiz or veterinary student, which I'm guessing this guy is *not*. There are just too many weird little details to watch out for."

"Would a random Talent really be any better, then?" I asked. "You said a whole bunch of the kids died while you were trying to get their needs figured out. Considering all of what's going on, is there *anyone* you could really bring in? Could anyone realistically take care of them with just some written directions and crossed fingers?"

"No," the Warlock replied, his eyes downcast.

Opal sucked on her cigarette noncommittally.

"Then it seems to me that you've got to stay here to look after the family, Opal," I said.

Opal turned on me, scarlet-faced and scowling. "No *way*, I—"

"Look, I know you don't want to lose your man, *believe me*, I *know*!" I shouted back, meeting her fury. "But Cooper is the Warlock's only brother, his very own flesh and blood, and he is surely no less deserving of his love and help than you are!"

Opal was still shaking her head. "I can't—"

"If you have a better idea, I'm all ears," I said, exasperation making my tone harsher than I'd have liked. "Tell me how you're going to keep the kids from dying if you come with us. Tell me how you're going to come with us and single-handedly protect your man from everything Jordan might throw at us. If you can't tell me that, tell me how you're going to leave the Warlock here and lead me to the farmhouse. Answer any one of those and we're good. Otherwise, the best thing is for you to stay here and watch the kids. And I promise you, I will do all I possibly can to keep the Warlock safe."

Opal sucked her cigarette down to the filter. "Fine," she replied tightly. She almost looked like she was going to start crying. "I'll . . . I'll stay here. But you—" She turned toward the Warlock and shook the remains of her cigarette at him "—you *promise* me you won't get yourself killed. *Promise!*"

He crossed his heart. "I swear I'll do my best."

"Okay." Looking miserable, Opal tossed her spent cigarette into a nearby pile of butts. "Let's go eat some goddamn pizza."

chapter seventeen

Mysterious Ocularis

I took a nap after lunch on one of the smoky leather couches in the dark lounge and had Pal poke me awake when it was three thirty according to the bar clock. We went into the ladies' room to dump my anathema on the receptionist at the day-care center. I hoped it wouldn't bring the young woman any lasting bad luck.

The Warlock was waiting outside the restroom, slowly swirling the foam atop another tall mug of ale with his index finger. "That's a very pretty aura," he said to me.

"Yeah. I'm gonna try not to get anything on it."

He coughed into his fist, looking uncharacteristically worried. He stared at the bandage across my eye socket for a couple of beats, then let his gaze slide to the floor. "Did Cooper ever see anyone about getting rid of his nightmares?"

I shook my head. "Not that I know of. He just tried to ride them out."

"Figures. He was always so stoic about that stuff." The Warlock chewed a corner of his mustache and stared off into the distance. The dark circles had deepened around his eyes.

Pal sniffed the air and shifted on my shoulder. "Ask him how long he's been having the nightmares."

"Have . . . have you had a problem with bad dreams, too?" I asked.

The Warlock laughed humorlessly. "You could say that."

"For how long?" I asked.

He shrugged. "On and off, as long as either of us could remember. Cooper's had really flared up bad lately, huh?"

"You could say that," I replied. "I started having them, too, but I can't really remember them. Not sure I really want to. I got the impression that he tried to get rid of them a few years ago, but they wouldn't budge, so what could he do?"

"He could have seen someone to have them amplified and illuminated," the Warlock replied. "He could have done what I did and gone to see a dream specialist. It was hard, and not much fun, and yeah, a lot of the time it was a crapshoot. But after I learned about the little 'problem' with my soul, I started to wonder about what else I might be missing, and how my ignorance might end up biting me in the ass. So I went looking for people who could help me remember my dreams."

He took a long drink from his mug. "I know why Cooper wouldn't ever go with me to see the dream witch. It's not easy learning things you never wanted to know. It was hell to bring all that crap up day after day. His soul was fine, far as either of us could tell, so I quit bugging him about it. But maybe it would have helped him head some bad stuff off at the pass, you know?"

Where's he going with this? I wondered to Pal.

"I can't fathom it yet," my familiar replied.

"Do you think Cooper could have kept the accident downtown from happening if he'd had his dreams examined?" I asked the Warlock.

He ran his free hand through his curly hair and scratched his scalp, as if the subject made him itch. "It's possible. No guarantees, though. Dreams for people like us are seldom pure prophecy. Glimpses of possible futures get jammed together with old memories and pure fantasies, and it's hard to make useful sense of it all even if you can remember everything perfectly. But . . ."

I prompted after he'd been quiet for several seconds: "But what?"

"But. This day, the one you and I are having right now? I've dreamed a lot of this. At least fifty, sixty times. I've met you at this restroom door before. I know that I take you back upstairs next. I know what I'm going to show you next. And the dream *always* turns into any of a few nightmares after that."

"Oh dear," said Pal.

My mouth went dry. "So let's do something else. Let's not go upstairs. Let's get out of here."

He smiled at me grimly. "I learned to be a lucid dreamer. I've tried plenty of other paths before, and you know what? The nightmare's worse if I don't follow the script.

"So let's go on up to my closet. If you're going to Coop's hell, we better kit you out properly."

Should I go with him? I asked Pal, feeling shaken.

"I don't have a good feeling about this," he replied, "but if you're still determined to find Cooper, I'm not sure we have many other options at the moment."

I followed the Warlock upstairs into the apartment. He led me back down the impossibly long hallway to a wooden pocket door on the left side. The door unlatched at his gesture and slid open.

Beyond the doorway was a spacious room of polished oak cabinets, shelves, and wardrobes. Clear, square skylights showed a majestic blue mountain vista—whether it was the Rockies or Himalayas or someplace unearthly I couldn't tell. Boxes and books were stacked neatly on the shelves, and a variety of clothes and costumes hung from gleaming brass closet bars arranged in staggered layers from floor to ceiling.

"Nice closet," I said.

"Thanks," the Warlock replied. "Come on in and have a seat." He made another gesture, and a red upholstered stool slid from beneath one of the shelves. I sat down while the Warlock opened a set of wardrobe doors. The brass handles were made to look like dragon's heads.

"You can't go to hell in a pair of old jeans and Chuck Taylors. What you need is dragonskin." He reached inside the wardrobe and pulled out what looked like a frogged, high-collared Chinese jacket and drawstring pants made from smooth, iridescent brown leather instead of silk. They looked like they were tailored for a Mongol marauder the size of an NFL linebacker. "Here, try these on. I won't look, promise."

"Uh, those are like twenty sizes too big . . ."

"They'll be fine. Trust me. King Arthur would've given his right nut to own leathers like these."

I looked from the Warlock to the dragonskin clothes. *Do you think I should?* I asked Pal.

"I don't see any danger in this so far," he replied. The Warlock turned around. Pal ran down my right arm and hopped onto a nearby shelf, and I shucked off my shoes and jeans. I took the dragon-skin pants off the steel hanger and pulled them on. To my surprise, they fit perfectly. I pulled off my sling and carefully slipped on the jacket. The left sleeve immediately shrank up to match my truncated arm.

"That's pretty cool," I said, looking at the inside of the jacket; there were several small pockets sewn into the lining, two of which I could access by slipping my hand between the frogs when it was buttoned up.

"Good dragonskin is way more expensive than regular leather," the Warlock said. "It's waterproof, and resists fire, cold, and corrosives, and it'll stop a knife blade or a .44 magnum. Do you think anyone wants to run the risk of their kit not fitting anymore just 'cause they started hitting the gym or started toss-ing down one too many beers and burgers? Any decent set comes with a sizing enchantment."

He ducked back into the wardrobe. "If you'd been wearing that when you faced the Wutganger, you'd probably still have your arm."

"Then it's a real shame you didn't drop this little ensemble off for me a couple of weeks ago," I said, bitterness filling my voice despite my best effort to keep it down. "Or warn me and Cooper not to go downtown in the first place."

"That's the bitch of dreams," he agreed, still rum-maging in the wardrobe. "Most times you can't tell a serial nightmare from a precognitive alarm until the shit's already dribbling onto the fan. Believe me, if I'd realized what was happening I would have got-ten the word out to you two. Ah, here they are."

The Warlock backed out of the wardrobe and straightened up, holding a pair of dark gray knee-high leather hobnail boots with English firedrakes embossed on the vamp and shaft. "These are older, and from a different dragon. Better protection from heat and cold and acids."

He tossed the boots at my feet. I slipped them on over my pant cuffs, and they molded comfortably to my feet and calves.

"So how much did this stuff cost you?" I asked.

The Warlock laughed. "I won most of my dragon gear in card games when I was on my walkabout overseas. It pays to have a good bluff."

"So how much would it cost you if you found it in a shop someplace?"

"Oh man, that's hard to say . . . I'm guessing maybe fifty or sixty grand."

"Sixty thousand dollars?" I felt the blood drain from my face.

"Right in that vicinity, yeah. It's all a couple of centuries out of style, and well used—obviously— but wild dragons are a lot rarer than they used to be, so new stuff is really expensive."

I stared down at the warm, shimmering leather. "I couldn't pay you back in a zillion years if anything happened to this outfit."

He laughed again. "Darling. Honey-buns. Sugarpie. *Please*. I'm taking you to a *hell*. I don't need another chunk chiseled off my immortal soul because I sent you in with less than all the protection I could give you. And it's not like I'm using the gear for any death-defying heroics these days." He looked a lot less cheerful than he sounded.

"Okay," I replied, doubtful. I stuck my hand in the square front pocket and felt a piece of folded leather. Upon pulling it out, I saw that it was a thin, elbow-length dragonskin glove. I used my teeth to pull it on, then shook my sleeve back into place to cover it.

"Does he have any head protection for you?" Pal asked from the shelf. "You do have an unfortunate tendency to lead with your face."

He barely managed to dodge the sneaker I threw at him.

"What's that all about?" the Warlock asked.

"Pal's being a smart-ass. Yet he has a point. Do you have a helmet I can borrow so I don't lose both eyes?" I asked.

"I have a lot of helmets you can try out. But . . . funny you should mention your eye." He shivered, suddenly looking like a man on his way to the gas chamber.

"What's the matter?" I asked.

"There's . . . something I have to show you." The Warlock went to an ornate wooden chest on a nearby shelf and unlocked it. He pulled out a red velvet bag, opened it, and dropped a pale green cat's-eye chrysoberyl orb into his palm. It was about an inch in diameter. He held it up, the bright line in the middle of the silky stone glowing in the sunlight filtering down from the skylights. I could feel positively ancient magic humming inside the orb.

"That's a most unusual piece," Pal whispered from his perch, his eyes huge.

"I picked this little gem up twelve years ago," the Warlock said, sounding strangely distant as he stared at the stone. His eyes seemed to go out of focus. "You ever see something and know you had to have it? Yeah. Only I knew it wasn't really for me, it was for a girl I hadn't even met yet. A girl with one eye. Funny . . . how . . . these things . . . work out . . ."

I couldn't pull my own gaze from the gem. Mesmerized, I peeled the bandages off my face and head and dropped them on the floor. Popped the plastic ball out of my eye socket and carelessly let it fall to the carpet, then stood up and stepped toward the Warlock.

"Jessie, no!" Pal squeaked. "I can't tell what that thing does!"

The Warlock dropped the orb into my outstretched palm.

"Jessie, for God's sake stop!" Pal leaped off the shelf onto my arm. He bit down as hard as he could, trying to break the trance, but his small teeth didn't even dent the dragon leather.

I impassively shook him off and slid the enchanted stone into my socket. It was like sticking a live wire into my raw skull. My head was humming, crackling with a witchfire net of fey lightning. Suddenly I was able to see through my dead socket, but what I was seeing couldn't be the inside of the closet; it was way too bright, too many colors.

I let out a wordless scream and stumbled backward, clutching my socket, tripping over the stool, landing hard on my back. *What the hell just happened?*

The Warlock shook his head and blinked rapidly. His trance seemed to be broken. "Are you okay? Is it hurting you?"

"Get it out!" I pressed on my temple, but the orb didn't budge. It didn't hurt, not exactly, but it was sending an unpleasant electric buzz through my head into my spine. My tormented optical nerve was sizzling with hallucinatory ghost-images.

The Warlock bent over me and pulled my hand

away to gaze down at the gem in my skull. He appeared in a weird double exposure. I saw him normally through my good eye, but the gem showed me a glowing black outline of his body with a small undulating blue torus floating inside. A section of the torus's smooth surface was pitted as if a mouse had bitten into it and gnawed off a small piece.

"I think I'm seeing your soul," I said, dazed.

"You're supposed to be able to see a whole lot through that gem," the Warlock said. "I never tried it out myself; didn't feel like scooping out a perfectly good eye. But the guy who sold it to me said you change the magical aspect view by blinking hard. I mean *hard* hard; wouldn't do for the thing to get triggered every time you get a bit of dust under your lid."

"I can't blink. I lost my eyelid along with my eye," I replied, feeling increasingly upset as I realized what had just happened. I'd been charmed, tricked into putting a strange magical device inside my own body. The situation was a hundred shades of wrong.

The Warlock frowned. "But your eyelid's right there."

Pal ran up onto my chest and peered at me anxiously. He was outlined as a spider through the gem, his soul a blooming rose of intricately looped rotating golden chains. "He's right. Your eyelid's grown back."

"For real?" I tried to close my eye; the muscles didn't respond right away, as if the nerves had been miswired, but after a couple of seconds I managed a hard blink. When I opened my eye, the gemsight showed the room glowing in various shades of gold. I was fascinated despite myself. "Weird."

Pal cocked his head at me. "I have to say that eyelid looks a bit, er, *abnormal* . . ."

"Abn—oh fuck me." I lurched to my feet. Pal scrambled to cling to my shoulder. "I need a mirror."

The Warlock beckoned me to a jewelry chest and raised the lid so I could look into the mirror inside. I tried to ignore the gemsight as I stared at my socket. The eyelid that had grown back didn't look like anything that ought to be on a healthy human being. The skin was red, the ragged lashes pointing out in all directions. At first glance the lid looked as though it might simply be scarred, but I realized the skin was mottled and covered with a fine layer of translucent gray scales. I pulled off the dragon-skin glove with my teeth so I could touch my new eyelashes; they felt more like spines than hairs.

Suddenly feeling very, very cold, I grasped the orb with my thumb and forefinger and tried to pull it out. It was firmly rooted in my head.

"It's hooked into your muscles and nerves by now," the Warlock said, sounding resigned. "It's not going to come out without surgery."

I turned on him, scared and furious. "What the hell did you put inside me?" I hollered.

"I didn't—"

"Yes you *did*! It was yours and you *knew* what would happen! It took me over and now it's stuck and I *hate* it!"

"But in the dream—"

"Fuck you and your dream!" The bright ghosts from the orb lit my rage like a blowtorch on dry tinder. I hauled my arm back and socked him in the mouth as hard as I could.

"Jessie!" Pal exclaimed.

My punch rocked the Warlock backward on his heels, his lower lip split. He tried to grab my arm. "Whoa there—"

I stepped forward and kneed him in the groin. The Warlock grunted and doubled over in pain. I kneed him in the side of his head, knocking him over, and fell on him in a blind rage, punching him in the head again and again. I felt his nose crunch beneath my fist. Blood spilled down his face onto his chest and his velvet bathrobe.

"Jessie, no!" Pal shrieked, clinging to my collar and trying to avoid the Warlock's defensive flailing. When I didn't stop, Pal bit me on the ear, hard.

"Ow, crap!" I exclaimed, swatting Pal.

That was enough distraction for the Warlock to knock me sideways and get my arm and wrist in a joint lock behind my back. I swore at him long and hard and struggled to get free, but he forced me down on my knees.

"Cool. De fug. *Down*," he said sternly. "You broge my node."

"So did your dream warn you about *that*?" I snapped.

"Yes, as a madder of fag id did."

"Jessie, for goodness' sake calm down," Pal pleaded. "You're not helping anything."

I trembled in the Warlock's grip. "What's in my head?"

"No more hittig?" he asked, shaking me.

"No more hitting," I agreed, slumping forward.

He released me and pulled a crumpled light blue bandanna out of the left pocket of his black jeans and gingerly blew some of the bloody snot out of his nose. "I godda get Opal to figs dis. Stay here. Don' touch anythig."

He strode past me out the door as I tried to shake off the soreness in my fingers, wrist, and arm. My knuckles were swelling red and blue, bruised despite all my heavy bag work at the dojo. Hoping the pressure would keep my hand from swelling up too much, I pulled the dragonskin glove back on. I blinked through several gem views until the room around me looked mundanely normal.

"Well, that could've gone better," Pal said. "I understand your being frightened by the compulsion charm on that stone, but our allies are in short supply right now. It's best not to attack them, yes?"

"I know, I know. I'm sorry. I don't know what got into me."

"Your apologies are best given to the Warlock when he comes back."

"Yeah. I know." The gem was still jittering little waves of not-quite-pain through my head. I pressed against it to see if pressure would make it stop. It didn't help a bit. "What *is* this thing, anyway? Should I be worried it's going to take over my brain or something?"

"Well, it's obviously an ocularis; they used to be much more common centuries ago when people were more prone to losing eyes than they are now. Back then, it was often far cheaper to purchase a used ocularis than to seek the assistance of a master healer. The most common types simply gave the user normal sight; multiple viewing modes are hard to enchant, and expensive to acquire. They typically do *not* come with compulsion charms, much less charms strong enough to influence trained Talents. That's certainly worrisome," Pal replied.

I continued to press on the stone in the vain hope it would stop humming. "So do you think this ocularis was built with the charm from the start, or re-enchanted?"

"I couldn't say. I'm far from an expert on these things, I'm afraid."

I wished the Warlock would come back soon so I could get more information about where and how he'd found the ocularis. "He said he knew when he got the stone it wasn't for himself, but for a one-eyed girl. Is that charmy metaphor, or literal? Did he mean he got this thing twelve years ago, way before I even came here, specifically for me?"

"I'm at a loss as to what any of this might actually mean," Pal admitted. "Did anything happen to you twelve years ago?"

"I'd have been eleven, and my mother . . ." I trailed off, realizing that the Warlock found the ocularis around the time my mom had died saving me from inoperable cancer.

"Dammit dammit *dammit* I don't *like* this fate bullshit!" I yelled, smacking the floor with my palm in fear and frustration. The impact made my knuckles ache sharply, but I didn't care. "I don't like pre-destination even as . . . as a *concept*. 'Cause the big take-home message there is we don't have free will and never did. It means we're nothing but a bunch of puppets."

"That's an extremely negative view," Pal protested gently. "Certain things are meant to come to pass, but not *everything*. Many of us see destiny as a positive guiding force in the universe, a thing to be embraced."

"Fate, destiny, whatever . . . it makes us nothing better than marionettes," I insisted. "And I don't like getting jerked around, even for the good of the universe."

I was silent as I considered the primary string-puller in my world. "Do you think this ocularis could have been planted here by Jordan? Could he have cast some kind of memory-change spell on the Warlock to make him believe he got the stone twelve years ago? When in reality Jordan's men slipped the thing into his box just a couple of days ago while he was out cold? Could this thing be transmitting everything I see to Jordan's crystal ball?"

"That's . . . an exceptionally paranoid hypothesis, although I can't immediately dismiss it," Pal admitted. "But really, that would require an incredibly intricate set of enchantments. And why would he give you the benefit of sight through it at all, much less extrasensory views?"

"I can't figure out why he's done half the stuff he's done," I grumbled. "We never did a thing to him, ever. We don't deserve what he's done to us."

A faint, cool breeze ruffled through my hair and kissed my neck and cheek.

The sight-stone is a gift for my best girl. The voice was a faint, dark whisper inside my ear, inside my head. *Jordan doesn't know its secrets.*

I spun around. "Who's there?"

"Who what?" replied Pal, looking perplexed.

"Did you hear that?" I asked, looking around the room and quickly blinking through different gemviews to try to catch a glimpse of the entity that had spoken to me. On one view, I thought I saw something like a faint violet mist fading into a skylight. It disappeared so quickly that I couldn't be sure it wasn't my imagination or a trick of the light.

"I didn't hear anything. What's the matter?" Pal asked.

"I . . . something just . . . crap. I don't know. Maybe I'm hallucinating."

"Hallucinating?" the Warlock asked from the doorway. His nose was straight and his face unbruised and unbloodied; Opal had made quick work of healing him. Probably this was far from the first time someone had broken his nose. He'd changed out of his bathrobe, black jeans, and slippers and put on a dark gray T-shirt, a clean pair of olive-drab cargo pants, and a pair of black cowboy boots.

"Or not," I said. "I just had a new invisible friend whisper sweet nothings in my ear. 'Best girl' my ass. Cooper gets to say that, *nobody* else, and that sure as hell wasn't him."

The Warlock was silent, looking puzzled. "I never—"

"I want this thing out of my skull," I said firmly. "I'm sorry I went off on you, but for all I know this thing is going to blow my head right off my shoulders in an hour. Where's your bathroom? And I need a spoon."

The Warlock closed his eyes and took a deep breath. He pulled a clean stainless-steel cereal spoon out of the pocket of his pants. "Please don't do the spoon thing. That never turns out well."

I got up and took the spoon out of his hand. "Bathroom?"

He nodded sideways, looking deeply pained as if

he wanted to refuse me but knew he'd have another fight on his hands. "To the left, on the left."

I pushed past him, Pal padding after me. The bathroom was luxurious, bigger than the bedroom Cooper and I had shared in the apartment. I flipped on the lights above a big marble-topped vanity sink and leaned into the mirror to examine the ocularis.

The burn-scarred skin around my eye and on my cheek had thickened and darkened. Patches of the fine gray scales had begun to sprout in places. I poked at my scars; they weren't nearly as sensitive as they'd been that morning.

Pal clambered up the handles of the vanity's drawers onto the chilly gray stone of the counter. "You're not planning to do what I think you are planning to do, are you?"

"Yes, I am." I raised the gleaming spoon to the ocularis, trying to decide if I should scoop in from the side or from the top.

"But the Warlock said it's connected itself to your muscles and nerves—"

"All the more reason I should take it out now before it does anything else to my body," I replied, deciding to go in from the top.

I pressed the bowl of the spoon against the round front of the ocularis and slid it up under my eyelid. My probe was met with a sharp jolt of blue pain that took my breath away. I pressed my face against the countertop, hoping the cold marble would soothe my inflamed nerves. Stone squeaked against stone.

"Damn," I gasped.

"Seriously, don't try that again," the Warlock said from the doorway. "In one dream you put yourself in a coma trying to dig out the stone. In another you bleed to death."

"Bleed to death? How?" I stood up, frowning at him. "There aren't any major arteries—"

"Dammit, I should *not* have to talk you out of sticking a spoon in your eye!" The Warlock threw his hands up in exasperation. "I am telling you to leave it *alone.*"

"But where did it come from?" I pressed.

"I picked it up in an antiquities shop in London. The proprietor, a personal friend of mine, told me it's originally from Egypt, probably made in 200 BC. I have no reason to disbelieve her. And I have no reason to believe the stone will hurt you."

"But—"

"Stop with the 'buts,' okay? You'll need the sight through that thing to stay alive where you're going. Are you listening to me? You *need* that stone in your head, so leave it alone."

"Why do I need this thing so badly?"

He sighed as if he were trying to explain income taxes to a grumpy fifteen-year-old fry cook. "Hells aren't realms of the flesh. They're spiritual. Magical. They'll overwhelm and deceive your senses if you don't have magical help. We can usually ignore our ears, but seldom our eyes. If you can't see through whatever illusions Cooper's hell is going to throw your way, you'll be trapped. And then you'll die in there. So will my brother."

"I'd heed his advice," Pal said. "I, too, have lingering doubts about the true nature of the ocularis. But I must agree it would be far more dangerous to venture into any hell without it. And it seems unlikely you can remove it without seriously hurting yourself."

I tossed the spoon into the sink and took a deep breath to calm myself. "Okay. Fine. What now?"

"Opal told me she's almost done with the engine. Apparently the Einhorn was just what she needed," the Warlock replied. "Did you still want a helmet?"

"Yes, definitely," I said.

"Okay, follow me."

He led me back down the hall to another closet, a narrow room filled from floor to ceiling with wooden racks of hats, caps, and helmets from different eras. This room had mundane incandescent track lighting and beige carpeting. The Warlock reached onto one of the racks and pulled off a gleaming round bronze helmet.

The helmet had a half-circle dome with a quilted leather lining affixed by wrought-iron rivets to the rim. A one-piece soft leather neck/cheek protector was riveted to the lining on the rear half of the helmet. A buckled leather chin strap was riveted to the base of the ear sections. The helmet occupied stylistic space somewhere between something a medieval foot soldier and a 1940s motorcycle bandit might have worn.

"This doesn't have a sizing charm, but by my eye it ought to fit. What it *does* have is a charm to nullify poisonous gases and provide oxygen in dead air. It won't let you breathe underwater, but it would help in a sand- or ash-storm . . . unless the hell Cooper's in squelches magic. But that's a risk with anything I could give you. No matter what—" He rapped on the crown with his knuckles. "—it'll stop a pretty good whack with a bat or sword, and it'll bounce a bullet."

I took the helmet from him and put it on my head.

It was a little loose and smelled like stale hair spray, but I deemed it a fit. "Hey, thanks, I think this'll work fine."

"Great," he said, scratching his beard. "There's something else I wanted you to take a look at while you're up here."

"What?" I asked.

The Warlock reached up onto another shelf and pulled down what looked like an old hatbox. When he took off the lid, I saw that the box contained a pearly glass ball about the size of a grapefruit nestled in a bed of old-fashioned paper Easter grass. Something about it made my ocularis itch.

"You probably haven't seen one of these before," he said, lifting the glass ball. "It's an odeiette. They were popular with wealthy Talents up until the late 1800s, when everybody started going to the movies instead."

"It's making my ocularis tweak out a little," I said. The itching was getting worse.

"Well, that's good, actually, 'cause that means maybe I didn't get ripped off when I bought it. The guy told me that the visualization enchantment got screwed up, but you could still see into it if you have ghost-sight or some other kind of clairvoyance. Which I don't have, but who am I to turn down a good deal on a real antique?"

He held the ball out to me. "Blink through and tell me if you see anything."

I took the ball from him and took a look inside. On one of the middle gemviews, the glass cleared and I could see two striped ginger kittens playing: wrestling on a patch of green grass, leaping at a blue butterfly, over and over, tirelessly cute. I realized that I could hear them mock-growling and mewing as they tussled. Apparently the ocularis was sending more than just visual information to my brain.

"It's kittens playing," I told him as I passed the ball back to him. The ocularis had stopped itching. Evidently the irritation was some kind of built-in alert for whatever kind of vision I'd just had, and once seen, it went away.

"Oh good," he said. "It's something nice. The guy said it was cats but that could mean almost anything."

Something nice. I squinted at the ball. "What's in that thing, exactly?"

"Kitten spirits. Ghosts under glass."

I was starting to feel a bit creeped out. "How did they make it?"

"Well, in the early days odeiettes were used as duppy jars by spiritualists . . . they'd just sort of hunt around for loose spirits, capture them, and use these glass balls to observe them. Nobody but hard-core collectors wanted those; wraiths and poltergeists aren't a happy bunch, so generally you'd just see the person inside endlessly screaming—"

"Person? They put *people* in these?"

"Well, yeah, it was mostly all people at first, but the necromancers who made 'em started looking for scenes that might be a bit more, you know, fun to watch. So they'd set up scenes with animals or slaves fighting, or having sex, or playing, and when everybody involved was really getting into it, the necromancer would flash-kill the participants and scoop their spirits into the glass and voilà! Portable entertainment. These things were like the video iPods of the Victorian era."

I stared at the pearly glass, feeling my stomach tighten. "That's *horrible*."

"But it means you can see ghost-loops through that stone eye. And that's pretty sweet," he said.

I wasn't going to be sidetracked. "It's horrible and just plain *wrong*."

The Warlock shrugged. "It was a different era. The kittens in this thing would have probably ended up in a sack at the bottom of a river if they hadn't ended up in here. They wouldn't have even been aware of their own deaths, if that makes you feel better about it."

"How do you free spirits from these things?"

"Just break the glass, usually," he replied.

"Then break it. Let them go."

"But this is an antique—"

"I'll pay you whatever for it! Seriously, it's wrong. Let them go."

The Warlock gave me a look of consternation, then shrugged and sighed. "Fine, if it'll make you happy. But for the record, you owe me a thousand bucks."

He pulled a folding knife out of his pocket and rapped the glass sharply with it. The glass cracked, and I saw two small glowing wisps and a third, much tinier wisp escape and disappear into the air.

"Satisfied?" he asked.

"Yes."

"Well then. I'm pretty sure Opal's done with the truck by now. So if you need to get another snack, grab a bottle of pop, use the facilities, get your sling back on, or anything like that, go for it," the Warlock said. "And then we can head downstairs and get this show on the road."

chapter
eighteen

The Road to Hell

When Pal and I got down to the garage, we found Opal loading an arsenal of a dozen-odd grenades and a couple of wands and pistols into a box on the floor of the passenger side of the Land Rover.

"What's up?" I asked.

Opal straightened, squinting at my sling. "You weren't a lefty, were you?"

"No, I'm right-handed . . . what's all that?"

"Insurance," Opal said. "Warlock knows what everything is. You just gotta throw straight and hard as you can."

"Okay . . ."

The Warlock came around the back of the Land Rover. "You get something to drink upstairs?"

"Just water," I replied. "My stomach's feeling a little touchy."

"Well, I got some ginger ale in a cooler in the back, in case you feel like something later."

"This'll take, what, about an hour to drive out there?" I asked.

"Traffic's heavy on Fridays, so call it an hour and a half, provided we don't run into trouble," the Warlock replied.

"That's all I got," Opal said as she put a small string of what looked like firecrackers in the floorboard box, then turned to the Warlock, her face a tight mask of dismay. "Don't go. Please?"

"Baby, you know I have to. I'm sorry," he replied.

Looking like she was going to start crying, Opal grabbed him by the back of the head and pulled his face down toward hers. They kissed so deeply I felt myself start blushing. When they came up for air, Opal released him and backed away, her arms crossed.

"Get the hell out of here," Opal said softly, staring at her boots. "Don't get killed."

"You heard the lady," the Warlock said to me. "Let's get going."

I nodded toward the Land Rover. "What's the plan to get that out of here, again?"

"Well, I'm all for doing this as quickly as possible," the Warlock replied. "Driving it will obviously be a problem once we're immaterial, so I figure we can both take our potions and go through the barrier on foot. And then once we've rematerialized, Opal can put the Rover in neutral and roll it out onto the street, and I can hop in, grab the wheel, brake, and then you can get in, and we're on our way."

"Um," I said. "Isn't that overly complicated? Not to mention dangerous?"

"Not really," the Warlock said. "It won't be going more than five or ten miles per hour when it clears the barrier, and if we wedge the door open—"

"But it's the middle of rush hour. And what about all that?" I pointed at the box of stuff Opal had loaded. "Most of that's magical, right? Won't that trip whatever sensory alarms are in the sphere?"

"Uh." Judging from the expression on his face, I guessed the Warlock hadn't considered that problem.

"She has a point," Opal said.

"Seriously, just let me shrink the Rover down and put it in my pack . . . we can walk it out of here and find someplace where we can expand it without any random people seeing us."

"But it'll get bounced around—all the ice and drinks'll spill out of the cooler," the Warlock protested.

I looked at him and cocked my head. "Surely you have some duct tape or bungee cords around here?"

"What about the engine?" he asked. "The gas'll slosh everywhere inside it. It's gonna get flooded, and we won't be able to start it."

"Won't," Opal said. "Figured it might end up ass-over-kettle. Charmed it so the fluids'll stay put."

"Okay, then?" I asked.

The Warlock shrugged. "I guess so."

The Warlock, Pal, and I resolidified in the alley across the street from the bar.

"Urg. Dematerialization's just as nasty as I remembered," the Warlock said after he finished heaving near a pile of milk crates. "That potion could have stood a few more hours' brewing, I think."

"Gimme a break, it was my first time making it." I shrugged off my knapsack and set it on the pavement. I took off my helmet and awkwardly strapped it one-handed to the side of the bag. Pal wobbled over to me and crawled up my jeans and shirt to my shoulder.

"You guys keep an eye out for pedestrians and cars." I pulled the miniaturized Land Rover out of the zippered main compartment of my bag and set it on the pavement.

I felt Pal stiffen, his claws scratching against the dragonskin.

"Oh dear. Cold and Fear," the ferret said.

"What?" Still kneeling, I turned my head in the direction Pal was staring. Two men in dark suits stood in the entrance of the alleyway, both holding pistols. They were fifteen or sixteen yards away.

I heard a car pull into the other end of the alley. Doors opened, and I looked over my shoulder to see another pair of men in suits emerge from a maroon Ford Taurus. They checked their watches, smoothed their shirts, hitched up their Sansabelt slacks, taking their time. The rat bastards had probably been lurking near the bar all this time, just waiting for me to come out with the Warlock.

A small granite pebble lay near my hand. Acting on sudden instinct, I set my hand down on the pebble to unobtrusively palm it between my index and middle fingers. I picked up the truck and stood up slowly. Clutching the Rover to my chest, I turned to fully face Cold and Fear.

"Put your hands up where I can see them, Warlock," said the man I assumed was Cold. "You, girlie, set down that toy."

His partner Fear was hanging back, giving me a look midway between discomfort and pity. *Pity*. Like I wasn't really a threat to them . . . and never could have been, because I was just a girl and a cripple and I wasn't ever going to find that boyfriend of mine anyhow and wasn't this a big waste of everybody's time? *That* kind of pity.

"Aw, fuck," muttered the Warlock, slowly raising his hands in the air.

"You've got no place to go," Cold continued.

"Come quietly, and you won't get hurt. Mr. Jordan is prepared to forgive your crimes against the community if you'll just end this nonsense."

I stared at Cold and Fear, at their suits and CIA-wannabe haircuts. Something about Cold reminded me of my stepfather. I remembered every time he'd treated me like a loser freak, every time he'd acted like I was a worthless burden he couldn't wait to unload. I felt the blood rise in my face.

Damn Cold and his supercilious smirk. Damn Fear and his gun-toting pity. Damn the jerks strolling up the alley behind me. Damn them *all*. The stone eye hummed in my skull. A cold, hard rage crackled adrenaline through my body.

"We totally give up!" I said loudly, then tossed the Range Rover wheels-down at Cold and Fear in a flat underhand pitch. "It's all yours! Catch!"

The men stared at the little truck, momentarily baffled. I whispered a dead word for "big and heavy" as I let the palmed pebble fall to the ground.

The Rover expanded midair and the three-ton vehicle slammed down onto Cold and Fear. I didn't wait to see what happened to them; I whirled on the two other men, pointed at them and whispered a word for "fire." They shouted in surprise as their clothing burst into flame.

"Stop, drop, and roll, jackass!" I hollered as I snatched up my knapsack and started running for the Land Rover. Pal held on to my jacket for dear life, and the Warlock was quick behind me.

I yanked the passenger-side door open, my foot slipping slightly in something that had spilled from beneath the vehicle. I didn't look down as I threw my knapsack in the back and hopped in.

The Warlock jumped into the driver's seat, slammed his door shut, and cranked on the ignition. His face was white. "Jesus H. Christ, Jessie. You totally pulped those two guys."

"Get us the hell out of here," I replied as I heaved my own door closed. The Warlock did as I asked, slamming the Rover into gear and stepping on the accelerator.

As we sped out of the alley, I looked back through the rear window at the men I'd set on fire. They'd managed to extinguish themselves; one was running back to the Taurus and the other was hurrying to tend to the two men I'd crushed. The crushed men were hard to look at, but their arms and legs were still twitching.

"Jesus," the Warlock repeated. "That's a murder charge if those guys die. That's the death penalty for sure. Jesus."

"They're still alive. The other guys can put them in stasis, and Jordan can get them healed up. Right, Pal?" I asked.

"Perhaps," Pal replied. "I didn't get a good look at what you did to them. They surely have broken spines and legs and probably massive internal injuries. That's a challenge for even a very skilled healer. Best to hope they don't have too much brain and skull damage."

"Well, that's just too fucking bad for them," I said, trying to keep myself angry so I wouldn't get sick. The image of the twitching, broken men wasn't leaving my mind easily. "That's what they get for being thugs. They should have left us alone."

"Even if they survive, it's attempted murder for

sure," the Warlock said tightly, shaking his head. "We're gonna get prison for this."

I realized my own hand was trembling in my lap; I smacked the dashboard with my palm. "Don't fucking pussy out on me *now*, Warlock. You knew shit like this was gonna happen."

"I'm driving, aren't I?" he shouted back, the tires screeching as he turned onto Summit Street. "If I was pussying out, I'd have stopped the truck and left you here by yourself!"

"Then stop with the 'oh no, you crushed them!' 'oh no, we're going to prison!' crap, okay?"

"It's not crap, it's a real problem—"

I kicked the side of the box at my feet with my booted heel. "No. Stop right there. This box does *not* contain party favors. You had your girlfriend pack us guns and grenades. Those two guys would be just as mangled if I'd had to use one of these on them. And we'd both be leaking brains right now if they'd had the chance to take us someplace nice and quiet and plug us like they'd planned."

"You can't be sure—" the Warlock began.

"Yes. I *can*. They have not given Shit One about our lives since this whole thing started. They were gonna squish us like bugs. It's just their bad luck I got to do the squishing first."

I took a deep breath. "Look, I'm not happy I probably just killed two guys. Believe me, I'm not. But they should have left us alone."

"Unfortunately," Pal said, "they most certainly won't leave you alone after this. More to the point, they're not going to leave *me* alone. You're likely to find yourself without my services before nightfall."

"What? Why?" I asked.

"They just obtained positive eyewitness proof I've been helping you break the law. They can go to my overseers with their complaint. The overseers will demand a memory scan from one of Jordan's witnesses, which will take only a little time. And then I will be forcibly withdrawn from this body. The shock will probably kill the ferret, but the little creature hasn't had its own life for quite some time."

"What will happen to you?" I asked.

"My overseer promised a punishment that is 'most severe,' but he was not forthcoming with details."

I was mortified. "Is—is there anything we can do?"

"Sadly, no," he replied. "Helping you was a gamble I took of my own free will, and I've lost. Please make sure my help has not been in vain, all right? Find Cooper. Bring him back."

"Okay," I said. "How much time do you think you might have?"

"Two hours if I'm fortunate. An hour if I'm not," he replied.

"What's going on?" the Warlock asked, signaling and speeding up to merge onto I-71.

"Pal's busted. He's gonna get yanked back to prison in an hour or two. How fast can you get to the farmhouse?"

"It'll take me a little less than an hour, if I speed and we don't run into any trouble." The Warlock dodged between two semi trailers to make it onto the I-70 eastbound exit ramp. "Jordan's people wouldn't dare do anything while we're on the interstate; there'd be way too many mundane witnesses. But he might call the police and have them try to stop us."

"Joy." I stared bleakly at the traffic, then glanced at the clock on the dashboard. It was seven fifteen. I shifted my gaze to the box at my feet. "So which of these should I use to stop a cop car?"

The Warlock gave me a quick, pained glance. "We're in enough trouble already—I really wouldn't point a gun at a police car. Just . . . blow up his front tire or something. That's nice and surreptitious. You Babblers can do that, can't you?"

"I expect I can try," I replied, then reached down and picked an antique pistol out of the box.

"What are you doing with that?" the Warlock asked.

"This." I pointed the pistol at the side of his head. "I demand that you drive me to the farmhouse without stopping, and I will kill you if you don't. There." I primly set the pistol back in the box. "If they ask, you can in complete honesty tell them I held a gun to your head and threatened to kill you if you didn't obey me. So maybe now you'll get parole instead of prison."

"You realize you're seriously starting to lose it, don't you?" the Warlock asked, looking irritated and nervous.

"I think I'm handling the situation with sangfroid and joie de vivre and je ne sais quoi and all other kinds of Frenchy cool," I replied, rolling down my window to get some fresh air on my face and neck. The dragonskin suit was making me sweat like crazy, and the warm, damp leather was giving off a musty stink that made my nose itch. "It's not like they cover this kind of stuff in charm school, you know."

"You never fucking went to charm school," the

Warlock replied. "And don't ever, *ever* point a gun at me again unless you want to eat it for dinner."

Suddenly the cars in front of us were slowing down; the highway was a sea of red brake lights. Ahead, I saw flashing blue-and-red visibar lights across both lanes.

The Warlock touched the brake, craning his neck at the police cars. "Dammit, it's a roadblock."

"Screw this noise," I said, hunting the floorboards for a piece of fluff or a feather or a foldable piece of paper. I found something better: a little toy airplane from one of the kid's meals the Warlock had started consuming in his effort to eat less at drive-throughs.

I held the plastic plane in front of me, closed my eyes, and started chanting ancient words for "flight." The Rover lurched once, twice, then hurtled up in the air with all the grace of a dead elephant flung from a catapult.

"Whoa Jesus!" the Warlock exclaimed as the vehicle listed alarmingly from side to side. "Keep 'er straight! The drinks may be tied down but my lunch sure isn't!"

I steadied the grenade box between my feet, still chanting. We were sailing over the roadblock, the white-shirted police below shouting, some pointing as others drew revolvers—

—I was flung back against the seat, the inside of my head seeming to explode in a bright firework of agony. My tongue twitched in my mouth. I only half sensed that we were falling.

"Jessie, wake up!" Pal squeaked.

"Keep it together, keep it together!" the Warlock hollered.

I fought past the stunning pain and got my chant

going again, barely in time. The Rover bounced down hard on the pavement fifty yards past the police cars. The engine had died from the force of whatever invisible magic barrier we'd passed through.

The Warlock cranked the key in the ignition as seven cops ran toward their cars. Nothing.

I desperately tried to think of a chant to save us, but my mind was blank. I reached into the box at my feet, grabbed a grenade at random—the yellow tin bomb body was made to look like a fat bee— pulled the pin with my teeth, and flung it as hard as I could at the pursuing policemen.

The grenade skipped across the pavement. The cops scattered, backpedaling. The little tin bee popped in a huge explosion of sticky honey goo. Five cops were slimed, slipping at first and then sticking fast like insects bogged in thick amber tree sap.

The two nimbler cops skirted the goo and advanced on the Rover more carefully, shouting orders as they trained their guns on the Warlock and me.

The Warlock cranked the key again, and the engine coughed awake. He slammed it into gear and stepped on the gas. "Throw a red one!" he yelled.

I grabbed one of the red copper grenades, yanked the pin, and pitched it behind the speeding Rover. The grenade went up with a loud bang that rattled my teeth and made my ears ring. When the purple mushroom cloud cleared, I saw an enormous, yards-deep crater in the highway across both lanes. The two quick officers had been knocked off their feet and were struggling to get up.

The Warlock and I drove on in silence. I stared glumly in the rearview mirror, watching for police cars screaming up in pursuit. But none came. The Warlock passed Buckeye Lake and took Exit 132 onto Johnsontown Road. I half expected another magical barrier to crash down on us the moment we were off the highway . . . but once again, none came.

Just south of Fleatown, the Warlock turned right onto an unmarked gravel farm road that wound east and lost its stones past Hog Run. The rutted road dove down into a thicketed ravine for several miles until it reached a crossroads with a narrow, weed-choked dirt road that had probably looked exactly the same for the past fifty years.

The Warlock slowed to turn left onto the road. The thick, knitted branches of the yellow and black birches looming over the trail made it seem like night-fall.

I was about to ask how much farther he thought the farmhouse would be when the road took a left-ward bend and suddenly the blighted field spread in front of us like a carcinoma on the skin of the world. The only char that remained was on the limestone rocks lining the pit of what must have been the farm-house's basement and the jagged fang of the shattered chimney. A full half acre around the basement was nothing but bare dirt and mottled bits of rusted metal. Sickly-looking poison ivy and a few desiccated toadstools grew on the border of the dead land.

The Warlock pulled the Land Rover up to the edge of the dead field and killed the engine.

"Well, this is it," he said, his jaw set in a grim line. He nodded toward the ruins of the house. "We better get to it—might not have much time before the cops or Jordan's people find us here. I think that opening the portal will be easiest down in the basement."

I shivered despite the heat.

The Warlock fingered the bronze sword-and-shield pendant at his neck, then took off the necklace and held it out to me. "Here. I think you should wear this."

"Why? What is it?" I asked.

He squinted at me. "It's a necklace."

"Duh. What *else* is it?"

"It's . . . I don't know. I think I . . . got it from my mother." His eyes seemed to go out of focus for a moment, but he quickly recovered and smiled at me. "Call it a good-luck charm."

I hesitated, staring at the gleaming pendant. "Did your dream tell you I should wear this?"

"Yes."

Should I take it? I thought to Pal.

"As far as I can tell it's just a necklace," my familiar replied. "It has an odd magical residue, but I can't sense an actual enchantment."

I took the chain from the Warlock's outstretched hand and slipped it over my head.

"You should wait in here while we go to the basement," I said aloud to Pal.

"I really think I ought to come with you and help as long as I can," he protested.

"The girl's right," the Warlock said. "There are probably lots of copperheads slithering around in the weeds out there, and you're just the right size for a snack."

Pal reluctantly climbed off my shoulder and sat on the top of the headrest. I fetched my helmet from the backseat, put it on, and buckled the strap in place under my chin.

"Hey," I said to Pal as I rolled down the passenger window for him. "Thanks for everything you've done. I'm really sorry that you're in trouble for this."

"I'm glad I could help," Pal replied. "It was the right thing to do, and this has been a far more worthwhile cause than the error I committed that got me indentured in the first place."

"What *did* you do?" I asked.

"That's a long, embarrassing story," Pal replied. "If we meet again, I'll tell you."

"You don't have long before they come for you, do you?"

"No, not more than half an hour, I expect."

"I hope things go as well for you as they can. I hope—"

"Please don't worry about me—focus on getting Cooper and yourself back here safely. That is what's important now."

"Okay." I paused, then reached out and scratched Pal between his ears. "You might really be a spider, but I love ya just the same. Thanks again. I don't think I can say that enough. Good-bye, and I hope I have the chance to hear that story someday."

I turned to the Warlock. "Let's do this thing."

The Warlock opened the driver's-side rear door and nodded down toward the untouched cooler. "Want a drink for the road? Not to be negative, but it might be your last chance."

I shook my head. "I'd rather go to hell thirsty than have to pee when I get there."

The Warlock pulled the bungee cords off the cooler, opened the lid, and pulled out a root beer in a dark glass bottle. "Hope you don't mind if I have one."

"Nope."

We left Pal gazing at us sadly from his perch on the headrest and stepped toward the dead field. As we reached the graying edge, the Warlock stopped me with a hand on my shoulder, then moved around behind me to stand at my right.

"Take my hand," he said. "Just in case. If you haven't felt this before, it can be pretty bad . . . better hold on to me."

He gripped my gloved hand; I took a deep breath and stepped onto the dead earth.

It felt as though lightning ran up my leg and out the top of my head. My mind flashed on darkness, pain, and a sudden panic jerked through my core, an orgasm of abject fear. My breath caught in my throat, and I thought I'd go down on my knees.

"Steady," the Warlock said through gritted teeth, holding me up. "Keep moving. It'll go away. I hope."

He marched me forward toward the basement, my knees rubbery but the terror slowly ebbing, leaving behind a foreboding that made my stomach clench into a cold acidic knot. The basement was a big L-shaped depression, thirty or forty feet on a side. The house that once sat above it must have been huge. A set of crumbling concrete steps led down into the basement, and as they reached the basement's edge, I saw that in the middle was a fieldstone pit or well, about ten feet in diameter, the round walls maybe a yard higher than the concrete floor. The pit was topped by rectangular rusted metal doors, the kind you usually see on old-fashioned storm cellars

The hinges had been hammered into the stone lip of the pit, and the rotting remains of plywood planks covered the gaps between the sides of the doors and the stones.

"I wonder what they kept in there?" I found myself saying. The hairs on the back of my neck prickled; there was some seriously bad magic coming from the pit.

"I wouldn't want to know," the Warlock replied, "but I expect you'll find out. That's your portal."

He dug in one of the thigh pockets of his pants and pulled out a small brown leather bag from which he produced a lighter and a lock of hair. "I got this off Cooper a couple of years back. Never knew when it might come in handy, but I had a feeling I was gonna need it someday."

He paused. "Once we get you in there . . . you know not to drink or eat anything while you're there, right?"

I nodded. "I knew that one."

"Good," he said. "Breathing the air's bad enough, but you can't help that. Don't touch anything in there with bare skin if you can help it. Stay aware of your surroundings at all times. Don't fall asleep; that's even worse than eating. Get in, find Coop, get back here fast as you can."

"Um. And how do I get back here?"

"Right. That'd be important, wouldn't it?" He set his root beer on the floor and used his free hand to pull a pair of corked glass cylinders out of another pocket. Each was about as wide as one of my fingers and four inches long. They looked a bit like test tubes with runes etched on the outsides of the glass.

He bent down, filled the vials with dirt, ashes, and dead leaves that had drifted against the pit wall, recorked them, and handed both to me.

"When you're ready, break one of these open and say 'Return.' It should snap easy as a glow stick. The important thing is to not lose them, or let them both get broken before you're ready."

"Seems easy enough." I took the vials and tucked them between my buttons into separate interior pockets of my dragonskin jacket.

"Okay," the Warlock said. "Are you ready for this?"

"As ready as I'm ever gonna be," I replied.

The Warlock heaved the pit's rusted doors open. The cold, foul air trapped inside swirled out, the interior of the pit black as a bullet hole in a moonlit skull. He closed his eyes and began a chant in Latin; I regretted that I could understand none of the words. The air got colder, denser, and I began to shiver in my stifling jacket. Clouds began to gather overhead, darkening the evening sky. Just as frost began to blossom on the pit's rocky lip, the Warlock flicked on the lighter and ignited the lock of hair.

Cooper's lock went up in a purple flash, and a slow shock wave rolled from the pit like a grenade exploding in heavy water. I kept my feet, but the gust blew stinging grit in my face and I had to shut my eyes.

When I was able to see again, the pit was glowing with the same bad magic, the same reflected hellfire as the portal Cooper had opened in Taft Park. Through my good eye, I could see nothing inside but vertiginous blackness. Through my stone eye, the pit was a maelstrom of colors I didn't have names for.

"If the spell worked right, this thing won't stay active more than a minute, but it'll be receptive to your return indefinitely," the Warlock said. "But you've got to go through now, while it's active."

"Okay," I said.

I took a deep breath, and remembered Cooper. Remembered his smile, his laugh, the feel of his warm skin against mine on a winter morning. *I love you, honey. I'm coming for you. Don't be dead when I get there.*

I stepped up onto the lip of the pit, gave the Warlock a trembling wave good-bye, and let myself fall into the portal.

chapter nineteen

Palimpsest: The Sting

From my vantage in the Land Rover, I could no longer see Jessie and the Warlock once they descended into the basement, but I certainly felt the telltale shock wave when the portal to Cooper's hell was opened. It was simultaneously frightening and elating to see the basement lit in that brief dark flash; I knew she had gone inside. And my slithering bastard of an overseer hadn't hauled me out of the ferret yet. Whatever happened next was up to Jessie and Cooper. I was determined that I could endure whatever punishment was in store for me with the comfort of knowing I'd done the right thing, done my job, and been true to my mission. My personal sense of honor was one of the few things I had left, and I wanted to preserve it if I could.

My relief was doused like a match in a tsunami: Somewhere nearby, a stranger shouted a staccato charm I recognized as the counter to a mass hiding spell.

Two of Jordan's men—the pair that Jessie had briefly set aflame—shimmered into view at the edge of the dead field. They wore pistols in police-duty holsters at their hips and carried pump-action shotguns with pistol grips; the short chromed barrels gleamed dully, reflecting the overcast sky. The guns hummed with fierce enchantments. A second later, a motley assortment of half a dozen Talents appeared in the grass near them. My dread deepened as I recognized Mother Karen and her teen protégé Jimmy among the group.

The air twenty yards above the basement shimmered, and a fifty-foot-long orange firedrake became visible, flapping in an awkward hover as a bald man in dragonskins and welding goggles pulled back on the steel tow chains serving as reins. The firedrake angrily gnawed the steel playground post bit in its enormous crocodile jaws and clawed the air with its buzzard-like feet. It let out an irritable squawk along with a puff of blue flame.

"Rosko, what the hell are you doing here?" the Warlock yelled from the basement.

"I'm air support," Rosko yelled down.

"Air support?" the Warlock called back.

"My name is Deputy Titus Wilson," the first of Jordan's men shouted. "Warlock, come out with your hands clasped over your head. By the power vested in me by the Central Ohio Governing Circle, you are hereby under arrest for attempted murder, helping a fugitive escape justice, and magical malfeasance."

"Rosko, you snaky bastard! If I get out of this I'm going to kick your lardy ass to Cleveland!" the Warlock hollered.

"Sorry 'bout this, man, but they busted me with a shitload of contraband relics this afternoon," Rosko replied, not really sounding very apologetic. "I can't do prison again. Just don't have the disposition for it anymore."

"Fuck you and your disposition!"

"Warlock, we're warning you, come out *now* or

we'll consider you hostile," Wilson shouted. "Hands up!"

"Don't make me hafta barbecue you, bro," Rosko added.

Muttering obscenities, the Warlock did as he was ordered, stomping up the concrete stairs with his fingers laced above his head.

"Get over here to the grass and get down on your knees," Wilson ordered, training his shotgun on the Warlock's midsection.

The Warlock goggled at the assorted Talents. "Mariette? Oakbrown? Paulie? Ginger? Jesus, guys, what—*Mother Karen?* What the fuck, guys!"

"These men came to the house and ordered Jimmy and me to come with them, or they said we'd be arrested for refusing to render aid." Mother Karen looked deeply distressed. "They wouldn't tell us anything—still *haven't* told us anything, in fact—and I assumed they needed a healer. I never imagined I was supposed to help arrest you."

"Dammit." Wincing, the Warlock crossed the dead field onto the grass and got down on his knees, his hands still on his head.

"You," Wilson said to a woman with a zippered canvas bag slung over her shoulder; I guessed by her red hair that she might be Ginger. "Open that bag I gave you, and put the gag on him. And you two"— he jerked his head at the two men who had to be Paulie and Oakbrown—"put the cuffs she's got on him. Make sure they're tight."

Looking confused and unhappy, Ginger unzipped the bag and pulled out a pair of heavy old handcuffs that hummed with magic-dampening charms. She held the cuffs out to Paulie and Oakbrown, neither of whom approached her to accept them.

"Sometime today, people!" Wilson snapped. "Don't make me explain the situation to you all again."

The man I thought might be Oakbrown by his fringed suede boots and oak-leaf pendant took the cuffs and went over to the Warlock to bind his wrists behind his back. Relieved of the cuffs, Ginger pulled a black leather ball gag out of the bag. Looking deeply ashamed, she carried it over to the Warlock and gently brushed his hair back before she strapped it in place across his mouth and head.

I saw her mouth "I'm sorry, honey" as she tightened the buckles.

"What *is* the situation, exactly, and why do you need us here?" Jimmy asked, his voice shaky. "Don't you have your own guys for this kinda stuff?"

Wilson gave Jimmy a dark glare. "The situation is, you're doing your civic duty in bringing a wanted criminal to justice. More to the point, you will drink a nice tall glass of shut the hell up and do what I tell you, kid, if you know what's good for you and your foster mom."

Wilson turned to Oakbrown, Paulie, and Mariette. "You three, get out those spells I gave you." They obeyed, pulling narrow scrolls of parchment on mahogany sticks out of their pockets.

"Take those down to the basement and get that portal closed for good," Wilson continued. "I don't want so much as a bad smell getting through that thing from the other side."

My hackles rose as I realized that Jordan meant

to trap Jessie in the hell. This was no spur-of-the-moment scheme; this had taken careful planning. Jordan had known the location of the ruined, cursed farmhouse well in advance. Who could have told him? Or had Jordan known about it all along? I desperately wished that I could engage my telepathy with the Warlock, but that was impossible.

The trio of Talents let out pained gasps as they stepped onto the dead field; Oakbrown seemed to faint briefly and nearly fell, but the others grabbed his thick arms and hauled him up.

"Shake it off," Wilson said. "Keep going. Those scrolls will take a dog's age anyhow; the sooner you get done, the sooner we can all go home."

Wilson turned to his partner, who had fallen to the back of the group, apparently to block the way if any of the Warlock's shanghaied friends made a run for it.

"Go check out the SUV, Bruce," Wilson told him.

Bruce gave him a casual two-finger salute, picked up a sack at his feet, and headed toward the Rover. I quickly hid behind the backseat where I could keep an eye on what was happening in the front of the vehicle.

Bruce pulled on a pair of disposable latex gloves, leaned in through the passenger window, and laid the sack on the seat. He pulled out a large black device in the shape of a black eyeball. I recognized it as a homemade bomb full of concentrated vitreous humor draco niger; if it had been made to the usual recipe, it was powerful enough to destroy most everything in a half-mile radius. Bruce set the bomb in the middle of the box of pistols and grenades, picked up his sack, and headed back toward Wilson, whistling.

"All clear," Bruce announced.

I climbed up onto the back of the passenger seat and stared out at Mother Karen and Jimmy through the window. There was no possible reason for Jordan's men to have brought the witch and her foster son along . . . unless it was to eliminate possible witnesses who'd seen and heard Jessie's side of the story.

I felt absolutely petrified at that realization. Jordan's men had rounded up known associates of Jessie and the Warlock on the pretext of needing assistance. When the portal was closed and she was trapped for good, Wilson and Bruce would likely teleport away as they detonated the VHDN bomb. Mother Karen, Jimmy, Oakbrown—everybody else would be killed. Murdered in the coldest blood. Jordan and his men could easily blame the homemade bomb on the Warlock and Opal—who was, no doubt, under arrest back at the bar—and then call the whole thing an unfortunate accident caused by reckless renegades. Nobody would be alive to claim otherwise.

Something had to be done, and quickly. Perhaps I could find a way to warn Mother Karen. But what could *she* do? She was unarmed, and afraid for her foster son. No matter; I had to try.

I hopped down into the front passenger seat, clambered up the door to the sill, and leaped out, landing painfully on the packed, dried mud of the overgrown roadway. I began to run through the dry grass toward Mother Karen—

—and felt my spirit yanked out of the ferret into the aether, then into my true quamo form in my overseer's lair.

The old white wyrm was a knot of indignant rage on his ottoman, his tail stiff as a butcher's knife. He stared at me balefully, his sapphire eyes glittering.

"We don't appreciate being lied to, spider. The depths of your subterfuge plumb straight down to rank stupidity. I do wonder if you appreciate how *very* much trouble you've gotten yourself into."

"Wait," I said. "Jordan's been lying to you—"

"You accuse Benedict Jordan?" the wyrm replied, his voice caustic. "That's a fine laugh. I've seen the cerebral recordings from his servants. I know what you and the Shimmer girl have been up to. You're most fortunate the men she attacked have not perished from their injuries."

"Innocent people are about to die," I insisted. "If you don't believe me—"

"Indeed, I *don't* believe you, and that's perhaps the first true thing that's come from your ugly duplicitous mouths—"

"Come to Earth," I said, panic scrabbling in my very core, "and you'll see—"

"No. I shall do no such thing. You're planning some trick, some escape from your just punishment. I'm not about to be fooled twice by the likes of you."

"Sir, please—"

"Quiet, or I shall cut those vile flapping calliope valves from your belly! You're legally entitled to fifteen minutes to say your good-byes; after that, you will be recalled to your true body and returned to prison for intensive reprogramming. I hope to never see your chitinous grotesquery or hear your disharmonious piping ever again!"

I came awake inside my ferret body, swinging limply midair, suspended painfully by my tail. Bruce was holding me at eye level, squinting at me suspiciously. I continued to hang limp, breathing shallowly, eyes half closed and unfocused.

"I found the girl's familiar," Bruce called to Wilson. "I think it got recalled. What should I do with the body?"

"Wring its neck," Wilson replied. "Just in case it gets sent back here."

Oh dear, I thought. *We're completely fucked now.*

chapter twenty

Underworld

I had no idea what was happening to Pal, but I had plenty of my own troubles to deal with. As I traveled through the portal, I was crushed on all sides by an oppressive darkness as I felt a vacuum try to tear the air from my lungs and boil the blood from my veins. At one point I wasn't sure if I was falling or simply spinning in place, trapped in some horrible spot between worlds and time where I'd go on dying forever.

Abruptly I felt myself jerked sideways, and I tumbled out into chilly moonlit air and hit snowy ground feet-first. I might have been able to stay upright but suddenly something yanked hard on the back of my neck and I fell forward, flailing to catch myself. My right hand jammed into a padded convex surface, and I felt the chain at my neck snap free.

I hit the ground, jolting my knees and wrists painfully. *Wrists?* I looked down; my good right eye saw nothing but buzzing darkness, but my stone eye showed both my hands before me. My right gloved hand gleamed faintly in the moonlight; it rested on a big upholstered plate the size of a manhole cover.

My left hand was sunk into a few inches of snow, ghostly pale but apparently completely intact. The snow looked normal enough in the half-light, and it was certainly cold, but it felt weirdly spongy. The air hung stale and icily humid.

Oh crap, I'm touching the snow bare-handed, I realized in alarm, remembering the Warlock's warning. I scrambled to my feet, scrubbing my freezing palm furiously on the front of my jacket as I stared around me. I was in a small clearing amid dark woods. The trees looked like larger versions of the kinds I'd seen near the dead field. I wondered if their trunks would feel as strange and unreal as the snow. Nothing seemed to move within the snow-blanketed woods; as far as I could tell, I was alone.

The full moon hanging in the sky was twice as large as it should have been. The satellite had been shattered in two by some terrible cosmic accident. The ragged halves ground soundlessly against each other, sending a constant stream of meteors streaking down into the atmosphere, flaring red like lunar blood.

Unnerved, but satisfied I was safe for the time being, I raised my left palm up close to my stone eye to inspect it. The skin was uninjured, unscarred, the lines and whorls completely normal and familiar. It was indeed my own hand, though I could still feel pain deep in the bone in the spot where my arm had been bitten off. The jacket sleeve had magically extended to cover my arm to my wrist.

I wiggled my fingers and flexed my wrist. The Warlock had said that hells were realms of the spirit; had my arm actually regenerated, or had my phantom limb simply become more solid in this place? I stared down at both my hands and blinked through several gemviews. Some views were utterly bizarre and I could make no sense of what I was seeing, but others gave me a fairly normal view of myself. In those, my left hand was translucent while my right remained solid.

I decided my renewed arm was probably just a spiritual extension. Possibly it wasn't something I should trust to hold me if I found myself hanging for dear life from a cliff or tree limb. But who could tell? I dug out my other glove and slipped it on, just to be safe.

I knelt to examine the object I'd fallen on. Moonlight gleamed on bronze edges. The inside, I soon realized, was padded leather. My hands found straps; I tentatively lifted the object out of the snow, and realized it was a shield. The remains of the silver chain I'd worn on my neck still hung from a fist-width loop at the top. A leather-wrapped hilt stuck out diagonally from the top of the shield: A sheathed short sword was affixed to the front with copper wires.

I slipped my left arm through the shield loops and carefully pulled the sword free with my right. The sword had good balance and nice heft; the blade was about thirty inches long. We'd had a couple of sessions on sword fighting in my hapkido class after the ninja- and pirate-crazy youngsters pestered the sensei. I was no swashbuckler, but the weapon felt comfortable.

The Warlock said his mother had given the necklace to him; had her metaphoric protection simply become literal in this dimension? Or had the necklace been enchanted in a way that Pal couldn't sense?

Either way, so far this place doesn't seem that bad, I thought, staring up at the shattered moon.

Suddenly I heard someone crashing through the underbrush nearby. I turned, sword raised, and saw a pale young man with long, curly blond hair and a fringed buckskin jacket stumble into the clearing, panting hard, his breath steaming in the icy air. The guy bent over, resting his hands on his knees, trying to get his wind back. He wore a gray or red T-shirt beneath his jacket—it was hard to tell the color in the moonlight—and faded jeans tucked into tall suede lace-up boots. He reminded me of the Who's lead singer; I guessed he'd been trying to play up the look.

"Benny!" he exclaimed, looking up and seeing me for the first time. Wait, he was certainly looking *at* me, but didn't exactly seem to see me. "I told you to go home, man! This shit ain't right! We gotta get outta here!"

He ran up to me. I couldn't quite bring myself to take a swing at him, so I stepped back. Frowning, he grabbed the sleeve of my shield arm and tugged me sideways.

"Don't stand there like a jerk, we gotta *go,* Benny," the young man insisted, starting to jog again and pulling me along behind him. "Bad storm's coming!"

A wind rose in the trees, and I thought I heard hail hitting the leaves, but it didn't sound right. The hissing was far too loud, and I thought I could smell smoke. I looked up.

The meteor shower from the shattered moon had intensified, and fiery moonstones were streaking down into the trees. Steam rose where they struck snowy branches. Dark leaves flashed into orange flames.

I stopped resisting the young man and matched his pace.

"You ain't supposed to be here," he told me. "I

thought I got you home safe. I—I shouldn't have brought you out here. I'm sorry," the young man gasped, running faster.

"It's okay," I said reflexively, feeling lost.

"It was a terrible thing your dad did, but nobody needs to know. We gotta do what my mom said, and keep it quiet. You didn't tell anyone else, did you?"

"No," I replied.

"Good boy," the young man said, looking relieved.

We broke out into a freshly plowed field, kept running. The hiss and thump of the meteorites sounded closer and closer.

The young man stumbled, doubling over in pain. "Oh God. They're comin' for us."

"What's coming?" I asked, peering over my shoulder as I ran. The front edge of the meteor storm was emerging from the trees. The cooling moonstones turned black as they tumbled earthward, their crusts cracking . . . and dark, winged things were hatching from them in midair, shaking off the rocky shells and flying toward us through the trees.

As the first few darted out into the moonlight, I saw that they were big crows with cold, shiny black eyes and cruel curved beaks and talons. More and more flew from the woods in a dense flock swirling toward us, strangely silent but for the rush of wind through black feathers.

The young man looked back at the horde and let out a shuddering sob. In his moment of inattention, his foot fell through a hole hidden by the snow and he went tumbling headlong.

I hurried over to try to help him up; the snow was thicker here, and running was difficult. "Are you okay?"

"No, don't touch me! Get out of here!" The young man's face contorted into a profound grief I dared not imagine.

The crows were less than fifty yards away and gaining fast. "Let me help you up—"

"No! Benny, go, get out of here! It's too late for me." He rolled up onto his knees and threw a hunk of ice at me, which I easily dodged.

I hefted the shield in front of me and closed my eyes, beginning a chant to cast a protective sphere around the two of us. But the words wouldn't come; the ancient languages were blocked in this place, and my magic with them.

The young man was staring at the snow. Tears spilled down his cheeks. "Oh God. I shoulda known what he was doing. We shoulda stopped it, shoulda done something to help Siobhan and your brothers. All I did was burn the damn house down so nobody would find out, but I can't forget."

He reached inside his buckskin jacket and pulled out an old revolver. Before I had a chance to protest, he put the barrel of the gun against his chest and pulled the trigger. His whole body jerked as the gun went off. He collapsed sideways in the snow.

"Get outta here, Benny," he gasped, clutching the wound near his heart, struggling to breathe. "It's a sin to kill yourself."

I began to backpedal, shield raised, sword clenched in my gloved fist, staring at his dying form.

The mob of crows slowed as it reached the young man, hovered, and dove on him as if he were a tasty bit of roadkill. He weakly tried to shield his face as they pecked and tore at him. The birds were eerily silent in their attack. Their talons and beaks sheared through his leather jacket and jeans like steel razors. The flapping mass of birds smothered his body. Soon, only his right hand was visible, his fingers clawing at the snow.

A crow flew down beside his hand and eyed his fingers hungrily. The bird grabbed the skin between his thumb and forefinger in its beak and pulled. His pale skin came cleanly off as if it were just a glove, and beneath it was not human bone and tendon but a slender hoof.

The young man thrashed, rose up on all fours, shaking off crows and shredded clothing. He was no longer a man but a spotted fallow stag, a yearling buck with short antlers. Through the flocking crows I could see that the terrified deer bore the fresh gunshot wound on its chest, blood dark on its white fur.

Most of the crows attacked the stag with fresh savagery, but about twenty turned their beady eyes on me.

I turned and began to run as hard as I could. The field arced around a small copse of trees, and after I rounded the curve I saw a big three-story Victorian house at the end of the field. The windows glowed with yellow electric lights, the rooms inside indistinct through gauzy curtains.

The house, I realized, had the right dimensions to be an intact version of the burned farmhouse. I didn't much want to go inside, but knew I had to if I expected to find Cooper. And the crows closing fast behind me weren't giving me much of a choice.

I pelted across the field into the front yard, up the broad wooden front stairs onto the wide front porch. I slid to a hard stop against the front doors and pounded on the red-painted wood with the pomme of my sword. My bruised knuckles ached sharply, but I didn't care. "Hello! Is anyone in there?"

A tall, clean-shaven man in a flannel shirt and jeans answered the door. His brown hair was buzzed close to his skull, but I could see a touch of gray at his temples. Something about the set of his jaw and broad shoulders reminded me of the Warlock, but his smile and glacier-blue eyes made me think of Mr. Jordan.

"Hello, what can I do for you?" he asked, looking completely unperturbed that a woman with a sword was standing at his door. He glanced past me at the winged murder bearing down on his house. "Looks like a bad storm tonight, eh?"

"Yes, a very bad storm," I agreed anxiously. "May I come inside, please?"

"Oh, sure, I suppose so," he said. "Wouldn't be very neighborly to leave a pretty girl like you out on a night like this, would it?"

The man held the front door open wide, and I dashed inside under his arm just as the first of the crows reached the porch.

"My name's Lake," the man said as he shut the door and bolted it. Two seconds later I heard a solid thud as a bird hit the door, then the scrape of claws and beaks against the wood.

"I haven't seen you around here before," Lake continued. "You move into the Murphy place down the road?"

"No sir, I'm from the city." I stared at the house around me. It appeared to be a very nice, pleasant country home decorated with folksy knickknacks and colorful handmade quilts on the backs of sofas and chairs and woven rag rugs on the gleaming hardwood floors. "I came out here to find a friend who got lost in the woods."

"Well, I hope your friend found a dry place for the night! You're welcome to stay; we have a guest bedroom upstairs. My wife and I were just sitting down to dinner . . . care to join us?"

"Sure," I said, intending to just sit politely at the table and not consume anything.

Lake led me into the dining room. The rectangular six-seat table was laden with a country feast: mashed potatoes, a boat of sausage gravy, green beans, fluffy biscuits, and an enormous roast turkey. The food smelled delicious; my mouth started watering despite my determination.

A pretty, gray-eyed woman in her mid-thirties wearing a green-checked gingham A-line dress sat at the far end of the table. Her long, curly black hair was pulled back in a ponytail, and in her lap she held a large china doll dressed in a blue satin jacket and knickers. The doll had to be at least thirty inches tall, and looked like it was intended to be a replica of the figure from Thomas Gainsborough's *Blue Boy* painting. The woman did not react when Lake entered the room, keeping her downcast gray eyes fixed on the top of the doll's head. Something about the set of her nose and cheekbones reminded me of Cooper.

A crow rammed the window behind the sad woman's seat. The noise made me jump, but neither Lake nor the woman seemed to notice it. More thumps and claw-scrapes; the whole mob had reached the house, and the birds were trying to get in. Although the windows rattled alarmingly, at least it seemed the crows weren't striking with enough

force to break the glass. I hoped the house's chimney
had a grate.

"Have a seat anywhere you like." Lake settled in
the chair at the head of the table near the sad
woman.

"This sure is a lovely dinner," I said, trying to keep
my voice steady and not really making it. There was
no room to sit down with the shield, so I sheathed
my sword on it and pulled out two of the rail-back
chairs opposite the woman. I carefully propped my
shield up in the left chair and sat down in the right.
I rotated the shield so I could quickly grab my sword
if the need arose.

"I know it might seem like a lot for just two
people, but my son Benny will be home tomorrow
from boarding school, and we wanted to cook up a
nice big bird for him," Lake said. "That boy could
eat his own weight in turkey sandwiches. He's on the
lacrosse team now; he was voted best midfielder in
the eighth grade last year. He was on the honor roll
every quarter, and he's the tallest boy in his class."

"I bet you and your wife are very proud," I said,
looking around at the room.

What was this place? My gut told me it was definitely a re-creation of the farmhouse as it existed
thirty years ago, right before it burned down. I knew
a little about hells, and this looked like the kind
where tormented souls re-experienced the events
leading up to their spiritual catastrophe over and
over again in an endless loop. It was a living serial
nightmare, partly metaphoric and partly real.

In a hell like this, tormented souls would eventually get some kind of epiphany or catharsis from
their self-inflicted loop of pain, and then they'd move

on to the Beyond. Or maybe they simply got bored, and went off to haunt something instead. Either way, three decades was a long time for a purgatory hell to exist. Was something keeping them here? I couldn't tell.

If Cooper and the Warlock had come from this house, it would stand to reason that their parents or guardians had lived here as well. I couldn't see anything of Cooper in Lake. But I could easily believe the man might be the Warlock's father, and the sad wife looked like both brothers.

But who was the young man who'd transformed into a stag? And who was Benny? Clearly the souls trapped here in the hell had expected him to join them someday.

"Oh, we're proud as brass buttons," Lake said. He gave his wife a wide, toothy politician's grin. "Benny's going to be a big man in this state someday, just you see."

My heart bounced. I'd definitely seen that same smile on Mr. Jordan's face. The realization hit me: Benny could be short for Benedict. Could Mr. Jordan be Cooper's half brother and the Warlock's full brother?

Something rapped sharply at the window. The battered, bleeding young stag had staggered up to the glass, apparently trying to drive the crows away. His horns squeaked against the pane, and I could see that his muzzle was covered in scratches. He stared at me through swollen eyelids and gave a couple of hoarse barking cries as if he were trying to warn me of something.

Lake didn't seem to notice the stag. He lifted the

bowl of mashed potatoes and offered it to me. "Try these; we grew 'em right here on the farm."

I took the bowl, trying to be polite, and put a spoonful on my plate. I figured I could push them around and make it seem like I was eating.

Underneath the sounds of the stag and the crows battling at the window, I thought I could hear someone sobbing. It sounded like it was coming from the basement beneath my feet.

My right eye, blind in the woods, was sending flashes of *something* to my brain now that I was in the house. The stone eye was starting to itch as it had when I held the odeiette at the Warlock's apartment. My current gemview, I suspected, wasn't giving me the whole story. Bracing myself, I stared at the sad woman and her pretty china boy and blinked to the next view.

The woman was dressed in a long purple satin dress that had clearly once been regal, but now the fabric was stained and the ermine trim was moth-eaten and tattered. She rocked in her chair, weeping, her face dirty and her curls a ratty mess that looked like they hadn't seen a comb in weeks. Her wrists were chafed as if she'd been wearing shackles. She clutched a large, naked ball-jointed doll made from pale wood. The doll's face was a smooth blank plane except for two eyes made from dark blue glass.

Lake was standing at the head of the table dressed in a ragged ermine mantle over a dirty red surcoat and white tunic. A tarnished brass crown sat on his head.

He shouted at the weeping woman: "I can't believe my son came out of a faithless witch like you!

You were just going to abandon him, weren't you? But my son's going to rule the world someday, and you're going to help him. He'll have magic so strong no one will believe it, you hear me? Look at me when I'm talking to you!"

I turned away from Lake's insane fury, and finally noticed that the room had changed. The walls were the dark gray stone of a medieval castle, and the dinner table had turned to old oak planks on trestle legs. Torches smoked and flickered in wrought-iron sconces. The food had turned to wood; the turkey was a painted burl, and the mashed potatoes were nothing more than sawdust.

King Lake turned his fury on me. "Why aren't you eating?" he barked. "My food not good enough for you, is that it?"

"No sir, I'm just not very hungry—"

"Liar!" he snarled at me. "How *dare* you lie to me in my own house!"

He came around the table at me, his fist raised. I grabbed the sword, but as soon as I touched the metal a warning rose in my mind. This version of Lake, though strange, felt more real than the polite dinner host, but I couldn't kill a man who was surely already dead. My stone eye flashed a vision of King Lake throwing me off the front porch to the hungry mob of crows. I quickly blinked back through a dozen dark, strange views until I saw the tidy country home once again.

Lake was sitting in his chair, calmly buttering a fluffy biscuit. The woman sat silent, not eating, gazing down at her china doll. I slowly released the sword, my heart still pounding.

"You don't have to eat if you're not hungry," Lake

told me. "You look like you've had a long day; would you like me to just take you up to the guest room so you can get some rest?"

"Sure," I replied. Maybe once he'd left me alone I could figure out a way to sneak down to the basement. "That sounds like a good idea."

I picked up my sword and shield, and Lake led me out of the dining room back through the foyer to a staircase.

"Benny will be home tomorrow around noon; my nephew Reggie is driving him out here. We've got a wonderful birthday surprise for Benny," Lake said as he led me up the narrow stairs. "He's almost a man now, by my reckoning. It's going to be a very special day for him. You should stay for the party; I bet Benny would love to meet a pretty woman like you."

Nephew Reggie. I remembered what the young man in the woods had told me before his transformation, remembered his 1970s-era clothing. The stag was Reggie, I realized, still trying to protect his family from the evil that had driven him to suicide. I was more convinced than ever that this house was the place Cooper and the Warlock had lived before Cooper lost his memory.

"A party sounds like fun," I said, being careful to not overtly promise Lake anything. I wasn't sure if a casual promise in this place would be spiritually binding, but I didn't want to take any more risks than I had to.

He pulled open a door that led to a small bedroom with a single bed, a writing desk, and an old-fashioned sewing machine in the corner. A narrow door led to a closet-sized half bathroom with a small green night-light in the electric fixture by the sink.

"It's nothing fancy, but it's comfortable," he said.

"This is great, thanks." I stepped inside.

"Sleep tight! Don't let the bedbugs bite!" He abruptly shut the door behind me, and I heard a bolt click.

Dammit!

I turned and tried the doorknob. It was locked fast. I leaned my full weight into the door, but it wouldn't budge. Great. Just great. I set my shield down on the bed, then knelt to inspect the knob to see if it had any screws that might be removed. The brass knob ring was smooth and featureless. The hinges were on the other side of the door, so I couldn't pry them loose.

I stood and took a deep breath. There *had* to be a way out of the bedroom, hopefully a *quiet* way that wouldn't let Lake know what I was up to. I glanced toward the window. A big crow hovered awkwardly outside, cocking its head to stare at me with its cold black eyes. It pecked the glass fiercely as if to emphasize that the exterior of the house was indeed a very bad place to be. There'd be no sneaking out across the roof and down a drain spout to the storm cellar, at least not for me.

I stared back at the crow. More and more of its brothers were arriving to hover beyond the glass or lurk on the windowsill. All stared at me balefully. Soon there would be so many crowding at the window that they would block out the light from the shattered moon.

Acting on a hunch, I blinked to the gemview that had shown me insane King Lake and the wooden feast. The cozy guest room around me turned into a stark medieval gaol cell. The bed was a dirty burlap sack of straw on a wooden bench; the bathroom was nothing more than a narrow alcove containing a filthy pine bucket and a crude floor drain. The window had become a tall, narrow opening through the stone, far too stingy for an adult to squeeze through. Nonetheless, it had been covered with a rusty iron latticework.

The creatures pressing against the lattice no longer appeared as birds. At first glance they looked like sponges soaked in black india ink. I pulled one of the torches out of its sconce and brought the flame to the window to get a better look.

They still looked like sponges, but in some of the larger pores I could see small, probing, tentacle-like tongues. In other pores I saw tiny, circular grinding mouths. I thought of the slimy jaws of hagfish. And in others shone beady eyes a deeper black than their porous flesh. I felt a deep, primal hatred toward the weird creatures, the sort of animosity I supposed a mongoose raised in a laboratory might feel when it finally laid eyes on a cobra.

I squinted at the spongy little monsters, wondering if I might remember some long-forgotten bit of information that would explain to me what they were. Something nagged in the back of my head, just below my conscious recollection, a shark in murky water that refused to surface. Perhaps I'd read of creatures like these in some arcane bestiary years ago. Whatever the case, I could no longer recall their proper names.

But as I continued to stare at them, I realized that whatever they were, they were giving off the hungry, heedless energy of very young creatures. They were larvae, perhaps, or hatchlings.

"So where's your mother?" I asked them through

the window. They answered me by sucking at the iron bars, tiny teeth chattering silently.

I jumped and nearly knocked over the lamp when the lock clunked and the thick oak door swung open.

The sad woman's ball-jointed doll stood in the doorway, the torchlight shining on its dark glass eyes. It raised a wooden finger to its blank face in a shushing motion, then set a wooden toy block down in the doorway. The doll stepped into the room and let the heavy door swing almost shut behind it, kept from locking by the little block.

"What are you?" I whispered.

"I am Blue," it replied. I realized I was hearing it telepathically, as if it were a familiar. "And I am not an 'it,' I am a boy."

Blue didn't sound irritated; his tone was one of patient correction.

"My father put me to sleep, but I woke up after the monster trapped us here. It made me so angry seeing my mother get hurt every day that after a while it felt like there was nothing in me but bad thoughts. I sent the angry part away so I could try to think of a way out of here," Blue said. "My bad half hurt you; that's why you can hear me in your head, because a little bit of me is still inside you."

The Wutganger. Blue was the other half of that monster, everything that was left of the original soul, the part incapable of feeling pain or hatred. I stared at his strange, featureless doll body.

What on Earth was going on here?

chapter twenty-one

Palimpsest: The Gamble

Bruce flipped me in the air and caught me by my neck; I felt the man's strong fingers closing around my tiny windpipe, threatening to crush the life out of me.

I bit the man's index finger as hard as I could while I raked the tender underside of the man's wrist with my back claws.

"Dammit!" Bruce dropped me.

I hit the ground running, racing toward the cover of some nearby bushes. Bruce cursed, and then I heard the slide of a pistol being drawn from a leather holster. The gun fired, a bullet kicking up gravel perilously close by. I dove into the cover of a wild honeysuckle.

"Leave it," Wilson ordered. "Don't waste your bullets; it doesn't have long to live."

I barely had time to catch my breath from my mad sprint when I felt a sharp, tugging pain deep in my core. I'd never felt that kind of pain before, but I instantly knew what it meant: My jailers were tearing my soul from the ferret's body so they could drag me back to prison.

No. No, no, no, I thought. It couldn't happen *now,* not when Jessie and Mother Karen and Jimmy needed me most. But what could I possibly do to stop it?

I thought back to the night I'd awakened in the ferret's body, the night Smoky had transformed into a blended version of his true self. I hadn't thought that sort of thing was possible. Instead of being dragged back to my true body in prison, could I somehow reverse the process and pull my true form into my ferret self? Smoky *had* gone insane in the process, but that might have been from the shock of the explosion rather than the trauma of his transformation.

I felt desperate enough to take the risk; I was far too small and weak in this body to do anything to help save Jessie and the others. But was that kind of transformation possible here?

Another sharp spasm rippled through my body, and I vomited onto the dead leaves beneath the honeysuckle. The ferret's body was going to die. My jailers would take me soon; resisting them could prolong things, painfully, but only for a few more moments.

Had the reality shift caused by the portal enabled Smoky's accidental transformation? Would the portal in the basement of the farmhouse ruins generate a similar effect? Would there be a way to control it, keep my mind intact? I shook myself; there was no way to know any of it until I tried.

I peeked out from beneath the bush. No one was looking in my direction. I took a deep breath and started running for the dead field and the basement beyond.

When I leaped across the edge of the dead field, the pain was astonishing. I nearly lost consciousness, and I couldn't stay on my feet—

—I opened my eyes, and I was in my true quamo body, chained down to a bare concrete floor. Gray-

uniformed human guards stood nearby with wands
and pain-staves—

No!

I opened my eyes again, seeing a double exposure
of the prison and the poisoned field, feeling the little
heart in my chest shudder, beating weak and erratic—

"He's almost through," one of the guards said beside
my quamo body. "When he's fully awake, we're to
take him to Fifth Level for intensive deprogramming."

They meant to sap my powers and wipe my mind,
turn me into a simpering drudge they could set to
work on a host of mundane tasks. There'd be no returning to my nestmates, no respectable position in
academia, and no saving Jessie from being trapped
in Cooper's hell. Everything I'd done on Earth the
past few weeks would have been wasted. There'd be
no heroism in my future, no redemption for my past
sins, and not even a marker for my grave.

Goddess save me, I thought, my mind racing like
a rat in a cage to think of a way to escape the living
death that awaited me.

An idea came to me, one so simple, one so pure, I
was shocked by its diamond clarity. In my quamo
body, I began to sing a variant of a teleportation spell
I knew by heart. In my ferret body, I beat a little charm
on the dirt with my front paws that would normally
allow a spirit to enter my body during a séance.

"What's he doing? Somebody stop him!" one of
the guards shouted.

But whatever they planned to do, they were too
late. I felt my quamo body collapse in on itself as my
ferret body began to swell, the furry skin splitting and
healing faster than the mind could think. My spine
cracked and elongated, sprouting flat ribs and bony

girdles where none had existed, extra legs bursting through the flesh of my abdomen, my tail falling away like a lizard's. The transformation was a sweet itching agony, an adolescent's years of growing pains compressed into three seconds. I was becoming something not-quamo, something not-ferret, something completely new and possibly never seen in the universe before, something uniquely myself.

I blinked my four eyes in the gray light of the dead field, shook my shaggy head, and rolled my bulky abdomen over onto my eight legs. The pain of the cursed land wasn't so bad now; I had my full powers back, and the ambient magic was just a distraction.

I looked down at my two front legs; they were covered in fur, and the musculature and bone structure didn't look right. But at least I had proper hands, though this time I had five digits instead of four, and they ended in crude mammalian claws instead of delicate needles. Still, they were far more useful than what I'd had as a ferret. I'd make do.

"What in the great blazes is *that*?" I heard Wilson exclaim.

"What should we do?" asked Bruce.

"Kill the damn thing," Wilson replied. "I gave you that shotgun for a reason, you idiot."

Bruce and Wilson both trained their enchanted weapons at me and fired. I made a quick gesture to raise a fiery force shield before me. The enchanted pellets sizzled into the field and vaporized.

Bruce and Wilson gave each other an *Oh crap* glance.

And now, gentle sirs, it's my turn, I thought, giving them my best saber-toothed smile.

Siobhan's Children

"My brothers are sleeping. We have waited a long time for someone to help us," the ball-jointed doll told me.

Brothers? "How many of you are there?"

"We are seven, but not all are trapped here. The firstborn has never been more than an idea in this place."

Firstborn. Mr. Jordan was easily seven years older than Cooper. "Do you mean Benedict?" I asked.

"Yes. Father waits for him forever, but Benny has never come. He could have saved us from this fate. The second-born escaped with the seventh, who is just a shadow here. But Father's grip on the second-born was too strong, and it pulled him back here because Benny never came."

"Is the second-born Cooper?"

"Yes."

"Is he still alive?"

Blue cocked his blank head at me, his wooden neck creaking and his eyes glittering. "Are you still alive?"

I paused, my heart bouncing into my throat as my mind flashed on the sudden irrational notion that perhaps I'd died entering this hell. After all, how would I really know if I was actually alive or dead until I tried to leave?

"*Yes*. I'm alive," I replied firmly, as much to convince myself as him.

"Then yes, he is. For now. As are my brothers."

"The young guy I met in the forest—is that Reggie?" I asked.

Blue nodded. "He saw what happened here, and it made him sick to his soul. The guilt was never his to bear, but he bore it anyhow."

"How—how old are you?"

"I was almost two years old when Lake put me to sleep. Then he stored me like a doll on a shelf until it was time for Cooper to sacrifice me."

"*What?* Cooper would never hurt a baby!"

"He was just a child himself, and did not know what Lake was training him to do." Blue paused. "But no, he did not hurt me, nor did he hurt my brothers who are trapped here. We were in enchanted sleep when the monster drew us into this not-home. Cooper killed only one of us, our brother who escaped this place, leaving his shadow behind."

At first I had no idea what he was talking about, but then I thought of the Warlock and his missing piece of soul. It fit. But Blue was saying Cooper had murdered him.

I shook my head, biting my lips. "No. I don't believe you. You . . . you're not even human. And if you're just two years old, how can you speak so well? This is a trick."

"But I cannot speak, not at all." Blue touched his blank face. "You are just hearing my thoughts in your mind. Your mind is turning them into words.

Your mind is giving my spirit visual form. I cannot control how your mind chooses to see me."

I shook my head, still refusing to believe.

"You cannot help any of us if you do not believe me. Not even Cooper. You need to go down to the basement. You need to see the monster who trapped us, and you will believe me. You need to see what happened here. What *still* happens here, over and over and over again, to our mother and father."

Deep inside, I knew Blue was telling the truth, but I also knew that I had to see it for myself.

"Fine," I said, picking my sword and shield up off the crude straw mattress. "Let's go down to the basement."

Blue pushed the door open, then nudged the block out of the way and locked it once I was in the hallway. "Be very quiet. Lake will be angry if he hears us. I made a secret passageway where you can see everything.

"Lake put me to sleep like the others, but after a while my mind woke up even though my body slept. Once I sent my bad half away I was able to think well enough to make a plan. And when Cooper came back here, I was able to borrow some of his power when nobody was looking.

"When my bad half attacked you, I felt it; it was like a dream, only I was awake. And then I knew you would come here, or at least try. So I made this place just for you, so you could understand this place and find a way to get us all out."

Why me? I thought despite myself.

"Because you can resist what happens here." Blue could apparently hear my thoughts. "I can only do things while the monster is asleep; when it is awake, I have to go back to being the sleeping doll in my mother's arms. Cooper could not resist at all; his guilt was too great once he remembered what he had done to his own brother. He should have sent his bad feelings away like I did."

Blue stopped, trembled. "It is time for me to sleep again. Go to the end of the hall, pull out the panel in the wall to get to the secret stairs to the basement. Put the panel back when you're inside so it stays hidden. Whatever you do, do not let It hear you."

And in a blink, Blue simply disappeared.

"It"? What "It" had Blue meant? I got the feeling he wasn't talking about mad Lake. I licked my dry lips, wishing I could risk a sip of water, and began to creep down the dark hallway. I reached the wood-paneled wall without incident; I felt around in the dark until my fingers found a loose edge. A tug, and the panel came free.

The stairs were low and quite narrow, indirectly illuminated from the basement. It was difficult to pull the panel back into place once I was in the passageway. I had to hold my shield sideways and push it in front of me as I crawled down the stairs. The dim passageway smelled of dust and rot, and debris crunched beneath my gloved palms and leather-clad knees.

The stairs opened into a wood-paneled hallway with a cold stone floor. Flickering candles in several iron chandeliers hanging from the ceiling lit the hall. A dozen narrow windows were set into the walls. I got to my feet, glad that there was room to stand. The windows were set low so that I had to stoop a bit to see through them, but at least they were built more with an adult's height in mind than the stair-case.

Gripping my shield, I approached the first window and peered inside. I saw Lake's wife cowering at the foot of the bed, a baby in a blue blanket clutched in her arms. Lake stood in the doorway, scowling, holding an unconscious man by the back of his collar.

"You really thought I'd never find out the baby wasn't mine, Siobhan?" Lake demanded.

He muttered a charm under his breath, and the unconscious man was flung across the room to land at the woman's feet. The man groaned, rolled over; his face was battered and swollen, but still bore a noticeable resemblance to Cooper's.

"Speak up, woman!" Lake barked. "You'd rather be with Corvus here? You'd rather abandon your husband and firstborn son and live with this philandering fuck?"

"No," the woman wept. "It—it just happened."

"Oh. I see. You just, *oopsie,* slipped in the kitchen and happened to land on his dick, is that it?"

"It was only one night," she pleaded. "My mother just died, and you were in Europe." Her voice cracked with desperation and fear. "I'd never abandon you, or Benny. I love you."

His handsome face darkened with madness that frightened me even through glass. It was as if a cold shadow of evil was seeping in through the walls, eclipsing the entire room.

"*Love* us? That's a laugh. You've shamed me, shamed your firstborn son. I'm going to have to send Benny away to boarding school, just to keep him away from your bad influence. You're nothing but a white-trash whore."

"Please don't hurt us," she begged.

"Hurt *you*? My lovey-dovey wife? And your ittle-wittle bastard? Oh, not I. I'd never hurt *you*. I'd only ever want to give the love of my life what she most desires. And if actions speak louder than words—and believe me, they most certainly do—what you want most in this world is to fuck this piece of dogshit as often as possible and spawn his brats. And you're gonna get your wish, dear wife, you can count on that."

The window went dark; I moved to the next looping memory-scene. Lake was standing in the basement, looking angrier and crazier than before, a whiskey bottle clenched in one hand and a wand in the other. Corvus labored with a shovel in a dirt pit in the floor.

"Keep going, asshole," Lake said as Corvus paused to rest. "I didn't tell you to stop."

"Please, man," Corvus begged. "I'm sorry I did your woman. I was drunk. It was only once. I didn't mean for her to get pregnant."

"You can be sorry all you want; you're still gonna dig that hole as deep as I tell you."

Corvus held up his blistered, bleeding hands. "For God's sake, at least let me have some gloves!"

"You'll get gloves when I hear that handle grinding on bone. Not before."

I moved to the next window. Here the pit was finished, about six feet in diameter, twelve feet deep, and lined with fieldstones. I recognized it as the same pit I'd used to enter the hell. Corvus and Siobhan stood naked in the pit, staring up at Lake, who stood at the edge with a dark-haired baby in his arms. The baby looked healthy and well cared for, and didn't seem aware of the peril his parents were in.

"I wanna see you two fuck. *Now*," Lake ordered, his voice low and even.

"This is crazy." Corvus was much thinner than he'd been before, his hipbones sticking out sharply, his arms and back scarred with fresh cuts.

"*Now*, studmuffin. Your boy Cooper here needs a little brother to play with. Don't oo, oo little bastard oo," Lake cooed to the baby.

"Honey, *please*." Siobhan looked as if she'd been crying so much she'd run out of tears. "I'm sorry my friends came looking for me; I sent them away, just like you asked. They don't suspect anything, and they won't come here again."

Lake seemed to not even hear her. "I better see some baby-making down there real soon, or lil' Cooper's going straight out the attic window onto the driveway. Think he'll live? Think your boy can learn to fly all on his own?" Lake began to bounce the baby in his arms, singing "The window, the window, the third-story window! High-low, low-high, throw him out the window!"

Shuddering, I moved on. At the next window, a toddler in a diaper was playing with wooden blocks on the concrete floor in another part of the basement. A large Raggedy Andy doll lay near him. The floor had been chalked with complex signs and sigils; I recognized some of them from Cooper's tattoos.

Nearby, Lake knelt beside Cooper, who looked to be about three years old. The man handed Cooper a sharp stiletto blade.

"Now, be careful, don't cut yourself. Do you remember those words I taught you?" Lake asked.

"Uh-huh." Cooper turned the knife over in his hands, fascinated.

"And what are you going to do while you say those words?"

"Cut the doll's neck and belly," Cooper replied obediently. "And not myself."

"Very good!" Lake exclaimed, as if all this was a delightful game. "You're such a good boy, and your big brother Benny will be so pleased that you're practicing to help him be such a big man someday."

"How I make him big man?"

"Blue has power; he was born with it, like you. But he doesn't deserve it, so after practice today I'm going to put him down for a nice long nap so he doesn't get any bigger than he is now. And someday, when *you're* bigger—but not *too* big—and when Benny's old enough to be a man, we'll do all this for real. And the words you say will give you Blue's power when you cut his neck. And then your job is to give the power to Benny. He can't know what we're up to—it has to be a surprise present. And then all that power you've saved up will help make him the biggest man in the whole wide world, and he won't have had to hurt his soul to do it."

"Will he be giant big?"

"Giant big, for sure!" Lake stood up and went over to a worktable on which a polished music box sat. He lifted the lid, and "The Twelve Days of Christmas" began to chime through the basement.

"Benny fav'rite song!" Cooper hopped up and down, excited.

"Yes it is! Now, go get Raggedy Andy and show me what a good little brother you are . . ."

I stepped away from the window. Jesus H. Christ. Lake had hatched a plan to turn Cooper into some kind of living magic battery, training him to perform black magic death rituals to absorb his younger brothers' magical powers. What kind of twisted freak would think up something like that?

I went to the next window.

Siobhan was weeping in the corner of one of the upstairs bedrooms, wailing "Oh baby Blue . . ."

Lake came in with little Blue, now locked in an enchanted sleep, as still and beautiful as a china doll. "Stop your crying, woman, he's not hurt, he's just asleep. I'd never let anything bad happen to the little guy until it's time to kill him!"

I flinched and moved along.

Corvus was in the bottom of the pit, staring up at Lake, his eyes red from weeping.

"You crazy fuck," Corvus sobbed.

"Can't have you trying to run away again." Lake impassively threw down a hacksaw and two lengths of rubber hose. "I want those legs off above the knee. And trust me, you don't want me to come down there and do it myself."

I fled the window and went to the next.

Lake led his nearly catatonic wife into a bathroom and pulled off her filthy dress. Her emaciated body was covered in sores.

"Hate to have to do things this way," he told her cheerfully, "but I don't have much choice now that Corvus up and died on us, do I? There's got to be a seventh son, or the spell won't work. So I've got to do my husbandly duty for a change."

I moved on again.

Cooper was six or seven years old, sobbing into his pillow. He lay on a single bed inside an eight-by-eight-foot chain-link dog pen in the corner of the basement. His cinder-block walls were bare.

"It's not right; I don't want to hurt them," the boy wept.

"You'll do as I tell you, or I'll have to kill your mother," Lake replied, standing somewhere in the shadows beyond the boy's locked pen door. "And you don't want that, do you?"

"N-no."

"It's bad enough I had to put you in here to keep you from running off." Lake stepped into the light, shaking his head. "Like father, like son, I guess."

"I see him at night. My father. He's mad about what you want me to do to my brothers."

"Well, of course he is, dumb-ass!"

"Can't we bury him proper? He don't like the freezer."

"I don't care what he likes or doesn't like." Lake was finally sounding angry, and I could feel Cooper's fear intensify. "Shut up and do as you're told. All this will be over soon."

This scene, unlike the others, did not go black; it simply looped, an unending scene of misery for the boy. After a few minutes of watching, feeling profoundly sad for the child and more and more furious he'd been put to such a monstrous task, I moved on to the final window.

Cooper, just a bit older, was on the sacrifice floor. He was kneeling, staring down at the body of a baby who looked to be about nine months old. A sword-and-shield pendant—the one the Warlock had given me—was almost unrecognizable under the baby's blood. The old music box tinkled the hateful Christmas carol. Lake stood nearby, arms crossed over his chest, looking satisfied. Siobhan lay dead at his feet;

a short distance away four infant brothers lay still and beautiful in their enchanted sleep.

Cooper's eyes filled with tears, his jaw working wordlessly. Something was building inside him, something dark and far too strong for such a little body to hold.

"Good work," said Lake, who apparently couldn't sense the growing danger I felt. "One down, four to go. Benny will be home tomorrow, and you'll never have to do this again. When he gets here, you attack me like I told you, and Benny will save me. He'll have to kill you to do it, but by now you're okay with that, aren't you, boy? The dead don't have bad dreams.

"And my son will be a big, brave hero doing good by saving his loving daddy from his crazy half brother, so he'll inherit all the power you've saved for him without any of the ghosts. He'll get the best birthday present a father could ever give a son."

Cooper dropped the knife, threw his head back, and howled. Lake clamped his hands over his ears and fell to his knees. A hot rose bloomed in Cooper's chest, exploded outward with a storm force that blew the boards off the floor above them. The blast threw Lake into the cinder-block wall; he fell in a broken heap onto the concrete.

When the dust cleared, Cooper touched his little brother's slashed neck, and the wound sealed. The baby's eyes fluttered open. Looking stunned, Cooper carefully lifted him to his shoulder.

"I'm sorry, I'm so sorry," Cooper whispered to him, awkwardly patting his back. "I didn't mean it, I never wanted to hurt you, I'll take good care of you always like Momma told me to . . ."

The boy carried the baby up the smoking stairs toward the bright light of the open front door.

A living shadow seeped out of the walls, touched the bodies of Lake and Siobhan and the four sleeping children, then drew them all into its darkness.

The windows went black, all but the loop of young Cooper weeping in his bedroom. I went back to that window and blinked through several gemviews.

In one, Cooper was an adult curled on the tiny bed, holding his head in his hands and shivering.

I was elated. Cooper was really in there, and it looked like he was still alive. I banged on the glass with the palm of my hand.

"Cooper! It's me, Jessie . . . get up! I'm here for you!"

He didn't seem to hear me, or if he did, he was too far gone to respond.

I beat the window with the pommel of my sword, hoping I could shatter the glass. It wouldn't even crack. "Cooper, snap out of it! We've got to get out of here!"

The hallway shuddered like a living thing. The bare bulbs flicked out for a moment, and when they came back on the ceiling was impossibly high, the candles distant stars, and a huge oak door that looked like the entrance to a giant's castle had sprung up where the stairway had been.

The door swung open, and King Lake stepped inside, monstrous and dark in leather armor and sable robes. He was twice my height, at least, as big to me as he'd surely seemed to toddler Blue. He carried an executioner's ax, the rust-mottled head almost as big as my shield.

"My hospitality not good enough for you?" Lake

rumbled. "You've got some nerve snooping around where you don't belong. Maybe your daddy couldn't teach you proper manners, but I sure can."

Lake crossed the hall impossibly quickly for something of his size, and I barely had time to raise my shield as his ax came down. The clang of steel on bronze made my ears ring. The shield held, but the blow knocked me sideways into the wood-paneled wall.

I leaped to my feet and stabbed Lake hard as I could through his leather trousers into his thigh, right where his femoral artery ought to be. But it was like sticking my sword in a sawdust-filled dummy. No blood, no pain, no reaction.

My sword stuck fast in his leg, he pivoted sideways, jerking the weapon out of my hand. Another swing, the ax coming down at the back of my neck fast and hard. I ducked. His blow caught the rivets on the rear edge of my helmet and knocked it clattering across the stone floor.

Immediately, the air felt cold and suffocating in my throat. I scrambled forward to retrieve my helmet, realizing there was almost no place for me to go, no way to escape. It was a mistake to fight Lake, but he'd come at me so *fast*. If I could get back to his polite version, would he stop his attack? Or was the refuge of that vision lost to me now that I'd fought back?

I dodged another blow from Lake as I snatched up my helmet and slapped it back on my head. Relieved to be able to breathe again, I began to blink back through gemviews—and stopped on one of the strange, dark views that had made no sense to me before, but now that I looked around at Lake and the hallway through it, I realized I was seeing *inside* things, seeing the strange geometries that formed this place, and this place wasn't a place at all, these walls weren't made of wood, they weren't made of *anything,* and giant King Lake with his ax was no more substantial than a doll made from dreams.

The Lake-doll swung his filmy ax at me again. I took a deep breath and blew at him as hard as I could. He flickered like a candle flame and puffed out, wisping away like a bad smell, but my sword fell solidly to the floor at my feet.

I saw the sword now for what it was: an instrument of vengeance imbued with spilled magical energy from the Warlock's death ritual and the power of a mother's fear. My stone eye itched, and I blinked to the ghost-view. In the mirror of the blade, I saw Siobhan's last rational act: She blessed the pendant and put it on Blue's neck before he was taken to the basement, hoping it would save him, but her magic didn't work as she'd hoped. Lake, to mock her and her failed spell, put it on the necks of the other babies he put into enchanted sleep, and then finally on the infant Warlock, perhaps intending to eventually give the pendant to his beloved firstborn son, if he intended anything at all.

My mind turned over everything I'd seen in the basement, letting the scenes flash before me like facets in a cursed gemstone. Reggie's strange transformation, Cooper's unrelenting anguish, Lake's monstrous acts . . . and here in the hell, Blue's demon and the adults' compulsion to repeat the horrors of the past. I'd thought at first that Lake's hateful spirit was the driving force in this dimension, that he was the one compelling the others to relive their worst experiences over and over. But now I realized Lake's spirit was so degraded there was practically nothing left of it. He was just a shadow puppet, empty of soul or will, and perhaps he'd been one long before he died.

What, then, was the hand guiding Lake's inhuman cruelty?

I blinked back to the architecture view and looked around me, seeing through the illusion of the walls. Cooper lay nearby, curled in a fetal ball, shivering in the throes of whatever nightmare plagued his senses. He was tormented and insensible, but solid and quite real. In the background were four child-like shapes, just as solid as he was: the enchanted brothers shining brightly, still alive. In the distance I saw three other spirits, weak and flickery: Corvus, Siobhan, and Reggie, dead but still with hope of escaping to the great beyond.

One of the child-shapes turned in my direction: "Do you see?" It was Blue's soft, papery voice.

I looked up past the hazy illusion of the house and saw the dark sponge-creatures swarming outside, solid and real.

"Where's your mother?" I whispered to them.

Instinct told me to look down, and when I saw the grotesque monstrosity there, I almost jumped. A corpulent *thing* was lolling beneath the floor, a vast, flaccid version of the little monsters I'd seen at the window, a tooth-pored black sponge as big as the hell itself.

My brain finally dredged up information from the diabology class I dropped my freshman year. The huge creature was an algophage, a Goad, a thing that fed on negative spiritual energy, a parasitic devil that drove other creatures into violence and sadism. If the hell was a kind of web, the Goad was the fat spider right in the middle of it.

Siobhan's wispy spirit flickered at me; she was trapped where she was, but it seemed that she was trying to get my attention. I blinked to the ghost-view. I saw Lake confront her over her lonely dalliance with Corvus, a lover's argument simple and common as the hills. It should have just caused tears and angry words, a few resentful months the couple's love could overcome. But the hungry Goad was in the woods nearby and felt their savory pain. It smelled the seed of darkness in Lake, tasted arrogance and a potential for hard violence he'd never acknowledged to himself, a potential the Goad could cultivate and exploit. I watched the Goad squeeze itself into a crack in the home's foundation, creep up between the spaces in their walls, poisoning the air, damping their magic, infecting Lake's brain with malignant madness.

"I see you," I told the Goad, blinking back to the architectural view. "And I see what you've done. You can't fool me anymore."

The vast thing rippled, angry. "What do you want?"

"I want you to let these souls go."

The Goad bucked beneath my feet as if it was trying to shake me off. "This is my hell. I made it! Get your own if you want one, mongrel!"

I did not flinch at its rage, nor wonder what it meant by its epithet. My mind, for once, was perfectly focused on what I knew I had to do. "Let them go, or I exterminate you and your children like the nasty little tapeworms you are."

The Goad let out a noise that might have been a laugh. "Destroy *us*? Impossible."

"Remember that I offered you mercy," I said, snatching up Siobhan's sword and slashing the point into the Goad's body. It felt like cutting into greasy mud, and the open wound steamed like a volcanic vent.

The Goad shrieked, and from the corner of my eye I saw its larvae diving down to protect their mother. I pulled the sword from the gritty, oily flesh and swung it in a wide arc into the first wave of goadlets as I hammered others with my shield. The nasty little monsters popped like flies on a windshield.

Slashing and swatting, I sidestepped through insubstantial walls across the bucking Goad to the spot where Cooper lay surrounded by his brothers. I'd killed enough of the larvae that the others were hanging back, hovering uncertainly. Apparently they weren't quite as mindless as they'd first seemed.

"Honey, *wake up*!" I yelled at Cooper, as loud as I could. "I know it hurts, but you're not a child anymore! It's not *real* anymore! I need your help to get us out of here!"

His eyes opened slowly, glistening with tears.

"I wanted them to live," he whispered.

"They're still alive! Get up and hold on to me!"

Cooper wasn't immediately able to get up farther than onto his knees, but he reached out and grabbed my leg. I flung my shield into the thickest part of the larvae swarm and used both hands to drive the point of the sword deep into the Goad, carving the blade back and forth to try to get to the devil's heart.

And I saw it: a red-orange lump of pulsing magma, a burning lava auricle. I grabbed Cooper's wrist with my right hand as I plunged my left deep into the Goad's heart.

The devil screamed as I plugged myself directly into the source of its dark power, and it hummed through me, stronger than a lightning strike. The monster had been feeding off human pain for thousands of years. I felt the spells the creature used to keep magic and the real world at bay, the spells that kept the hell running as a well-oiled agony factory. My stone eye showed me the devil's machinations inside and out.

The stink of the Goad's flesh and my burning dragonskin glove filled my nostrils. My heart-bound hand was in nerve-rending, fiery agony, but I knew I was no longer affected by the Goad's magical suppression. No amount of physical pain could stop me now. I began to chant the ancient words to turn off the spells, one by one. The whole dimension wracked with tremors as it began to collapse.

Still chanting, I filtered the Goad's power into Cooper. He sucked in his breath as the magical current coursed through him.

Figure it out, I thought, hoping that on some level he could hear me. *Help your brothers. You can do it. You've lived your whole life needing to do this— don't fail them now.*

Cooper began to chant, a clear, powerful spell of life and love and forgiveness, a spell he could only have begun now that I was there to help and protect him. The brothers clustered close to him, drinking the power I fed him.

The goadlets suffocated and shriveled as the hell disintegrated around them. I dug my hand deeper into the flaming heart, simultaneously trying to crush it and suck the last of the power from the dying monster.

The vast bulk of the steaming Goad began to contract in on itself like a foul sun turning dwarf, growing hotter and hotter, the pain singing in my hand and arm more than I could imagine. It felt as if the devil's heart was being crushed into my bones. I wasn't sure I could draw my hand away even if I wanted to.

Cooper was drawing power fast, and so were the brothers, glowing children of light awakening and condensing into pale delicate flesh. He reached out to them, and they took hold of his arm.

I could see holes opening in the sky; the adult spirits wisped away to whatever lay beyond. Any moment now, the hell would collapse completely and we'd be crushed. Still gripping Cooper's hand, I gave my trapped arm a mighty pull and finally jerked it free. I stuck my freed hand inside my dragonskin jacket and found one of the Warlock's dirt-filled vials.

"Return!" I shouted as I snapped the glass.

chapter twenty-three

Palimpsest: Easy as Peanut Butter

My jaws closed on Deputy Wilson's neck; I gave the man a hard shake and felt his spine break with a satisfying crunch. I tossed Wilson's body aside and stared up at Rosko astride the irritable firedrake. Rosko shrugged, gave me an exaggerated salute, and reined the drake away across the sky.

The Warlock lay trussed on the grass beside Mother Karen, Jimmy, and Ginger. Out across the field in the ruined basement, Oakbrown, Paulie, and Mariette were reading scrolls to permanently close the portal. Jordan's other man Bruce was running toward a brown Jeep partially hidden in the trees. I wondered if Bruce was going to call for reinforcements, or if he was going to teleport away and set off the VHDN bomb he'd left in the Warlock's vehicle.

I couldn't risk the bomb going off, but I also couldn't risk the Talents shutting Jessie's portal. I searched Wilson's pockets until I found the handcuff keys, then loped over to the Warlock. The others stepped back, looking scared as I approached and freed Cooper's brother from his bonds.

The Warlock unbuckled the ball gag and tossed it into the bushes, working his jaw and spitting on the grass. "Man, I never thought I'd be this glad to see a face as ugly as yours."

I jabbed a clawed finger toward the basement, then tapped my wrist as if I were wearing a watch.

"Yeah. I'll go stop them," the Warlock said, seeming to understand my pantomime. "Karen, Jimmy, come with me—Jessie and Cooper will probably need your help if they can get back at all."

"What should I do?" Ginger was staring at me, her voice a nervous quaver.

"Go with Spiderboy; he might need your help if any more of Jordan's goon squad shows up. Just . . . try to be useful, okay?" The Warlock turned away from her and hurried across the dead field, hollering "Knock it off, guys, stop the spell!"

I loped back to the Warlock's Land Rover and pulled out the VHDN explosive Bruce had planted. The black metal eyeball weighed about three pounds and fit in the palm of my hand. It had no obvious seams or any apparent fuse that could be separated from the rest of the device.

Ginger ran up beside me. "Is that a bomb?"

I nodded.

"Can you defuse it?"

I made my best approximation of a shrug. It's difficult if you don't really have shoulders.

"Let me look," she said, then blushed slightly. "I, um, made some of these in high school. Little ones, I mean. I had *nothing* to do with that nun who got blown up at the Catholic school across from my house—that was totally that Lautermilk kid's fault. Uh. Sorry. I babble a little when I'm nervous. You're, um, kinda big and scary and stuff."

I put the bomb in her outstretched hands. Ginger bit her lip, frowning as she inspected the bomb's smooth body. She ran her finger over one spot on the case that to me looked identical to every other spot on the case, and pressed. A fuse popped out of the pupil.

"See? Easy as peanut butter." Ginger pulled the fuse out and tossed it into a nearby shrub.

Not sure how to thank her, I gave her a gentle pat on the head. I steeled myself to cross the dead field, and ran to join the Warlock and the others at the basement.

Halfway across, I felt the ground ripple, the air turn icy. The door to Cooper's hell was opening; I hoped that meant that Jessie was coming back.

chapter twenty-four

Jessie's Return

The return through the portal was fast and brutal. One moment I was crushed against Cooper at the heart of a roaring cold vortex, and the next I was flung forward onto my hands and knees on the dirty concrete floor. For one brief, wonderful moment, I thought my left hand had been magically restored. Then dead leaves smoked and caught flame around my fingers, and in the same moment my hand and forearm burst into a bright lava glow, the glow of the slain devil's heart.

I rocked back onto my knees. My left was looking less and less like a hand, the fingers subliming into twisting tongues of red and purple plasma. The arm of my dragonskin jacket had retreated to the scarred stump where my true flesh began, but the cuff was smoking, my flesh blackening. There wasn't any pain, not really, but a strong buzzing heat was moving through me, and every heartbeat sent a dark tormented flash through my mind, an image of the evil the Goad had wrought upon its countless victims in the hundreds of hells it had nested in and sucked dry.

It took me a moment to realize that some of the noises I was hearing weren't just inside my head. I looked behind me, and saw the naked forms of Cooper and three very-much-alive squalling infants lying beside the pit wall. Cooper wasn't moving, wasn't even obviously breathing. A blond, blue-eyed toddler stood beside him, the boy's face impassive and curious.

I scrambled over to Cooper and yanked my surviving right glove off with my teeth—discovering too late that the glove and my dragonskins were spattered with the Goad's foul, bitter black ichor—and checked the pulse at his neck. He took a ragged breath and moaned a little at my touch, but did not awaken. I brushed his curly hair away from his forehead and felt along his scalp and neck for injuries. Superficially, at least, he seemed unhurt.

"Jessie?" Pal's voice was strangely distorted.

I looked up. Standing at the top of the cinder-block wall was a huge, shaggy monster with an eight-legged body vaguely like that of a spider. Valved spiracles ran in double rows on the underside of its black, chitinous abdomen. It had a four-eyed head that reminded me of a saber-toothed tiger by way of a mescaline hallucination. But its fur bore the rough coloring of a ferret.

I blinked hard several times, my stone eye shuttering through several unhelpful views, hoping that what I was seeing was a hallucination and it was all just a matter of getting my head clear of the Goad's psychic poison. But the monster at the edge of the basement wall didn't change one tiny bit.

"Jesus," I croaked, my throat aching like I hadn't attempted speech in years. "Pal, is that you?"

The monster nodded. "I'm afraid so."

Mother Karen appeared next to Pal, looking refreshingly just the way she ought to look. She gaped at me and the others.

"Oh my goodness," exclaimed Mother Karen, hurrying down the steps toward the infants. "Who are these babies?"

"They're . . . Cooper's little brothers," I replied, squinting up at the horizon as I realized I was hearing the distant flap of leathery wings.

A dozen armored dragons with human riders were flying toward the field. More enforcers from the governing circle. They were perhaps three or four minutes away.

An image burst through my attempts to keep it down: A dragon writhed, shrieking, impaled on huge stakes above a burning field. Goadlets gnawed on its flesh. I felt my knees go rubbery, and my left arm glowed hot. What had I absorbed from that monster?

"Are you okay?"

I realized I had doubled over, and Mother Karen was peering at me, concerned.

"I'm fine," I lied through gritted teeth. "This . . . it's all . . . long story. Dragons. Gotta take care of that."

I forced myself to stand up straight. My arm was blazing now, flames crackling like a tree in a wildfire, and I was feeling real pain deep in the bones of my upper arm and shoulder. Part of the Goad's lava heart had stuck to my flesh, and was devouring me. I didn't know how much time I might have left.

Karen had picked up one of the infants and was rocking him in her arms, trying to quiet and comfort him. "These babies—"

"Take care of 'em. Lots of love. Gotta leave now."

I marched myself up the stairs, and Pal stilted around to meet me.

"Are you okay?" he asked in that weird voice of his.

Oh Lord, I'm not even close to okay, I thought

back, afraid I might start screaming if I tried to speak. *I think I'm dying. But Cooper's alive. I got him out. Him and his brothers. Fucking Jordan left them there. He knew they were in there, but he just left them there.*

"What happened to them all? What happened to Cooper? Where did those children come from?" Pal asked me.

Do you really want to know?

He paused, blinked, then nodded.

Trying to describe what had happened seemed impossible; there wasn't time, and I simply didn't have the words. The dark images were coming too hard and too fast to suppress. They crowded every edge of my consciousness like the goadlets crowding at the farmhouse window. I raised my blazing hand, whispered an old word for "relic," and released a single memory the Goad had taken from Corvus. It emerged as a tiny curl of blue plasma that floated toward Pal, settled on his forehead, and disappeared.

Pal stumbled backward, flinching, shaking his fearsome head as if he'd been stung. He fell, retching. While part of me sympathized with his revulsion, the rest wished I could've passed off a larger memory, and with it greater relief from the hideous pressure in my mind.

It was an algophage, I thought to him. *And I heart-jacked the fucker before I killed it so we could use its energy to free Cooper's little brothers and give them the life they deserved.*

The dragons were visible now, great red beasts with bronze armor, their hide-clad riders armed with magic staves, shotguns, and grenade launchers. Clearly they'd armed themselves to thoroughly annihilate any fell beasts and foul demons that the governing circle had supposed might have emerged from Cooper's hell.

I took a deep breath, intending to shout up at them that there were children down here, dammit, they needed to back off and let me explain, but instead what came out was a long string of angry expletives. Unable to stop myself, I shouted hair-curling English curses that morphed into inhuman Goadspeak as the men on the dragons started taking aim with their weapons and before I knew it I'd raised the burning hand.

The words wouldn't stop coming, and the diabolic energy I'd absorbed from the Goad was coming with them. Purple globes of plasma exploded from the palm of my distorted hand toward the men and burst around them like fireworks. Burning memories of torment showered down on them. The men and dragons at the periphery scattered, fleeing, and those hit worst vainly fought the empty air, shrieking with madness, their sophisticated weapons and mission forgotten.

I felt a brief bit of relief before more horrors swarmed up inside my mind to replace what I'd cast off. Was there no end to them?

A bright crack rent the sky above me, and a lightning-framed hole began to open. A crystalline Virtus as wide as an Olympic swimming pool began to descend.

"Sweet Goddess, can this get worse? We've got to get out of here," Pal said, coming up behind me and tugging at my jacket.

"No. I don't think I'm leaving," I heard myself say, pulling away from his strong grip.

The Virtus's cold diamond eyes fixed on me. "You

have disobeyed our orders," it boomed. "You have violated the prohibition against grand necromancy. You and all who emerged with you from the algophage dimension shall be expunged."

"Wait," I shouted. "Mr. Jordan—"

"Nothing you have to say is relevant."

The cold dismissal shocked me to the soles of my feet. It took me a moment to find my voice. "But he's been tricking you! He's why this happened!"

"His past actions are of no present concern to us."

"How can you fucking say that?" I screamed at the Virtus. The blood was humming in my ears.

The Virtus responded by hurling a bright plasma tentacle straight at my head, fast as a bullet. There was no time to duck. No time to run. I acted on instinct and raised my left hand.

The tentacle connected with my fiery palm in a shower of sparks, slipped off, lancing toward my heart. I grabbed the Virtus's sting and whipped it around my forearm. The sparks were a bright blue fountain, hot and cold at the same time, and I had to shield my face with my right arm to keep from being blinded. My dragonskin jacket was smoking under the cascade. Not knowing what else to do, I yanked the tentacle as hard as I could.

The Virtus jerked me high into the air. I held on for dear life.

"What happened here matters!" I screamed as it tried to fling me off onto the ground. "Jordan was supposed to help—"

"Jordan has kept order." The Virtus's booming voice seemed to be all around me. "Or he did until you interfered. You are disorder. And I shall expunge you. That is all that should matter to *you* now."

No. I'd make this cold-blooded spirit of the air acknowledge the injustice Jordan had perpetuated on his own family if it was the last thing I ever did. I chanced a glance upward—the Virtus's pulsing magma heart loomed above me, big as my car.

A part of me was chilled to realize the core similarity between our supposed guardian spirits and the Goad I'd killed. The rest of me had no time to wonder. I began to chant. Released my grip on the tentacle and began to pound the worst of the memories straight into the spirit's core.

I was falling back, straight toward the ground, but I kept hammering the Virtus with the vile energy I was desperate to be rid of. The spirit was too pitiless to feel the primal horror any human would feel, but I could see it stilled, shuddering. Too bad I was about to hit the ground and get splattered all across the field—I was sure I was close to making a real impression on the imperious bastard.

Somewhere below me, a creaky, out-of-tune organ started playing a weird melody.

The tiny hairs on my skin rose at the touch of friendly magic. My fall slowed, stopped, and then I began to rise back toward the Virtus, buoyed on the calliope charm.

"What worked on the Goad might work on a Virtus," Pal told me. "Don't hesitate, or we're all dead."

I rose to meet its heart and plunged my left hand inside. The jolt threatened to knock my teeth right out of their sockets, and the Virtus made a noise like two freight trains colliding at full speed.

My head was flooded with alien mathematics, cold equations it might take me a hundred years to comprehend, the technomancy of true future divination and probability. I could grasp just a tiny drop of the fire-hose blast of image and information. It was baffling and exhilarating, awful and wonderful. So many worlds, so many futures, and humankind lay close to the center, Talented primitives the Virtii feared as much as they were capable of fearing anything. But the Virtii had been given a holy task as shepherds, so they'd reluctantly resisted wiping out Talented humanity. All the restrictions, all the interference—the Virtii were managing their own risk while adhering to the letter of their ancient duty to help the naked apes rise past the squalor of their origins.

But who ruled the Virtii? I still couldn't see.

And in there was a different kind of fear. A fear specifically concerning *me,* a fear they'd held long before Cooper had ever been sucked back into the family hell.

I tried to explore further, but the mortally wounded Virtus twisted away from me. It tumbled Earthward, threatening to yank me down in its wake.

Pal's tune strengthened, pulled me safely away.

I watched as the giant living orrery crashed onto the field, its diamond eyes cracking, its punctured heart steaming on the dry ground. Its power still tingled inside my flames, a live current connecting me to the last of the life inside its body. I concentrated, raised my hand, twitched my fingers. The remains of the Virtus rose a few feet from the ground, reassembled into disjointed orbitals, danced in response to my movements.

Then I lost my concentration, and the Virtus's corpse collapsed again, dissolving into glowing mathematical mist that evaporated into the sunset sky.

"Did you just do what I think you just did?" Pal

asked as he sang me down to stand beside him on the grass. "Did you just make the Virtus your . . . your *puppet*?"

"Well . . . yeah. I guess I did."

The flood of logic from the Virtus had illuminated every dark corner of my mind in an icy perspective. The horrors the Goad had left behind were scorpions trapped in amber, twisted specimens preserved in jars. I could hold them up to the light to examine them, or push them to the back of my brain and ignore them. They'd been rendered inert, but I knew they'd come alive if I broke them from their cold shells. They were *my* weapons now.

I looked down at my flame hand and forearm. The fire had stabilized, no longer scorched my dragon-skins, no longer threatened to consume the rest of my flesh.

But my own fury at what had been done to me, Cooper, and the children had not diminished. Not even a little.

"Humans shouldn't have that kind of power," Pal said, sounding amazed and a little afraid.

With my right hand, I absently rubbed the scaly scars beneath my stone eye. Remembered how the Goad had called me a mongrel. "Maybe I'm not as human as I thought. The Virtus . . . I could feel it was worried about Cooper and me both. Worried about what we might do."

"And oh look, you killed it." Pal's telepathic voice was tight with near hysteria. "So I think its fears were rather well founded, weren't they?"

"So I killed it. Big deal. Surely sorcerers get off lucky shots every now and then, right?"

"Actually, no. This is the first I've heard of any

mortal creature seriously damaging a Virtus, much less killing one."

"Oh." I looked back across the field. Mother Karen and the Warlock had brought the survivors up from the basement. Karen and a couple of people I remembered seeing around the Warlock's bar held babies and toddler Blue. The Warlock and a guy in fringed boots were carrying Cooper, who hung limply between them, apparently still unconscious. All the Talents were staring at me and Pal with mixed expressions of shock, awe, admiration, and fear.

"Are the Virtii going to come after me in force?" I asked Pal.

"It's possible, but honestly I don't know what they're likely to do," he replied. "And so I don't know what *we* should do."

"Well, crap." I looked down at my boots.

Mr. Jordan's parchment and quill lay by my feet.

I burst out laughing.

"What?" asked Pal.

"Oopsie. We let my anti-anathema spell run out," I giggled, pointing at the magical contract. I blinked to the gemview that had shown me the architecture of Cooper's hell. Subtle enchantments swirled around the document. "What kind of dumb legal magic keeps on going after it's been rendered completely pointless? Or do you think that if I sign this, he'll call off the dogs? Better late than never, right?"

I knelt, picked up the quill with my right hand, and wrote "Go screw yourself" in neat cursive on the blank signature line. My writing disappeared. It was replaced briefly with the words VALID SIGNATURE REQUIRED, and then the space went blank again.

"If you insist," I said, signing my name, then

snatching up the contract and crushing it into my flame palm.

"What on Earth are you doing?" Pal asked.

"I think this thing's gonna phone home," I said. Staring through my stone eye at the burning contract, I whispered an ancient word for "trace." I got a flash of Jordan in his fancy library, sitting at a mahogany desk flanked by bookshelves and antique suits of armor. It was his mansion in Bexley, the ritzy part of the city people like me didn't get invited to very often. I'd never been there, but I knew I could follow the enchantment back to its source.

"Hey! Karen, Warlock!" I yelled. "Are you guys okay to get everyone back to the city?"

"I think so," Mother Karen called back. Her voice shook. "What—what are you going to do now?"

I waved the quill pen at her. "I think Mr. Jordan and I need to have another little chat."

I turned to Pal. "They're gonna need the Land Rover. Do you know a flying tune?"

Pal nodded.

"Got enough juice to get us back to the city?" I asked.

"I think so," he replied.

Pal knelt, and I climbed up onto his shaggy thorax, eventually finding a comfortable seat between the crests of two vertebrae. He began to sing a new melody, flexed his legs, and leaped into the sky.

chapter twenty-five

A Little Chat

I rode Pal toward the sunset, my hair blowing in the wind, my heart thrilling at the feeling of being aloft above the world. The flight would have been great fun except that I was gritting my teeth, expecting a whole host of Virtii to descend on us at any moment. But none came, so halfway back to Columbus, I began to relax a bit. And then I started to sense that other creatures in the air were pacing us. But the others, whatever they were, didn't approach. I suspected they might be more men on dragons, hidden behind an invisibility spell.

Invisibility.

"Oh crap, the mundanes can totally see us up here," I shouted to Pal as we began to descend toward Bexley.

"I can't do more than one spell at a time," he replied. "You'll have to take care of that one."

I imagined the people below sitting on their front porches, enjoying the evening breeze, sipping sweet lemonade or perhaps frothy cold beer. And then they'd look up to see a woman with a flame arm flying through the air on a giant spider monster. Would they point and scream? Dial the cops and the TV stations? Decide to switch to O'Doul's?

Or maybe they'd just give them a passing glance

and mistake spider and rider for a weather balloon in the dimming light.

"Oh, the hell with it," I told Pal. "They can see us if they want to. Screw the rules."

Screw Jordan, too. I hadn't decided what I was going to do when I finally saw him, mainly because I was trying to think of him as little as possible. The merest memory of his patronizing smile infuriated me. And then the fire of my arm flared bright, and I had to hold it above my head to keep from scorching Pal's fur. The Statue of Liberty impression made my much-abused shoulder ache, so I was doing my best to think about other things. Like what I was going to do if Pal and I ever had to deal with more than one Virtus.

Following the trail of the tracking spell, I directed Pal down onto a round, pavestone courtyard before a plantation-style brick manor with a wide, white-pillared front porch. An elderly man in white gloves and a dark suit—a mundane by the feel of him—stood on the porch. Behind him were red double doors with twin brass Egyptian lions set into them.

"You are Miss Shimmer?" the man asked as I dismounted. He had a proper British accent. It figured that a guy like Jordan would import his own butler. Elitist son of a bitch. My arm flared up along with my anger.

"Where's the rest of Jordan's . . . crew?" I asked, trying to stay calm, trying to minimize the flames crackling against my sleeve.

"Master Jordan's associates have retired for the evening; in anticipation of your visit, he has sent his wife and children to stay with friends. I do not know their location, so I cannot reveal it, no matter how much . . . duress I might be put under."

His tone took me aback. What kind of a monster did this guy take me for? I looked down at my ichor-spattered leathers and sighed. "I didn't come here to hurt you. Where is Jordan?"

"Mr. Jordan is waiting for you in his library. If you will please follow me? I'm afraid your . . . companion won't fit through the doorway."

I looked up at Pal. *Are you okay staying out here?*

"I'll be fine, but will *you* be okay?"

I bit my lip and tugged at the chin strap on my helmet. *I might need backup, depending on what happens. Can you—*

"I'll know where you are. If you need me, I'll be there right away. I'll break through the roof if I have to."

Okay. I stepped toward the butler. "Let's go."

The old gentleman led me into the airy, chandeliered foyer. "Would you care for refreshment? I recently made the master a pitcher of sangria."

"No, thank you," I said, warily looking around as he led me through a hallway. I'd fully expected to find a small army guarding the house. But if word had gotten back that I'd killed a Virtus . . . well, at least Jordan cared about *some* of his own family. I was appalled that he apparently thought I might hurt one of his kids to get back at him, but that just went to show what a small-minded creep he really was. He sure as fuck wasn't above letting innocent children suffer if it suited *him*.

My arm blazed and almost caught a nearby tapestry on fire. Crap. I took a series of deep breaths to calm down. He'd *expect* me to trash his place, because he'd done the same to me. Not that setting the mansion on fire wouldn't be viscerally satisfying, but in the end I thought that perhaps taking the high road might help me sleep a bit better. Maybe.

"Master Jordan awaits you inside," the butler said, opening a set of French doors that led into the large, wood-paneled library I'd seen in the brief vision from the burning contract.

I stepped inside. Jordan was sitting very still behind his desk at the far end of the room, his back to the window. His hands were flat on the desk in front of him.

"Hello, Miss Shimmer." He gave me what I guessed must be the best of the swell-guy smiles he'd practiced on countless judges and juries.

I glared at him. "Hello, *Benny.*"

"I'm pleased to see you've survived your recent adventures."

"Pleased, my rosy pink ass." I stalked toward his desk, gratified that the arm was staying under control, at least so far. "I'm surprised you're still here."

"After all that's happened, I thought I should see you. Privately."

"How thoughtful," I replied. "But really you should've come to the farmhouse like a man instead of sending your dragon riders and the Virtus. Wouldn't have had to kill the poor thing, you know?"

"The Virtus attacked you of its own accord. I had no control over its actions." He paused and took a deep breath. "I admit that I have handled things poorly. I was acting on information and advice that has turned out to be gravely inaccurate. I would like to . . . make amends for all you've suffered these past few weeks."

"Amends? That's a laugh." My glare deepened to a scowl. "But please, go ahead, tell me how you think you could possibly make up for all you've done. I might be amused."

"First, all charges against you and Cooper Marron will be dropped. I guarantee that neither of you will suffer any criminal or civil consequences, because we recognize that you felt you had no choice but to act as you did."

"What about the Virtii? Are they agreeing to this?"

"They will take some convincing, but I'm sure I can bring them around."

He flashed the swell-guy smile again, and the rage rose up inside me. My arm flamed, and I didn't try to stop it. "You'll have to do *much* better than that."

Jordan didn't miss a beat. "We will bring in the best magical healers to cure you of that unfortunate curse you've picked up," he nodded toward my flame hand, "and restore your body to normal."

"I suppose that's a better start, but only a start," I said.

"All confiscated property will be returned in perfect working order, and all your damaged property will be replaced. You'll be awarded extensive experiential credit toward your degree," he said. "And to compensate for the unpleasantness with your apartment and the destruction of the shack in the woods, we have located a very nice town house in the Short North that you can stay in as long as you like. Rent-free."

"So what about that job you got me fired from?"

He didn't even blink. "Because you've demonstrated you're a Talent of unusual creativity, intelligence, and power, I'd like to offer you a position on the circle's paranormal defense team. You'll help protect the mundane population from demons, werewolves, vampires, and other malevolent entities.

"What do you think of my offer?" he finished.

"Wow. It's like Christmas in July," I said. "But what about your brothers?"

Jordan paused. "Cooper, of course, will receive the same excellent healer care and counseling that you do. And of course he will benefit from the property compensations, and if he wants a job I will certainly do my best to locate a suitable position for him. As for the Warlock . . . well, any financial losses he suffered as a result of his bar being closed will be more than compensated for."

"I meant your *other* brothers."

A shadow of fear flickered across his face before it returned to his normal placid expression. "I'm afraid there's nothing anyone can do for souls trapped in a hell."

I felt weirdly elated. He didn't know I'd brought back the babies! Either his dragon squad had been too freaked out to relay that bit of information to Jordan, or they hadn't seen the kids at all.

"Liar," I growled, pointing at him with my roaring fiery hand. "You're a lousy chickenshit liar."

His eyes widened ever so slightly. Was that sweat I saw on his forehead?

"What?" he asked, sounding utterly calm. Breezy, even.

"You know good goddamn well that you could've gone in there yourself and brought them back to Earth. But it was so much *easier* just to cover it all up and pretend it didn't happen, wasn't it? You gutless jackass. You left those kids in there to suffer, and you could have saved them."

Jordan's façade broke, and for the first time I saw real fear in his eyes. Fear of *me*. "I didn't have anything to do with what happened! I . . . I didn't know my father was . . . was doing those things. I *didn't know*! There was *nothing* I could have done to fix what happened."

"You dickless coward. You've had every day of your life since you became a big-shot wizard to make things right for those kids. And when I stepped up to the plate, you could have grown some balls and helped me out, but no. You just tried to shut me down. And you couldn't even do *that* right, could you?"

"I tried to stop you for your own good. For God's sake, just look what it's done to you! I made my decision in the best interest of public safety—"

"Bullshit. You were just covering your own ass."

"There was nothing anyone could do to help my brothers, you have to understand that!"

"Liar."

"I'm not lying!"

"If you're not lying, then you're one hell of a shitty wizard. Because Cooper and I brought them back."

The color drained from Jordan's face. "What?"

"We rescued your brothers from hell and brought them back alive, you asshole."

Jordan leaned away from me, shaking his head. "No. Impossible. There's not enough magical energy—"

"Did you *see* the Goad running the show in there? No, of *course* you didn't, because you're a fucking coward and you didn't even *try* to see what was going on."

I leaned in close to his face. "It had *plenty* of power. It had been tormenting innocent people for thousands of years. It would have been in the best interest of the *public fucking safety* for you to have sent your little paranormal defense team in there to kill it if you didn't have the guts to try the job yourself."

His jaw worked soundlessly for a moment before he got any words out. "They—they can't be *normal* after that, they'll be no better than demons—"

"If they go bad later I'll send them right back where I found them. But until then, they deserve the chance to grow up in a nice place with decent people who love them. They deserve the chance to laugh and grow and learn that the world is a pretty cool place to be. They deserve it way more than you *ever* did."

I stood up and stared down at him. "So before I accept that oh-so-awesome deal from you, I want to know what you're going do for your baby brothers. Are you going to welcome them into this cozy family home of yours? Are you going to change their diapers, wipe their tears? What, exactly, are you going to do to make things right for the brothers you abandoned in hell?"

Jordan stared back at me, looking completely horrified. Through my stone eye, I saw the aura around him shift; he was subvocalizing some kind of spell. An offensive charm, or perhaps teleportation magic.

I barked an ancient word for "tongueless" and slammed my flame hand down on his right, pinning it to the desk. He gave a wordless scream, his eyes bugging out. There wasn't a trace of guilt or regret on his face, just raw animal fear and pain.

"You think *that* hurts?" I shouted, the smell of his sizzling flesh and scorching mahogany filling my nostrils. "I'll show you real pain."

I closed my eyes and willed us both into the remnant of the Goad's hell that existed in my fire.

When I opened my eyes again, Jordan and I were standing beneath the bare yellow bulb in Cooper's chain-link bedroom in the empty, cold basement. Jarred memories glowed in the dark under the narrow bed.

"Where are we?" Jordan asked, his face gray.

"In a piece of the hell you dodged all these years," I replied. "And as far as you're concerned, I'm the Devil."

Jordan whirled on the chained, padlocked door behind him, futilely rattling the cage as he tried to muscle it open. When it wouldn't budge, he started shouting for help.

I gave a soft, bitter laugh. "Nobody can hear you in here, Benny. Save your breath."

I knelt and pulled a jar from beneath the bed. The swirling memories inside flashed and strobed like red and black lightning. I could tell by the feel that they had belonged to Reggie Jordan. "Maybe you're some kind of sociopath like your dear ol' dad and you aren't built to feel sympathy for anyone but yourself. But maybe you just grew up like any spoiled mundane rich kid and now you got a bad case of self-ish. Either way, we're going to see if we can't make you feel a little something for your family's suffering, okay?"

I held the jar toward him. "These are Reggie's

nightmares. They got so bad he finally killed himself. What exactly did you do to try to help your beloved cousin before that happened?"

"He—he never talked about his problems—"

"Or maybe he tried to talk but you never wanted to hear it?"

"He never told me what happened," Jordan insisted. "We got to the farm, and we both knew something was wrong. Reggie made me wait in his car while he checked out the house. Then he opened a mirror to talk to his mother, and she told us to burn the place down. I never went inside. He never told me what he found in there. *Never*."

"Someone once gave me a pithy little lecture regarding my aunt Vicky that I think very much applies to your situation, Benny. What was it? Oh, right: 'A big part of knowing what's going on is being *interested* enough to try to find out.' And it doesn't seem to me that you were very interested in Reggie's life. Fortunately, you have me to clue you in."

I dropped the jar onto the concrete floor. It shattered, splashing the contents in an irregular circle that quickly melted into a glowing silver pool.

Jordan was no match for me in this place. I grabbed him by the back of his neck, forced him down to his knees, pushed his face forward into the pool.

"Take a good long look, Benny," I said as he struggled in my grip. "This is your sin of omission. This is how you failed your cousin. This is what you let happen."

I pulled him from the nightmare pool when I felt him start to go slack, rolled him coughing and gagging to the fence.

"N-not my fault," he insisted. "Not my fault."

I materialized a fresh jar and swept the pool into it with a quick motion of my hand. "It seems that vintage didn't broaden your horizons. How about Corvus?"

I reached under the cot and found Corvus's memory of being forced to cripple himself.

"You weren't responsible for their deaths, or their suffering, not at first. But the moment you became a real wizard, the moment you decided you were so important you should run the whole city, the day you decided you knew what was best for the rest of us—every day after that, what happened to them was *entirely* your fault, because you were the one who should have stopped it."

I smashed the jar onto the floor and forced him down into the new pool.

"Can you feel that?" I said. "Can you feel what it's like to push the saw through your own flesh and bone?"

Jordan shrieked in the pool, his hands scrabbling at the concrete, but I held him fast.

"His spirit had to relive that every day! *Every day!* You could have saved him, but you just let him suffer!"

I pulled him from the pool and lifted his head.

"No . . . I never . . . no . . ." he said weakly.

Disgusted, I threw him against the chain-link fence.

"So you're not moved by the suffering of your cousin and Corvus? Fair enough." My voice dripped with sarcasm as I put Corvus's memories away in a fresh jar. "After all, Reggie was supposed to be the responsible adult. If he wasn't man enough to take what the world dished out, then he was just a weakling, right? Doomed. You couldn't have helped him if you tried, so why try? And Corvus, well, he's not any blood relation to you, is he? He's just a stranger. He might as well have been some mundane kid in a Chinese sweatshop putting the laces in your deck shoes. Out of sight, out of mind, not your problem, right?"

I went to the cot and pulled another jar from the darkness beneath.

Jordan's eyes widened when he saw the glowing vessel.

"No, not that one," he said, his voice cracking.

"Ah, this one you *do* recognize, don't you, Benny? Every man should recognize the pain of the woman who gave him life."

Jordan tried to crab-scramble away, but there was no place to go. I put him in an arm-bar, hauled him to the middle of the floor, and flipped him onto his back. I stepped on his neck to keep him down while I unscrewed the jar. He gasped in pain, grabbed my boot but couldn't pry my foot away.

"This is the hell your mother was in while you were jacking off in boarding school," I said as I slowly poured the contents of the jar straight down into his gaping mouth. "This is the hell she had to endure for decades because of your cowardice. Every Christmas, every Easter, every Mother's Day, *this* is what she was enduring because of your cowardice. Justify it to me. Go ahead. Justify it."

Jordan couldn't speak under the bitter silver stream, couldn't take a breath, and soon his eyes rolled up into his skull. I tossed the empty jar aside and willed us back to his library.

We reappeared in the same positions as we'd left.

The air was thick with the stench of charred flesh. Jordan was still sitting at his desk, slumped in his chair, out cold. I released his nearly cremated hand and checked his neck for a pulse. He was still alive. Whether his mind was irretrievably broken, I didn't know. And found I didn't much care.

I turned his head to the side, then gently patted his cheek with my flesh hand.

"Sweet dre—on second thought, maybe not so much. Nighty-night."

I stepped away from the desk. My rage was gone, but my arm still blazed. My eye fell on a nearby suit of German gothic armor, and an idea pinged. I went to the suit, pried off the steel gauntlet, vambrace, and greaves, then slipped the armor onto my arm. The metal quickly turned hot to the touch, but contained my flames nicely.

I left the library and found the butler sitting in a chair in the hallway. He looked supremely worried.

"Is Master Jordan . . . ?"

"He's alive," I replied curtly. "But I'd call a healer if I were you."

I strode past him and went to the courtyard to find Pal.

chapter twenty-six

Ever and Ever

Pal landed on Mother Karen's front lawn, and I swung my legs over his head and slid to the ground.

"I'm hungry," he said.

"Okay, I'll bring you something from the kitchen after I check on Cooper. I don't think you'll fit in the house. What do you want?"

"Erm." He scratched the ground with one leg. "Ham, I think."

"Ham you want, ham you get. I bet she's got one in her freezer."

I jogged across the grass toward the front door.

A cool breeze ruffled my hair, and then I heard the same faint whisper that had spoken to me in the Warlock's apartment. "You've done well, my girl. Your mother will be so proud of you."

I stopped, spun around. "Who's there?"

"There will be plenty of time for explanations later. We'll soon have the chance to meet properly," the voice replied. "That man of yours has a bright soul, hard as a diamond. Not a scratch on it, even with a murder before the age of seven."

"That wasn't his fault," I said. "He was forced to do what he did."

"In the end, weren't we all?" The voice faded away.

I shivered, continued on to the house. Mother Karen opened the door before I reached it.

"Is everyone okay?" I asked.

The witch nodded, looking tired. "It took me forever to get the babies to sleep. They're a real handful."

"Sorry about that. I did offer Jordan the opportunity to take care of his family responsibilities, but unfortunately he declined to take custody of the kids." I paused. "I couldn't have just left them down there . . ."

"No, no. Of course not. That would have been a monstrous thing to do. You did the right thing." Karen wiped her hands on the front of her apron. "Cooper's asleep in the guest room. I'm making a late dinner for everyone. Do you think you can eat something, or are you too wound up?"

"I can eat. Could you cook up a whole ham for Pal? I've been working him pretty hard."

"Consider it done." Mother Karen grimaced as I looked at the greasy ichor on my dragonskins. "But you are *not* bringing all that into my house. Wait out here, and I'll find you some fresh clothes. I'll tell the Warlock to hose these off and leave them to dry on the back porch . . ."

Cooper was fast asleep under the homemade quilt. I gently brushed his hair away from his forehead, then leaned down and planted a kiss on his lips. His eyes opened, focused on the elbow-length gray satin opera glove that the Warlock and Mother Karen had enchanted to contain my flames.

"Ooh, silky," he said, his voice slurred. Mother Karen had probably given him a heavy-duty pain killer. "But do you really think it goes with those khakis and the Hello Kitty T-shirt?"

"It goes better than the armor. The metal was starting to chafe."

"Huh?"

"I love you, too, goofball," I replied.

He looked at me with amazed adoration. "You are the best girlfriend *ever*."

I laughed. "Why, thank you."

"I can't believe you came after me. That was . . . incredibly awesome. I'm taking you to dinner in Paris. Rome. Wherever you wanna go." He cleared his throat. "I heard Mother Karen talking . . . are we in a lot of trouble with the Circle Jerks?"

" 'A lot' might be an understatement, but whatever happens, we'll manage."

He looked out the window at the bright harvest moon. "So much is going to change."

"But not everything . . . you still love me, right?"

He gazed up into my eyes. "Forever and ever and ever."

I crawled onto the bed beside him. We kissed deeply, passionately, until Mother Karen stuck her head in and told us dinner was ready.

epilogue

There's more to our stories, of course. A lot more. I haven't even gotten to the parts where I've changed the course of your life, have I? I mean, you're probably *not* that guy who saw me and Pal flying to Jordan's house, thought I was some kind of angel, and consequently had a religious epiphany that inspired him to quit his job and start an apocalyptic cult in Marysville. Seriously, you're not him, right? Because that would be pretty weird.

Anyway. I'm out of paper and shotgun shells, so I need to make a run for fresh supplies. Wish me luck if that's in your heart. If I make it back here, I'll get to work on the rest. Which would have happened way before you found these pages, actually, so check my sock drawer. And if you *are* that guy . . . hands off my undies.

Want to delve back into Lucy A. Snyder's world
of dark and sexy magic?
Read on for a glimpse inside
Spellbent's gripping sequel

THE DEVIL IN MISS SHIMMER

by Lucy A. Snyder

All things considered, it had been a damn busy
Friday. In the previous seven hours, I'd run police
roadblocks, battled dragons, and literally gone to
hell and back as I rescued my boyfriend, Cooper, and
his little brothers from a fate considerably worse
than death. Every muscle in my body ached, and I
was looking forward to getting some rest, if perhaps
not much actual sleep. I'd seen some things that
evening that would probably give me insomnia for,
oh, the next decade or so. And there was the little
detail that I'd put our city's head wizard in a coma
and killed a major guardian spirit. They both richly
deserved it, but I'd broken about infinity plus one
laws and surely the authorities were going to hunt
me down with extreme prejudice. So I had prison
and perhaps execution to look forward to as well.
Yay, go me.

But, so far, it appeared I was safe for the night. I
was definitely looking forward to the late dinner my
witch friend Mother Karen was making for me and
the other Talents who'd helped in the rescue.

Whatever she had cooking in her kitchen smelled wonderful. And I knew my familiar, Pal, was plenty hungry.

I carried a platter of savory, steaming ham and a wooden bucket of water down Karen's back steps out into the moonlit yard. It probably looked the same as most other backyards in the neighborhood: rattan furniture and a shiny steel gas barbecue on the brick patio, a wooden picnic table on the lawn, a scattering of oak and buckeye trees bordering the tall dog-eared-plank fence bordered by softly glowing solar-charged lights. However, I suspected this was the only place in the entire state of Ohio sheltering a shaggy, six-foot-tall spider monster.

Who, based on the circles his clawed legs had torn in the turf, had spent the past half hour stalking his own posterior.

"Hey, Pal, I got your dinner," I called.

He stopped going around in circles and blinked his four eyes at me, licking his whiskered muzzle uncertainly.

At least, I *thought* Palimpsest looked uncertain; as a ferret his emotions had been pretty easy to read. But now that his familiar form had become magically blended with his true arachnoid body . . . well I didn't exactly know what "happy" or "sad" or "puzzled" was supposed to look like on such an alien face.

"Having troubles over there?" I asked, setting the platter and bucket down on the picnic table.

"I . . . have an itch," he replied gravely, his voice strange and muffled in my mind. Our telepathic connection was slowly improving, but that, too, was taking some getting used to.

"I could reach every part of my Quamo body and my ferret body," Pal continued, "but strangely these new rear legs aren't very flexible. I can reach my underside but not my back."

"Maybe you just need to do some yoga."

Through the valved spiracles on his abdomen, he blew noisy chords that sounded like a child randomly banging on the keys of an organ. Laughter? Oh-please snorts? I'd only known Pal for a week, and already I had to get to know him all over again.

"That doesn't help me at the moment," he said.

"Horses back into trees and fence posts to scratch themselves," I replied. "You're tall enough to stand on tippy-toes and scratch yourself on the low limbs of that oak over there."

"How dreadfully undignified."

"Or you could just roll around on the grass."

"And that's more dignified *how*?"

"Oh, hush. It's not like anybody can see you back here," I pointed out. "Otherwise you'd have flipped the neighbors out already and the cops would probably be here."

Long ago, Mother Karen had put her house and its yards under a camouflage charm to keep her foster children's magical practice sessions out of sight of the neighbors. So at least there would be no panicked suburbanites dialing 911 to report a monster prowling through Worthington.

I glanced up at the sky, half expecting to see a Virtus silently descending, ready to smite me like a curse from Heaven. One of the huge guardian spirits had already tried to do a little smiting earlier that evening. Mr. Jordan, the aforementioned now-comatose head of the local governing circle, had convinced the Virtus that I was committing some kind of grand necromancy instead of simply trying to rescue Cooper. I'd defended myself, not expecting to win the battle, but win I did.

It was still hard to believe: I had killed a Virtus. *Nobody* was supposed to be able to do that. Not with magic or luck or nuclear weapons or *anything*. It was as if I'd thrown myself naked in front of a speeding freight train in a desperate, unthinking attempt to halt hundreds of hurtling tons of iron . . . and had somehow stopped it cold.

Miracles had abounded that evening. But I doubted the Virtii would see me as anything but a threat. They'd be coming for me, and from what I'd seen so far, they were as merciful as black holes.

I squinted up at the dark spaces between the stars, wondering what lurked there.

"Speaking of things that shouldn't be seen by mundanes, how is that working for you?" Pal asked.

"Huh?" I looked at him, confused.

He nodded toward the gray satin opera glove on my left arm. "The gauntlet. Is it keeping your flames contained?"

"Yes, Karen and the Warlock did a good job enchanting this," I replied, looking at the thin curls of smoke that were trailing from the cuff of the glove, as if I'd used it as a place to stash a still-smoldering cigarette. So far, that was the only sign that the lower half of my arm was a torch of hellfire, courtesy of my having had to plunge my arm into the burning heart of the Goad, the pain-devouring devil that had imprisoned Cooper and his family.

"It slips down a little sometimes—I might have to find some double-sided tape or superglue to hold it in place."

Sheathed in the glove, my arm functioned more-or-less normally but still had a squishy unreliability. Fine finger movements were still difficult. And that wasn't surprising, considering the arm was boneless from my elbow down. I'd had to rely on a natural talent for spiritual extension to give it any kind of solidity; Pal had referred to the ability as "reflexive parakinesis."

And it was pretty close to true reflex. My crysoberyl ocularis—a replacement for my left eye, which I'd lost the week before in a battle with a demon—still hurt a bit, and I was constantly aware that I had a piece of polished rock stuck in my head. But a couple of times that evening, I had completely forgotten my left arm was no longer entirely flesh. And fortunately I hadn't dropped anything important as a consequence.

"With luck we may be able to find someone to remove the underlying curse, and you'll have your regular arm back," Pal said.

I frowned. Everyone was treating my flame hand—and its power—like a curse. If I were an evil person, somebody bent on destruction and domination, my hand would have seemed almost purely a gift from the gods. With that kind of power literally at my fingertips, so what if having a fiery hand presented a few practical problems? That would be like complaining that you had to move a few boxes out of your garage to make way for the new Porsche. Or in my case, the new tank with a seemingly unlimited supply of surface-to-air missiles.

I was pretty sure I wasn't an evil person. Though I'd certainly made some regrettable decisions—crushing a couple of Mr. Jordan's men under the Warlock's Land Rover was currently at the top of my growing list—I'd been trying to do the right thing at the time. Evil, certainly, was bad. But the power in my hand had saved us all from the Virtus, hadn't it? I was getting pretty annoyed that everyone seemed to think I ought to be in a hurry to get rid of it.

"I should go back inside before they all start dinner without me," I said. "And anyway, your ham's getting cold over here . . . did you want anything else for dinner? Karen's got pie."

"Let me start with the ham and see how it sits first," he replied. "Wanting to eat something and being able to digest it are two different things."

I left Pal to his dinner and went back inside to the guest bedroom. Cooper lay thin and pale under the covers, dead to the world. Dark curly bangs obscured his eyes. He'd lost a scary amount of weight during his time trapped in the hell; he'd always been on the skinny side, but now I could see every rib, every bump on his sternum.

"Wake up, time to eat." I gently shook his bony shoulder.

He grunted and pushed away my hand. "Don' wanna. Wanna sleep."

"C'mon. Potions only go so far—we gotta get some real food into you. We can sleep after."

"Where's Smoky?" he mumbled. "I can't feel him."

My stomach dropped. I hadn't yet told him that his white terrier familiar died the night he was pulled into the hell. "He, um . . . he's not with us."

Cooper seemed confused. "You left him at the apartment?"

I took a deep breath. "He didn't make it. The night you disappeared . . . he got killed. It was quick. I don't think he suffered."

A bit of a lie, that; being torn apart by a demon was quick but certainly not easy. I felt horrible about Smoky dying, because it was my own damn fault for not knowing what to do.

Cooper's features twisted in pain and sorrow, and he covered his face with his hands, pressing the heels against his eyes, I guessed to try to keep himself from crying. "Dammit. Poor little guy."

I wanted to weep, too, but if we both started with the waterworks we probably wouldn't stop for a while.

"Hey, everyone's waiting on us; we better get to the dining room." I hauled him up into a sitting position and helped him pull on a black Deathmobile T-shirt.

"This isn't mine," Cooper said, staring down at the flaming death's-head motor band logo.

"It's Jimmy's," I replied, referring to Mother Karen's eldest foster son. There are spells to create clothing, but fewer and fewer Talents have bothered with that kind of magic since the Industrial Revolution made fabric cheap. "Your pajama pants are his, too. All our stuff is shrunk down in a safety deposit box at the bank, so you may be wearing his hand-me-downs for a couple more days."

He blinked bloodshot eyes at me. "Why's our stuff at the bank?"

"The farmers wouldn't pay me for the rainstorm,

so I missed the rent and we were getting evicted. Also that rat-bastard Jordan bugged the apartment, so I figured it was best to pack up and go underground for a while."

"Benedict Jordan? He bugged our place? Why?"

"He wanted you to stay gone in the hell. You're the secret half brother he was scared everyone would find out about. Because then everyone would find out his father was a batshit crazy murdering son-of-a-bitch and people would start questioning his family's authoritah or some crap like that."

"Whoa, wait . . . he's my brother?"

"Yep. Same mother, different father. Thank God. The Warlock, sadly, is his full brother."

"Huh." Cooper stared down at his knees, his eyes unfocused as if he was remembering something long forgotten. "Benny's . . . Benedict Jordan. Ain't that a kick in the head."

"Yep. Ol' Benny knew what was going on long before either of us did; he could have prevented your getting trapped in hell, or tried to. Or he could have helped us get you out. But instead he tried to cover everything up and screwed us over to protect his family's reputation."

Cooper swung his legs over the edge of the bed and slowly stood up, leaning against my right shoulder for balance. "Please tell me you kicked his ass."

I gently pulled his head down to mine and planted a kiss on his nose. "Oh yes. I'll probably go to prison for it, but his ass is well and thoroughly kicked."

My mind flashed on Jordan lying broken on his desk, his hand a horrible burned mess. My stomach twisted into a knot, but I angrily forced my guilt back down. I would not feel bad about giving that creep a taste of his own magic.

I helped Cooper down the hall toward Mother Karen's dining room. The scents of garlic steak, fresh rolls, and sweet potato pie wafted through the air. Cooper's stomach growled loudly.

The Talents who'd helped bring Cooper's infant brothers to Mother Karen's house were already seated at the long cherrywood dining table. Oakbrown and Mariette sat across from Paulie at the far end. Mother Karen and Jimmy were ferrying plates of food in from the kitchen. The Warlock and Ginger sat across from each other at the near half of the table, arguing.

"I *am* tolerant," Ginger protested, twisting a lock of her red hair around her index finger. "But fundies get on my every last nerve. It's like they think the free expression of female sexuality is going to cause the Apocalypse or something. They're totally threatened by it, and it's stupid. I hate stupid."

"Ginger-pie, it doesn't matter what the mundanes believe, does it?" the Warlock replied. "How do their beliefs touch us? The fact is, they don't. It's been centuries since they were a real threat to us. We don't have to deal with them if we don't want to."

"But what about the Talented kids who get born into mundane families?" Ginger asked. "What about them? Are we just supposed to let them swing in the wind when their crazy stupid parents decide they're possessed by Satan and go all Spanish Inquisition on them?"

"We take care of our own," the Warlock said, looking up at me as I helped Cooper into the empty chair beside Ginger.

Lucy A. Snyder

"Maybe," I replied, unable to keep the bitterness out of my voice. "Not all Talents are in a hurry to do the right thing, not even for their own kids." I moved around the table to sit across from Cooper in the chair to the Warlock's left.

"You were in a rough situation with your mundane family in Texas, right?" the Warlock said. "And your Talented relatives got you out of there, didn't they?"

"Yeah. My stepfather was going to have me locked up in a mental institution, but my aunt Vicky found out and brought me to Columbus. She was really cool," I said, swallowing against a fresh swell of sorrow and guilt. No matter how much I told myself that Vicky's suicide wasn't my fault, my heart just wouldn't believe it. "But for what it's worth, my stepfather isn't religious."

"See?" the Warlock said to Ginger. "Jackasses come in all faiths."